"Tom Wing has done it again! This fast-paced naval adventure is a highly entertaining education in naval history from the perspective of a captain and crew as they navigate many complexities and dangers associated with taking the fight to Britain on the high seas as American privateers during the Revolutionary War."
—Isaac G. Lee, LtCol, USMC (Ret.), award-winning author of *Hangar 4*

"With *In Harm's Way*, author Thomas Wing's beautiful prose captures the rhythm of the sea itself. Hypnotic, lyrical passages describing the dance between ocean, wind, and ship are punctuated by nerve-shattering naval pursuits and battles, bringing to vivid life the Revolutionary War battlefield of the Atlantic Ocean. Wing grounds his protagonist, the colonial privateer Captain Jonas Hawke, by giving him a family to defend and care for, and Hawke's relationship with his young son is especially well-drawn. Fans of naval adventures by Patrick O'Brien and Sean Thomas Russell will be thrilled to discover an exciting new voice in the genre."
—Laura Rader, author of *Hatfield 1677*

"It has been said many times throughout the annals of maritime history that sailors belong in ships and ships belong at sea. Tom Wing has taken us from the steel decks of a modern destroyer at war with the gallant crew of USS *Nicholas* in *Against All Enemies* to the wooden decks of the Virginia privateer *Resolute* taking the first steps towards building the maritime power of the United States. Again, Tom relates a gripping saga with a knowledge gained only by having experienced the deep emptiness of leaving families behind, the inner courage of facing the dangers and majesty of the sea, and the thrill of seeing the first lights of home again. I hope this is only the first of many adventures for Captain Hawke."
—Don Ditko, CAPT, USN (Ret.)

"Captivating. Powerful. Well-written. Thomas Wing masterfully places you onboard an American square-rigged ship in an ocean ruled by the British Royal Navy. You can almost hear the creak of the blocks and smell the gun smoke. It is a gripping story capturing the fierce spirit of American sailors during the Revolutionary War and immersing you in the raw, high-stakes drama of privateering. But beyond the battles and strategy, it's the emotional depth of the sailors' experiences—their moments of doubt, defiance, and brotherhood—that truly resonate."
—David Wallace, LCDR, USN (Ret.)

"Gripping, compelling, and impeccably well-researched, *In Harm's Way* is a vibrant work of historical fiction and a must-read follow up to Wing's debut novel, *Against all Enemies*. Drawing on his decades of experience sailing the high seas, Thomas Wing takes his readers on a dramatic voyage that explores the political divisions of colonial America, paints the Revolutionary War in a new and fascinating light, and leaves members of his fanbase asking the same tantalizing question—where will Captain Wing whisk us away to next?"
—Patrick Holcomb, LtCol, USMC (Ret.), award-winning author of *Where the Seams Meet*

THE SEA HAWKES CHRONICLES
BOOK ONE

In
HARM'S
WAY

THOMAS M. WING

ACORN PUBLISHING

Helping talented writers publish exceptional books

In Harm's Way
Copyright © 2025 Thomas M. Wing. All rights reserved.

Printed in the United States of America. For information, address
Acorn Publishing, LLC
3943 Irvine Blvd. Ste. 218, Irvine, CA 92602

www.acornpublishingllc.com

Interior design by Kat Ross
Cover design by Damonza

ISBN-13: 979-8-88528-120-1 (hardcover)
ISBN-13: 979-8-88528-119-5 (paperback)
Library of Congress Control Number: 2024922615

To my late writing mentor, Richard Keith Taylor, author extraordinaire

PREFACE

The major events in and around Norfolk and Newport are true. I have inserted my fictional characters to show the impact these incidents and battles had on ordinary people. Additionally, the relocation of the Continental Congress to Baltimore from Philadelphia is historically accurate, as are depictions of the buildings. This includes the cannonball embedded in the wall of St. Paul's Church in Norfolk. It is still there.

The quiet support provided by the Spanish and Dutch in the Caribbean is also factual, though the specifics utilized in this novel are fictional. While it's well-known that the French initially supported American independence under the table, then openly for years, less has been written about the support of the Dutch and Spanish in the Caribbean, other than by Barbara W. Tuchman, in her 1988 book *The First Salute: A View of the American Revolution*.

My intent is to present authentic history, put into context by my characters. The only fictional (for the story) major events are *Resolute*'s battles with other ships, and those ships. The exception is the real Royal Navy sloop *Otter*, and her actual commander.

Personalities and conversations with historical figures are obviously made up from whole cloth. However, contemporary writings or descriptions of those persons, for example, Esek Hopkins and the other members of the Marine Committee of Congress, were used to portray those persons as well as what they might have said as accurately as possible.

With respect to locales, I have also used the old names and spellings. For example, Cape Henlopen was Cape Hinlopen in the 1770s. Likewise, Falmouth, Massachusetts is now known as Portland, Maine.

The quote near the end of Chapter Four is from *The Way of Duty*, by Joy Day Buel and Richard Buel, Jr., W. W. Norton and Company, 1984; page 32. The original is from a letter by Reverend Joseph Fish to his daughter, Mary Noyes, upon the death of her firstborn son. (Used with permission.)

The cover is adapted from an 1863 painting by William Bradford (1823-1892) titled *Brigantine on a Lee Shore*.

"I wish to have no connection with any ship that does not sail fast;
for I intend to go in harm's way."
    — John Paul Jones

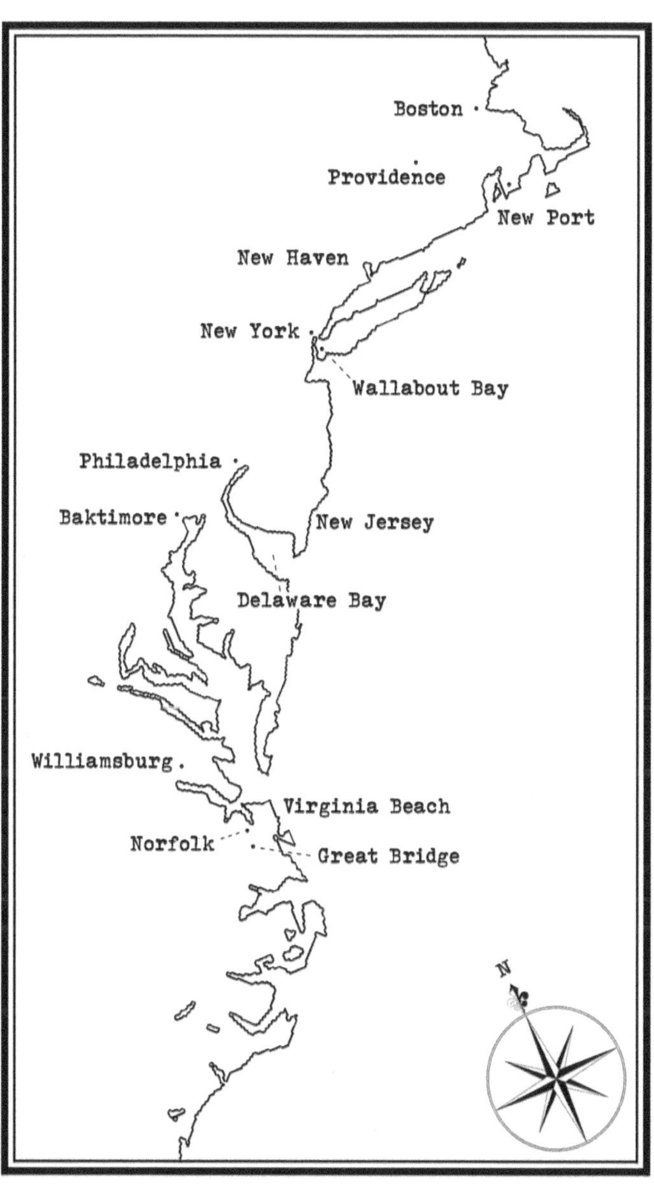

Boston
Providence
New Port
New Haven
New York
Wallabout Bay
Philadelphia
Baktimore
New Jersey
Delaware Bay
Williamsburg
Virginia Beach
Norfolk
Great Bridge
N

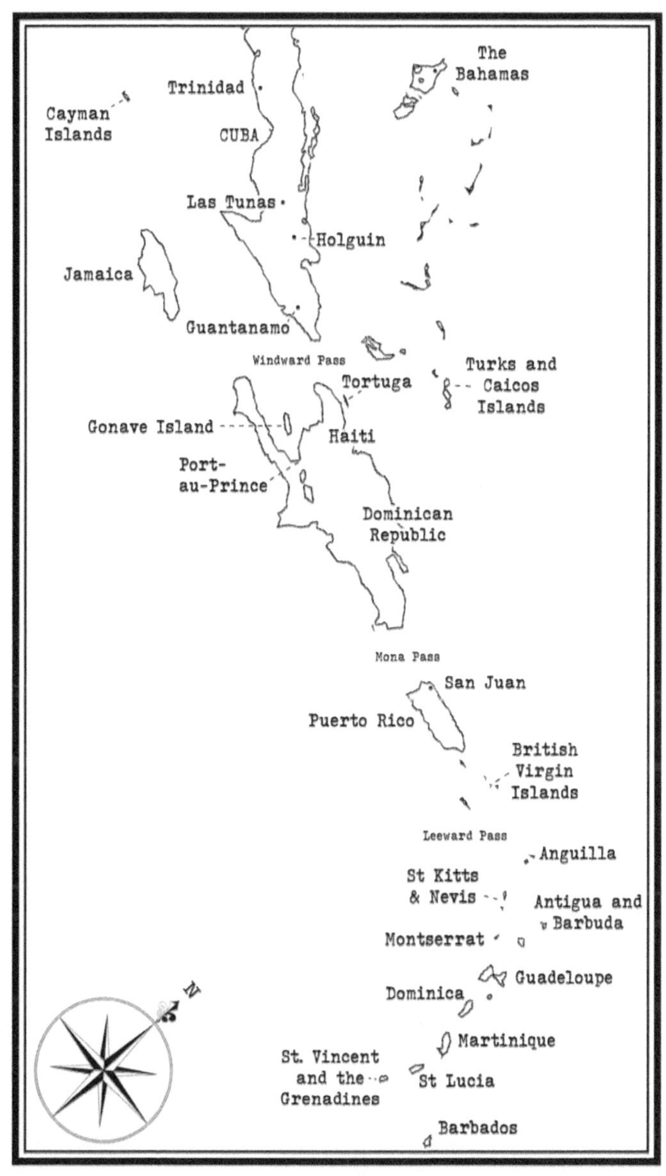

The
Bahamas
Cayman
Islands
Trinidad
CUBA
Las Tunas
Holguin
Jamaica
Guantanamo
Windward Pass
Tortuga
Turks and
Caicos
Islands
Gonave Island
Haiti
Port-
au-Prince
Dominican
Republic
Mona Pass
San Juan
Puerto Rico
British
Virgin
Islands
Leeward Pass
Anguilla
St Kitts
& Nevis
Antigua and
Barbuda
Montserrat
Guadeloupe
Dominica
Martinique
St. Vincent
and the
Grenadines
St Lucia
Barbados
N

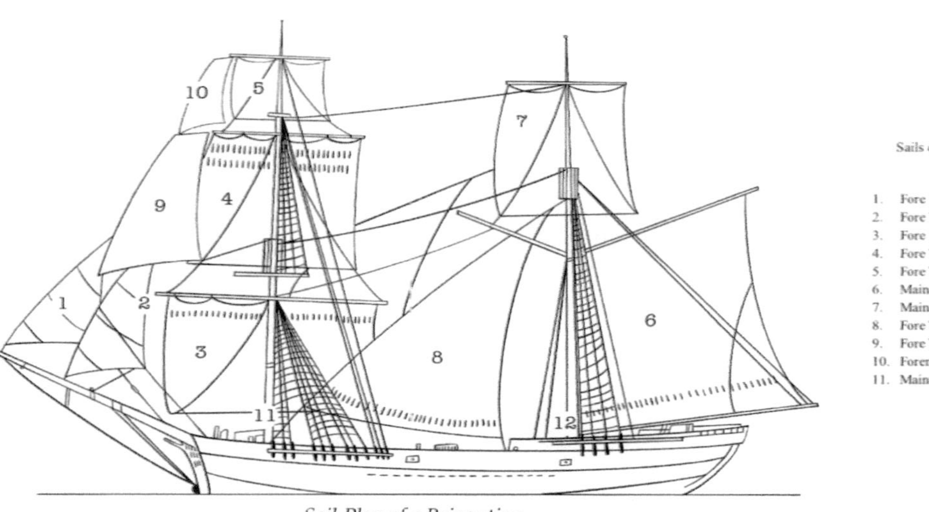

Sail Plan of a Brigantine

CHAPTER ONE

30 SEPTEMBER 1775
NORFOLK, COLONY OF VIRGINIA

"Get the printing press, typesets, ink, and paper. Leave nothing."

The Royal Marines spread throughout the poorly lighted shop to begin the tasks ordered by the Royal Navy lieutenant in command. Their bright red jackets faded to the color of blood in the shop's dim interior.

Four of them disassembled the large printing press that stood in the center of the room. The odor of dried ink permeated the warm fetid air as more marines searched large cupboards at the base of the back wall, seeking quarter casks of ink. Two more seized wooden-framed trays of typeset from shelves next to the press. Others dragged burlap-covered bundles of blank newsprint toward the door. They collided with those carrying trays of type. Finally, two men overturned boxes, pulled out drawers and spilled them, and generally disarranged the contents of tables, desks, cupboards, and cabinets, ostensibly looking for printed papers.

The Marine sergeant moved to untangle the groups near the

door, then stepped back to the center of the room to oversee the action. The lieutenant came and stood next to him.

Seeing the men at the back shake their heads after they'd opened the last of the cabinets, the sergeant said, "Beg pardon, sir, we canna find any ink."

"Hmph. There must be some here. Keep looking. Have the men search the rest of the house. Did you find that bastard Holt yet?"

"No, sir. Corporal Coates says he heard a door in the back slam after we started lookin' around. He and Williams went back there, quick like, but they couldna see anyone. House's deserted, sir."

The lieutenant fumed. He was supposed to obtain a fully operable printing press, and that required ink. He was also supposed to deliver a fully cowed and silenced newspaper's owner. That didn't appear likely, either.

"Keep at it."

"Yes, sir."

The sergeant came to attention, then moved off to further motivate his men.

The *Virginia Gazette & Norfolk Intelligencer* was to be put permanently out of business. The lieutenant was also to escort Mr. Holt aboard ship to meet with Lord Dunmore's secretary. They would discuss Holt's unreasoned and senseless attacks against both the Royal Governor and the Royal Navy; in particular, on Captain Squire, *Otter*'s commanding officer.

Lord Dunmore's orders on those points had been very direct and strongly worded. He desired John Holt himself so he might ensure more favorable coverage of Lord Dunmore's activities in the region. The fact that the newspaper had been printing mostly truthful articles — only slightly exaggerated — didn't concern the lieutenant. Nor did he care that the Royal Navy had ravaged the countryside and the coastline, seizing fishing boats and small trading schooners without even the pretense of legitimacy.

In tit-for-tat retaliation, the colonists had seized a tender from

Otter, removing all its fittings and furnishings. The Navy had gotten the empty hull back eventually. This, however, *had* angered the lieutenant.

Loath to disappoint Captain Squire, the latter being somewhat difficult when his orders weren't carried out to the fullest, no matter the reason, the lieutenant turned and walked out to the street. His neck cloth cloyed at his throat as beads of sweat ran down his body beneath his jacket.

Situated in a semi-circle centered on the door, another eight marines held loaded muskets across their chests, fingers rigid beside triggers. Beyond them stood a silent crowd, almost exclusively men. The few women stood at the back. Most of both wore scowls, but no one spoke.

The lieutenant hoped someone would provoke his men, goad them into conflict. The young officer was looking for a fight. He'd grown tired of hiding aboard ship, foraging for scraps during short raids ashore. He was particularly tired of the people who'd caused him such discomfort. Life in these colonies was irritating enough without having to deal with the colonials. They were mean-spirited, vengeful, and had long memories. They still smoldered over events of more than a decade ago, when the lieutenant had been but a schoolboy. How they retained such anger, he couldn't understand, least of all when it was directed at him, his governor, or especially his king. He'd be grateful to be shut of them when *Otter* returned to England in thirteen months. In the meantime, he wished for one, just one, to open his mouth.

He sneered in the direction of the crowd. None did, though murmurs broke out then died quickly. *Cowards.* He turned away and went back inside.

THREE HOURS LATER, THE LIEUTENANT STOOD IN THE cabin aboard His Majesty's Ship *Otter*.

"Well, what have ye to say?" asked Captain Matthew Squire.

Seated behind a table, Squire gazed coldly up at him, the corners of his mouth downturned.

"Sir, as ordered, we marched to the office of the *Virginia Gazette and Norfolk Intelligencer*. I stationed my men—"

"Damn your eyes, Lieutenant, I want to know whether you carried out my orders, not a blow by blow description of marching." Squire's gravelly voice cut sharply into the lieutenant's narrative.

Resisting the desire to grind his teeth, the lieutenant changed tacks. "Yes, sir. We entered the office and seized the printing press and what supplies we could find. A crowd of perhaps fifty or sixty of the damn—" He paused, swallowing hard. "Beg pardon, sir. I meant fifty or sixty colonials. They stood quiet-like, sir, and watched. I had my men keep a close eye on them, but there was no trouble."

"So, Lord Dunmore can print and publish papers from his flagship, then?"

The lieutenant licked his lips. "Ah, no, sir, not quite." Seeing Squire's mouth open, he quickly interjected, "There wasn't any ink, sir. We took everything in the place apart, sir, and there weren't no ink in the whole place. The printer hisself was not to be found, sir."

The officer's carefully cultivated speech collapsed under his sudden burst of fear. He pushed on. "Sir, my men searched the houses around, but he wasn't there. He must have been warned, sir."

He stopped, waiting for the explosion. When it didn't come, he added, "But we did capture the bookbinder and a journeyman printer, sir. A Mr. Joseph Conant and a Mr. Alexander Cameron."

The sun slanting through the stern windows reflected off a wave top, directly into the lieutenant's eyes. He blinked.

Squire smiled coldly. "Well, no matter. We've got the press and we can find ink tomorrow or the next day. Lord Dunmore will have his newsprint, and we'll finally have the truth out. And one of the first things to print is his order closing the ports of Norfolk, Portsmouth, and Suffolk. Not a single ship will be allowed in or out without a permit signed by Lord Dunmore. And I will recommend he not grant any. These damned colonials are going to pay for the damage they've done to the Navy, for what they've stolen from us. In money, in property, and in lives."

Squire stood in dismissal. He turned to look out the stern windows. Gray smoke rose from the distant town of squat houses and shops, blending with the low clouds overhead.

As the lieutenant stepped out, he heard Squire say, "Yes, indeed, they will pay."

CHAPTER TWO

Coming up on deck in the predawn darkness, Captain Jonas Hawke turned and looked west. The bright gibbous moon lay only half an hour below the western horizon. Where it had sunk into the sea there remained a silvery sort of twilight. Somewhere in that direction was Cape Henry and home. Above, the stars shone starkly in the crisp air, hard points of light in the ink-black expanse.

In a few hours, by his reckoning, they would pass abeam the cape, then on to Hampton Roads where the James and Elizabeth Rivers merged into the Chesapeake Bay. By nightfall, he would be home with Mary and the children. They'd gather in front of the hearth and he'd show them the trinkets he'd brought. He'd meet his new twins. Later, he and Mary would sit alone in front of the fire....

He shook such thoughts from his mind. He was close, yet there was a full day's activity ahead. Jonas didn't think himself superstitious, yet he was a sailor to the core. He didn't want to imagine about the homecoming lest he jeopardize its realization.

A tall, solid man, heavy but not fat, Jonas nevertheless moved easily with the ship's motion. Legs long accustomed to the motion of a ship in a seaway effortlessly, unconsciously, shifted his weight back and forth, forward and aft. His dark brown hair was tied in a queue at the base of his neck, but as usual a few wayward strands fluttered round his face in the gentle wind. Unlike many sailors, he didn't braid it or coat it with tar. Instead, he bound it with tarred marlin, more in the style of a genteel landsman, the tarred marlin a nod to his seafaring nature. Wearing the long white canvas pantaloons he favored aboard ship, and a loose flowing blue cotton shirt, today he also wore a light tarpaulin jacket. His deeply tanned face marked a man who'd been many years at sea.

Elizabeth herself mimicked Jonas, rolling gently in the long swells, sails slatting as her masts swung to and fro. A light breeze off the land kept her hove to under fore and main topsails. She was, to the uninitiated, wide and ungainly, what sailors called beamy. A full-rigged ship, with three masts and square sails on all, she looked to be from an earlier era with her exaggerated poop deck sloping upward to a high stern. She was younger than she looked, being only twenty years old. She remained well found. Rising tall out of the water with great freeboard between waterline and deck, her tumblehome rolled a man inboard gently as he ascended her sides. Jonas was fond of her. Not fast, she was steady, a good sea boat, sailors said.

He strode the hard wooden deck slowly, forward then aft, unconsciously avoiding ringbolts and other fittings strewn in his path.

On deck earlier than was his wont, he paced rather than toss and turn in his cot. Up and to starboard, Polaris lay framed between the graceful curve of the foot of the main topsail and the hard line of the main yard. The star slowly migrated left, then right as the ship's head swung back and forth. Pacing didn't satisfy, however, so he moved to the rail on the windward side and leaned over to watch the barely visible wake. *Elizabeth* first surged slowly ahead, turning into the wind. Then, as the fore topsail was taken aback, she lost headway and gathered sternway, the bow falling off the wind. Thus with the wind generally on her larboard side, she moved gently to starboard, away from the longed-for shore.

Jonas stood mesmerized by the smooth stretch of inky water left on the surface by the sideways drift. The pattern repeated endlessly and would continue until he gave the order to alter course homeward. That order would come soon. Once the sun rose and began to warm the land, the winds would shift toward the shore and grow in strength.

"Good morning, sir, I'm about to strike three bells. Mr. Masefield left orders to call all hands at five bells."

Ship's bells rang each half hour during a watch. Three bells in the morning watch was five-thirty in the morning. All hands would be called an hour later, at six-thirty.

A voice issued from the darkness at Jonas's elbow.

"Very well, Mr. Pierce," Jonas replied.

Pierce turned and ordered the seaman to strike three bells, then returned his attention to Jonas.

"If I may, I took a sight on the pole star just after I came on deck. Latitude thirty-six degrees, fifty-three minutes north." Originally from Charleston, a slight drawl softened his speech.

"Very good. We'll have a fair run into the Bay," Jonas responded.

Forward, one and a half double strokes of the bell indicated it was now five-thirty. His sailor's subconscious reminded him the sunrise would come in just about fifty minutes. He contemplated the navigation situation.

They'd been continuously at sea for seven weeks, with no landfall in the last five. That had been the island of St. Peter and St. Paul's Rocks in the mid-Atlantic. Despite being certain of his latitude, he'd ordered the bottom sampled last evening with the sounding lead. They'd pulled up mud and broken shells at fourteen fathoms. Based on depth and bottom composition alone, he estimated Cape Henry lay no closer than ten nautical miles nor more than fifteen, though the continental shelf had a very shallow slope at this point. He'd hove to just slightly south of the right latitude for the entrance to let the Gulf Stream push them slowly north through the night.

To starboard the horizon grew perceptibly lighter. He fancied he even felt warmth. Approaching footsteps drew his face from the rail. "Good morning, John," he said.

Jonas's first mate moved toward him. Masefield had had the watch from midnight until four, so Jonas was surprised to see him on deck again after only two hours below.

"Good morning, sir."

A short and balding man, Masefield was also lean and hard. His face was the color and texture of old leather, accented with piercing blue eyes that peered out from eyelids perpetually half closed against decades of bright sun. An excellent seaman, he'd been a sailor longer than Jonas had been alive.

"Cape Henry in the offing, sir?" asked Masefield.

"I am hopeful we will find it visible once the sun is up. Mr. Pierce confirms the latitude."

The water slapping the sides of the ship produced a calm, normal, peaceful sound. The two stood peaceably and silent, waiting, watching.

"Land ho! Land broad on the larboard beam."

The cry galvanized all hands and brought up most of those below deck. Every man hoped to catch a glimpse of shore, of home. Those already aloft crowded the larboard yards while others lined the rail. Though he strove to remain businesslike, even Jonas's heart lifted and his pulse quickened. Feigning nonchalance, he pretended to study the set of the sails.

When he could wait no longer, he hefted his body into the rigging and climbed the main shrouds hand over hand. Hanging back downward as he climbed over the edge of the top, he continued up to the topgallant mast crosstrees and seated himself.

Wrapping an arm around the mast, he settled his telescope and looked for the land.

"There, sir, just a hair's breadth aft o' the larboard beam," said the lookout. He'd climbed farther up the topgallant mast shrouds to make room for Jonas.

It was Cape Henry, all right, closer than expected, in fact only six or seven miles off, emerging from the darkness and haze of humidity that cloaked it. It always cheered him to have his navigation confirmed.

Jonas remained aloft, enjoying the sunrise at his back and home to his front. Finally, he twisted around and watched as the sun ponderously heaved itself into the firmament. For the first time in well over a year, surrounded as he was by the familiar smells of tar and hemp, the motion of the mast, and with home under what would soon be his lee, he felt truly happy.

As all good things must, his time aloft needed to end. Reluctantly, he closed his telescope and grasped the shroud for the return trip. Reaching the deck, he moved aft.

To Pierce, he said, "Cape Henry, it is. Call me when the wind shifts and we'll stand in. I'm going below for some breakfast." To Masefield, he added, "Please join me when you can."

As the morning aged, the wind veered first north and then northeast. Soon *Elizabeth* bowled along under topsails, courses, and fore topgallant, wind firmly on her starboard quarter. Three headsails and the spanker completed her homecoming ensemble. The creamy froth at her cutwater leapt out to either side as if dancing in joy itself, then streamed along her waterline to disappear swirling astern. Heeling gently to leeward, she seemed to strain to get home herself as if she too wanted to rest her weary bones. The rigging creaked and sang. The breeze freshened, the growing chop giving rise to whitecaps. Above, the sky

WAS SO BLUE IT HURT, WITH ONLY AN OCCASIONAL fluff of cotton to mar its cold perfection. It was ideal for coming home.

Jonas and Masefield stood to windward on the poop deck. Cape Henry lay far astern now, and the great expanse of the Chesapeake Bay stretched out to starboard as *Elizabeth* approached Sewell's Point. Halfway home. Ahead lay the long bend south to run up the Elizabeth River to Norfolk. The tide would turn to a flood about then, helping them along. For the moment, the last of the ebb increased the steepness of the chop with the wind blowing against the outflow of tide. As *Elizabeth* put her shoulder into the backside of a wave, a rainbow of spray flew to leeward.

"Looks like a warship coming down the bay, sir," said Masefield. The lookout had reported an unknown sail before, but Jonas hadn't bothered to more than glance at it.

Now he swung his telescope around. The narrow entry and row of gunports along the main deck confirmed its status. "He's got something in mind of importance. He carries more sail than prudent in this breeze," Jonas said.

The two men watched as the ship skirted the channel edge near Horseshoe and Thimble shoals, then approached Point Comfort, obviously making for the river entrance. Jonas allowed it'd probably enter before they did, though not by much. *No great matter*, he thought, *the channel is wide enough for both*. He turned his mind to tallying the myriad of things to be done in preparation to either anchor or warp alongside the quay.

"Is that a signal?" Masefield asked.

Jonas raised his telescope again. Perhaps three or four flags flew from the stranger's mizzen halyards, but they blew right at *Elizabeth*.

"Perhaps to a friend farther up the bay. He must know we can't read it."

Both men started at the sound of a gun. They barely had time to see the powder smoke before the wind whipped it away.

Jonas shook his head. "See what you can make of that signal."

While Masefield climbed a few feet up the mizzen shrouds, Jonas ran forward and climbed halfway up the foremast shrouds to scan the water ahead.

"Lookout, there. Harper, d'ya see anything ahead? Sandbars, a wreck maybe?" he called aloft.

After a long moment and another gun from the sloop, Harper called back, "No, sir, nothin'. Nor no ripples like might be somethin' on th' bottom."

They were approaching the spit to the south but were easily in the middle of the channel. A relatively recent addition to the topography of the southern bay, the spit had been raised during a hurricane a bit more than ten years before. But there was no sign of any new changes that posed a danger. The buoys looked to be in the right places.

Still, they'd been gone more than a year. Jonas ordered sail shortened while Masefield stationed a man in the forward chains to heave the lead. The crew grumbled as they took in and furled topgallant sails and fore course. They wanted nothing to slow their return. *Elizabeth*'s speed rapidly diminished, now under topsails and headsails alone.

"If I may, sir, I think they mean us to heave to. I canna say for certain."

All doubt was removed, however, for when the sloop fired once more, a splash erupted ahead of *Elizabeth*. Shortly thereafter, the warship's remaining ports opened and a row of guns appeared.

"Clew up main and mizzen tops'ls. Put your helm down and bring her head into the wind. Cast loose the heads'l sheets. Set and back the spanker." Jonas flung angry orders at his now bewildered crew. This time they hurled themselves to it. The sooner they obeyed and settled whatever business the Royal Navy had with them, the sooner they would be once more homeward bound.

Jonas shared their puzzlement. The sounds of flapping canvas and squealing blocks enveloped the ship.

As *Elizabeth* rounded up and hove to, the sloop did likewise. As it drifted slowly down on them, Jonas hailed her with his speaking trumpet.

"The warship 'hoy. What is the meaning of this, sir? Forcing me to heave to here hazards my ship."

"This is His Majesty's sloop *Otter*. Anchor your vessel and stand by to be boarded. All your crew to be on deck for my officer," came the response. Most unusual, they'd not asked *Elizabeth*'s identity.

Jonas had never been stopped like this before, nor had he heard of this happening except under a blockade or to press men. It was unlikely *Otter* was looking to press sailors this close to port. There hadn't been a press in Norfolk for more than eight years, not after the riots the last time.

Jonas waited, face set in a scowl.

As soon as *Elizabeth's* anchor was set, *Otter* followed suit, placing herself so as to keep her guns trained on *Elizabeth*.

Otter's longboat came alongside and hooked on to the main chains. A very young, gangly lieutenant bounded up the ladder to *Elizabeth's* deck. Twelve armed sailors quickly followed. All drew their pistols or cutlasses as they gained the deck. Ten of them covered Jonas's crew, gathered in the waist. The remaining two stood behind their lieutenant. The officer scowled broadly, silently pointed at Jonas, then at a spot immediately in front of himself.

Jonas did not move. Silence reigned, broken only by the flap of sails and the creak of the ship's hull. Tension flooded the deck like ice water.

"You did not greet me with proper honors, Mister. You owe respect to the Navy and by God, you will show it. Now, get over here and speak to me," he bellowed.

Ignoring the outburst, Jonas remained where he was and asked, "What is the meaning of this, sir? I protest the stopping of my ship." He tried to keep the anger out of his voice. He'd learned long ago that a cautious yet firm hand in dealing with naval officers was prudent. He paused, then moved slowly nearer the officer, carefully avoiding the spot indicated.

"You are in no position to protest anything, and you'll keep a civil tongue in your head. Else I will have you bound and gagged." The lieutenant leered. He made no effort to hide his anticipation of doing just that, if only Jonas would do something, anything, to precipitate it. He quite obviously enjoyed his perceived position of power.

"You rebels must learn manners, Jonathan. Let me see your permits." At Jonas's blank stare, he added, "You do have your permits, don't you? The ones that authorize you to trade into Norfolk? From Lord Dunmore?"

"Of course not. What permits? Norfolk is a free port. And who is 'Jonathan'? My name is Captain Jonas Hawke."

The officer snorted, smiling smugly. "I don't care what your name is. You are a lowborn rebel colonist, a Jonathan." He raised his voice. "This vessel is now prize to Captain Squire of His Majesty's sloop *Otter*. You are to consider yourselves under arrest for violation of Lord Dunmore's orders in council. I am Lieutenant Alder, and I am now in command."

Jonas stared, unable to speak. Forward, a seaman moved to secure a halyard. In the haste to heave to, it hadn't been made up properly and had worked itself nearly off the belaying pin. One of the British sailors promptly clubbed him with the butt of a pistol. Hinckley fell unconscious to the deck. Blood pooled under his head. Two more of Jonas's crew moved to help him, but the British sailors growled and readied to strike. Jonas's men snarled and bent forward, ready to leap.

Jonas found his voice. "Hold! Stay where you are."

Turning, Jonas moved toward the lieutenant, who backed

away, scrabbling for his sword. The sailor behind him raised his pistol.

Jonas stopped. "What in God's name are you doing? By what right do you assault my crew and seize my ship? We are loyal subjects of his majesty the King."

"Subjects? Ha. No, you are colonists, with only the rights his majesty sees fit to grant. Under the laws of war, this ship is now a prize and you are my prisoners. Do you state your intention to resist?" Alder asked, voice slightly wobbly. He let go the pommel of his sword and moved his hand to the butt of his own pistol. He licked his lips.

Jonas harrumphed. The boy had found his courage, facing an unarmed man.

With no choice but to acquiesce, Jonas withheld an answer. His body, tensed and ready to lash out, uncoiled, and he stood straight. Pausing to steady his voice, he said, "At least let my men tend to Hinckley. Or do you think an unconscious man a threat?"

Lieutenant Alder seemed to consider refusing. But then he nodded.

Chapman and Scott moved to tend to Hinckley.

Jonas continued, "You are in the wrong. I shall protest when we return to port. What is this about us being 'rebels'? We are from Norfolk, not Boston."

"I have seized your ship for commerce with the enemy. No trade is permitted into Norfolk."

"What the devil are you talking about? There's no war here. I've spoken both French and Spanish ships, as well as English. They've nought said anything of war. Virginians are loyal."

Alder snorted. "No war? Perhaps you're right. There's no war, least not with the Frogs or Spaniards. And if they know what is good for them, they'll not interfere. Not a real war, just a rabble in arms." He glared. "Loyal subjects do not attack royal soldiers or threaten the royal governor. And they most certainly do not attack His Majesty's Navy."

Alder puffed out his chest and rose to his full height. "This rebellion will be put down most harshly. You bastards will pay in blood for the killing you've done." Alder spun on his heel and went forward to organize his prize crew. He ordered his men to gag any man who spoke.

Jonas chose not to follow.

The British gathered the rest of the crew then came for Jonas and the mates. Jonas ordered them not to resist. *This will be righted when we gain the shore.*

None were allowed to gather personal possessions but instead were put into the longboat. Two of Jonas's men picked up Hinckley and carried him.

The trip to *Otter* was quiet and wet. The wind remained a fresh breeze and the swells continued to build, with whitecaps now prevalent. At nearly every stroke a wave slammed against the windward bow and soaked the occupants. Jonas's men were unprepared to ride in an open boat loaded to the gunwales. By the time they arrived, all were soaked through and some shivered.

Aboard *Otter* they were hustled below into the hold. Hinckley wasn't with them. Jonas hoped he'd been taken to the sickbay. Once in the hold, the hatch was slammed down and battened, and they were alone in the dark.

Chapter Three

It took time for their eyes to adapt to the darkness. It took even longer to adjust to their imprisonment.

The space had been prepared for prisoners. Small, down low and all the way forward in the bow, the triangular space spanned about eighteen feet on the long sides and twelve along the short one. Completely cleared of ship's equipment save for two large coils of cable, it still did not easily accommodate twenty-two men. The stench of unseen waste and unwashed bodies permeated the space. Mixed with the more normal ship smells of decaying wood and hemp rope and not-quite-dried sea bottom one expected, it became noxious. Jonas nearly gagged.

"Sir, there's a bucket here needs emptying," said Masefield.

Jonas shouted up to the midshipman, who now stared through the grate. "Have one of your men take care of the bucket we're going to hand up."

The midshipman looked to be about twelve. His eyes went wide and his mouth opened and closed, but no sound issued. One of the British sailors pulled the youngster away and called down, "None o' that, you. You don't give no orders here." They were left alone.

The smell of their own wet clothing added to the fetid air,

which quickly warmed with the crowding. The stench was not improved by the added heat.

Jonas stayed bent at the waist until his eyes adjusted, then sat on one of the coils. There he could at least sit straight, head between the deck beams above. As was usual in the hold of anything smaller than the largest man o'war, no one could stand. Men claimed space where they could, leaving the presumably more comfortable rope to the officers.

Pierce took charge and organized the men into watches. It gave them routine and discipline they were used to. It also promised they'd not be caught unaware if something advantageous happened.

The rest of the morning dragged by. Most slept while others groused about the possible ancestry of the British sailors, especially as to how closely their mothers might have consorted with dogs. Masefield and Pierce remained silent, lost in their own thoughts.

Jonas sank into a foul anger.

At eight bells, a face appeared above. Jonas demanded to see the captain but received only a laugh and curse in response. The hatch opened and a pot of thin oatmeal dropped unceremoniously amongst them, spilling some of its contents. Fortunately, the nearly overflowing waste bucket was taken away.

Masefield organized the sharing of the meager ration. Later, the guard collected the pot and returned the empty waste pail.

After the pot had been collected, Masefield approached Jonas. "Well, sir, what do ye think? This war talk, I mean."

"I don't know. I wouldn't have imagined fighting in Virginia. Not even the radicals in the House of Burgesses would be so foolish as to take up arms. Certainly not against the Royal Navy. Too many of us make our living from the sea. We need the protection the Navy provides."

"Aye, but here we are. Some might not have the limits you and I do." Masefield stared into the blackness. "And if the British were to push hard enou', there might be others who'd join 'em."

"But they couldn't stand against the British Army and Royal Navy."

Masefield lowered his voice. "Aye, mebee. But my wife's family's been vocal about their feelin's. They've got friends who think we shouldn't just manage our own affairs under the king, but be free of the king. My family, now, that's a different story. My parents came to make a better life than they could'a made in Wales." He shook his head. "But when men get big ideas, they can't always see what's starin' 'em in the face."

AS THE DAY WORE ON, THEY MADE OUT THE BELLS FROM on deck. The incremental and interminable drag of the afternoon watch ended in eight bells struck again. Throughout, the ship heeled first to starboard, then port, and then starboard again, half an hour on each tack, as *Otter* maneuvered back and forth. The burble of water alongside was punctuated with an occasional *thud* as she nosed into a swell.

Finally, as the afternoon watch came to a close, the familiar sound of heavy rope running out the hawse told them *Otter* had dropped anchor.

She drifted for moments, then jolted as the anchor pulled her up short, starting a repetitive motion that dulled their senses. At eight bells they were presented the worst excuse for boiled salt meat any of them had ever seen. Hungry as they were, most refused to eat.

Jonas's opportunity finally came while the food was handed down.

The same midshipman's pimply face appeared. His voice broke as he tried to sound authoritative. "Captain says th' commander of th' prize lay aft and report at once to 'im in 'is cabin." The face hung there for a moment blinking, then vanished. The hatch gaped.

As Jonas's eyes came level with the deck, he squinted. Even the dim light of the berth deck was brighter than the hold. Two guards stood near, pistols aimed at the ready. A mounted swivel gun between them was set to fire into the hatch. From a bucket rose the telltale smoke of slow match for the gun.

Severe precautions for the small, simple crew of a merchant.

He faced the midshipman, who promptly turned and marched aft with an air of self-importance. In different circumstances, Jonas might have laughed.

At the cabin door the midshipman knocked, entered, then loudly announced, "The rebel captain." Stepping aside, he said to Jonas, "Captain Squire, His Majesty's Sloop *Otter*."

Squire sat behind a table that faced the door, back to the stern windows and head down over papers. After a time, he looked up and dismissed the midshipman.

Without preamble, he said, "Well, what have ye to say?"

A spare man, Squire was older than Jonas had expected. A study in contrasts, his entirely white hair hung to his shoulders, yet lay thin at the top. His darkly tanned narrow face clashed with the color of his hair. The old face sat above a new uniform coat, gold epaulets resplendent.

The cabin reflected similar ostentatious splendor. A mirror hung on the bulkhead above a polished dark wood chest of drawers. In the corner a small set of shelves held beautifully bound volumes, none of which looked as if they had been opened. A narrow bench ran the width of the cabin beneath the stern windows. On it lay rich cushions of some shiny scarlet fabric, silk perhaps. A small portrait of a young woman decorated the port bulkhead.

Jonas stepped into the cabin and began. "Sir, I protest the seizure of my ship."

Squire stared for a moment, then spoke softly. "I do not for a moment care about any protest. I enforce the orders of the royal governor. I will carry out my duty. That duty at the moment extends to seizing all vessels trading in and out of Norfolk, Portsmouth, Suffolk, and Gosport, unless they carry express permission from Lord Dunmore. You, sir, do not have that permission." He clasped his hands on the table.

"I know nothing of orders closing Norfolk to trade," Jonas said.

"Then you are ill-informed or lying. Either is of no consequence. Both allow me to make your ship a prize." Squire leaned back in his chair. "Now, answer my question. Who are you?"

Jonas was about to retort angrily when the door opened. A sailor — the captain's clerk, he suspected — slipped quietly in. The man's identity was confirmed when he took paper, pen, and ink from a drawer, and sat to write. The interruption gave Jonas time to take a deep breath and calm himself.

"Captain Jonas Hawke of Norfolk. I am returning from Batavia where I dealt in a cargo of tobacco and other goods. *Elizabeth* carries a cargo of spices, silks, and other items from the Orient. We left Norfolk 24th August last year. She is owned by George Scoggins of Norfolk. And what of my injured man?" As Jonas spoke, the clerk made notes.

Squire peered at him. "That's a long time for a trip to the Indies. Perhaps you made an undeclared stop along the way? Do you carry contraband, smuggling tea, perhaps? Arms for your rebel friends?"

"Sir, your men have had ample opportunity to verify my cargo. My logs are in your hands. I believe they sit at your elbow. No, I am not smuggling. I had troubles expected of a trip of that length."

"Very well. My crew will verify the cargo," responded Squire. He'd shifted uncomfortably when Jonas had pointed to the log books. As an afterthought, he added coolly, "Your man is in my sickbay. He's quite well, or will be. He's lucky to be alive after attacking my men. I'd have ordered him shot."

"He did not—" Swallowing the anger that threatened to burst from his chest, Jonas continued, "I have committed no crime, sir. These permits were not required when I left. I have been inspected and paid required duties in Cape Town." He took a breath again. "Furthermore, I protest the treatment of my crew. We were crammed below deck like slaves. Were we far at sea, I might understand. Therefore, I request we be put ashore in Norfolk. And under the Articles of War, seizure of personal possessions is not permitted."

Squire snorted. "I'm sure Lieutenant Alder made adequate provision for the safekeeping of personal property." Sneering, he added, "Seeing as how personal property means so little to your rebel friends by the way they steal and destroy, I'm surprised to hear of your concern. I suppose it means you care only for your *own* property. That of loyal subjects is unimportant."

Jonas ignored the last comment. "This day, sir, we've also had nothing more than a half ration of oatmeal and the worst ration of meat, surely the bottom of a spoilt cask. This is beneath the Royal Navy, sir."

Squire smirked. "Well, you and your crew received the finest in shipboard food, and you should be damned glad to have it. You are in no position to demand anything. It is you who have no rights here. How dare you question my authority?"

"Sir, I insist you release us to our own ship immediately and allow us to return home. There is no legal right of seizure here."

"You insist? Ye insist? Ye shall insist nothing. How dare ye, ye rebel whoreson," shouted Squire, rising to his feet. A short man, nevertheless he automatically moved slightly left to allow himself to stand straight. He pounded his fist on the table. He paused to breathe, then sat and picked up his pen. "As to the law, do not presume to lecture me. Your opinion means nothing. The prize board will determine the law. And I believe you will find that I am being truthful when I say they will condemn your ship as a lawful prize of war. This rebellion must and will be put down. We will take what measures we deem necessary to do so."

Jonas spluttered. "We are not—"

Squire angrily cut him off. "Don't bother. I've heard it all, and I do not believe it. Ye may not have been carrying contraband. It doesn't matter. Ye may or may not have known of the permit requirement. It doesn't matter. Ye did not have the permits, and *that* matters. Yer vessel is seized, and ye are a prisoner. Yer vessel will be sold. The prize court will decide what is to be done with ye. I personally hope they hang ye." Squire paused expectantly.

Jonas stood silently for a moment, breathing hard. The angry beast inside threatened to overwhelm him. He decided to pursue a different tack. "Sir, the injury done to a member of my crew was needless. He was beaten when he moved to make fast a line. No man on my ship would attack anyone without my express order."

"Bah. Mr. Alder reported the circumstances of his injury. He grabbed a belaying pin and swung at one of my sailors."

Surprised Alder had lied so blatantly, nevertheless such an accusation would bear no fruit. Instead, Jonas said, "You can be sure I will file charges, sir. There will be an accounting. When I left, Virginians were loyal to His Majesty. But with the heavy hand I've seen today, I don't wonder that some would choose to protest in a more violent way. I and my crew are loyal to our King. But that does not imply that I will quietly abide the abuses heaped upon me and my men by petty tyrants."

"Ye and yer rebels will dangle at the end of a rope. Get out. Sentry. Take the prisoner back for'ard."

The sentry nearly fell into the cabin as Jonas threw open the door and pushed his way out.

Jonas fumed as he strode forward. He would see this corrected and Captain Squire ruined if it was the last thing he did on this earth.

The sentry followed him forward. The guards opened the hatch and thrust him coldly below, nearly slamming the grate on his head.

"Well, sir?" Masefield and the crew gathered 'round him.

"They thought us to be smugglers. They know now we're not, but it doesn't matter. We are to be treated as prisoners of war, and the ship as their prize."

"War, sir?" asked one of the able seamen.

"There's been some changes since we left. Lord Dunmore

ordered the ports of Norfolk, Portsmouth, Suffolk, and Gosport closed. To land cargo, or even to enter the port, you've got to have permits from him," Jonas said.

"And I'm sure you've got to 'render honors' to the fine gentleman to get them permits," Masefield added bitterly. Many a ship's profit margin had been severely cut, even disappeared as a result of bribes paid to customs officials and others.

Jonas added, "He claims the lieutenant will guard our belongings and the court will return them to us. But our ship and cargo are gone."

Low whistles, growls, and groans greeted Jonas's last remark. They'd put fifteen months of their lives into bringing this cargo home. With the cargo gone, how would they be paid? He really couldn't commit his owner to anything, but he needed to say something.

"Don't worry, men. Mr. Scoggins will make good on your pay somehow. He's a fair man."

THE SOUND OF BATTENS BEING REMOVED ROUSED THEM early next morning. The hatch lifted and a seaman called down, "Up and out, the rebel captain. Yer goin' aboard the flagship."

As Jonas climbed, sounds of commotion filtered down.

Not quite sunrise yet, something brighter than twilight bathed the main deck. Patches of mist rolled by as he was led across the waist to the entry port. An older midshipman ordered him down into a longboat, clearly not from *Otter*.

Jonas couldn't see through the fog well enough to be certain, but it appeared they lay anchored near Craney Island, only a few miles upriver from where his ship had been taken.

Once Jonas and the midshipman were seated in the stern-sheets, the boat shoved off and rowed around *Otter*'s stern. As they did, another larger ship emerged from the fog, anchored a hundred yards or so away. The trip was cold and wet, though not as rough as the day before. Once aboard, a lieutenant pointed at Jonas, said, "You, come with me," then turned and walked aft.

In the stern cabin, a naval officer and another man sat. The officer wore the uniform of a post captain. He was older, certainly in his second half century, though the fringe of unusually short hair that remained was still mostly dark mottled with gray.

The other man was well dressed but did not wear a wig. Younger than Jonas, his brown hair was tied neatly in a queue, framing a callow, pockmarked face. His silk cravat and vest marked him an official of some kind. The two sat behind the table, a pile of paperwork in front of them. Jonas recognized his own handwriting on some. His bill of lading at least had made it to these men. There was no third chair. Jonas was expected to remain standing.

"Is your crew list accurate, Mr. Hawke?" asked the younger man, getting right to business. He kept his eyes on the paper in front of him.

Jonas bristled at the man's rudeness but held his tongue. He refused to give him the satisfaction. "Yes, it is. May I ask who you are? And have our families been informed that we are returned?"

The man did not answer, lifting instead a disgusted expression to Jonas.

Sitting back, the captain took charge. "Thank you, *Captain* Hawke."

With a sideways glance at the civilian official, he continued, "I'm Captain Davenport, naval aide to Lord Dunmore. This is Mr. Williams. We serve as the governor's prize court. We are here to gather information for the purpose of determining the appropriate disposition of your ship and yourselves. Being unsure of your muster, we have not told your families your whereabouts."

He paused, then continued. "Now, Captain Hawke, about your ship."

The interrogation lasted nearly an hour, hitting upon every detail of the voyage just completed. Jonas quickly realized they must have perused his log, as their questions implied foreknowledge of *Elizabeth's* travels. Davenport did most of the talking, with Williams only asking for an occasional clarification of some point. Of the two, Davenport remained cool and professional. Williams, on the other hand, appeared to have a chip on his shoulder, his questions accusatory. However, neither would answer any further questions themselves.

Davenport turned finally to cargo that hadn't been on the manifest.

Jonas explained. "That is my personal interest. I'm sure you understand some owners permit captains to carry unmanifested cargo for their own personal profit. If you examine the logs and customs declaration in Cape Town, you will see it was properly noted and duty paid."

Williams spoke. "*Mr.* Hawke, it looks like smuggling to me. You say it's common practice. But *I* have never heard of it. Perhaps it is the norm in *colonial* trade, but in the honest business world..." he said doubtfully.

Davenport turned and glared at him.

Before Jonas could answer, Davenport abruptly stood, followed hesitantly by Williams.

"Captain Hawke, we will render a decision and inform you. Your ship will likely be condemned as a lawful prize. But your crew will be released, as you appear to be innocent of *intentional* wrongdoing."

"Sir, I protest. My ship cannot be a lawful prize, for no war exists. For reason of our innocence, the ship cannot be condemned. Do you honestly believe I would stand into Norfolk in broad daylight had I known of the permits?"

Davenport and Williams glanced at each other. Williams looked angrily up at the ceiling while Davenport turned back to

Jonas. Davenport answered. "No, I do not. However, this rebellion must be quashed. Norfolk is not yet entirely in our possession. The rebels must be taught a lesson. Making a prize of your vessel is one of the ways we shall instruct them. We will make an example of you. I'm sorry for it, but war does not bring with it fairness."

"What do you mean, Norfolk is not entirely in your possession?"

Davenport pursed his lips. "I would think you would have heard news at some point. Surely you know of the hostilities in Massachusetts?" When Jonas nodded, he continued, "The Army has rounded up dens of rebels and arms all around the colonies. There are often scuffles in the streets, even here in Norfolk."

"I cannot believe fighting could happen here," Jonas said.

"Ah, but it has. Unrest has spread amongst the radicals. A fortnight ago, Lord Dunmore saw fit to put an end to rebellious exhortation in the press. It was not, er, well received by the citizenry. As a result, the governor restricted trade into the city, though he has not occupied it. He felt some of those who remain loyal might be pushed away by placing soldiers in town. Though not all his staff agree with that decision."

Williams snorted with derision.

Davenport continued. "The House of Burgesses has been dissolved, again, and several of those rabble-rousers have become outright rebels. Lord Dunmore and his family were forced to take refuge with the Royal Navy after mobs in Williamsburg and Yorktown directly threatened their lives. Within a few days his family will return to England for their own safety."

Williams interrupted. "You claim to be a subject of the King. You are not. You are a *colonist*. You have not earned the rights of free men. You and your kind strut around in your homespun clothes and think yourself the equal of *real* Englishmen. You shall learn your place, Hawke. The sooner, the better." He turned his back on Jonas to stare out the stern windows.

Davenport closed his eyes for a moment. "Steer clear of politics, Captain Hawke. The traitors are cowards. They shelter not only behind rocks and trees, but behind families, businesses, and even the Church. They do not come out in the daylight to fight like men but hide in the shadows, emerging only when they find a weak target. They will be crushed. They must be made to understand that. If you find you know some of them, my advice would be to make it clear they cannot stand against the might of the British Army and the Royal Navy. It will cost them their livelihoods, and most likely their lives."

Pausing to let it sink in, Davenport continued. "You may, of course, appeal the condemnation to the Prize Court of the Admiralty. But I should think you'd accept your fate quietly rather than make enemies of men who can be of help should you wish to continue employment at sea. In any case, such an appeal would literally take years and cost you more than the cargo you seek to save. I think you'll see the wisdom of leaving the issue drop." He smiled.

Jonas felt his face flush. They were innocent, yet he and his crew would still be punished. The "friendship" of these men was not something he was concerned about saving.

"Then, sir, what can you tell me of my men's belongings? They have been withheld. Prize laws do not allow their seizure."

Davenport cocked his head to the side. "I am informed by Captain Squire that your crew was permitted to retain all their belongings. I trust that you are not accusing a King's officer of intentionally misleading me?"

"Yes, sir, I am. My men were allowed to take only the clothes they wore. I will file a formal protest."

"With the Governor? Very well, you may do so. However, Captain Squire assures us that there were no personal things onboard your ship when she was brought in." Davenport glanced quickly at Williams, who had turned his eyes to the wall over Jonas's head. Davenport sighed and turned his attention back to Jonas. "Is there anything else?"

"Yes, one of my men was needlessly beaten. There was no

resistance offered when the 'prize crew' came aboard, and therefore no reason to attack him."

Davenport sighed again. "The man is said to have reached for a belaying pin, intending to strike down Lt. Alder. He could have been shot, Captain. He was fortunate he was not." He shook his head. "This rebellion has led to much ill will, which can understandably lead to excesses. Remember that. Good day."

The two men moved around the table and departed, leaving Jonas alone with the guard.

While Davenport seemed sympathetic, Alder and Squire had obviously explained away every questionable act.

As he climbed back aboard *Otter*, he pondered the other duty that lay yet ahead. He must report to Mr. Scoggins that he had nothing to show for fifteen months at sea.

Two hours later, the hatch opened and a lieutenant handed down an envelope with a Royal Navy seal. Inside was confirmation that *Elizabeth* had been seized for "trading with the enemy." The second sheet informed him of their release.

Jonas and his men were trooped up on deck and once more into boats alongside. There was still nothing of the shore visible for the fog.

As the boats rowed upriver, two shots rang out from behind, accompanied by shouts. The former crew of *Elizabeth* ducked their heads.

As the yelling died away, the sailors at the oars looked nervously toward the midshipman in the stern sheets. Despite his pale face, he growled, "Keep rowing. We're to get rid of these prisoners and that's what we'll do. The ship'll be there when we get back."

The men obeyed sullenly. The midshipman relayed the order

to the boat behind them. No more gunfire interrupted their journey.

When the boats cleared the fog, the Norfolk quay lay a short distance ahead. Jonas's men began to raise a cheer but were quickly cut off when the midshipman raised his pistol.

"Silence. I'll not mind trimming the numbers of rebels in Norfolk before I land you, I won't."

As soon as the boats moored, Jonas and his crew climbed onto the quay wall.

It was a far different homecoming than anticipated a few days and a lifetime ago.

The quay lay nearly deserted this time of the morning. A few people hurried by on business. An elderly man took time to stare at the boats, now under oars headed back downriver. He shook his head and moved on.

The passage of Jonas and his men further roiled the fog as it swirled between the buildings. The growing light revealed the warehouses and wharves that lined the street on the water side. More ships than usual stood silently along the waterfront, and there was far less activity than he'd expected.

A small crowd awaited them. Jonas was pleased that Davenport had kept his word on that, at least. He searched the small, silent group. He spied Mary, William, and Rebecca at the back of the crowd. His in-laws, George and Elizabeth Scoggins, stood one to each side of Mary. He went to them.

Chapter Four

Three-year-old Rebecca hid behind her mother's skirt at his approach. When Jonas reached them, Mary's face broke. She sobbed while her parents silently held her.

"Oh, Jonas, Jonas, you're too late. Dear God, you've missed them," Mary cried.

Over her gasps, Scoggins said, "Son, I'm sorry. It's the worst news possible. The twins are dead these six months."

Mary's mother, Elizabeth, stifled a sob of her own.

Jonas's head reeled as he reached out to his wife. The children he'd anticipated coming home to were gone, lost to him, unknown and unknowable. Jonas could do no more than hold her as she gave vent to half a year's worth of sorrow in the street outside the Customs House. As they stood there, the dark clouds moving overhead matched what lay in his heart. A light rain began to fall. Around them the crowd swirled as families reunited and departed, careful not to intrude on the torment playing out on the cobblestones.

Minutes later they walked homeward, Mary still sniffling. Jonas turned to his father-in-law.

"I'm sorry, too, sir. I've lost you your ship."

"Never mind. I tried to send a letter to you, but no post was allowed out. Governor's orders."

"But—"

George raised his hand. "Don't think on it. You need to take care of your family. We will talk on the morrow or the day after." Turning to his own wife, he continued, "It's time we leave them to themselves."

Elizabeth hugged her daughter one last time. Mary smiled weakly at her. Jonas put his arm around her, and they proceeded homeward.

William spoke. "You were gone a long time, Father."

Resisting the urge to draw William into a hug, instead he said, "I know, son. I'm sorry." Softly, he asked, "What happened?"

Mary swallowed her tears. "Right after Christmas, the twins were born. They were healthy, happy babies." Drawing a deep breath, she continued, "They grew so fast. By Easter, they were fat and near sat up by themselves. Then, a mere week after Easter...." Her voice broke. Shaking, she sagged into Jonas' arms. Moments later, she pulled herself upright and resumed.

"The influenza was widespread last spring. It took many, especially children. I kept Sarah and Matthew in the house, thinking to avoid those who were sick. Still, they took ill."

She paused again and wiped her eyes. "It took only a few days. At the end, they just lay in their crib, trying so hard to breathe." Her eyes again welled with tears. Though she tried, she couldn't continue.

Rebecca felt the sorrow in the air, but she remained afraid. Holding William's hand, she snuggled under his arm. Mary picked her up.

Devastated for the loss of children he'd not met but had loved, Jonas mourned the sorrow his family had endured alone.

At home, William took Rebecca to play while Jonas sat with Mary in the parlor. A silence born of shared, but not shared, sorrow lay between them.

Jonas was unprepared for the change in Mary. A cheerful soul when he'd left, she was now embittered and sad. There was resentment, too, perhaps because so much sorrow had been visited on her.

"I'm sorry, Mary," he began.

She did not respond, staring into the fire he'd built against the damp chill. Outside, rain fell steadily.

Finally, she whispered, "Don't. Don't say you're sorry. 'Sorry' suggests that it won't happen again. It will. It will...."

Jonas rose and gazed into the fire himself. "I can't change it. God knows I would if I could. But I don't know what else to say, Mary." He turned again to look at her. "I truly am sorry."

She turned to him, eyes pools of torment. But they contained fire, too. Fierce, raw, pain-driven anger. It frightened him like nothing at sea did. In all their years together, he'd never seen such anger.

"There's nothing you can say, Jonas," she said, voice hard. "The twins are gone. You will never know them, and they'll never know you, because *you* were *gone*."

He did not, could not answer. She'd never been quite as understanding as her mother had been of her father's time at sea. Thus, he'd devoted his time to her and the children when he was home. The previously unspoken tension between them became a presence as real as the moist cloying heat in the kitchen, and much more powerful.

"There's nothing you can say or do to change it." She drew a deep breath and straightened. "But you must stay home for now."

She measured tea into two cups, and they lapsed into silence.

THE NEXT MORNING, JONAS STARED UP AT THE CEILING as Mary lay beside him in exhausted sleep. He admired the curve of her chin, her nose, her cheeks. Though unblemished youth had left her, she was still beautiful. He lay back.

Losing children was not uncommon. He mourned the children he'd never met, but in some small way, to him they weren't real. However, for Mary it was different. She'd known them.

Later that morning, he sat with his father-in-law in the study of the Scoggins' home.

In his youth his father-in-law had gone to sea as both mate and captain. The two sipped a fine old Madeira, mementos of Scoggins' life at sea surrounding them. A stuffed kangaroo from Botany Bay. A tortoise shell from the Galapagos. On shelf after shelf sat finely bound and well-thumbed volumes, amidst knick-knacks from the far corners of the world.

His seagoing days now in the past, his captains often brought objects back for him. A small chest had been aboard *Elizabeth*, filled with spices, sandalwood carvings, and some fine silk cloth.

I hope Squire enjoys the spoils of his piracy.

Scoggins waved off Jonas's concerns about the loss. "They've taken three other ships since the start of the war," he said.

Scoggins rose and stirred the blaze in the hearth.

"Is it really a war?" Jonas asked.

"Ah, Jonas, that's a fair question, isn't it?" Scoggins rubbed his hands before the fire. "What do you know?"

"Very little, it would seem."

Scoggins gazed at the wall above the hearth for a moment before he said, "It feels different this time, and not just because of the bloodshed. There's more anger, deeper, and nearly every-where. Times past it was a game to see how to best avoid interfer-ence from afar. But it's no game now."

"Folks have been angry before. The burning of the *Gaspee* three years ago. There's been bloodshed before, too, in Boston. How has it gone so far this time?"

Scoggins sat and sipped his wine. "We've always been a passionate people. But something has stoked a raging fire. Men I've known for decades no longer speak to each other. Others who've sailed together for years avoid each other on the water-front. I myself speak cautiously to avoid taking sides. And there's them who won't abide me not taking *their* side." Scoggins sighed.

"There's no knowing where it will end. New provocations occur near daily, each worse than the last." He turned back to Jonas and leaned forward.

"Yesterday, a dozen or so men shot at a schooner that lay at anchor in the river. The schooner fired back with grape shot. Two days ago, soldiers took William Hutchings's cannon, the ones he used aboard his privateer during the last war. Lord Dunmore has promised to find and capture every cannon in the area to prevent their use against his soldiers. A month ago, he seized John Holt's printing press. They barely missed seizing John himself." Scoggins's tone grew more somber with every word.

Jonas rose, walked to the window and gazed out at the muddy street.

Boston had always been a hotbed of radicalism. But in Norfolk? Yet he was a newly released prisoner of a war. Turning to face Scoggins, he said. "What can I do now, though? To care for my family. I know nothing but ships and the sea."

"We all find ourselves in that position. Most shippers cannot afford or refuse to apply for these permits, so ships sit idle, rotting. Davenport assures us as soon as the rebels are chased out of Virginia, they'll open up the port once more. However, the events of yesterday prove it will be harder than many thought."

"So you're opposed to rebellion, then?" asked Jonas.

"Of course. Though, I admit I agree with the principle of self-government. It did seem to me that Parliament overstepped its bounds. Still, we must pay our fair share. We enjoy the protections of the Royal Navy. You know as well as I do, sometimes merely flying the British flag assures safety."

Scoggins joined Jonas at the window. Men shouldered through the gentle rain, collars turned up against the chill. The windowsill oozed cold air. Both men shivered.

Scoggins said, "Some folks had hoped the Continental Congress would work out some kind of solution. They sent letters to Parliament, the King, and some ministers. As usual, Patrick Henry spoke in fiery fashion." Scoggins grunted. "That man knows how to stir up a crowd. Things grew worse after that."

Jonas shook his head. Virginia had been one of the few colonies that had remained loyal to the crown during Cromwell's so-called "republic." Its loyalty had been rewarded following the Restoration. The more Scoggins spoke, the more the walls seemed uncomfortably close.

Scoggins continued. "I thought the government in London would reconsider, that there'd be a negotiation. All would come to their senses. The fighting *should* have scared everyone. No one save the radicals seemed to want it. Now I am afraid of where it will lead, and afraid of what others do or might do. In my worst imaginings, I underestimated them." He breathed deeply and took a sip of wine.

"There have been fights at sea, as well. Rhode Island formed a naval militia. In May, another Royal Navy schooner ran aground and was captured and burned. In June, there was a huge battle north of Boston. Hundreds are said to have been killed on both sides. George Washington, from up north near Alexandria, was appointed to lead what they call the Continental Army. There's men from all over rushing to join, even from here. There's another army forming in North Carolina." He closed his eyes for a moment. "Men's worst instincts have come to the fore."

Jonas shook his head. "It sounds as bad as the reformation movement a few years ago. Lay preachers going round, raising Cain. The whole country was aroused."

Scoggins nodded. "Perhaps worse. The middling folks' passions are inflamed again. There's even militia companies here about. Lord Dunmore formed a troop of his own and began hunting the militias' stores of weapons and powder. He got reinforcements from New York. Despite all that, the mobs keep at it."

"Do so few remain loyal?"

"There are. My son Isaac is one. But it is dangerous to speak up."

Jonas sat again. He'd heard enough calamitous news for one year, let alone one day.

But Scoggins wasn't done. He poured himself more wine. "After yesterday, the governor may decide to land soldiers in town. There's many who fear it will draw the militias from Williamsburg or North Carolina." Scoggins sat and stretched his legs out in front of him. "The rebels here are loud, a rum lot. No respect for a man's property. So-called 'committees of safety' go about looting and burning in effigy those who disagree with them. Only last week in Hampton, they tarred and feathered a landowner when he came to town. It's the inoculation riots all over again. Most just keep out of their sights. It seems easier than fighting." George looked ruefully at his hands and sighed.

Jonas shivered. Norfolk reminded him of a pot with a rolling boil beneath a lid.

If the fighting came, where would they go? Would anywhere be safe? There were no clear lines between enemy and friend. *And to which side do I belong?* He'd always been loyal to the crown, but then the crown had never before done him personal injury.

"In the unlikely event the colonies succeed in breaking from England, won't we just trade one tyranny for another? You can be certain exchanging a king in England for a local one would be a bad trade."

Scoggins smiled slightly. "It seems in many respects that the majority of the Congress feel the same way, Jonas. They are careful never to go so far as to declare a break with the king. Despite the severity of their actions, they always make room for reconciliation. No matter how much they might disparage Parliament and Lord North, they never go so far as to berate the king. But the questions is, can they control the others, the men of action who seem to run things in some towns?" Scoggins sipped from his nearly empty glass. Silence fell.

When Jonas brought up the issue of paying off *Elizabeth*'s crew, Scoggins waved his hand. "Posh, don't worry. I will take care of them. I can't give them a lot of money, but I can take care of their immediate needs. I don't mind telling you, Jonas, there's many who wouldn't do so, but I just don't feel right telling them they get nothing after so long a voyage." He studied Jonas. "I must say, I had concerns about you. We heard nothing for so long."

"Ill fortune followed us nearly the entire voyage." He closed his eyes and imagined the faces of his twins. "But 'twas nothing compared to the ill fortune that befell Mary."

Scoggins swirled his newly-filled glass as he stared into it. "There is a quote that says, *These are melancholy steps, but the path to glory leads through the grave, and it is well worth while to undergo the pains of bearing and of parting with children if thereby we people the Redeemer's kingdom, for of such does His kingdom consist, as He assured us when He was here upon the earth.*"

Jonas nodded. But such words would bring no comfort to his wife.

They turned to discussing the voyage. Scoggins enjoyed the professional details and seamanship. As day advanced into afternoon, Jonas finally took his leave.

Scoggins cautioned him that, even with permits, he didn't dare go to sea. With the Royal Navy pressing against trade ever more closely, to be recaptured now could lead to being jailed as a smuggler or worse. But how would he support his family? Jonas wondered.

Chapter Five

At breakfast, he said, "I believe I will go to Hampton. To see Fred Payne."

Mary raised her eyes suspiciously. The dishes clattered as she abruptly began clearing the table. "A few months, eh?" she asked. "Is that all we get of you?"

Sensing shoal water, he responded cautiously, "No, not necessarily. But we cannot live without my working somewhere. Nor will I live off your parents' table."

She put the dishes down on the counter and stared at the wall for a long minute. When she turned, her face was dark. "Yes, I know. But your son needs you. Our daughter doesn't know you. I need you. Go to Hampton, but make no promises. There is too much uncertainty now and our children need a father." She turned back to wipe the dishes.

Jonas closed his eyes and took a deep breath. "You know I cannot promise. I also must provide for my family." He stood. "I will take William with me. It will do him good to get away for a night."

After a few more moments, Mary gave a slight nod. Jonas headed up the stairs to talk with his son.

They set out by foot to Sewell's Point, where they would take the ferry across Hampton Roads to Mill Creek. To the south, several of Dunmore's flotilla sailed downriver toward them. While they were miles away and posed no obvious threat, William nevertheless watched nervously.

Across Hampton Roads, two more Royal Navy schooners lay at anchor. But they made no move to interfere with the ferry as it approached the landing.

In Hampton, Jonas sought out his old shipmate.

Payne had been captain and Jonas his first mate in the Caribbean trade over a decade earlier. He'd owned his own ship, and it was Payne who encouraged Jonas to purchase *Mary Rose*. Now he owned three coastal vessels, moving whatever cargo was available both within the Chesapeake and without, but primarily between Savannah and Charleston to the south, and New York and Philadelphia to the north. A tall, thin man, he kept his white hair close-cropped. It was more comfortable under a wig, he said. His face matched his body. Today, he wore a green waistcoat and spectacles as he bent over a newspaper.

"Hello, Fred."

Payne looked up and the tanned leather of his face split into a wide smile, revealing long yellow teeth. "Why bless my soul, Jonas Hawke, pirate and smuggler," he rasped. Rising quickly, he moved to shake Jonas's hand. "And this must be Master William. Why, he's nearly a man. Are you ready to go to sea yet, son?"

William glanced up at his father.

Jonas smiled and turned back to Payne. "Not quite yet, Fred, but soon."

Payne waved them to a small round table at the corner of the office by the window. Pulling a bottle from a cabinet, he removed three glasses from a drawer and poured deep red liquid into two of them. Turning back, he looked a question at William.

"No, sir, I wouldn't like any. Thank you."

Putting the third glass back, Payne joined them at the table, gave Jonas the one glass and raised his own.

"To the best mate I've ever sailed with. And confusion to the English," he said, and drank.

Jonas raised his own glass as he heard the first part of the toast, and his eyebrows at the second half.

"I take it you're with the rebels, Fred?" Jonas asked.

"Aye, you may. I believe in choosing my own destiny, and I believe my country should also," came the reply. "But let's not talk of politics, Jonas. For what reason have you sought me out today? Aren't you newly home from a long voyage?"

"Yes, but it didn't pay very well." Jonas related his story to Payne.

Afterward, Payne studied him for a long moment. "I'm sorry, Jonas, truly I am. I hadn't heard how poorly you'd been treated. I knew the bloody bastard had closed Norfolk. There are plenty who've lost their vessels and their livelihoods. I'm sorry it's happened to you."

"Well, what's done is done. But I need to make a living, Fred," Jonas said.

Payne fixed Jonas with a pinched, sad look. "I can't help you, though I wish to God I might."

He stood and walked over to his desk and picked up papers. "These are the bills due to chandlers, the shipyard, and what I owe my captains and crews. I am able to pay many, but not all. Two of my ships lie idle here at the wharfs. The third is in St. Kitts, and I hope Tisdale can get her home without being captured. If he does, I may be able to pay the rest. Dunmore has put me out of business. You saw the Navy at anchor out there, didn't you?"

Jonas nodded. He also mentioned the three or four more they'd seen from the ferry.

"They know we aren't completely choked off here, yet. None-theless, I have no work, and neither do any of the other shippers here. It's not much better up north, and there are a dozen or more captains and tens of mates who've gone there ahead of you. Every ship that sails is plundered because no one will sell foodstuffs to 'his lordship', and every one that returns is seized for fear they carry arms to the militia. They're strangling us a day at a time."

"But then why fight? Surely if they are so much stronger, why place your head in a noose?" Jonas leaned forward at the table, his wine forgotten.

Payne gave him a sad smile and shook his head. "Because in the end, I think we will wear them out. Can we stand up and fight them? No, of course not. But if we make it uncomfortable enough for long enough, they must eventually give in and give us our freedom. It will take years. It may be our sons —" he pointed to William "— will have to pick up the mantle and finish it for us. I fear I will not live to see the day, in fact. But in the end we will prevail, for we must." Payne drained his glass. "And where do you stand, Jonas?"

Jonas shook his head. "I do not delve into politics. There's rocks 'neath the surface of every discussion, so I avoid it like a lee shore."

Payne pursed his lips. "You've lost your ship and your livelihood. What else will you let them take from you? One way or t'other, you'll need to take a stand one day, likely soon."

They continued to talk across another glass of wine. Then Jonas took his leave, strolling with William along the waterfront. He had intended to talk with other acquaintances. But the talk with Payne had convinced him of the futility of his mission.

"William, we shall head for home. There's no work to be found here."

"Aye, father. I listened." As they walked along the water, William asked, "Why does Mr. Payne hate the king?"

Jonas considered his son. William was none of the smiling, fun-loving lad he'd been before Jonas had left. The heartbreak of the past year had matured him, made him somber. Jonas worried it was too much but only time would tell. "He doesn't, son. But he and others believe the king's ministers treat us unfairly."

"Do you believe that?"

"Perhaps I do, sometimes. It's difficult, William."

The boy looked thoughtful, and they walked in companionable silence for a time. "But shouldn't the ministers always be fair?" he asked.

"Yes, and no, son. It seems to me that government isn't fair or unfair, it just is. The king's ministers must act as they see fit to protect the kingdom and keep it prosperous. You know the Royal Navy keeps piracy down and ensures our trade ships are protected." He paused, then said, "It's difficult to be fair to everyone. What benefits me and keeps my ship safe costs money. Thus, the government must levy taxes to pay for the Royal Navy. This may seem unfair to a man who makes his living plowing the earth and only sells his corn to the mills or to the people of his town."

William walked quietly, looking at the shops they passed. After a time, Jonas continued. "There is no easy resolution to this disagreement. Men's passions are aroused. When that happens, they often don't think clearly. They too easily take offense. The best we can ever do is to be fair in our own affairs. I pray that more thoughtful men will prevail and we will avoid more bloodshed."

"Is Mr. Payne not a thoughtful man?"

Jonas instantly regretted his choice of words, but there was nothing for it now. "He is, or always has been. But as you heard, his dander is up. He finds it hard to be unprejudiced. He is not a bad man for it. But when two men are angry and they see the issue from opposite sides, it makes for conflict. And when the issue affects a man's ability to make a livelihood and take care of his family, the strength of such passion can lead to violence."

"Could it lead you to violence, father?" William was looking up at him thoughtfully and with a hint of trepidation.

Jonas smiled. "No, son. Oh, if someone threatened you or your mother or sister with harm, I would be very much moved to do whatever I needed to do to protect you. And if someone took away everything we had and prevented me from feeding you all, I might be moved to fight. But that's not going to happen, son. We will be alright. I'll find something."

As they moved through town, smoke rose to the southeast toward the ferry landing, and filled Jonas with foreboding. Deciding to stay for now, he looked for a tavern where they might eat and get some news. The new sound of firing from beyond the harbor mouth confirmed they could not return to Norfolk.

As they lunched, two men seated near them described the previous night's events.

"They'll get through, I'll wager. They worked all night on that line o' ships we sunk. How our sentries failed to hear it, I can't say."

The other responded, "They be not done. There's boats with axes up to the barricade and th' sailors was working on it. The militia ought to get some sharpshooters up. Chase 'em off so they'll not get into the harbor."

Learning the Royal Navy was trying to breach the harbor was enough to motivate Jonas. "William, hurry and finish your meal."

Another man hurried in. "The Navy's a-marchin' from Mill Creek." His shout further stirred the diners. Several men rushed out.

Jonas and William joined them in the street. The intermittent musket fire swelled to a near continuous roar. The peak did not last long, only to swell again after several minutes. William said nothing, but his face paled. He walked steadily, though he moved closer to Jonas.

The thunder increased again, this time holding for nearly half an hour. Smoke from burning buildings now mingled with the haze of gunfire.

Jonas changed his mind again. They couldn't stay if Hampton became the site of a battle.

"William, we must find a boat."

William nodded shakily.

"We will be fine, son. Even if the Navy is out there, they won't shoot at a man and a boy rowing home. I know it's a long row, but it will be the safest." He led William toward the beach west of the harbor, away from the ferry landing.

The musket fire began again, closer. Jonas pushed William behind a building and looked around the corner.

Masts moved beyond the buildings, ships sailing into the harbor. Jonas started as the air was torn by cannon fire.

A line of warships fired on the town. *Otter* led, followed by *Fowey*. Behind them sailed two smaller warships. They loosed another ragged broadside at the waterfront. Clouds of splinters flew as shots struck home.

"William, we must get away," Jonas shouted. Grabbing his son by the coat, he half dragged, half pushed the boy along. Partway across the street, William regained control of his legs and ran. Jonas was close behind.

"When you get back to the tavern, run inland at least five streets, as fast as ever you can," Jonas called. He was about to repeat his instructions when William reached the next building and turned around.

"I want to stay with you, Father."

"You can't, son. I need you to be safe."

"Why are they shooting?"

"I don't know, but you need to get away. D'ya hear? Run. I will find you at the tavern when the shooting stops."

William's eyes were wide, his face chalky. But no panic.

He couldn't risk losing his boy, so Jonas spun him and pushed him in the direction of the tavern. The boy ran haltingly, but he went.

Jonas turned just as the ships fired again.

The waterfront filled with other men also come to see. One ran past him, carrying a musket.

"What do you hope to do with that?" Jonas called.

The man turned, eyes blazing. "I plan on sending as many of

those bastards to hell as I can before they cut me down." He disappeared down the quay. Other armed men followed.

Despite the cool air, sweat beaded across Jonas's forehead.

Here was civil war, and he didn't know which side he was on. He watched in dismay as the Royal Navy fired on civilian warehouses, destroying the livelihoods of Hampton merchants. He watched as men hid behind the corners of buildings, barrels, or wooden boxes, firing hopelessly at ships with muskets. Farther down the quay, warehouses burned. Acrid smoke burned his lungs and stung his eyes.

Boats filled with the redcoats of the British army appeared at the sterns of the warships, rowing for the quay. Judging it was no longer safe to remain in the open, Jonas moved behind a pile of disused old rope and found another man already squatting there.

"Will ye look a' that?" The man grinned and pointed at the rebel musketmen.

"Do they actually believe they can fight off the army?"

"Ah, not only can they, but they will. We've been spoilin' for this fight, we ha'," the man shouted over the din of the now unceasing cannonade.

Jonas carefully peered around the edge of the rope.

The musket fire was drowned out by the cannonade. Smoke rose from the guns ashore, more than one or two dozen. They were having effect, too. Several men pitched into the harbor from the boats and from the decks of the ships. A few fell from the rigging. One boat spun suddenly to starboard, the coxswain apparently shot. Its oars fouled with those of another boat and together they drifted with the current. The men in both struggled to free themselves. The musketmen ashore shifted their fire to the remaining boats.

The cannonade slackened, then ceased. The musketry filled the gap. Boatswains pipes trilled aboard the ships and *Otter* turned toward the quay. Jonas saw the boats had turned as well. The farthest passed astern of the last ship in line, hidden behind the ship's bulk.

"Hah. The' run, by God, the' run," cried the man. Jonas had quite forgotten about him. He clapped Jonas on the shoulder, grinning broadly. Then he stood and shook his fist at the ships. "Run, ye bastards, run. Ye're not welcome here. Go back and tell the king that." With that, the man ran down toward the musket fire. Others left their shelter and followed, shooting.

Jonas stood as well but ducked back down as the cannonade resumed. *Otter* headed back to sea, firing as she went. The steady west wind had enabled both their approach and now their apparent retreat.

Remaining behind the rope pile, Jonas looked once more down the quay. The man with whom he'd shared the shelter lay on the cobblestones ten paces away, writhing in pain.

Moving carefully to avoid drawing fire, Jonas moved quickly to the wounded man. He kneeled next to him.

"Where are you hurt?"

"Ahh, it's me leg," moaned the man. Blood dripped onto the stone.

"Let me help you stand and we'll get you out of here."

The man grunted, but Jonas got him standing. They moved behind the rope pile. He pulled back the trouser leg to examine the wound. A piece of stone protruded from a jagged rent in the flesh. As he pulled it out the man screamed and fell silent. Jonas checked to ensure he still lived, then bound the wound.

The ships completed their maneuver and rapidly distanced themselves from the waterfront. The men with muskets split into two groups. One headed down the shoreline toward the bay to continue harassing the ships. The second remained behind and organized bucket brigades to try to prevent the fires from spreading. Small groups tended to the wounded. Several bodies lay still on the stones.

The battle had lasted a little more than an hour, yet it was another high-water mark for the violence spreading through Virginia.

Jonas retrieved William, and they remained overnight in

Hampton. That evening they heard the ship that had carried Jonas and his crew to Norfolk following their release had run aground, been captured, and burned. In the fighting, her captain had been killed.

———

Jonas and William left their lodgings at dawn, hurrying through the wakening Hampton streets. Smoke still sullied the morning air, but the shattered glass and broken and splintered wood had been swept from the cobblestones.

They rented a boat at the docks for an exorbitant price and received instructions on who to leave it with on the southern side of Hampton Roads. They began the four nautical mile row homeward.

The gurgle of the water alongside the boat was accompanied by the gentle squeak of the oarlocks in their tholes as they rowed silently back to Sewell's point.

William stared off toward the expanse of the Chesapeake.

"What do you see, William?"

William didn't move for a moment, then turned toward his father and refocused. "Nothing, sir." Then he returned to his reverie.

Jonas tried again.

"Does what you saw yesterday frighten you? There is no shame in that. It frightens me."

When William didn't move or answer, Jonas waited. He was just about to speak again when William said, "No, sir. I mean, yes, sir. It frightened me." He turned to Jonas. "But I do not understand it, Father. They shot at the town. Men might have been hurt. Shops and buildings got knocked down. Why? You said when a man is wronged it can lead to violence. Did someone in Hampton wrong the Royal Navy?"

"God's honest truth, I cannot tell you what made the Royal

Navy do it. And yes, men were hurt. It is likely that some were even killed."

William's face blanched.

"You heard Mr. Payne. He cannot help his men support their families."

"Would it harm the Navy for us to be independent?"

"It's complicated, William. The colonies add wealth to Britain. We have good soil. That grows cotton, tobacco, trees for wood. We grow food. They need those things in England and elsewhere."

William looked down at the filthy water swirling back and forth around his shoes. "But they could still buy those things from us, and we from them, if the colony was independent."

"Yes."

William sighed. "Mr. Payne said it would be up to me to win a war. I don't think I am ready to die."

The rhythm of Jonas's strokes never broke, but his heart did. "I won't let them hurt you, or your mother, or your sister, William. I promise."

He only hoped he could keep that promise.

When they opened the door, Mary ran from the kitchen. Jonas caught her as she enfolded them both in her arms. "I heard there was fighting in Hampton. When you didn't come home, I feared the worst. I couldn't bear to lose both of you."

Jonas went inside with her where they sat in the kitchen.

"Jonas, you must promise me you'll stay out of this fighting."

"I promise I will only fight to protect you and William and Rebecca."

Mary looked sullenly at him. She shook her head. "Why does God allow this? Men lose their sanity, putting everyone in danger. Will no one cease the madness?"

More bad news arrived over the next days.

In the middle of the previous month, the Royal Navy had sailed into Falmouth, Massachusetts. When the local militia defied the order to turn over their arms, the ships opened fire with cannon, carrying out their threat to destroy the town. Later that same day, they landed marines to burn what remained. Over three hundred people were left homeless in the snowy fields of northern Massachusetts. Nearly every building lay in ashes.

Closer to home, in Williamsburg, a loyalist was tarred and feathered and his home set afire. The man died, leaving behind a widow and two small children.

Chapter Six

Faced with a seemingly insoluble problem, Jonas turned to something that had always helped him clear his mind. He took William down to the waterfront to help him work on *Mary Rose*.

Jonas had paid an old sailor and his young grandson to look after her while he'd been gone, but there was always more to do than a caretaker could get to.

William was half a foot taller than when Jonas had left, the top of his head now reached midway up Jonas's chest. His face was leaner though still baby-skinned. His dark brown hair covered his ears and he was forever unconsciously pushing up a wild lock that fell across his forehead. Jonas marveled at how his son had matured while William methodically checked the deck and bulwarks for rot.

Jonas removed the battens from the main hatch to go below to check the berth deck and bilges. The sound of a bosun's pipe made him turn and look downriver. A line of ships sailed toward him, *Otter* in the lead. She wore round, bringing the wind from her starboard quarter to the larboard quarter, steering east to follow the river. Guns run out, wisps of smoke rose from behind the bulwarks.

When the fourth ship in line hove into view, his heart nearly stopped.

He couldn't mistake the lines of her hull nor the cut of her sails. It was his own *Elizabeth*, the ship he'd taken to Batavia and back. The ship they'd taken from him.

Elizabeth's cargo had been sold, the funds used to buy food for the men aboard Dunmore's flotilla. To see her sail past him in the hands of the Royal Navy cut him to the quick. He wondered where they might be headed.

Oh, no. Not again. His heart raced. Running forward, he called, "William, get ashore now. Run."

William looked up and the color drained from his face. Jonas grabbed him. "Run home. Tell your mother I'll be right behind."

William dashed ashore and disappeared between the buildings.

Jonas turned back to the ships and prayed. He continued to watch as they sailed around the bend into the east branch of the Elizabeth River, their masts visible above the rooftops for long minutes. Then he, too, hurried off *Mary Rose* and headed for home.

***

At home, Mary and William stood in the doorway.

"Where did they go, father?" he asked.

"I'm not certain, son. They were prepared for battle. I don't know who might be upriver for them to fight." Inside, a dinner of dried venison and corn cakes awaited.

Later, they returned to the waterfront. They had just walked onto the wharf when a man on horseback galloped up. Dismounting, he hurried into the tavern across the street. Jonas told William to stay put and went across.

The darkness after even the watery sun made him pause just inside. A booming voice drew his attention.

"They march on Kemp's Landing. Hutchings and Lawson are there with the Princess Anne militia, but they need more men. Dunmore landed at Great Bridge this morning."

"Ach, Dunmore canna ha' more than a hundred men hisself. Tha' militia's more than enou' ta send them back to theys ships," said a man seated at a table. He was rewarded with a general muttering of agreement.

"Well, now, that's a fine kettle. You're saying you'll not come?" asked the rider.

"No, we're no' needed. 'Tis a waste o' time an' shoe leather, 'tis."

"If the militia is defeated, what is there to stop Dunmore coming here? From taking Norfolk?"

The seated man stared at his tin cup. "Well, then he'll be here. There's no much us can do abou' that." He took a deliberate slow draft.

Having heard enough and being in a hurry to find reinforcements, the horseman pushed past Jonas. He led his horse down the street.

Jonas rejoined William on the wharf.

"What was it, father?"

"He brought news. It appears there might be a fight at Kemp's Landing."

William shivered. They hadn't talked about what had happened in Hampton. He'd tried to bring it up but William demurred. So Jonas had let it be. Now he spoke. "Son, what happened in Hampton didn't resolve anything. The militia killed sailors and Royal Marines. The Navy battered the waterfront. They destroyed men's livelihoods. Neither side forced the other to give in. It just made both sides angrier."

"What do you think?" William asked.

The river meandered slowly past the wharf and the ships moored there. Would that the affairs of men moved so slowly, he thought.

"There are good and bad arguments on both sides. Men fear

change. I do. Would any man prefer things remain as they are, or that they change? What would you decide?" he asked.

William, too, stared off across the river. Jonas wondered what he saw.

"I don't like how things are. I wish things were as they were a year ago, after the twins were born. But I wish you were home then, too."

Jonas reached out to touch the boy's shoulder. This war would mean William and boys his age would grow up much faster.

Later in the afternoon, they heard a few bursts of musket fire at a distance, but it died off quickly and silence reigned.

<hr>

THE BRITISH SHIPS SAILED AS FAR UPRIVER AS THEY could, then disgorged their soldiers. Despite having the advantage in numbers and having laid an ambush, the militia ran when Dunmore's men marched into Kemp's Landing. Moreover, the British captured the militia commander, Joseph Hutchings. The fighting was short-lived, and the royal governor's men next moved toward Norfolk.

"Can we please not discuss the fighting at table, Father?" Mary blurted as George and Jonas discussed the city's impending change of hands at the Scoggins' dinner table.

Both men lapsed into silence, then Jonas said, "We can't ignore what's going on around us. We're in the midst of a war. We have tried not to take sides, to not give offense and go about our business. But once Dunmore's soldiers are here, what if the rebels attack the city? What if they lay siege, as they did in Boston? People there starved."

"I'm sick of war talk, Jonas. We're not Bostonians and our fellow Virginians are not monsters. They will not allow children to starve."

Elizabeth laid her hand on her Jonas's arm. "We are not blind.

But Mary is right, it *is* different here. New England is filled with rebellion. Virginia is not." She looked at her husband, then continued. "What happened in New England can't happen here."

Jonas looked at Scoggins, who gave him a slight shrug.

His mother-in-law continued. "We're British subjects. We are protected by custom and constitution. The fractious men will be arrested, and the rest will go back to their farms and shops."

Jonas shook his head. "I'm not so certain. Mr. Williams of the prize court insisted we are not subjects of his majesty, but 'mere colonists.' He does not believe we are his equals."

Mr. Scoggins joined back in. "I've seen that, too. Lord Dunmore's men treat us uncivilly, as if we are lessers." He shook his head. "It is that, more than the acts of Parliament themselves, that drives the anger and frustration. A man may abide many things done to him by government. But when it treats him as less than a man, that he cannot and will not abide."

Jonas turned to Mary. "I want the fighting to end as badly as any man. Nonetheless, I can't ignore it. The governor seems uninterested in anything beside crushing dissent. The rebels are the same. How is that different from New England?"

Mary looked down at her plate. "I don't know. I only know it must be different. This cannot happen in our home. It cannot. I fear for the future. I fear for the children. Where will the madness end?"

THE NEXT DAY SAW DUNMORE'S MEN MOVE INTO Norfolk proper, quartering officers in homes and setting up a camp for the soldiers outside the city to the south. They appeared to be settling in for the winter. Dunmore ordered over thirty homes destroyed to construct a fortress meant to defend the city from the rumored body of rebel troops moving up from North Carolina.

The approach of the rebel force brought near panic to the

city. Several families, outspoken loyalists, left town to the north, unsure that Lord Dunmore's force would try to hold the city. Boat traffic from Sewell's Point greatly increased, ferrying people and their belongings across Hampton Roads.

As November drew to a close, the fighting grew more organized, the lines more clearly drawn. The British constructed another earthen stronghold at Great Bridge on the north side of the river. Called Fort Murray, it was reinforced with the Ethiopian Regiment, formed of slaves who had responded to Dunmore's proclamation of freedom for those owned by rebels.

Upon arriving, Colonel Woodford, leading the North Carolina militia, also built a fortification on the south side of the river. There the two forces faced each other, neither side willing or ready to move. The year stretched into December. Though the two sides traded musket fire almost daily, an uneasy peace settled over Norfolk.

It wasn't to last. Upon hearing rumors that cannon moved north to reinforce the colonials, Dunmore acted. The evening of the 8th he sent further reinforcements to Fort Murray. Arriving at three in the morning, they found the Ethiopian Regiment was not at the north end of the bridge where it was expected to be. Indeed, the fort was manned only by the small force of regular British foot soldiers. Shortly after dawn on December 9, despite not being fully prepared and his men exhausted from three days of preparation and the march, the captain in command ordered an attack.

Chapter Seven

Behind the house, Jonas worked to fix a chair. Later, there were ashes from the fireplace to clear out. He looked up at the distant sound of cannon fire.

Mary came out of the kitchen. "Is it battle?" She held William's trousers in one hand, a needle thrust halfway into a patch on the knee. She'd been interrupted mid-stitch.

"I believe so. I heard musket fire earlier. I thought perhaps the militia turned and ran when faced with regulars. But now there's cannon fire, I expect they're standing and fighting."

"Please God they change their minds." Mary returned to the house.

As the morning wore on, the sound of battle grew. The cannonade tapered off once, but surged again half an hour later. The musket fire didn't slacken until nearly noon.

Jonas was torn. A man of action nearly his whole life, it was difficult to be uninvolved. He badly wanted news but didn't want to leave Mary and the children alone.

Using a drawknife to finish rounding the new leg, he looked up at sudden silence. The cannon fire had ended abruptly, replaced with a few randomly spaced musket shots.

As he fitted the leg into the seat, the clop of hooves from the road caused him to miss with the hammer. Cursing quietly, he stepped quickly round to the front of the house.

John Langdon, who owned a general goods shop near St. Paul's church, rode along, followed by a wagon piled with hastily packed belongings. His wife and son bounced in the seat.

"What's the news, Mr. Langdon?" he asked.

Langdon pulled up his horse and moved out of the road. He motioned for his wife to keep going.

"Tha rebels are comin', Captain Hawke. Some'ow, they beat the bloody cowards o' tha army, and now they're comin'. We're headed for Lynnhaven Inlet. There's ships anchored nigh what will take us off. 'Tis said the rebels mean ta burn the town. You'd best get your family packed and get out." Langdon's Scottish brogue was more pronounced than Jonas had ever heard it. "Near half a thousand o' th' bastards. They're comin' hell for leather ta burn and loot. Get ye gone, sir, and your family, too. Tha's nothin' twixt them and here ta stop 'em." Turning his horse, he galloped off after his family in the wagon.

The Langdons weren't the only ones leaving in a hurry. As the afternoon wore on, several more families, mostly loyalist Scots, passed by. Finally, at mid-afternoon, he told Mary to gather essentials. Packing them in their own wagon, he still waited.

As evening approached, the traffic moving north slackened. Despite occasional shots from the southeast, no flames or smoke rose.

Finally, he strode into the parlor. Rebecca slept in front of the fire. William sat near her, reading silently. Mary sewed a new frock for their daughter.

"I think it's safe. Nothing seems to be happening in town and no one else has passed this way in the past half an hour."

"This madness must stop. There is nothing to be gained from sending good people fleeing into the night." Mary thrust the needle through the fabric, jerking it tight.

"As long as the fighting continues, there can be no reconciliation. I hold no hope of the King or his minister suddenly deciding they've been unreasonable, nor do I see the rebels deciding to give in. This war will require one side to be defeated and the other side to recognize they've been beaten."

"Bah. And which side will surrender, Jonas? Surely you don't think the rebels can compel England to surrender, do you? Could a child compel a bull to kneel? These small, sparsely populated colonies against the might of England?"

"There is another way to look at it. Perhaps it is David and Goliath." He rose and went to her side of the table. He put his arms around her neck. "I know. I wish it were not so. When a man fights for his family, he cannot accept surrender; it will take death to defeat him. The English cannot kill all the rebels."

Sleep avoided them until the wee hours of the morning.

THE NEXT DAY COLONEL WOODFORD'S MILITIA occupied Norfolk. Dunmore's small fleet sailed away and anchored in the mouth of the York River. A few ships remained anchored in Hampton Roads.

Tensions ran high between those who remained loyal to the crown and the new occupiers.

With the city in rebel hands, local independence advocates grew bolder, and everyone generally knew who was a loyalist. As December wore on, occasional attacks took place on Tory homes and places of business, intended only to drive the targets out of town. Occasionally, someone died.

Following his retreat, Dunmore continued to forage in the area, demanding supplies as he and his troops huddled aboard their ships. Depending upon their sympathies, local residents either refused or were not permitted to comply.

Rebel troops insisted on being called the Continental Army, and actively patrolled neighboring towns, plantations, and farms. For the most part they kept Dunmore from obtaining food, and the surreptitious trickle that did make it wasn't sufficient for the number of men and civilians in the small fleet. Hunger raised the level of violence.

As fall weather gave way to winter, the numbers of those who desired to remain neutral dwindled.

At last, just before Christmas, the snow came and covered the dirt and grime of the city. Incidents became more infrequent, and a nervous peace settled over Norfolk. Many hoped the spirit of Christmas would hold well into the New Year.

A pallor of gloom still hung over the Hawke home as life had returned to some semblance of routine. The ports remained closed as the Royal Navy controlled the southern Chesapeake. Food now came from North Carolina along inland trails, despite the worsening weather.

The only true shortages were what most considered luxury goods – primarily things imported from England. While the demand in England for cotton kept the port of Charleston open, transporting trade goods that far by road was impractical. So for those in search of an iron pot, there were few to be had and those for an exorbitant price. For someone in search of something to put in the pot, there was relative plenty.

Christmas at the Hawke home lacked for little.

The children were appropriately grateful for the small sweets they received. The house smelled pleasantly of cedar boughs. All hands were scrubbed clean on Christmas Eve, and on a bright, sunny, though cold Christmas morning, they donned their finest and walked to St. Paul's Church.

The golden brilliance contrasted splendidly with the hard blue of the sky. Just a few clouds dotted the horizon. If one stared solely up toward the heavens, he might not see the scattered heaps of ash that represented what had once been homes, and thus forget the cruelty of war.

In his sermon, the rector called on his flock to reflect Jesus's love for his enemies, and for peace in Norfolk. He especially emphasized charity for those who'd lost everything. Jonas expected to hear grumbling from over the high pew partitions but there was none. At least here, people kept their silence. Afterward, the family enjoyed the warmth of the sun as they strolled home, avoiding where the thawing ground had already turned to mud.

Later that afternoon, they called on Mary's parents. The children were lavished with more sweets. A rather sumptuous feast with a local ham and Christmas pudding graced the table. Mr. Scoggins expressed the family's thankfulness and desire for peace in the New Year in heartfelt prayer.

After supper, the women and children withdrew. The men turned their conversation once more to current events.

"Do you think Dunmore will make good his promise to take back the city?" Jonas asked.

"Who can foretell? The rebels are dug in quite thoroughly. I worry about a long siege, though I am uncertain if Dunmore has sufficient force at this moment. However, I'm told he's written to General Gage, petitioning for yet more soldiers. If they come, that could change everything."

"I often wonder why he doesn't operate against Williamsburg. That's where the rebel leaders are."

"I suspect it's because not only does he not have the soldiers to try to go so far inland as to take Williamsburg, but also because it would be far too easy for the Burgesses — sorry, the Convention now — to escape. We are the largest city in the colony. We have the best port from which his ships can operate, and good roads for bringing supplies in from the countryside. What he will do with his newly arrived frigate, this *Liverpool*, I wonder." Scoggins gazed up into the ceiling, as if it might answer.

Jonas sipped a local strawberry wine. "This guessing how far either side will go drives me mad. We are caught in the middle."

Scoggins sat silently. Finally, he said, "We are trapped, all of us. We do not control events, but neither do they, really. We can only attempt to remain out of the line of fire."

"That could prove exceedingly difficult," Jonas replied quietly. "I'm ashamed every time someone's house is burned by these rebels, while I stand by doing nothing."

"What would you do? Fight? How would you take care of Mary and the children if they burned *your* home?"

Jonas had no answer, as events dragged him deeper into the wildly spinning morass of conflict.

On New Year's Eve, as the sleeping city passed from 1775 to 1776, the former royal governor's fleet sailed silently upriver.

CHAPTER EIGHT

Jonas started at the sound of hooves in the muddy road. *Three, at least.*

He moved around the corner of the house, where he'd been splitting logs for the fireplace. One of the riders pulled up while the other three continued at a fast clip.

"You have a wife, children here?" the rider asked. Seeing Jonas nod, he said, "T'en best get t'em away. Ta redcoats is coming. T'ere's four ships anchored in t' river. Ta captain says he's a-going ta blast the town. We got hours ta get t'e women and children away."

"There's always rumor they're coming. What is different now?"

His horse turning under him, the rider said, "Tis true. I seen 'em. Colonel Howe and Woodford got the letter from t'e captain t'emselves." Swinging his horse back around, he flicked its reins. Over his shoulder, he called, "Stay if you want. Upon your head be it."

Closing his eyes, Jonas stood quietly for some time. Shrugging, he went to the back of the house. Making a bundle of several split logs, he carried them into the house.

As he stacked them in the kitchen, a mad clanging of church

bells, accompanied by a deep thunder, broke over the house. Sighing, he climbed the stairs to get his thicker coat. Pausing, he looked out the window.

Smoke rose from the direction of the wharves. His heart began to pound, and he broke into a cold sweat.

Mary came in. "Where're you off to?"

"There's another fire in town. I'm going to see if I can help," he said. He pretended a calm he didn't feel.

"A fire? Where is it?"

"Not toward your father's house. More down by the waterfront."

"They're burning houses again." Her voice caught.

"It could be it's just a fire."

"If there's a fight, come home."

He looked at his watch and said, "It's just past three, now. I should be back for supper."

He leaned over and kissed her. Then he pulled on his thick peacoat and hurried out into the icy afternoon air. Only a few clouds floated above, the sun hanging low in the western sky. Patches of leftover snow reflected sunlight like diamonds.

As he moved down the dirt road, he joined the flow of other men brought out by the pealing bells and sound of cannon fire.

"All you men with muskets, we will muster in front of St. Paul's." A shout came from ahead. Several men moved toward it. Jonas stayed clear.

The hastily organized fire party moved through town toward the growing conflagration. Flames soared above the buildings ahead.

Nearing the harbor, the sound of cannon fire grew louder. Some warehouses were already fully engulfed. The ghostly outlines of anchored ships materialized from the cannon smoke. When the big guns fired, an orange glow gave them an evil tint.

British troops drawn up on Main Street raised their weapons. The men of the fire party stopped in their tracks.

"Withdraw, in the name of the Royal Governor," shouted the

officer in charge. "We're here to enforce the rule of King George and his lawfully appointed officials."

"Be gone, you devils. You'll rot in hell before long." The shout came from somewhere behind Jonas.

"Disperse now. This is your last warning." The soldiers took aim.

Jonas dropped to the ground. *This is not my fight.*

Around him, the crowd melted away.

"Aye, run you cowards." The British officer's voice dripped with derision.

A shot sounded behind Jonas. The soldiers returned fire. The air filled with musket balls. One of the British troops grasped his belly and cried out, falling to his knees.

Men scampered to find shelter. Jonas crawled behind a stack of barrels across the street from the wharves.

The battle did not last long. Hopelessly outgunned and outnumbered, the rebels retreated at a run. When the firing stopped, the British marched farther into town. Three of their number lay on the ground. Two groaned loudly. The third was silent.

Four sailors, hitherto unseen, rose up from below the quay and moved quickly to the soldiers. They picked them up and lowered them to unseen hands.

More musket fire erupted from the direction the soldiers had gone. This time, more guns were involved. Out on the water, cannon fire continued. Crashes spoke of the destruction the balls wrought.

Jonas peeked cautiously from behind his barrel. A few others had also hidden to avoid being shot. The majority found discretion the better part of valor and fled. A man with night clothes beneath his coat lay in the street. Another man knelt beside him as two more hurried toward them.

The ships stopped firing. His ears rang in the silence.

Warily, he stood and moved back toward the wharves. Inland,

the musket fire continued, periodically swelling then dying down. The cycle repeated every few minutes.

Jonas made his way down to where his ship floated alongside the farthest pier. The heat made his skin prickle as several of the ships and the wharf nearby burned. His heart pounded as he hurried past the inferno. Intense heat melted small mounds of snow piled where shovelers had left them. Massive showers of sparks rose into the cold air, spreading the fire from ship to ship. Tar in the rigging caught first, flames racing up shrouds and masts. As the gaskets and robands burned through, sails dropped from the yards. Finally, the sails themselves flared, burning remnants dropping to a blazing deck or overside, extinguished when they hit water.

A firestorm raced toward his *Mary Rose.* He ran.

The farther nests of ships weren't yet wrapped in blankets of flame. He held his breath as he neared them. Untouched thus far, *Mary Rose* heeled moderately over in the flame-fed wind.

Men around him stood and stared at the burning ships, some sobbing. He grabbed each in turn, crying, "Let us save what we can. Cast off those already afire."

Moving pier to pier, they loosed mooring lines not already burned through. The ebb current began to move the flaming pyres downstream.

As they drifted into the harbor, the British shifted and resumed their cannon fire, with new targets. The flaming hulks had to be sunk lest they spread fire to the flotilla.

Urgent pipes called crews to weigh anchor and move away from the drifting mountains of flame. Gunfire from the ships slackened but did not stop as they made ready to get underway.

Finally, Jonas and his makeshift crew reached the last of the burning ships. Faces and hair singed, they released the mooring lines that held its stern against the pier.

As it, too, drifted out into the harbor, Jonas stood back. For the first time he noted the musket fire in town had tapered off. Only occasional gunshots could be heard above the crackle of flames. The eastern horizon darkened as dusk approached. Above, a no-longer blue sky, instead stained yellow and brown. A queer yellow light covered everything.

He turned back to the warehouses. Products from all round the world and around the colony went up in flames. A roaring inferno, the front wall of his father-in-law's warehouse had collapsed into the street. A few men threw desultory buckets of water in the direction of some of the blazing buildings. All the waterfront, and for dozens of yards inland, the town was aflame.

On the river, boats full of British soldiers appeared from just beyond Town Point and rowed out to their ships. The enemy flotilla moved downstream on the receding tide, still avoiding burning derelicts.

Jonas surveyed the rest of the harbor. Some of those burning ships had gone aground. Others were sinking. Occasional explosions threw debris high into the air as fire reached gunpowder, a loaded cannon, or some other volatile cargo.

Mary must have heard the shooting. He turned and hurried toward home.

This attack against the largest city in the colony was worse than the attack on Hampton. There, the ships hadn't fired indiscriminately into the town.

As he walked, the damage from cannon fire lay all around him. Moving up Church Street, he passed St. Paul's. A cannonball lay buried in the southeast corner of the wall, just below the roofline. Crossing Freemason Street, a house stood with part of its roof caved in, the chimney having been hit. He joined a man and a boy frantically digging through the rubble.

"Me wife 'n youngest son. They be in here somewhere." Snot ran from the man's nose as he pleaded for help, all the while lifting timbers and brick from the pile. Two more men joined the effort. Soon enough, they found the family. Her skull crushed in, her arms wrapped around a young boy. Pulling her off, they hoped for the best. But his neck made an impossible angle to his shoulders. The husband crumpled, his older son standing mute, patting his father's back.

Jonas moved on. Another home had large holes in the wall, yet another in the roof.

Gaining Fenchurch Street, a group of men tried to save a home. He inserted himself into the bucket brigade and began the mechanical process of passing full buckets of water along.

The drudgery continued for over an hour before they finally tamed the flames. The snow and wet helped. Moving from this home to another, they joined another effort. And another. And another. The sun disappeared. Fires provided sufficient light to move easily about the rubble-strewn streets. Mist mingled with smoke from fires. Wailed laments followed wherever they went as men and women found lost loved ones.

By midnight, Jonas's hands and arms were numb and he was soaked to the skin.

George Scoggins stumbled past him. Jonas called to him. The two men converged to move down the street together.

"Jonas. Have you been down to the waterfront?" George asked. He shivered and rubbed his arms.

"Yes, sir. It wasn't a pretty sight..." Jonas stopped, not knowing how to tell him his warehouse was gone.

Scoggins waved his hand. "Aye, I know. There's naught can be done now."

They staggered on in silence.

The rattle of musket fire interrupted Mary's supper preparations. Arising from where she'd been sparking the fire, she looked toward town. Individual tongues of flame seemed to lick the sky. As the gunshots moved closer, she brought William and Rebecca to the kitchen. *Just like Jonas to not be here.*

The fire lit, she put a kettle on. They waited.

Outside, other families fled the fighting. Most headed north as

Mary watched from the kitchen window. Minutes later, she started to a knock on the door.

When she opened the door, her mother stepped in and said, "Mary, dear Mary. Are you and the children all right? Did Jonas go down there?" Elizabeth moved to the hearth.

Mary replied. "We are fine. If the fighting gets close, we can head for Isaac's home near Lynnhaven Inlet." Rubbing her eyes, she added, "Jonas went. Did father go down, too?"

Elizabeth Scoggins smiled sadly. "Of course. You know your father, he cannot let well enough alone. He's much too old to be out like this, but to stop him is impossible. Very sensible, planning to go to your brother's. As always, we sit and wait. I thought it better to be here with you and the children. "

They waited in silence. Soon after Elizabeth's arrival, the musket fire died out. Hope grew, but still no Jonas or George.

As the smoky gray dusk came, Elizabeth and Mary set to making a meal. "We'll need to feed the young ones. Their appetites aren't affected by such doings as are ours," Elizabeth opined. Mary did not answer.

As William and Rebecca ate quietly, more smoke hung low over the town. They'd smelled it for some time, but now visible tendrils moved through every room of the house. Their eyes burned.

From the window, a large part of the city could be seen burning. Huge billows of dark gray smoke, lit below by the orange glow of flames, climbed into the dark sky. Flames leapt high, dulling the full moon trying to break through.

Back in the kitchen, Rebecca cried. William's leg jiggled furiously as he sat.

As fire raged, so, too, grew the tide of those who sought refuge. Mary began to invite them to take shelter. By full dark, the house was full of women and children and some old men. The crowd pushed aside fear. As night wore on, others joined her and Elizabeth in the kitchen, from which they fed the throngs.

As relative calm spread through the house, worry resurfaced.

Women huddled in small groups, wondering in low worried tones what the future held, and what might have happened to their husbands, fathers, and sons.

As night fell on the other side of town, Jonas and his father-in-law found themselves at the scene of yet another fire. As they began to fill buckets at the wagon that held large casks of water, three men ran at them, shouting. "Leave it burn, you. The devil take the man who helps these loyalist bastards. Leave it, I say, or I'll shoot every last one o' you."

The fire party retreated.

"We nee-need to get shelter, Jonas." Scoggins shivered uncontrollably.

Exhausted, they headed for Jonas's home. The men stumbled into the house, filthy, dead tired, frozen, and starved.

Jonas rose the next morning, intending to help fight fires.

Scoggins took his arm and shook his head. "No, we'd best stay here. What fires burn now have been set by the rebels. The British have gone."

Staring at Scoggins, Jonas finally nodded. Dropping his head, he stared at the floor. "How have we come to this?"

Through the next day, and the next, the Scoggins and Hawkes shared their home and food with those less fortunate. Friends whose homes had been spared returned home. They were replaced by less known faces whose homes were gone.

George broke the news to Elizabeth that they too had lost their home. Elizabeth smiled mistily. "Well, Mr. Scoggins, I'd grown tired of that house, anyway. 'Tis time we had a new one."

Chapter Nine

In all, the city burned for more than fifty hours. Four of every five buildings were destroyed. Those few of the city's inhabitants who had not gone elsewhere began the painful walk home from wherever they had sheltered. Most found nothing left, their homes and lives shattered.

Jonas sat with Mary after breakfast. Two weeks had passed since the fires had finally died out. Dunmore's flotilla now harassed Hampton and Yorktown.

"Mary, this town is dying."

Mary munched her biscuit in silence for a moment and contemplated her teacup. "It hasn't yet. There are still shops open."

"There's some life left, but there's also a steady ebb of folks going elsewhere. Fewer than a few hundred remain. There's no work. The rebels will not allow the town to be rebuilt. In the Bay, no one can even fish freely. The Navy seizes the catch to feed the soldiers. Those self-same soldiers plunder inland, tearing up farms, seizing seed stores and animals. There will be nothing to eat next winter."

Mary moved to the window and looked out. Norfolk had been their home all their lives. Now much of it was ash and rubble.

"We need to leave ourselves," Jonas said.

"Where would we go? The Navy stops all trade along the coast, if what we hear is to be believed. You cannot sail, in any case. Without trade, it's unlikely there's work anywhere else for strangers," she said, turning now to face him. "For that's what we'd be, Jonas. We'd be strangers. How would it be different or better?" Mary asked.

"To Newport. With my sister and her husband. He and his father are shippers, but they also own distilleries. Perhaps they have work or know of someone else who does. 'Tis better than remaining here. I will not live on credit from others. 'Twould be better to be indentured."

"Their trade is still in slaves. You have said many times, you will not truck with slavers. Do you mean to say now you'd sail on a slave ship?"

She had him with that, and she knew it. He looked down at his own cup, swirling the last of the coffee in the bottom. "No, no, I won't. I know my ideas about slavery don't fit there. But many of their ships do not carry slaves. I do not have to carry rum to Africa. I can serve in a ship that brings molasses, cotton, rice, and tea back from the West Indies or the southern colonies. At least I'm familiar with that trade. I sailed it for almost three years."

"But his trade is still based around slaves." Mary knew shipping from years of listening at her father's knee. That was one of the many reasons Jonas trusted her instincts.

He sighed. "We must do what we must to survive. I sympathize with the rebels. But right now, I fight to keep my family alive. And I cannot do it here."

She turned to him. "Then we will go to Newport. But you will not sail in Mr. Trimble's slave ships. You will do whatever you must, but you will not betray what you believe." She sat. "Nor must I. What will we do to fight, Jonas? For I am convinced we cannot any longer remain wedded to King George. He has forsaken us, allowed his governors and ministers to murder us. That cannot happen anymore. God must forbid it, and we must help him."

Jonas sat mute. Very much her mother's daughter, Mary was strong-willed when she chose to be.

She gave him a slight smile. "What will you do with *Mary Rose*?"

He breathed deeply and sighed. "The cannonballs knocked the tiller to splinters and holed the berth deck. The only shipyard now is in Gosport. I have no crew to move her there, and to do so invites capture by Dunmore." He rubbed the back of his neck. "Dunmore seems content to leave those few ships that float to rot at the piers. I see no alternative save to leave her. I will hire old Mr. Snodgrass to look after her. He intends to remain."

"Very well. So we will go." She reached out and took his hand.

George and Elizabeth Scoggins came to say goodbye before they moved to Williamsburg. George maintained a small set of rooms in the colonial capital for when he had business there. It would be their home for the foreseeable future.

Jonas leaned back in his chair. "You really should move in here. Thus, you may have the house when we go to Newport."

"No, son, we won't put you out like that. Perhaps we will move back and stay, someday. But there's nothing for us here now. Mayhap, I can find usefulness in Williamsburg." After sipping tea, he asked, "What is in Newport for you?"

"My brother-in law Jonathan's trade is large enough he holds local sway. I've informed him we are coming, and why we must leave. He will have heard what happened here. Perhaps he can find me a berth."

Scoggins regarded Jonas over his cup. "What if he cannot employ you?"

"I will see if someone else might do so. If need be, I will leave Mary and the children there and seek other fortunes." He looked down at his own cup, avoiding Scoggins's gaze.

His father-in-law's eyes narrowed. "What are you not saying, Jonas?"

Jonas sighed and set his cup down. Standing, he moved to the fireplace and held out his hands to the flames.

"George, you know I have been loyal to the King." He paused, then took a deep breath. "However, what happened here and in Falmouth is beyond reason. Every time the British commit some excess, I excuse it or blame it on the rebels as instigators." He turned to face his father-in-law. "But I can't justify this."

He waved his hand as Scoggins began to speak. "Oh, I know, sir. The rebels taunted those on the ships. And they were responsible for most of the destruction. I cannot excuse them, either. But it was Dunmore who fired into the town with cannon. More than a dozen women and children were murdered. Not by rebels starting fires. By British shot. How can I accept that? Excuse that?"

Scoggins pursed his lips and gazed into the fire for a long moment. "We cannot." Sighing, he continued, "I also wanted to believe we should not make a break with England. Pshaw. We have heard and made all the arguments, you and I. The arguments against still prevail: we cannot provide protection for our own merchant shipping. We have no real manufactories here in the colonies, certainly not to provide for our own needs, at least not yet." He set his glass on the table beside his chair and leaned forward. "But perhaps that is the most important word. Not *yet*."

Joining Jonas at the fire, he continued. "But I believe most who remain feel as I do, as you do. A man cannot be convinced he is wrong by beating him with a stick. To convince him of his wrongness requires argument, persuasion, discussion. When he is pummeled, one of two things must happen. Either he must be broken into submission. Or he will fight back, as long and as hard as necessary." He thumped his fist into his hand. "I have reached that point. And it sounds as if you have, too." He stared Jonas in the eye.

Turning back to the fire, Jonas studied it for a lingering time before answering. "I have." He flexed his shoulders. "I will see Mary and the children set up in the Trimble household. Then I will seek a berth, perhaps in Washington's naval militia."

Scoggins remained silent.

Jonas continued, "He has several ships at sea. Mayhap they need additional captains. I would even sail as mate." He turned back to see Scoggins smiling ruefully.

His father-in-law said, "Aye. I cannot argue with you. If the Lord wills that the British be swayed, that they change their behavior, then let us make amends and remain one. But if they will not treat us as men should be, then by God I support a complete break with them. Better we chart our own course than be meekly led to our ruination. Does Mary agree?"

Jonas grunted. "I believe she would prefer I go straight to General Washington alone and offer my services. But she allows that she and the children would be better looked after in Newport."

Scoggins chuckled. "She has always been headstrong, even as a girl. You do well to at least listen and consider what she says."

Jonas closed his eyes and put his head back. Bringing it back down, he opened them and looked levelly at Scoggins. "I think we are rebels now." He smiled, but it didn't reach his eyes.

THE HAWKE FAMILY APPROACHED NEWPORT ON A rainy, cold, windy evening in early February.

A storm that had followed them all day finally overtook them, drenching them with cold rain. The roof of the coach leaked, leaving Mary and the children cold and wet. Jonas rode on top and huddled in his sea jacket. The closer they got to their destination, the uglier the weather became.

Emotionally, the trip had been exhausting and turbulent. The children had been quiet and dispirited since learning they would leave Norfolk. William was frustrated by the madness adults visited on each other. Rebecca, too young to understand, felt the stormy emotions of those around her and withdrew. Even the adventure of traveling hadn't improved their outlooks. Naked fear stared out from the faces they passed along the way, especially other children.

As they pulled up to the front of the house, Jonas's sister came out the door and down the steps. She met them with smiles and welcome.

"Mary, Jonas. Children. Come inside. I'm so glad to see you. Jonathan will be home soon. There's a fire and soup for the children. You're most welcome in our home."

Chapter Ten

One of the wealthiest men in Newport, Jonathan Trimble descended from one of the founders of the Rhode Island colony and had engaged in trade in Newport for over a hundred years. As the oldest scion, Trimble had learned the business from the bottom up, first at sea, shipping as a boy, then seaman, then mate. He was also an outspoken, ardent supporter of the independence movement.

Trimble had bold visions of how life could be in the American colonies if only England were out of the way.

"I tell you, Jonas, without England's meddling, we would march inland, all the way to the Pacific. We could conquer the entire continent. Evict the French, too. One American nation, from sea to sea, from Hudson's Bay to the Floridas. Send the Spanish back to Europe, too. We don't even know what riches lie beyond the Indian lands. And it should be ours for the taking." He drained his grog mug.

"It has taken us more than a hundred years to explore more than five hundred, perhaps a thousand, miles inland. How far is the other ocean?"

"Who knows? If it takes another century, does it matter? I,

and others, believe these colonies, joined into a single nation, could eventually rival Great Britain, were we only free to do so."

Jonas snorted. Seeing Trimble's eyes narrow, he said, "Do not mistake me. I believe in open trade. We have resources that England, and elsewhere, need. But we are few in number. It would require thousands of thousands to populate a continent."

Trimble nodded vigorously. "Yes, it will. And if we are free, others will come. Why did your family come here?"

"My grandfather was a sailor. His ship brought colonists to Jamestown, and he remained. Here, he was able to become a captain, and eventually to buy his own ship."

"Exactly. You see? My family came for a land grant. Opportunity. That brings people here. More to the point, it will bring more. We will draw people from all over Europe." He smiled. "One day, we will be more important, more powerful, than England herself."

Jonas listened raptly, amazed at one man's imagination. He also had a difficult time believing it possible, though he admitted Trimble could sell it.

Mary and the children adapted to Newport. Though colder, the late winter and early spring weather was not too different from Norfolk. The Trimbles' friends accepted them into their social circle. Mary and Martha got on well together, making it easier for Mary to be away from her parents.

A few days following their arrival, Jonas sat with Trimble at the Black Pearl tavern. "Who can I approach that might enable me to join the naval militia?" he asked.

Trimble leaned back and took a pull from his pewter mug, filled with grog. Eyeing Jonas, he said, "You are no firebrand. What has changed your mind?"

"I haven't, not really. After what happened, I find I must take a side."

"But you do not believe in what I've said we could do, could be."

"It is hard to conceive, I grant you. I believe in what is before me, what I can see. I cannot foresee such things." He rubbed his hands together. "But I know we cannot remain as we are. I must contribute. I cannot live on your charity, either."

Trimble waved his hand. "Bah. You are Martha's brother. Your family is mine. You have suffered and my conscience, let alone my Christian duty, requires that I aid you. I do so gladly. Do not concern yourself with that." He looked around the room. "I'll warrant that one in four men in this room also seek employment. The British are killing our trade, our livelihoods." He looked back at Jonas. "Half of those men are also unwilling to commit themselves to the glorious cause."

Leaning back, he eyed Jonas for a long moment. Then he said, "I will introduce you to Esek Hopkins. He is the commodore of what we now call the Continental Navy. He is the man you must speak with."

Hopkins' graying brown curls framed his round face. Dark circles and thick bags below his eyes betrayed weariness. Seated behind a desk covered in piles of parchment in the small cabin of *Alfred*, converted merchantman and Hopkins's flagship, he more resembled a clerk than a captain.

"You are the fourth captain this week who has sought me out for a commission. What are your qualifications that I should give you favor over the others? Or over those already appointed?" Hopkins asked.

"I have commanded vessels of nearly all sizes. My last was a six hundred ton full-rigged ship, which I took to Batavia and back."

"I would think such a trip would leave you in good straits, financially. Why do you need employment? The navy does not pay well. A lieutenant commanding receives but thirty Continental dollars per month."

"The Royal Navy took my ship and cargo as I approached Norfolk. We received nothing." Jonas shifted in his seat. "I accept that I am one of many who find themselves on a lee shore. I do not require that I command. I am willing to sail as mate if need be, to contribute to the cause."

Hopkins smiled for a moment, then frowned again. "I would not want as mate a man who had sailed as captain. There can only be one captain, as you should know. Again I ask, what special qualifications do you have?"

"I spent two years as midshipman in sloop *Endor*, Captain Whitmore, prior to the late war with France. I had charge of two guns, larboard broadside."

Shaking his head, Hopkins said, "Unless you participated in battle, that is entirely inadequate." He leaned back in his seat. "All the officer berths aboard my ships are filled." He picked up a parchment from his desk and waved it. "This is a list of those who also wish a commission. You are more qualified than some, but less than others. You are also not from New England. Nearly all my crews are. You acknowledge that could present difficulties?"

"I do. However, are we not all engaged in the same endeavor?"

"We are." Hopkins leaned his head back and closed his eyes. "Yet, I cannot offer you anything." Leaning forward again and opening his eyes, he clasped his hands before him. "I am in sympathy with you and all the rest. However, at the present time, there is nothing I can do. In a year or two, we will have thirteen new frigates constructed, along with several smaller vessels. Come see me then, and I may be able to offer you an appointment."

Jonas' shoulders sagged. "I thank you for your consideration, Commodore. But my family cannot wait that long. I will take my leave, sir." He stood and turned toward the door.

"Just a moment, Captain Hawke." Jonas turned back to face him. Hopkins stood as well. "Have you considered manning a private ship of war? The Congress hands out Letters of Marque by the dozen, as do several of the colonies. There are few ships to be had in Rhode Island, Connecticut, or New York. Perhaps in Massachusetts you may find something. I was rather successful as a privateer during the last war. I like to think we helped defeat the

French. Privateers will be of at least as much use as this navy of mine, if we are to be victorious. Have you considered that?"

"I have not. My ship is in Norfolk. There is no yard left to repair her."

Hopkins leaned forward, his knuckles on the desk. "Thomas Nelson, from Yorktown, related to the Maritime Committee just two weeks ago that Gosport and Portsmouth yards are eager for work. *He* is eager to get funds for them." He straightened. "Of course, Congress's money cannot pay to repair your ship. But if there are wrights, wood, and, for now, a dearth of work, then this could be your opportunity."

Jonas bowed slightly. "Thank you, sir. I wish you a good voyage."

Walking back through town, he stopped at the quay and stared out. The afternoon sun sat low on the horizon and gave the bay a shimmer, the wind waves reflecting its light in all directions. *To be at sea again.* As the golden orb sank below a cloud, he turned and walked home.

That evening as they prepared for bed, he told Mary what had happened.

She continued to brush her hair. "Then you must return. We will be safe here." Setting the brush on the table, she reached out to him. He held her in his arms, then together they climbed under the covers.

CHAPTER ELEVEN

In late March 1776, Jonas returned to Norfolk.

Stopping in Williamsburg to visit his in-laws, he learned they'd returned to Norfolk. He journeyed on.

Upon his arrival, he found Elizabeth Scoggins in the kitchen. "Oh, Jonas. We didn't expect you."

"I did not expect to return so soon. Where is George?"

Elizabeth hesitated. "Well, you'll find out soon enough. He's down at the Gosport waterfront. You'll be wanting to talk with him."

She returned to her baking when Jonas turned and left.

He found George in the ship chandler's shop.

"Jonas, it's good to see you. What news do you bring of my daughter and grandchildren?"

"All are well. They'd be happier were they all here at home, of course. What brought you back to Norfolk?"

He looked keenly at Jonas, then shrugged. "Let's walk down by the water."

Approaching the river, the smell of rain-soaked burnt wood drifted across the water from Norfolk. Skeletons of warehouses, taverns, and shops had fallen in on themselves through the worst of the winter months, leaving only piles of burnt timber. All the usable wood had long ago been scavenged. The tragic view reminded them of the catalyst that had changed their lives.

"Why have you returned?" Scoggins asked.

"There is nothing for me in New England." He told him of his interview with Hopkins, and others with whom he'd spoken.

Scoggins stared across the river, then turned and walked to the water's edge. He made his way along the muddy path upriver. Jonas followed.

The mud squeaked and protested their passing, their footprints filling with water as they passed.

"We are in much the same position, Jonas. There's nought for me to do, either. And I'm much too old for soldiering." He waved his hand and shook his head. "All the militia do now is march and drill. They accomplish nothing. Dunmore still sits in his fleet as he did in January. Were it not for the fact the British think nothing here worth the effort of destroying, there is little to stop them."

"Is there any hope of driving them away?"

"Little enough. There's not much of Norfolk left. St. Paul's is the only building standing in the town proper. And there's no one who really wants to rebuild, not yet. Many remain in Gosport and Portsmouth. New homes are built weekly." He stopped and turned to Jonas. "This is why I wanted to talk here, for what I tell you is confidential. The Continental Congress will allocate moneys to build ships for the new navy here. There will be work, and small ships to command."

"When? It will take time, and I do not have time. And how will they construct ships with the British fleet so near?"

Scoggins shrugged. "There is hope that the enemy will leave. What food they steal is not likely enough, or so it is believed. After they do, if they do, then yes, it will take time. I believe it will be worth the waiting."

"Commodore Hopkins told me much the same. He also told me what he had done during the war ten years ago." Jonas took a deep breath. "The army needs supplies of powder, muskets, cannon, and of money, too. There's only one way to get those.

The Royal Navy cannot stop all trade. If we put privateers to sea, they'll have to spend more time protecting their own trade. They will have even fewer ships to attack ours." He pointed across the river to the few ships against the bank. "I will fit *Mary Rose* out as a privateer. She's fast and she's big enough to take ships that trade in the West Indies. Even one or two prizes slipping back in to supply the militia would make a great difference. It did with Washington's army in New England. We do not have to defeat the Royal Navy. We must simply pry the blockade ever so slightly loose. How will we win, if we do nothing?"

Scoggins smiled broadly. "My boy, it happens that I can assist in your endeavor. Not only do I represent Norfolk to the Convention, I issue the Letters of Marque for the new Commonwealth of Virginia. And I can arrange for Boothby's yard to complete whatever work you need on *Mary Rose*." Scoggins grasped Jonas's arm. "Perhaps it is God's will that we should meet today." His face took on a frown. "It is not my business, son, but there is something I wish you to consider. The Convention requires a five-thousand-dollar bond for a Letter. If you find yourself unable to provide, I will loan it to you. Eagerly."

Jonas smiled but said nothing. There would be time to discuss it.

They turned and walked back. Along the way, Scoggins said, "John Masefield has inquired of you. I saw him in the Gosport Tavern just three nights ago. His family has set up here. You should speak with him."

"Hello, John."

Masefield looked up and a big grin split his face. He stood and grasped Jonas's arms. "Captain Hawke, bless my soul. 'Tis good to see ye, sir." He indicated the chair across the table from him. "Pray, sit with us."

"I thank you." Jonas sat and Masefield introduced his two

companions, both sailors. Jonas knew one by reputation and had sailed with the other several years past.

"Mr. Scoggins told me ye'd gone to Newport. When did ye return?"

"Just yesterday. I found there was no more likelihood of a berth there than here, and myself at a disadvantage, being from Virginia."

"Aye. But there's no berths 'ere, neither, not wi' Dunmore's fleet forever anchored hereabouts," said one.

Masefield nodded. "He's right. There's no' even permits to be had now."

"I don't plan on getting any permits." Jonas looked around. "John, I'm staying with my wife's family, in my old house. Can you come by tomorrow?"

Masefield stretched and leaned back. "Aye, I can. But ye can speak freely here. These two —" He indicated his friends. "— love the English as little as any Scotsman ever did." Sweeping his arm around the room, he added, "And everyone here is a friend. We don' tolerate strangers."

Jonas stared. *In for a penny, in for a pound.* He explained his intentions for *Mary Rose*. When he finished, he waited.

"Well, sir, ye've never shied away from trouble since I've sailed with ye. This is looking for trouble, mind ye," Masefield said, slapping his palm on the table. "But I'll sail with ye. I tol' ye that once before, and I meant it." He turned to his companions. "What of ye? Captain Hawke has asked. Now I ask. Will ye join us?"

Both men nodded grimly. "Aye, sir. I'll sail with you again. But how will we get your ship to Boothby's yard?"

"We cannot, not until Dunmore leaves. Meantime, we will do what work we can on her at night. One thing we can do is remove her rig, even in daylight. It will look to him as if we are dismantling her. They will pay less attention, then."

Masefield shifted in his chair. "That's fine, sir. Now, what plans have ye for taking water, food, refitting?"

"You know I used to sail the Caribbean trade years ago, right?" Jonas asked.

Masefield nodded.

Jonas smiled. "Well, there's a man in Puerto Rico I've come to know well, an agent. I intend to see if he'll help us dispose of prizes. The Spanish have no love of England. It may be, so long as we don't make our arrangement known, that they'll be willing to assist us. Therefore, we will water and take on provisions in San Juan. I'll meet with him then. And if he won't do it himself, he knows the other agents there. I'm sure he will know someone who will take on the task."

Masefield looked up at the ceiling rafters, perhaps seeing Puerto Rico and the illicit arrangement Jonas had outlined. It could be no other way but illicit. To the English, the colonials were rebels. Anyone assisting the rebellion could not do it legally. Slowly, he nodded.

"Aye, sir. Will we use San Juan as our homeport, then?" he asked.

"Not as such. We'll water there when it makes sense to, but I don't want the English agent there to see us too often, lest he realize the Spanish are helping us. We'll pick our prize crews up on the windward side of the island, near a small island called Vieques. We can come close inshore there and draw less attention. There's nothing there but sugar plantations and few people."

"I've been there, sir," said one of their table mates. "Good place for keepin' one's business quiet-like."

Jonas nodded and continued. "They have a good yard in San Juan, with capable riggers and spar makers. I put in there after a blow one time. They had us set up well and on our way quickly enough, though we did some of the work ourselves. The local people are a mix of the natives that used to live there, but the authorities are all Spaniards. They've the habits of the Spaniards, too, taking a nap midday. It was summer and so it was just as well, as it's hot and wet by then. The men drooped with fatigue just climbing aloft, and you'd find yourself dripping near as soon as you stepped out on deck. But this time of year it should almost be pleasant." He sat back and took a pull on the beer that had just arrived. "The harbor's near perfect for protection. It's guarded by a massive old fort the Dutch couldn't reduce a hundred and fifty years ago, and it's been strengthened since. Ten years ago, when the British took Habana, the Spaniards took note, and strengthened the rest of the harbor defenses even more, as well as the city's walls."

"Aye, but best we not need those protections," Masefield said. "True enough. If Spain and England go to war, everything will change."

Hazleton, the man who'd been to San Juan, added, "Once inside the harbor, the wind gets variable, eddyin' 'round the point with the fort. Unless it's blowin' some, there's no' much wind inside. Most anchor just inside the mouth."

They spoke well into the evening. When he left, Jonas felt more confident than he had since before *Elizabeth* had been taken from him.

As spring moved toward summer, however, the militia did carry out some attacks against the British, finally driving Lord Dunmore and his troops out of the Norfolk area.

In late May, the enemy took refuge on Gwynn Island. Without sufficient strength to attack the fortified positions, the militia settled for laying siege. Despite small boats of raiding parties that snuck out at night to forage from local farms, the British still did not have sufficient food. Disease continued to ravage their forces.

Shortages of war materials also plagued the Continentals. Some fought with farm implements or homemade pikes. Others carried muskets, but no powder or ball. Bayonets were virtually non-existent. One Norfolk brigade had three cannon with no ammunition.

THEY SUCCEEDED IN REMOVING *MARY ROSE*'S RIGGING and damaged planking. Thus, when Dunmore's fleet departed, they easily moved her to the yard. There, shipwrights eagerly began the work of repairing damage and modifying her cargo spaces to carry ammunition and larger quantities of stores. Cutting four additional gun ports in her side gave her too warlike an appearance, so Jonas had her painted to hide the extra guns. Boothby's carpenters and caulkers worked to get her in fighting trim.

All the while, Jonas and Masefield recruited a new crew, leveraging Hawke's reputation as a fair captain and a good seaman. Those of *Elizabeth*'s crew, who hadn't left the area, eagerly signed on. The rest of his new crew were unknowns, and a few seemed a right foul lot. But he needed three times the crew of a merchant so he took what he could get. Though competing with other privateers fitting out, he quickly filled his rolls with nearly a hundred able seamen, whom he put to work getting stores aboard and reaving new running rigging.

ON JULY 4, 1776, JONAS RENAMED HIS BELOVED brigantine *Resolute*. His Letter of Marque from the Continental Congress arrived, authorizing him to "sink, burn, or destroy the ships and vessels belonging to the United Kingdom of Great Britain." Shortly after came his commission from the Commonwealth of Virginia, making him a captain in the seagoing branch of the militia. With it came a Letter of Marque from the colony.

On July 9, news of the Declaration of Independence arrived.

The next day, militia attacked Gwynn Island. Dunmore and the few healthy men he had left evacuated ahead of Virginia forces. He'd left behind a camp of death. Smallpox had ravaged it, leaving horrible desolation behind. Unburied corpses spotted the landscape, those who'd been left behind to die alone and unattended.

The militia transported the very few survivors to the north side of the island where they set up a hospital. Then they buried the bodies and burned the camp.

Within just a few days, the survivors died and were buried, and the hospital burned.

Chapter Twelve

Jonas made his way to *Resolute*'s deck two hours before sunrise.

He longed for the normal fog to come in. Thus far, the weather had not been normal this fall. Unseasonably warm at first, it had changed abruptly to cold and dry. But there'd been encouraging signs the past few days. While still cool, the moisture had returned.

As he stepped off the ladder and onto the deck, a drop of cool water landed on his brow and ran down his cheek. Another caught the back of his head, running down into the hair he had tied in a queue, and then onto his neck and down his shirt. *A good sign*. He wiped away what he could.

Only darkness greeted him. The waxing sliver of a crescent moon had set long ago, leaving behind a bright blanket of stars and giving depth to the sharp blackness of the void. The feeble lights of Portsmouth shone dimly off the starboard quarter. A making tide neared its height. *Resolute*'s bow pointed toward the Chesapeake, as if straining to run. Just before sunrise, the tide would turn and the current shift, beginning the long run to the sea beyond Cape Henry. There was as yet no sign of the coming dawn. He leaned on the rail near the main shrouds.

It would be good to get back to sea. He'd been ashore nearly a year. The old familiar excitement and anticipation coursed through him, stronger than he'd ever known.

Most privateers lurked in the waters off New England or prowled the British fisheries off Newfoundland. The Royal Navy, he reasoned, would concentrate in those areas. The Caribbean would be lightly defended with some fat cargoes to take. Therefore, he would go there.

"Sir, I believe the fog is risin' up." Masefield slipped up beside him.

"We shall wait until it is good and thick, weigh anchor as soon as we can't see the shore. Who will you have in the chains?"

"Wilson, sir. He's the best hand with a lead. I don't mind telling you, sir, I'm not lookin' forward to this. I've never been out the channel in the fog."

"Aye. It's a damn sight better than trying to get past a frigate's guns."

"Aye, that I'll grant, sir."

A barely perceptible lightening graced the eastern horizon. The bow swung gently toward it, signaling the tide was at its highest and the current would soon ebb. North toward Hampton the fog rolled in from the bay, first in whiffs, then in a bank. Stirrings of a breeze ruffled his hair. Westerly, perfect for putting out to sea.

Like a gray cotton blanket, the fog moved in with the increasing light, as if the rising sun herded it. At first, it swallowed only the riverbank, leaving the trees emerging above like the masts of a wreck stuck from the water after the storm has cleared. By the time the sun should have peeked over the horizon, the fog completed its work, swallowing even the trees and *Resolute* herself. Dawn came as a feathery grayness, slowly transitioning from half-light to something a bit more.

"It's time, John. Call the hands."

"Aye, aye, sir. Bosun. Call all hands."

Dawn was shattered by the shrill call of the pipe and the

pounding of feet on ladders as his crew raced to stations to weigh anchor and set sail. All were experienced seamen. No landsmen to be led by the hand to their stations, no ordinary seamen limited in what they could be trusted to do alone, and no need for shouted orders.

He shivered. With the fog came a chill. Drops from the rigging came faster now, soaking everyone and everything. The fog muffled the noises of getting underway, yet strangely amplified some sounds as the ship came alive.

"Let fall," Masefield called.

Setting the square fore topsail took advantage of the wind from astern. The jib swung the bow around to larboard. Soon it would be over the anchor. The hands nearly ran around the capstan, the anchor cable fairly flying in as fast as the nippers could make fast the messenger to the cable.

"Sheet home."

Three hands on each side hauled the topsail sheets aft, bringing the clews, the lower corners of the sail, down to the fore yardarms. Three more men then raised the topsail yard up into place, then made fast the halyard. As it began to draw, *Resolute* surged forward. With so many men at his disposal, setting sail went faster than Jonas was used to. He felt a thrill of satisfaction.

The Bosun called out, "Anchor's aweigh." Then, "Anchor's clear." He followed it with the fact that it was catted and fished; then that it was stowed for sea.

Jonas turned his attention to navigating out of the anchorage. "Make your course east nor'east."

"East nor'east, it is, sir," returned the helmsman as he moved the tiller to comply. The fog parted ahead as the ship gathered way. The wind lay now dead astern. When he turned east, it would move to the quarter, right where she liked it best.

"By the deep four," called Wilson. More than four and a half fathoms, twenty-seven feet — plenty of water since *Resolute* drew only twelve feet.

The channel would shallow to three fathoms as he passed near the Tail of the Horseshoe, but it would deepen again, remaining at least four fathoms the rest of the way to the Chesapeake itself. Once in the bay, the channel deepened to five fathoms and more.

The fog thickened, blurring even the lines of the headsails only a hundred feet away. *Be careful what you wish for*. He didn't want the fog to be so thick that he ran into something. *Resolute* continued to gather speed. All the while, Jonas listened intently to the calls of the leadsman. The crew, oblivious to the rivulets of cold water running down their hair and faces, coiled down lines or strained to see through the fog.

"And a quarter four."

Resolute was now passing through the eastern end of Hampton Roads. Soon Jonas would order the turn east.

"Quarter less four."

"Hands to the braces. Put down your helm, steer due east."

"Steer due east, aye, sir." The helmsman gently guided the tiller to larboard while watching the compass. Masefield watched the yards on the foremast as the ship slowly turned, ordering them braced around at just the right speed to ensure the sail harnessed its wind.

With the wind now on the starboard quarter, Jonas ordered the jib taken in and the fore course set.

"And a half three."

So far, so good. The next several minutes should see the channel shoal to three fathoms, perhaps a foot less, then increase.

"By the deep three."

"By the mark three."

A sudden loud thump jarred the deck, startling Jonas. "What was that?" he demanded.

"Sorry, sir. Jenkins dropped a block from the fore shrouds."

"We must have quiet."

"Aye, sir."

"Quarter less three."

"Larboard your helm, steer east by south."

Resolute made slightly more leeway than he'd anticipated. It was just past the new moon, so the current would be faster than normal. That would tend to push the ship to the northern side of the channel. Steering more to the south should bring her back into the channel.

"And a half two." Urgency sounded in Wilson's voice.

Taken aback, Jonas hesitated. Then, "Larboard your helm. Brace around. Stand by the anchor." Something was wrong. He needed to be ready to drop the anchor. Perhaps he'd still underestimated the current. Or perhaps it had rained farther west, swelling the James and Elizabeth Rivers.

"By the deep two." Jonas barely had time to digest the new information. A sickening shudder ran through *Resolute* as she touched bottom.

"Start the sheets. Strike the topsail and course. Put up your helm. Steer east nor'east." The orders flew hard and fast. Masefield obeyed instantly. Sail disappeared. Men ran in seemingly chaotic fashion, yet with purpose.

Jonas looked at the binnacle. *Resolute*'s head was nearly east southeast but was swinging back to the east. She must have run into a bar sticking out of the north side into the channel, or perhaps the channel had shifted.

He waited, but no more bumps made themselves felt. They were clear, at least for now.

"Get the squares on her again, Mr. Masefield. And set the main to larboard. Put down your helm, steer sou' sou'east."

"Aye, sir."

Men rushed to the mainsail, casting off the gaskets that held the sail and gaff to the boom, loosing the folds of canvas. Other men took the halyards off the belaying pins, ready to haul away as soon as they were able.

"On the peak and throat, haul away." The sail began to rise, slowly at first, then more quickly. "Keep her level, now, keep her level." It would not do to jam the jaws of the gaff against the mast.

Forward, the square sails descended again from their yards and were sheeted home. The ship began to move ahead as the topsail and course flapped, filled, and drew taut.

How stupid to run aground.

"By the deep three." Jonas heaved a sigh of relief. This was payment for his year ashore.

"Perhaps it's good to put bad fortune astern, sir. With that done, we may have a good voyage, God willin'."

"Quarter less four. By the mark four."

He ordered the course made east. Removing his telescope from its sling near the binnacle, he made his way to the main shrouds and climbed. At the mast-head, patches of blue passed above him. Scanning from the larboard beam across the bow to starboard, he saw nothing. Closing his eyes, he calmed himself, subconsciously adapting to the leadsman's chant.

"And a quarter four."

He wouldn't feel comfortable until they were into the bay. Once there, the greatest danger would be running into an anchored ship.

"And a half four." Wilson still called out depths.

Jonas mentally calculated the ebb current and *Resolute*'s speed through the water. They should be passing abeam the eastern end of the Tail about now.

"Boat ho. Rowing boat two points off the starboard bow."

Jonas pointed his telescope in the direction indicated. There, a cable's length off. Few would, or should, be out in the fog who had aboveboard reasons for it.

"Mr. Masefield. We will stop that boat."

"Aye, sir." Below, Masefield ordered two hands to arm themselves, drawing a pistol himself.

If the men in the boat turned out to be hostile, he would seize it, or at least prevent its escape. At all costs, he needed to ensure word of his sailing did not reach British ears. As a last resort, he would fire into the boat.

Meanwhile, the five men in the boat heard the commotion.

Three turned and stared at this ship that had suddenly emerged out of the fog. They quickly began rowing back south.

"Avast there. Stay put. Who are ye?" Jonas demanded from aloft.

The men froze.

"Fishermen from Norfolk, sir. We laid up off Sewell Point through the night and are just going out."

"Where are your nets?"

Loaded with crates and barrels, Jonas suspected them of running supplies to the British. If they were, he decided he would seize them.

"Hullo, Jerrod." A voice rose up from the forecastle.

Jonas looked down, his face turning red. "Who is that? Who is that shouting?"

"Silence on the forecastle," Hackett roared at the same time. He advanced on the man who'd called the greeting. The man turned and looked aloft at Jonas.

"Beg pardon, sir. It's me, Williams, sir. That's my cousin Jerrod in the boat, sir."

"Is that you, Joseph?" This came from the boat.

"Silence." To the boat, he shouted, "Come alongside now."

The boat did as ordered and hooked on to the main chains.

On his way down the mast, Jonas ordered Williams to lay aft to the quarterdeck. Upon regaining the deck, he addressed himself again to the boat. "Jerrod, get up here."

The men in the boat shivered from fear, cold, or both. Crowded with the supplies, the boat rode low in the water. Occasionally, a wave slapped the hull and splashed over, so the men sat with their feet in water, soaking wet. One of them bailed as best he could around their cargo.

Once the cousins were on the quarterdeck, he queried Jerrod, "What are you really doing out here?"

"We're taking food and water out to the militia, sir. At Point Comfort. When the fog's up, we move whate'er we can. They're trying to set up a fort over there, sir."

"Williams, is this true?"

"Aye, sir, I've made the run m'self with them a couple of times."

Jonas let the boat go.

As it disappeared into the fog, *Resolute* continued to stand out to sea.

CHAPTER THIRTEEN

Jonas woke to the sound of water sloshing on deck, and the familiar grind of holystones as they worked back and forth over the sand spread on the wet wood. The motion of the ship had changed. Clouds had rolled in the evening before and the glass had fallen steadily. He listened to the creaks, squeaks, and bumps as *Resolute* worked in the seaway. The compass hanging from the deck above his head showed Masefield had brought her about to the east-southeast sometime on the mid-watch. Rising, he groaned. Another day of crew training faced him.

In the three days since their escape from Hampton Roads, they'd seen not a single sail. *Another indication of how the British strangled the colonies' trade.* Before the rebellion, they'd have seen at least four or five ships in the same period.

Jonas had shaped a course directly east once they sank the land. He wanted to be well off shore, closer to routes ships might take bound from the southern colonies or Caribbean to Europe. He also wanted to get out of the great current that ran along the coast, taking everything northward. The weather had been good, the wind hovering just short of fresh, allowing *Resolute* to make upwards of a hundred fifty miles in a day.

During those days, Jonas drilled the crew mercilessly: setting and shortening sail, tacking and wearing, running guns in and out and pointing them, then calling away boarding parties and repelling boarders. Yesterday, he'd even fired one live charge per gun. Drills and ship handling exercises had started to drive the contamination of the shore out of his crew.

However, fighting drills had gone badly. Few of the men had experience with sea fights. While nearly all merchant ships carried guns, few used them or routinely trained their crews in their use.

The boarding drills proved to be even worse.

His crew developed some ability to defend the ship. However, organizing to board another vessel was a dismal failure. Each boarding party needed to function as a team, each man instinctively knowing how the others fought, and trusting each to perform individual tasks so as to move together to take an enemy ship. Unfortunately, Jonas found his crew to be a group of individualists. So when he'd launch boats to carry out a mock attack on *Resolute*, he invariably found those who got onboard ended up being separated and individually "killed."

Topside, a uniform gray greeted him. The dark gray sea merged with lighter gray where it met the sky. To the east the sun tried to make its presence known, to the west storm clouds threatened. Confused whitecaps stretched to the horizon as the swell from the southeast met wind waves from the southwest. This time of year, heavy weather could be expected as cold moist air blew down from New England to meet the warmth of the northward flowing Gulf Stream.

It will get worse before it gets better.

It was cold, too, the cold wind that presaged winter's coming.

The crew washed the last of the sand off with the deck pump, water splashing around the gear stowed on deck.

Jonas looked up. *Resolute* carried fore topsail, reefed fore course, mainsail, and jib. Forward, hands tarred the fore topmast shrouds.

Masefield greeted Jonas. "Morning, sir. Course east sou'east.

Wind backed again jus' afore seven bells, so I brought her 'round. Looks like it'll blow up some."

Masefield reported the binnacle list, men who were sick or injured. *Resolute* carried an apothecary who'd spent time apprenticed to a physician. "We ha' two men with pulls and one wi' a broken thumb. No'ing serious."

"Good. We will forego drills this day."

Midafternoon, Masefield ordered extra lifelines rigged as the seas continued to grow. The wind veered to the west and strengthened to a fresh breeze.

"Take in the fore course and main. Set the storm jib and rig the staysail. It will get worse before it gets better," Jonas ordered. Hackett had the deck as the afternoon wore on.

Soon Masefield came back on deck to join them as the wind continued to grow. By six bells, it was nearly a gale.

Despite reduced sail, *Resolute* plunged into the seas, rose again with streaming bows only to bury her head into the next roller. The wind waves grew as well, giving her stern a harsh kick just as her bow rose to the next swell. The new motion kept the helmsman busy. At the change of the watch, Jonas ordered a second helmsman stationed. The wind waves competition with the swell wouldn't last long. Until they merged, it would be a rough ride.

The weather continued to deteriorate. Gray day transitioned to black night. The only light on deck came from the binnacle. Just after sunset, the wind waves and swells merged; both now came from the west. Their combined heights gave the small ship a dizzying corkscrew as they passed beneath her.

At seven bells, Jonas ordered the course altered to the north-northeast. *Resolute* labored through heavy gusts of wind and sudden downpours.

By midnight, a black maelstrom of icy blowing rain, howling wind, and driven spray surrounded the ship.

"Mighty brisk, sir," shouted Hackett. They put their heads

together to be heard above the scream of the storm. Masefield remained forward to respond to emergencies.

"The glass is still falling. It'll get worse yet," Jonas yelled.

Hackett nodded. Still veering and now from the west-north-west, the wind whipped around them. Men huddled below the bulwarks on the windward side of the waist, trying to hide from the driving water. A lucky few huddled in the lee of the boat lashed amidships. No such protection existed for the officer of the deck or the helmsmen.

A large wave exploded against the starboard bow. A deluge tore the length of the deck. Seeking escape, it soaked all hands and carried the chicken coop far against the leeward side. The terrified clucking of the hens was lost in the tempest. Two men staggered across the deck to re-secure it inside the boat.

Masefield moved aft, holding tight to the lifeline rigged along the deck. Twice, grasping waves took his legs from under him. Reaching Jonas, he shouted, "Topsail's like to blow out, sir. The strain is too great."

"Get it in," Jonas ordered. To the helmsmen he called, "Mr. Hackett, fall off to leeward two points. Shorten sail."

"Aye, sir."

Hackett's voice was nearly lost in the wind, but the helmsmen carefully eased the tiller to starboard. Masefield moved back to the forecastle. Climbing carefully, men moved up the foremast shrouds on the windward side.

An eerie silent ballet followed. Men yelled to each other, responded to orders, and struggled with the canvas, yet Jonas heard none of it. The roar of the wind and the crash of the sea eradicated all other sounds. Even the rain pounding on deck was drowned out in the rush of noise that assaulted him.

The rolling and plunging of the ship was vastly magnified far above the deck. Each time the ship rolled, the men on the yards hurtled through an arc of twenty or thirty feet only to stop abruptly, change direction, and do it all again. As the stern rose to a wave, they were flung forward ten or fifteen feet, again to stop abruptly and return.

Standing on a single strand of line slung beneath the yard in the driving rain and freezing wind, they bent nearly double over the yard. They grabbed handfuls of madly flapping canvas, as if trying to tame some mad tethered beast determined to tear itself to pieces, raging against its tether and trying to take the men with it. Somehow, as they always did, they gathered the canvas to the yard and bound it with the gaskets that hung there, taming the beast. Then, in the blackness, they moved back along the footropes to the mast. There they hung precariously upside down as they passed over the top platform, feeling with their feet for the ratlines between the shrouds, then slowly made their way back down. Each step of the way, the shrieking wind tried to tear them off and pull them to their deaths.

The wind spilled from the topsail, the motion eased. *Resolute* no longer heaved and fell, but instead lifted over the seas. Less water drove across the deck. The watch finished furling the sail and coiling lines, then sheltered once more.

Two hours later, the night grew longer.

Resolute struggled through the storm when a massive "crack" broke through the noise of the storm. Shrouds and stays parted, then the fore topmast went over the leeward side and hung there.

Broken just above the cap where the lower mast ended and the topmast began, held only by the running rigging. It plunged into the sea as *Resolute* rolled, and then rose again. Each time threatening to turn the ship broadside, roll her on her beam-ends, sinking her. Forward, jib and topmast stays flew from the jibboom like streamers. There was no sign of the storm jib itself.

"Get the jibboom in," Jonas shouted.

Lacking the support of the stays, it too would break the first time it plunged into the sea.

At the same time, Masefield ordered topmen aloft and cut away the wreckage.

"Ease your helm, let her fall off. Steer southeast. Watch her, don't let her bow go under."

The helmsmen fought the tiller to windward. Putting the seas on the stern made *Resolute* harder to steer, but she'd be less likely to plunge her bow and break off the jibboom, possibly the bowsprit itself.

Hackett and his crew struggled to rig in the jibboom amidst the havoc. Just then, *Resolute*'s stern rose. The bow began a downward plunge.

The break of the wave caught her just under the counter. She spun to starboard. Jonas watched helplessly as the broken topmast came back aboard and tangled itself in the foremast shrouds. It now threatened the whole mast. He held tightly to the fife rail as she continued to roll.

With agonizing slowness, *Resolute* rolled back upright. The combination of wind on her side and the rudder hard over brought her head back downwind. But they still had to get a sail set forward to hold it there.

Hearing the mast go, the watch below made their way up on deck. Jonas called out to Tilton, the bosun, "Set the fore staysail, double reefed."

Tilton stumbled forward with others. Jonas turned to see how Wilson and Benton were doing at the helm. Only Wilson stood there, struggling mightily with the tiller.

"Where's Benton?"

"Against th' shrouds, sir. Arm's broke," Wilson replied.

Benton lay passed out against the bulwark. The seas washed over him, gushing up through the scuppers as the ship rolled. Jonas looked over. The bone stuck out at least an inch. In between soakings, blood poured out through the wound.

Jonas leapt to the tiller to help Wilson while calling for help.

"Barrett. Come help Wilson. King. Where's King?"

Seeing him, Jonas continued, "King, get Benton below. Take care of him."

King, apothecary and acting ship's surgeon, took one look at

Benton's arm and retched. Quickly recovering, he lifted him as carefully as he could. Then he lurched his way across the madly gyrating deck and took him below.

When Barrett arrived and took the helm, Jonas looked forward again. A scream came from aloft. It trailed down to the water and suddenly cut off.

He ran to the shrouds. Nothing. Heard nothing but the roar of the storm. There was no way to find a man in this, even without damage to the rig.

He cursed. *What else can go wrong?*

Aloft, Hodges had nearly finished cutting away the fore topmast. As each line was cut through, the yard became less tangled. If they were fortunate, they might free it without losing the lower mast.

By the bow, they finally gained the upper hand with the jibboom. Rigged in, they secured it at last.

Masefield managed to get the forestaysail set, and *Resolute*'s motion eased as it filled and pulled the bow around. *Resolute* flew downwind, and the seas no longer threatened to roll her to her death. As the final line holding the topmast wreckage was cut away, the topsail yard took three feet of bulwark with it. At the last moment, it looked as if it would try to come back aboard and stab the ship to its heart, but a wave broke over and carried it away.

Hours later, the storm peaked. The rain and spray became something solid, stealing breath and knocking men to their knees whenever foolish enough to attempt to stand without grasping something. The helmsmen were relieved every fifteen minutes. Each pair wearily dragged themselves forward to the shelter of the boats to recover whatever strength they could. The wind howled like the screech of a thousand banshees in chorus. Each gust reached new octaves.

As dawn approached, it began to subside. Black turned to deep gray. The wind moderated. By midmorning, the rain stopped. Spray no longer ripped from the tops of mountainous waves and flung itself bodily against ship and crew. Men slept uneasily at first, then found the deep slumber of the exhausted. No one went below, instead sleeping near their stations.

Jonas supported himself against the binnacle, hunched against wind and rain. Masefield and Hackett drooped nearby, hanging on either side of the mainmast. The helmsmen mechanically dragged the tiller back and forth in response as *Resolute* rose wearily over each succeeding wave.

Shortly after four bells, Jonas jerked himself awake for what seemed the thousandth time since sunrise.

The sky, still nearly black to the east, lightened to the west as the storm passed over. Looking around, devastation met his eyes. Sleeping seamen lay strewn about the deck like toys scattered by a child. The fore topmast shrouds still streamed from the top. The starboard shrouds on the lower foremast showed damage wrought by the topmast. Odd bits and pieces of gear littered the deck. One of the boats had come adrift in the night and now lay smashed against the larboard bulwark.

Jonas made his way across the heaving deck.

"John, get all hands fed. Then we shall begin the rigging work."

"Aye, sir." A simple response, an exhausted voice.

The word was passed, and the men slowly revived. The thought of a hot meal and the respite of going below, if only for a short time to eat, enlivened what could have passed for a group of corpses.

Jonas ordered the watch below dismissed. Masefield organized those on deck into three groups. One would go aloft to clear wreckage and set up to rig a new fore topmast. The second would break out new cordage from the hold and make new rigging. The third began splicing what rope could be salvaged.

In a remarkably swift time, there were coils of usable rope, both new and spliced, heaped on deck. By seven bells, the top was cleared and they were ready to lower the stump of the old fore topmast.

"Let the watch change before we shift the topmast," Jonas told Masefield. Turning to Hackett, he said, "Lay below. You and I will clear the rest this afternoon."

Going below to his cabin, he threw himself in his chair and reflected upon the events of the night. He said a silent prayer for the man who had been lost. A loose piece of rope had wrapped itself around seaman Eben Jones's foot and pulled him over the side. Jones had been a good sailor and had sailed with Jonas on two previous voyages. He had no family, something Jonas took little comfort in.

Jonas could visualize what a lonely death it must be. The horror as the ship sailed past. Calling to shipmates but no one hearing. Hopelessness as the ship disappeared over the horizon. The intense loneliness of a tiny man in the immensity of the ocean stung his eyes.

Jonas still remembered receiving word of his own father's loss at sea.

His father's ship hadn't returned from the Mediterranean. Jonas had returned home to take care of his mother and fifteen-year-old sister. A year later his mother died of a broken heart. Months later, his sister married. With nothing more to tie him to the shore, Jonas returned to the sea.

Chapter Fourteen

The next day, *Resolute* had mostly returned to her old self. Slightly shorter and thinner, the new topmast allowed her to once again spread her fore topsail and topgallant.

A brilliant sun shone on a blue-gray sea beneath a sky of searing blue. Big rollers still came from the north, but they were longer, giving the ship a gentler roll. With the passing of the storm front, the air turned bitterly cold. *Resolute* tore along under mainsail, reefed foresail, and jib alone. Whitecaps that still pocked the sea to the horizon provided an accent instead of a primary element.

Aloft the crew made finishing adjustments to newly set up rigging, applied final turns of serving to new shrouds, then tarred them. On deck, the carpenter and his mate repaired the jolly boat, the ringing of their caulking mallets pounding out a rhythm. The din combined with the creak of masts and squeal of blocks, and the rush of water passing alongside. A blissful symphony of the sea.

"Before dinner we should be able to set tops'ls and t'gallants on the fore, sir." Hackett stood alongside Jonas as both men watched the work aloft.

"Let us set them as soon as we can, then. We can make our southing, then."

Hackett turned to Jonas. "We'll be needing a yard sooner than we thought, sir."

Shrugging, Jonas replied, "We shall see what our friends in Puerto Rico allow. To them, we are but a merchant with storm damage."

"That's true enough, sir."

"Turn the glass and strike the bell," called the master's mate. The sailor at the tiller then turned the glass while the mate went forward to strike four bells.

The comfort of the seagoing routine helped lift Jonas's dark veil of worry. He relished the sheer joy of being at sea under a cloudless sky, his ship alive beneath his feet and flying through the water.

"Sail ho! Sail, two points off the starboard bow," the lookout called in a voice calculated to wake the dead, or the next best thing, a sleeping sailor.

The crew rose together as if jolted off the deck. Hackett grabbed the spyglass and headed for the shrouds. Jonas moved forward with his own glass.

From aloft, Hackett called, "A full-rigged ship, sir. She's seen us. She's crowding on sail, looks to be closing us."

Jonas's suspicions rose. The only captain who might do that was one who commanded a warship or a privateer and smelled a prize.

Still, his curiosity got the better of him. "Hands to the braces. We will wear ship and see who she is. Set the fore tops'l."

As the ships approached, Jonas's concern continued to war with his curiosity. When they closed to two leagues distance, Hackett called down again. "Sir, she's painted as a merchant, but I can see more gunport than she ought to have. Three are painted over, like if they were part of the hull."

Jonas decided discretion was still the better part of valor.

"Hands to the braces. Wear ship. Steer south by east."

Soon after, the other ship tacked, paralleling *Resolute*.

Resolute was faster. However, their pursuer was deeper and made less leeway. Thus, she decreased the lateral distance while losing the race to windward. The result was that the other ship could, if well handled, control the situation.

"Get the reef out of the mains'l. Set the fore t'gallant."

"Aye, sir." Masefield had come on deck with the lookout's call. Now he stood beside Jonas, studying the strange sail.

"Begging your pardon, sir, but those new topmast shrouds have not had time to properly stretch. I wouldna' like to find out how much the mast can flex."

"We need the speed, John. I have to take the risk. Look at her bow. She's one of those new 'clipper' designs late from Baltimore."

As the morning turned to afternoon, the race continued. Jonas sent the crew to dinner. If forced to fight it was better they'd been fed. Hackett called to him as he and Masefield ate on the quarterdeck.

"Sir, she's sent up an ensign."

Jonas raised his telescope. A yellow flag with some sort of design on it fluttered at the fore. Describing it to Masefield, he asked, "What do you make of it?"

"I dunno, sir. Not something I've seen nor heard of."

Jonas decided he could do nothing but ignore it and run.

The day aged and the sun sank toward the horizon. The two ships continued their dance, white water pounding from their bows as they parted the seas. *Resolute* continued to fall infuriatingly further to leeward. Jonas tried different sail combinations, setting the staysails, then taking them in when she felt pressed under too great a spread of canvas.

He shifted guns from leeward to windward to stiffen her in an attempt to reduce her leeway. He even ran the windward guns out. It helped, but not enough.

"If we survive this, we must find a way to cut her leeway," he told Masefield.

"Aye, sir. I'll think on it."

"That ensign continues to puzzle me. Would that we knew what it is."

"'Tis not a Royal Navy standard, sir. Least not one I've ever seen."

Jonas thought for a moment. Then he said, "But is it worth the risk?"

Masefield grunted. "'Tis no more risk than to continue to run. She gains on us, as surely as the moon follows the sun before 'tis full."

Finally, however, the other ship fired a gun to leeward. The same dread feeling overcame him as when they'd heaved to for *Otter* a year ago. "Round up," he ordered.

Blood running cold, he stared at their captor and swallowed hard. *This cannot happen again.* His fists clenched and unclenched. He didn't hear the grumbling of his men as they coiled down and prepared to wait.

The yellow flag had flapped behind the other ship's topsail, but now it streamed clear. Jonas just made out the words "Don't Tread On Me!" emblazoned on it. He closed his eyes and let his head fall back. Taking a deep breath, he said, "I believe they are friends. Run up our colors."

The continental colors quickly broke at the masthead.

"What ship is that?" hailed the other captain.

"*Resolute*, five days out of Norfolk, Virginia," replied Jonas. "What is that flag ye sail under? What ship are ye?" he continued.

The other captain glanced quickly aloft at his flag, then back at Jonas.

"*Vengeance*, twenty-two days out of Newport, Rhode Island. And it's a flag of the independent colonies. I sail under the authority of the Continental Congress and of General George Washington."

The faces of his crew reflected the release Jonas felt.

He hailed back, "Perhaps you'll join me aboard for a glass. I also sail under the authority of the Continental Congress."

As the two ships rose and fell, a gentleman by the name of James Weatherford came across by boat from *Vengeance*. Once in the cabin, Jonas queried Weatherford further about the flag.

"It's been used in Massachusetts, Rhode Island, Providence Plantation, and a few other places in New England. Congress has given the naval vessels they're commissioning that flag you fly. But it's not popular with some. I don't like it meself. Too much of the king's flag to be found in it. So we use this flag. The message has found favor with the men."

"Aye. It does get the point across. I shall have my sailmaker run one up. Are there any other flags I should know about?"

"Yes. There's another common one, white with 'An Appeal to Heaven' upon it. Washington's ships fly it. Some privateers use it."

Weatherford considered his glass for a moment.

"When you didn't take note of the flag and turned to run, I thought sure I'd found a nice prize, I did. When you ran out your guns, I thought maybe I'd run into a Loyalist privateer, God rot them all. I ran into one before. He fought hard. Took my main topm'st and got clean away while I cut away the mess."

"I didn't know any Tories had taken up privateering."

"Aye, though not many. Mostly wealthy men who can buy a temporary commission. England doesn't give out Letters of Marque. That'd give us legitimacy as independent folk. There's a few's got wise and asked for letters making them revenue enforcers, a kind of 'anti-smuggling' letter. Royal governors can grant them. In return, the governor gets a cut of the take." Weatherford snorted. "Just like always, hands in *our* pockets."

Jonas pondered that for a moment. He'd expected to face the Royal Navy. This was a new threat.

The two shared a bottle of wine and exchanged information.

A New Englander, Weatherford told of a victory won by the Continental Navy. They'd captured New Providence in Bermuda and returned with a cache of arms for General Washington. On their return, however, they'd run into a Royal Navy frigate, the

Glasgow. They'd bungled the attack on her, and *Glasgow*, though damaged, had escaped.

He also relayed that the British appeared intent on taking Newport.

Alarmed, Jonas leaned forward. "Do you think they can?"

Weatherford waved his hand. "Not a question of can they, but when will they. There's little enough to defend it. They took New York easily enough. The Congress seems content to allow the redcoats to take all of New England, so long as their quarters in Philadelphia are safe enough. Here's to the hope that the French might come to help us."

"The French?" There would be a comeuppance if they assisted the colonies to gain independence. Jonas couldn't help but think such assistance would be paid for many times over.

"Aye. They've got no love of the English, that's for sure. I've heard that Mr. Franklin is in Paris even now."

"There's risk in climbing into a French bed," Jonas commented. "They'll want something in return."

"Aye, but we'll be needin' friends before this is over." Weatherford looked past Jonas to the stern windows where the light grew dim in the late afternoon. "I'll also be needin' to go back before dark." He stood and gathered his hat and jacket. "Well met, sir, and I'm glad to see a friend at sea. There's damned few of us."

Jonas gave him two bottles of wine, escorted him back up to the quarterdeck, and saw him over the side into his boat. He stood and watched the boat row across to *Vengeance*.

As the two ships parted in the crimson glow of sunset, each gave a cheer to the other.

The next morning dawned clear and cold. The wind remained fresh from the northeast, and *Resolute* flew before it. The new shrouds had stretched overnight, so he ordered them tautened.

He also carried out another gun drill.

Something had changed. Men ran to their guns with a new sense of purpose and paid rapt attention to the lessons taught by the few among them with gunnery experience. The events of yesterday had gotten their attention, and they didn't want to risk being on the short end if the next time were for real.

After two hours of exercise, Jonas ordered the final drill conducted with shotted guns. The men enjoyed the sharp crack of artillery and the rush of excitement as guns flew past them on recoil.

After supper in his cabin, Jonas came on deck. A watery sun set to starboard. He watched it, reviewing the day's events in his head. Masefield joined him at the rail.

"Gun exercises went better, sir."

"Yes. Nothing like fear to motivate men. I think it finally came home to them, and to me, danger lies out here. Most of them likely thought we were going to capture a lot of prizes and come home with heavy chests of money. I don't think they thought of fighting at all."

The two men watched the sun settle below the waves, each lost in his own thoughts on patriotism, rebellion, and the wisdom of it all.

CHAPTER FIFTEEN

"Captain, Mr. Hackett's respects, and can you come up on deck, sir? There's a ship off the larboard bow, sir."

Jonas rolled toward the voice and slowly opened his eyes. "All right, I'm coming."

He stumbled to his clothes, donned coat and trousers, and moved out the cabin door.

On deck he could see nothing. The new moon left it near pitch black, light from the stars above muted by high haze. He finished buttoning his jacket, waiting for his eyes to adjust.

The wind had moderated. Still from the northeast, now no more than a gentle breeze, and warmer.

"Good morning, sir. It's just past three bells. I stopped strikin' the bell, so as not to wake the chase."

"Good. How far out is she?"

"About five cable lengths. She's a brig, looks like, just about our size. Her lookout ought to be flogged, begging your pardon, sir. Never heard them call out, even we being so close. From aloft, we saw her binnacle light so I sent Miller for you. We started to see herself just after that."

Jonas made his way forward, feeling his way more than seeing, using the rail as a guide as he worked his way to the forecastle.

"Good marnin', sair. She's just over thair, two points to larberd, she is," said Callaghan, posted in the bow.

Jonas's eyes had now adjusted. By looking just to the side of where Callaghan indicated, the darker mass of the other ship appeared in his peripheral vision. Soon he made out her outline against the stars and the horizon. Indeed a brig, she carried main topsail, and fore course and topsail.

"Is she closer than when you first saw her, Callaghan?" asked Jonas.

"Aye, sir, that she is, just a wee bit."

Jonas turned and moved back to the quarterdeck.

"Get the course in. She'll be less likely to see us. We want to just keep her in sight. Can she see our binnacle light?"

"No, sir. I checked just as soon as we saw her. Saw no point in giving ourselves away."

"Aye, we'll have to wait 'til there's more light. Come around. I want to be windward of her by the time she sees us."

Hackett turned and quietly gave the orders. *Resolute* swung round to the west. She would first pass under the stranger's stern, then slide gently to windward. It would be easier to run down on her should she prove to be British when the sun rose.

She did not prove to be British. As soon as she saw *Resolute*'s guns, she showed a French flag. Jonas continued to pursue her, signaling he wished to speak to her. Shortening sail, she allowed *Resolute* to approach.

Uncertain, Jonas remained vigilant as they closed the vessel. She proved to be *Hermione*, forty-six days out of Brest and eleven out of Philadelphia, on her way to Port-au-Prince. She carried no news Jonas hadn't already heard.

Their destinations meant *Hermione* and *Resolute* should sail within sight of each other for some time, perhaps days. But *Hermione* wore away from them midafternoon, and by nightfall was hull down over the eastern horizon. *Perhaps having a predator so close made her captain nervous.*

Seated in the cabin following midday dinner, he reflected on the voyage thus far.

He had expected disappointments such as this morning. The crew had spent the morning growing excited at the prospect of their first capture.

He'd done what he could to reduce their expectations. Nevertheless, when the "prize" turned out to be neutral, he'd felt their enthusiasm burst. He needed to get his officers involved in moderating the men's attitude and buoying their spirits in the face of disappointment. It fascinated him how quickly they'd forgotten the fear of their previous encounter, when *Vengeance* had chased them all day.

Jonas turned to the paperwork that went with command, the close records of the consumption of stores and gunpowder. It was funny, he thought. The paperwork wasn't that different whether he was carrying tobacco to Boston or the fight for independence to sea.

Paperwork bored him terribly. There was one difference now, though. He didn't have to maintain any pay records, at least, not until they captured something.

None of the seaman aboard were paid. They'd signed on for a portion of profits from captured prizes, termed a share. He'd determined that for this cruise, the owner, in this case himself, was entitled to one-third of the total. Out of that he would repay his father-in-law. The remaining two-thirds would be divided amongst the crew. One-third would go to the officers, including what in the Navy would be called the warrant officers — the bosun, the carpenter, the gunner, and the sailmaker. Thus, each of them would receive one-eighteenth of the proceeds.

The seamen would receive the remaining one-third, divided amongst the survivors. Each of the surviving members of the crew — officers and Jonas included — would give up five percent of their share for division amongst the families of any men killed in action.

The part that haunted Jonas was that those who were lost in

accidents, like Seaman Jones, would receive nothing. There might be some kindly men who would take up a collection, of course, but it wouldn't amount to much.

Jonas decided he would take care of them out of his share. It would never be part of the ship's articles, but he would see to it all his men's families were taken care of.

Jonas gave off thinking of money. It was bad luck. Instead, he reached for paper and set about to write a letter to Mary. He would post it from the West Indies when he watered.

Dipping his quill, he wrote:

Resolute
At Sea, 26 Oct 1776

My Dearest Mary,
I take pen in hand for the first time this voyage. As so oft seems the case, we were assailed by a storm nearly as soon as we cleared Cape Hatteras. The ship was not troubled too much by it, only losing the fore topmast. It is with great sadness I must say we lost a sailor, Eben Jones, of Portsmouth.
I hope to be able to report by the next time I write that the tide has turned in our favor. We have not been blessed by any prizes as yet, both ships we've sighted being friends. But England's trade reaches all throughout the world, so we should fall upon some of the enemy's ships soon....

Jonas wrote for two pages. He did not recount the chase he'd lost to *Vengeance*, not wanting to add to her worries. She had enough to be concerned about.

When he'd finished he went up on deck.

"Afternoon, sir," said Masefield.

"Good afternoon, John. How are the men's spirits?"

"Well, sir, they're a bit down about the mouth, I'll allow. It'll pass, though."

Masefield could be counted upon to have the measure of the men's souls. Jonas heeded him, relieved to hear Masefield's assessment.

"Well, I'm glad to hear that. They seemed very 'predatory' as soon as the sail was in sight. It seemed to take them badly aback when she proved French."

"Oh, I'll wager there's one or two who would like to have taken her anyhows, especially a Frenchie, sir. But it'll help 'em keep their heads about them next time, being disappointed this time." He knew what Jonas worried about. He was also certain the men, their men, would neither fail in their duties nor would they disobey orders.

It was the age-old problem of privateering. The kind of men willing to sign on were of a piratical bent to begin with. The lure of fortune attracted a certain type, and those would fight hard to earn their portion. They would die, if necessary. But they would make extraordinary efforts to make the other fellow die instead.

However, these kinds of men were also the weakest when it came to letting a ship go that wasn't a legitimate prize. They tended to see gold shimmering before them, and it was hard for them to let it slip through their fingers. They'd find ways to rationalize capturing them anyway. There were crews that had stepped quietly back and forth across the fine line between privateering and piracy. Once a man stepped across, it became slippery and more difficult to step back to the right side.

"Well, here's hoping the next chase is British, anyway, eh?"

"Aye, sir, here's to it."

Masefield leaned forward and lowered his voice. "Sir, there's somewhat else I been meaning to ask. We have spoken of what would be done with prizes and how we would find provisions where we're going. It occurred to me there will be prisoners to be dealt with, too."

Jonas turned and walked to the stern, motioning Masefield to join him. While he didn't feel it needed to be a secret, he still wasn't ready to share his plans with the rest of the crew. They'd know as soon as they made their first capture.

"You're right. I will not send them into Norfolk, or any other port in the colonies, unless the cargo is powder and shot. They'd be easy pickings for the Royal Navy, and not only would we lose the prize, but I'd be putting the men in the prize crews at risk of hanging. I can't do that." He wiped away some salt spray that had been thrown aft when the bow hit a whitecap.

"If the crew is small enough, we may keep them below on the prize. That is, if we send the prize to the closest land. I am open to suggestions, in the event we send the prize home."

Masefield continued to look to the horizon. After a while, he said, "We could send them ashore ta that same bitty island we pick up our prize crews at. Veekis, is it?"

"Vieques, yes. But that would mean keeping them aboard *Resolute* for perhaps a week. That bears risk."

Masefield nodded slowly. "Aye, sir, it does. And the first time we turn any o' 'em loose, the Royal Navy'll quickly know we're hereabouts."

They stood watching the wake disappear astern. A pod of dolphins played for a moment in their wake, then moved on.

"Can we run 'em into the nearest town, wherever we are?" Masefield asked.

Jonas considered it. "That might work, save for the English islands. Most are French, Dutch, or Spanish. It would be as if we put shipwrecked sailors ashore. Which, in a way, they would be."

"Aye. Doing such might keep word from gettin' out too quickly where we are, too."

"That will be what we do, then."

"I'll find out who in the crew has been in San Juan, beside

Hazleton, sir. If they are steady hands, then them's is the ones we'll use in the prize crews," said Masefield.

"Good. When we're in San Juan, I'll want you to meet Señor Martinez. I want him to know you speak for me, in the event I can't meet with him. In any case, it's best that I not always be the one he's seen with," Jonas said.

Carefully weighing his words, he spoke again. "And in case, well, just in case...." he finished.

Masefield grunted softly. "Aye, sir. There's that, isn't there?"

The two men looked back at where they'd been, thinking of where they were going.

Chapter Sixteen

Resolute sailed beneath the guns of El Moro, then past Fort San Juan de la Cruz, and into San Juan harbor.

Jonas guided the ship to an anchorage commonly used by American merchant ships south of the old town. His first call would be on the American agent. In every way possible, he would portray himself and his ship as a common merchant.

Jonas selected an anchorage a cable's length due south of the Puerta de San Juan. "Let go the anchor," he called.

On the fo'csle, the waiting seaman knocked loose the pin on the cat's head, sending the anchor plunging over the side and into the mud of San Juan harbor.

"Back the fore tops'l. Clew up the courses. Brail up the main." Jonas continued the litany of orders that turned *Resolute* from a moving, living entity, to one made fast to earth again. Her movements were now restricted to the radius established by the scope of anchor cable Jonas ordered let out.

When the anchor, its cable, and all running rigging were secure, Masefield requested to set the anchor watch and dismiss the hands.

"Give the order." Turning to Hackett, he asked, "Any sign of the customs officials?"

"Yes, sir. The lugger is just putting off now from the landing, the one just below and right of the church on the cliff." He pointed to a spot on the beach at the base of the massive walls that surrounded the town.

"Very well, Mr. Hackett. Thank you."

Turning to Masefield, Jonas said, "Now, we wait."

The boat rowed out to where the breeze flowed mostly clear of the city walls. Setting the lug sail, she made a quick run to *Resolute*. Once alongside, the customs official made his way up the side.

"Buenos dias, Señor. The day is new and you are here. I am Capitán del Puerto Ramos, at your service. You have the necessary papers?" he asked.

"Buenos dias, Señor. Si, tengo los papeles en mi cabana. Le gustaria algo beber?"

The official looked surprised, not having expected Jonas to speak Spanish, nor to be offered something to drink this early in the morning. Jonas was in no way fluent, but he spoke enough to conduct limited business. The ability had earned him respect among the shipping officials in Puerto Rico and elsewhere. He'd also learned Spanish customs for doing business, which almost always required refreshments.

"Ah, Señor, muchas gracias. Hace mucho calor; me gustaria beber algo. Por claro, su papeles estan en orden? Y, cuanto tiempo vosotros quedáis? It's quite hot, Señor, and something to drink would be nice. Your papers, Señor, are in order? And how long will you remain?" the official asked.

"Of course, Señor. You may examine them closely in my cabin, where we can also share something. We can discuss how long we will remain there," Jonas responded in Spanish as he led the way to his cabin.

When he'd boarded, the customs official appeared to be in somewhat of a hurry. The offer of refreshment slowed him down. He lingered over the light wine Jonas poured out. "You are from the British colonies, no?"

"Yes, though whether we remain colonies is not yet determined," Jonas replied.

"We have heard of your conflict. But it is not to be expected that colonies can defeat the might of an empire."

"There are those who believe it can be done, Señor. I cannot say what the future might hold. I simply navigate through the present."

"You are wise. We who work the sea must remain clear of rocks and shoals. Such are the matters of those whose lives are bound to the land."

After exchanging further pleasantries, Señor Ramos sighed and began with routine queries about illegal cargos and sickness onboard. Half-hearing the expected answers, and finding Jonas did not intend to land cargo, he declared *Resolute* cleared through customs.

"You have not answered my question, Capitán. How long will you remain with us?"

"I have business with Señor Martinez-Leon. I also require water and provisions. I do not think those things will require many days." Jonas leaned back in his chair. "Perhaps two or three?"

Ramos shrugged. "Who can tell? I believe the chandlers in town can provide what you need. But Señor Martinez, he is a busy man. He has been given great responsibility since you were last here. He now represents the Royal Governor's maritime interests."

Jonas smiled. "You remember me, then. It has been many years."

Laughing, Ramos said, "Of course, Capitán Hawke. Your conquest of my language alone would make me remember you." Rising, he moved to the door. But he paused as he regained the main deck. Turning back to Jonas, he said, "Capitán Hawke, it seems you have many guns? Perhaps too many to carry much cargo, eh?" He smiled, eyes twinkling in the sun. It wasn't a challenge but a sly observation.

"Well, one can never be too careful, Señor. A good captain never knows if there are pirates over the horizon. And oft times there is war somewhere, is there not?" Jonas returned.

"Of course, Señor, of course. Hay que no puede ser demasiado cuida, eh? One cannot be too careful." The official smiled and climbed down into the waiting lugger. Her coxswain ordered the bowman to push off, the sail was set, and the lugger rushed back to the landing.

Jonas turned to look at Masefield and Hackett, both of whom had remained on deck for the fifteen minutes or so the "inspection" had taken. "That was our first obstacle, and I think we've overcome it, gentlemen. Let's be about our business. Mr. Masefield?"

"Sir?"

Jonas said, "You and I will don our shore-going rig. We shall need the longboat at four bells. In town, we will find Señor Martinez and make our arrangements. Mr. Hackett, you have the deck. No one else goes ashore for now."

"Aye, sir."

Jonas went below to his cabin and changed into clothing more appropriate for meeting with the agent. When he came back on deck, the longboat was in the water and made off to the boat boom. Seeing Jonas on deck, the coxswain ordered the bow line cast off. Using the boat hook, he and the bowman maneuvered the boat aft below the entry port. Jonas motioned for him to wait.

"'Vast. Pick up that line again. We're not goin' yet," said the coxswain.

Moments later, Masefield emerged and the two proceeded to the side.

Masefield climbed down and took a seat near the stern of the longboat. Jonas turned to Hackett.

"We shouldn't be long in town, Mr. Hackett. Perhaps three hours, I should think. The Spanish begin their siesta about eight bells, so there's not much business conducted after that until evening. We'll first arrange for watering and provisions, so roust out the water barrels for filling and get the hold ready. We'll also see if we can buy a small amount of powder to replace what we've shot. We can't afford much, but we may need what we can get."

"Aye, sir. Good luck, sir." Hackett turned away to organize the working parties.

Jonas stepped over the side and dropped quickly into the boat.

"Gi' way. Out oars. Stroke," muttered the coxswain, and the longboat moved toward the same landing where the lugger had taken the customs official a few minutes before.

***

MINUTES LATER THEY STEPPED ONTO THE QUAY.

The first minutes on land always felt unreal. Both men swayed slightly, bodies compensating for the ship's motion that was no longer present. It is this that gives a sailor his unusual gait when he first sets foot ashore after a long time at sea.

Approaching a boy seated at the base of the wall, Jonas handed him a coin and told him to find Señor Martinez, give him Jonas's compliments, and a message. That done, he and Masefield began the climb up to the upper city to find a chandler and arrange for provisions to be delivered.

As they ascended, Jonas looked around. Little had changed since his last visit. In truth, not much had changed in the past century. Halfway up, a new church at the edge of the cliff that marked the end of La Calle Cristo drew his attention.

Pointing, he told Masefield, "That church is the Capilla del Santo Cristo de la Salud. Legend has it that the man who had it constructed careened down this street on a runaway horse. Seeing he could not avoid plunging over the cliff to his death, he says he prayed to God to save him. The horse then stopped short at the edge of the cliff. He built the church to honor God for saving his life."

Masefield climbed several more steps before he replied. "I

think I know how he must have felt, astride a horse he couldna' control."

Jonas considered it. "We do, don't we? I pray daily for God to deliver us and our families. I believe He will."

"Aye. But what will be the cost?"

Nearly an hour later, arrangements for water and provisions complete, Masefield strolled alongside Jonas eastward down Calle Fortaleza. Ahead, midway down the street, lay the home where he hoped to find an ally.

A hundred yards farther, they reached a blue pastel two-story house. Three balconies faced the street from the second story, each lined with a wrought-iron balustrade. Climbing the short steps, Jonas made use of a shined brass knocker.

An elderly man opened the door and invited them inside. In a raspy voice, he said, "Capitán Hawke?" When Jonas nodded, he continued, "Señor Martinez se estancia esperando. Por favor, por aqui en la biblioteca. Señor Martinez is expecting you. Please, this way into the Library."

They followed the butler into a dimly lighted, book-lined room in the back of the house. Above them, three large wooden blades swung back and forth, providing sufficient air movement to keep it relatively cool. Masefield's eyes traced the driving mechanism back to where a young boy pulled a single rope descended from a pulley in the ceiling. It was an ingenious arrangement.

Aurelio Martinez-Leon was a slender man, not very tall, thin hair grayed on top. His face was lined with experience, but he was quick to smile and radiated self-confidence. Jonas had found him hard when business required it, while he preferred enjoying life to its fullest, especially with his family. His success showed in his home and its furnishings.

Martinez smiled and advanced to Jonas, hand out. Jonas shook it, also smiling. The two men embraced.

The warm welcome relieved Jonas. As well-connected as Martinez was, he would know about events in the colonies, and so Jonas had worried he might not be welcome. The man had business interests throughout the Caribbean. Riling the British Navy would harm those interests.

"Señor Martinez, muchas gracias por vernos. Thank you for seeing us." Jonas continued in Spanish, "It is good to be back here in San Juan, Señor, with my friends. I pray I find you and your family in the best of health?"

"Of course, mi amigo, everyone is very well. We will speak in English, for your friend. He does not speak Spanish, true?" Martinez asked.

"No, Señor, he does not." Jonas shifted to English.

"Señor Martinez, permit me to present Mr. John Masefield, my first mate and my friend. John, Señor Martinez-Leon, the friend of whom I've spoken."

As he carried out the introductions, he purposefully portrayed the meeting as a gathering of friends, old and new. Business in Puerto Rico was based on relationships and building those relationships took time and care. One could not jump immediately to the business at hand, as in some other places. Instead, a man took time to learn about those with whom he planned to deal, building a bond and trust.

It was not easy. However, once established, it stood solid and unwavering. It required effort to break such a bond, effort that usually involved false dealing. Such a broken connection would also destroy relationships with others. A man's reputation, good or bad, determined whether he could do business with anyone on the island.

"It is with much pleasure I make your acquaintance, Mr. Masefield. I hope we will come to know one another." Turning back to Jonas, Martinez continued. "Captain, we have known each other for many years. Yet it has been some time since I have seen you. How are your wife and children? Well, I trust?"

Jonas paused before answering but decided in favor of

complete honesty. "They are well, Señor, though my wife mourns. We lost twins born two years ago to influenza. They were not yet a year old." He smiled. "But my boy and girl are well, growing fast. On my next voyage, perhaps my son will accompany me."

Martinez grasped Jonas's shoulder and squeezed. "I am sorry for the loss of your children. It is a great pity to lose children. They are our future, our legacy. I pray that your wife may find peace. I, too, lost a daughter years ago to yellow fever. There are times in the spring when I can see in Juanita's face that she still thinks of her."

"I am sorry for your loss, too. I hope your other children are well? And Juanita, she is well?"

"Oh, all are well. My oldest daughter has blessed me with a grandson, just six months ago. Children are wonderful, of course, but a grandchild. Well, they are special."

The three men continued to exchange pleasantries and discuss families. Masefield also had a single grandchild, and he and Martinez shared stories. Their host ordered cool drinks while they talked.

Finally, Martinez asked Jonas what brought him to San Juan.

"Well, Señor, you of course know of the conflict with the English?"

"Yes. I hope this conflict hasn't harmed you. It has slowed trade into your colonies, though a good businessman will always find ships to carry his goods. Do you come for a cargo? Rum, perhaps, or sugar?" The twinkle returned to Martinez' eyes. "Or do you have in mind something perhaps a little more, how would you say, *martial*?"

Jonas smiled. "As I expected, you are truly well-informed. You might say my purpose is martial, though not perhaps in the way you think." He grimaced. "My position as a merchant captain is lost, Señor."

He relayed what had happened with *Elizabeth*. "Thus, I cannot stand by while Britain chokes the life out of her colonies. I have decided to take a more active stance." He paused, then added, "My ship is now outfitted as a privateer."

"Señor Ramos took note of the number of guns when he went aboard this morning. This fact was relayed to those of us with whom you have done business. Others here, as well as myself." He sipped his drink. "But how can I help you if you do not seek cargo?"

"Señor, while the colonial armies need powder and shot, muskets, and cannon, they also need funds to pay for those commodities." When Martinez leaned forward, he said, "No, Señor, I do not expect to load such military cargo here and take them home. That would place my friends in grave danger. I will not do that. However, I am told that the Royal Navy presence in the Caribbean is reduced, with some ships sent north to more effectively prevent those items coming into the colonies. Thus, British shipping here is vulnerable. Through captures, I can hope to help fund our army."

"This is a bold endeavor you undertake. It is with despair that I admit the British Navy is quite capable, and their ships are numerous. Just last week, a frigate called here for water and rum."

Jonas nodded. "The risk is great, Señor. But my countrymen fight for our lives and those of our families."

Martinez smiled. "The man who fights for his family is far more dangerous than the one who fights for his king." He raised his glass. "I honor you for your stance." He set his now empty glass on the desk. "But, my friend, what do you want of me?"

"Little enough, Señor. I would not embarrass you or ask anything that might cause you or your king difficulty." Jonas sipped his own glass. "I cannot send any prizes I take home. Recapture is too great a possibility. Though I will take that risk with military supplies, of course, should I be fortunate enough to capture some."

Now to the heart of the matter. He leaned forward and plunged ahead. "But for the rest, I need a port here in the Caribbean where I can quietly sell ships and cargoes. Without attracting the attention of the British." Now he leaned back, his case having been made.

Martinez's expression had remained neutral. He sat quietly, considering. Finally, he spoke. "Captain, you are aware that Spain is neutral in this war. My king would not take it as a kindly gesture were one of his subjects to openly provide assistance to a rebellion against a European monarch. Our own colonies have been, at times, what you would call 'restive'. We cannot be seen to promote independence."

Jonas grinned. He'd caught the nuance. No one in San Juan would *openly* assist him. However, that left many opportunities.

"No, of course, Señor. Spain's neutrality must be protected. But I am hopeful that, were I to send in a ship periodically for a normal transaction, the cargo might be disposed of through very ordinary means. Quietly, of course, but ordinary. And if, upon occasion, a ship were to become available for sale, I would hope that such ship brokers as ply their business here might arrange a sale that did not attract a great deal of attention?"

"No, Jonas. You misunderstand. I cannot do this. Even if I pretend that your ships are simply selling their cargo, this will make for trouble between Spain and England." He rose and moved to the windows, looking out at the palms swaying in the light breeze. "I am sympathetic to your situation, Jonas. On occasion, I myself have felt that rule from Madrid is, shall we say, ill-informed and arbitrary. But to break with my king entirely? No, it would not work. This colony relies too heavily on Spain for all the things we cannot do for ourselves. We rely on our navy to protect us and our ships. The army defends us from attack." He turned back to his visitors. "And for me to help you to break with your king would not do. If nothing else, it might encourage that kind of thinking among our own people."

He returned to his seat. "I am sorry. Perhaps you counted on me. I am sorry to disappoint you. You are my friend, and I would do much to help. But this I cannot do."

Jonas sank into his chair. But he couldn't let it go without a fight. "Señor, I understand the position you are in. But it is not the same. The English king allows his soldiers to burn cities. To leave women and children homeless in winter. To steal from people's homes. Your king does not do this."

Martinez looked down at his glass and swirled his rum punch. "No, he does not. At least, not to Spaniards. Nevertheless, you must understand that Spain does not want, cannot fight, another war with England. If I am honest, we do not have a sufficiently powerful navy to fight the British crown. Trade would suffer throughout the Caribbean. They might even return here."

As Jonas began to speak, Martinez waved his hand. "No, I do not think they could conquer this city or island. But there are other possessions of my king they might seize."

Jonas's heart beat fast and sweat greased his palms. Everything hinged on this. He had no friends in other non-English ports, not like Martinez, nor did he have time to find one. "Aurelio, my friend. Surely your king would not be unhappy if events forced the Royal Navy to reduce its presence in the Caribbean? Would he not look the other way if the power of England were diminished? Perhaps he might not even need to know that you were helping me?"

Martinez spluttered. "That cannot be. I cannot do these things and 'hope' that my king does not find out. I am a man of honor, Capitán. No, it will not be done." He threw himself into his chair. "This does not even take into account that the British Navy plays a part in control of piracy throughout the seas." He stared at the wall to his left.

"Please, Señor, forgive me. I would not suggest anything that might damage your honor. If it appeared thus, it was not my intent."

Martinez closed his eyes for a moment. "I know that, Jonas. Perhaps I reacted too harshly." He rose and began pacing. "More than fifteen years ago, the French asked us to do as you ask me today, to help their ships in their war with England. Other men, some of whom I knew, agreed. The lure of money was strong, and the possibility of harming the British interests added powerful inducement. However, in the end, it did not benefit my country or my king."

He waved his arms as if pushing something bad away from him. "Oh, this was not the reason Spain joined the conflict. My king tried to aid his cousin in France and declared war. But as you recall, the British took Habana from us. Many here in San Juan were ruined, their investments in French privateers lost. Though Cuba was returned to us when the war ended, we have not regained what we lost. And without regard to politics, the English agent here is not a fool. It would not take long for him to discover an increase in ship brokering in San Juan, and then to understand why it was so."

Martinez sat once more. "I'm sorry. Unless my government informs me to the contrary, I cannot help you. Nor will anyone else in San Juan." His eyes reflected sadness but met Jonas's. He took a deep breath and exhaled.

Jonas sank in his chair, shoulders slumping forward. "Very well, Señor. I understand. I am grateful to you for listening. We must each do what our conscience calls for us to do." He rose to leave and Masefield followed his lead.

Martinez rose to his feet as well. "I will not ask what you will do instead. But know this. You and your own ship are welcome here. No one will turn you away if you come to buy stores or to obtain water. This I can also assure you." He held out his hand.

Both Jonas and Masefield shook hands with Martinez before they departed.

Chapter Seventeen

Jonas might as well have been alone as he and Masefield made their way back to the landing.

He already knew what they had to do. The decision had been taken from him when Martinez rejected his plan. The only thing left was to send prizes back to the colonies. But how to avoid recapture? Keeping well offshore, then running in, sounded good in theory, but would it work in practice?

Jonas went over the possibilities again and again. He was surprised when Masefield touched his arm to indicate they'd gained the quay where their boat waited.

Once aboard, Hackett reported, "We've got the water aboard, sir. The chandler's man told me the salt meat would be here by sunset, as would the dried peas and oat tuns. The rum and other sundries will be here at first light."

"Very good, Mr. Hackett. I'll be in my cabin. I'd like to know when the stores arrive."

He went below and sank into the chair, bent forward, head in hands and lost in thought. He was roused when the messenger knocked and informed him that the first barge loaded with meat was approaching.

The next morning dawned cool and humid. Jonas was on deck when the chandler proved to be as good as his word. The lighters with stores set off from the eastern mole, deep in the harbor, right after dawn. By noon, the deck was crammed with barrels, casks, tuns, hogsheads, and sacks. It took the rest of the afternoon and well into the evening to stow it all below.

Jonas had himself rowed around the ship every hour to check *Resolute*'s trim as the provisions were struck below. He had always wanted his ships trimmed for their best speed, but never before had their lives depended on it. So, he drove both his men and himself mercilessly, making them roust out and re-stow when he felt the ship was down too much by stem or stern.

Just after seven bells, the last barrel and sack was secured below. Jonas ordered Masefield to have the ship ready to weigh anchor shortly after dawn. As he went below, *Resolute* quickly quieted as the crew slung their hammocks.

The ship slept.

As *Resolute* prepared to weigh anchor the next morning, the lugger that had brought the customs official pushed off and slowly made its way toward them in the light morning air.

"Sir, the lugger's approaching," Hackett reported.

"Aye, I see it. Return to your duties, Mr. Hackett."

Hackett stared at him for a moment, then muttered, "Aye aye, sir." He went forward, ostensibly to see to the anchor.

Jonas closed his eyes. He knew he shouldn't take his frustration out on Hackett. But he'd put so much stock in his relationship with Martinez.

"Shall I wait for the boat to come alongside, sir?" Masefield's voice included a slight tone of admonishment.

"No. There's nought good to hear from these people now. We need to be away."

Masefield nodded slightly and moved forward. He ordered the anchor brought to short stay as he went.

The lugger continued at its snail's pace. Jonas turned his back on it and watched the preparations to raise the anchor and make sail.

"Anchor's aweigh, sir," reported Masefield a little while later.

"Very well. Tops'ls, stays'll, and main, Mr. Masefield."

The pipes twittered, blocks creaked, and canvas flapped as sails were set. *Resolute* slowly gained headway as she fell away from her anchorage. The anchor broke the surface of the bay, was hooked, catted, and stowed.

"Capitán. Capitán. Por favore, espere."

Jonas had almost forgotten the lugger. He rounded toward the source of the shout.

In the bow the customs official stood, gesticulating wildly.

"Mr. Masefield. Pray shape our course to the sea. I'll see what the gentleman wants."

Stepping to the stern, he gestured for the man to speak.

"Capitán, may I come aboard? I have an urgent matter to discuss with you."

"I'm sorry, Señor, I must get to sea. I believe we have been cleared by the port captain, yes?"

"Yes, Señor, but my message is of great importance... from Señor Martinez. It should be discussed aboard your ship."

Jonas shook his head firmly. "Please pass my deepest regards to Señor Martinez, but I have business to conduct. I'm certain he will understand. Good day."

Jonas returned to Masefield, leaving Capitán Ramos standing open-mouthed in the bow. *Resolute* was already faster than the lugger. Out of the corner of his eye, Jonas saw it finally turn back to the quay.

Watered and restocked with food and powder, but without

the allies Jonas had sought, *Resolute* ghosted past the imposing edifice of El Moro and stood out to sea.

Clearing the land, he shaped his course for the Anegada Passage east of Puerto Rico. He would patrol to the east of the passage where he expected to find the English ships that brought goods to England and Europe.

Chapter Eighteen

Three days after they'd stood out from San Juan, *Resolute* sailed calmly through the waters northeast of the Anegada Passage, just beyond sight of land.

The sun hadn't brought much warmth as yet, though the day had dawned clear. The wind was still steady, a fresh breeze from the northwest, contrary to the normal easterly trade winds.

The swells were longer and taller, likely generated by a storm somewhere to the northwest. Jonas hoped it would stay to the north. For the moment, the wind waves were small, only a couple of feet high, and the Atlantic possessed the deep azure color that has so enchanted sailors since St. Peter was a mere lad. A small cadre of clouds hovered above, so white they sparkled.

Resolute parted the sea gently with a soft burbling sound that crept down the side to disappear astern. Her motion was easy, heeled slightly to leeward, rising and falling in perfect harmony with the ocean.

Jonas was mesmerized, as he often was, with the gentle cacophony of sounds. His foul mood, however, remained.

"Sail ho! Sail two points off the starboard bow." The lookout in the fore top pointed toward the horizon.

"What d'ya make of her?" Masefield called.

"Perhaps a brig, sir, but 'tis hard to tell. She's still hull down. Methinks I'm seein' her larboard bow."

"Mr. Masefield, let's get the hands out of the rigging and clear for action. This is no time for gawking. Helmsman, put up your helm, steer two points to larboard."

"Two points to larboard, aye, sir, steerin' sou' by sou'west, sir."

The pipes squealed and the crew sprang into motion. To the unpracticed eye, it would have seemed pandemonium, but it was organized chaos as men ran to their guns, picked up the tools from their stowage along the bulwarks, and cast loose the frapping that held the guns in place.

Within minutes they were ready. Jonas kept them loaded at all times, as an enemy could heave into sight at any time.

"Mr. Masefield, run the guns out. I'm going aloft to look at the stranger."

Jonas took hold of the main shrouds and climbed. Hanging back downward, he clambered up the futtock shrouds, over the lip of the top, and continued up the topmast shrouds. Arriving at the main topmast crosstrees, he wrapped his left arm in the shrouds, used the glass with his right.

He could just make out the other ship's sails above the fore topsail yardarm. Though still hull down, she was definitely a brig. The chase being on a larboard tack, the two ships were on converging courses. *Resolute* made six and a half knots, so he estimated their closing speed to be as much as ten or twelve knots. It would be ten minutes or less before she was hull up. In another twenty or thirty, they should know her nationality.

Hanging his glass again on his belt, he swung out and grasped the topmast backstay, making his way down to the deck.

"Mr. Masefield, have the men stand easy on station."

It was nearer half an hour before Jonas, who had returned aloft, could comfortably say she might be an enemy. She'd seen *Resolute*, but appeared confident she either approached a friend, or an enemy she could fight off. This last gave Jonas pause, but he was not going to run.

The stranger was a little smaller than *Resolute*. The cut of her sails said speedy merchant. But even if she were a Royal Navy ship, she was unlikely to be heavily armed. In that event, the greater danger would be her crew, both in numbers and fighting experience.

Reluctantly he chose caution and shortened sail, since their quarry didn't seem inclined to run. He would fight under mainsail, fore topsail, and main and fore staysails alone. As the canvas was taken in, he remained aloft and ran through the calculus of battle.

He didn't want to take on a warship for several reasons. His men were as yet unblooded. Though of late his men had improved greatly in mock hand to hand fighting, he couldn't be sure how they would respond to the chaos of actual battle. But they might be more motivated than sailors of the Royal Navy, as their very lives depended on not being captured.

But the greatest factor would still be crew size.

Returning to the deck ten minutes later, he addressed himself loudly to Masefield.

"I think we may finally have found ourselves a chase." A murmur of excitement broke out, which was exactly what Jonas wanted.

"As we close, we'll come around to larboard and fire a shot. Number one gun, ready. Mr. Masefield, raise our ensign." Jonas watched as the yellow piece of bunting leapt to the head of the main gaff.

A few minutes later the chase also raised an ensign. Blowing freely from the halyard, it was visible from the deck. It was a British merchant standard with a house flag streaming below. Jonas breathed a quiet sigh of relief.

The enemy had their guns run out, but only three per side, as might be expected. The additional two ports were likely painted fakes to frighten pirates.

But as she drew nearer, Jonas abandoned his idea of a shot across her bow. He realized with a start he had a fight on his hands as the additional gun ports opened. The guns that pointed out of them were not fakes. Was she a man o'war after all? It was not uncommon for ships to hoist false colors when approaching a potentially hostile ship.

Jonas hoped this wasn't a ruse. Few merchants carried ten guns, though. It was too late to withdraw, however.

Resolute being upwind of the other vessel, in theory Jonas controlled the engagement. He could come around, away from the threat. But he was reminded of what George Scoggins had said when he'd bought his beloved ship: the brigantine rig had all the disadvantages of both fore and aft and square rig, and the advantages of neither. The enemy's rig was heavier, carried more sail, and she had a finer entry. All combined meant she was likely faster than *Resolute*.

Continuing to run downwind was also fraught with risk. If well handled, the enemy could remain with Jonas nearly indefinitely. The enemy would close on him, a perfect position from which to begin a chase. She could yaw and fire entire broadsides at his vulnerable stern or quarter. He could not respond, because to do so would allow her to come up with him.

No, there was no longer any way to avoid battle. He'd been cocky, assured his position would allow him to choose or refuse battle. He'd been wrong.

He could only pray it wouldn't be too costly. The enemy's ruse had worked, drawn him closer.

He ordered the larboard guns manned. It disconcerted his crew to man the guns on the disengaged side, but they obeyed.

The aft gunport on the brig belched smoke. A corresponding splash appeared fifty yards off the starboard quarter, followed by two more as the shot skipped across wavetops astern of *Resolute*. A second later the sound of the shot boomed across the water.

The brig hoisted the Royal Navy standard. A warship after all.

There was naught to do but attack, and vigorously. Jonas prayed their first action wouldn't also be their last.

Aboard Royal Navy brig *Mythos*, Lieutenant Tristan Bell was momentarily blinded by the sting of powder smoke. The enemy ship reappeared through his watery eyes.

"Load. Fire again when ready."

He had no intention of letting this stranger get away, nor of letting himself be caught unprepared. As soon as the enemy had turned toward him, he'd suspected it might be a rebel. It was slightly larger than his own *Mythos*, but Bell was confident they couldn't have the training or ability of his own crew. They'd only been together for a month, but Bell had driven them hard, preparing for battle against the upstarts should they ever be so bold as to challenge England at sea. The only thing that concerned him was his numbers. He'd sailed with only two-thirds the number of hands he should have.

A dispatch packet, *Mythos* was expected to run from fights. So when fighting ships in Kingston needed hands, his ship was one of the losers. It had cost her dearly.

Bell had passed very late for lieutenant, nearly ten years before as a twenty-two-year-old midshipman. Shortly after the peace had been signed, ending the Seven Years' War with France, Bell had found himself ashore on half pay, too junior to be assigned a ship in the quickly shrunken Navy. That had been far too many years ago, and with every year the chance of being promoted diminished.

The budding conflict with the American colonies had caused the commander-in-chief of the West Indies squadron to rethink the size of his flotilla. He'd ordered the conversion of some of the faster miscellaneous vessels at his disposal. Those ships needed captains, and Bell had leapt at the opportunity to get back to sea, even as the lowly master of a messenger ship.

Despite standing orders to avoid a fight, Bell sought one. He'd seen only one action during the previous war and felt shorted. He did not intend to miss whatever small opportunity for fighting there might be this time.

The aftermost gun on the larboard side of the gundeck spoke again. Then, again.

"Mark the fall of shot, Mr. Whipple," he shouted.

"A hit, sir. By God, we hit her for'ard."

"Below the waterline, Mr. Whipple? Or did we take down a mast or shrouds? A lower mast stay, perhaps?"

Whipple's head came down and he stared at the gun beside him, his face turning a shade of pink.

"No, sir. In the hull above the waterline."

"Then I suggest you look to improve your aim."

"HOLD YOUR FIRE, THERE. MOVE TO THE LARBOARD guns."

Masefield had seen one of the gun captains, who hadn't heard the order to move to the other side, lowering the match to his gun on the starboard side. The man froze, plainly scared.

Jonas felt the churning of his own stomach, the pounding of his heart. Many among the *Resolutes* were afraid. Something about the thought of six-pound balls of invisible iron flying at them worried a man. It made Jonas afraid.

He called loudly, "Men, a warship she may be, but she's no different than us. She carries four fewer guns than ourselves. We can take her. If we handle our guns fast and steady, we'll serve her out and she'll strike. Be steady and all will be well."

A few men returned half smiles. Most relaxed a bit.

Jonas turned his attention to the enemy. She tried another ranging shot, this time rewarded when the shot hit home, shattering a rail forward at the head. No one was hurt, though, since the starboard side guns were unmanned. A few splinters tore across the deck.

"Larboard your helm. Brace around. Brail up the mainsail, haul taught on the headsails."

Resolute quickly swung round to starboard. As she did, the enemy loosed a broadside into her starboard bow. A few shots missed but most struck home. The jarring of the deck told him at least one hit the hull. Two holes appeared in the mainsail as it was brailed up. Two feet of caprail forward of the hances shattered and disappeared. A man standing near the main fiferail screamed and collapsed. He grasped his left leg where a long splinter protruded.

"Lay square the head yards."

Resolute now had the wind nearly on her stern. As she continued to swing, her stern came through the wind. Jonas ordered the headsails loosed and shifted, and the mainsail reset.

"Brace around." The ship swung fast. She must not go too far. He had to be able to pass astern of the brig.

"Helmsman, meet her. Steady."

To the men at the guns, Jonas shouted, "Let her have it."

Resolute's larboard side exploded. A ragged broadside, it took a full five seconds for all guns to fire. Jonas ran to the side to see its effect.

Obviously still unnerved by their first taste of battle, most shots missed. Splashes appeared both forward and aft of the enemy. Some went high and one shroud on the brig's main mast hung free, the deadeye shattered. A single hole showed in the hull, well above the waterline.

The brig's side erupted as she fired her second broadside. Again *Resolute*'s hull shuddered as shots hit home. The bulwark between number four and six guns shattered. Splinters slashed at the men serving guns. Two fell dead, mangled by the passage of the ball. Three more went down with splinter wounds.

"Get those wounded down below. Reman the guns. Fire as you bear."

Resolute fired again, broadside more ragged. Perversely, this one was better aimed despite the carnage. His men were blooded now. The need to serve guns and ship displaced fear.

Two gunports on the enemy became one. A chunk of her mainmast exploded into splinters, the mast cut through by nearly half. Two more shrouds swung free, lanyards cut by splinters or ball.

"Hands to braces. Brail up th' mainsail." Jonas issued a steady stream of orders, wearing ship and bringing *Resolute* around to pass astern of the brig.

Not to be outmaneuvered, the brig rounded up into the wind to tack. But *Resolute* was faster as she ran downwind. *Resolute* would rake the enemy's stern.

"Hold your fire." Masefield kept the gun crews from wasting shots.

"Wait 'til we're on her stern," added Jonas.

Watching for the moment when the ship passed directly astern of the brig, he shouted, "Fire!"

Her stern shattered as all but two of the shots told. Jonas could only imagine the devastation wrought on the brig as the balls passed down the entire length of the ship.

But there was no time to reflect. Jonas ordered *Resolute* to wear again and pass up the brig's starboard side.

Then his heart soared. Either the brig's captain had tried to come back to his original course, or *Resolute*'s broadside had wrought more damage than hoped. She was in irons, bow stuck into the wind. Losing headway, the brig began to drift down on them.

"Back the tops'l," he called. Slowing would allow another broadside into the brig's vulnerable stern.

Resolute fired again, this time hitting her starboard quarter to great effect. The forestay on the brig parted, the sail blowing back against the foremast. More holes appeared in the hull and the bulwark, as well.

Someone on the brig shouted and the sails on the foremast

swung round. She began to swing back to starboard. As her guns bore, she loosed a ragged broadside.

Aboard *Resolute*, the main staysail blew freely over to starboard, the sheet cut through. Number six gun upended as its carriage shattered. Jarvis, stationed at the starboard braces, disappeared in a red mist, his remnants blown over the side.

Resolute swung to starboard. Jonas looked back to bark at the helmsman. He wasn't there. He lay against the starboard bulwark. He looked down to where his forearm ought to have been, screamed, and passed out. Two men picked him up to take him below.

Jonas grabbed the tiller. It was shorter, a full foot having been taken by the same ball that had taken the helmsman's arm.

Back on course, *Resolute* continued up the side of the brig. Fire from both ships was continuous now, each gun firing as quickly as the crew could load it. Splinters flayed men and sails. Debris littered the deck. The newly rebuilt jolly boat was cut in half. Three guns were now out of service on the larboard side, and another to starboard.

Jonas looked over at the brig. Her side was a mess with holes both at and below deck level. Aloft, half the starboard mainmast shrouds were cut through. Most of her lower sails had at least one hole in them. The forestay still hung straight down, the lower half of the sail draped over the fore fife rail. While he watched, one of her foremast shrouds was cut eight feet or so above the channels. More bulwark disappeared. Another hole appeared in the hull.

His attention was drawn back within his own lifelines by the sudden crack of canvas. Forward, the windward clew and leech of the fore topsail flapped in the wind. The foreyard below the sail was broken in two halfway between the yardarm and the foremast. Only the furled foresail kept the broken end from falling and smashing a hole in the deck or killing someone. It looked like it would hold for now. But they must get it secured.

Jonas was suddenly grabbed and thrown into the blood puddling on deck.

Invisible Death has come for me.

He shook his head to clear it. Rising and regaining the tiller, he checked himself.

Masefield called, "Ye hurt?"

"No. I'm alright," he answered.

But he didn't feel all right. A ball must have passed so closely that its wind had knocked him down.

"Get the fore topsail in before we lose the foreyard."

Masefield glanced aloft, then ran forward, dodging wreckage. "Clew down," he called. Men at the halyard eased their lines, those on the clewlines hauled, bringing the topsail yard to sit in its gear, hanging in the lifts at the yardarms. The middle of the yard rested on the cap of the foremast.

"Clew up." The men at the clewlines and buntlines hauled away. The sail rose to the yard, safe now.

Resolute reacted to the reduced sail area forward and tried hard to turn up into the wind. Jonas shoved the tiller all the way to windward to hold her on course. She was losing speed.

"Mr. Masefield, get the jib on her," he shouted, trying desperately to be heard over the incessant gunfire. To the man tending the mainsheet, he said, "Ease the mainsail."

With sail balance restored, *Resolute* regained her composure but not yet her speed. She still carried a heavy weather helm and was falling behind the brig. The enemy, recovered, picked up speed.

"Let fly the headsail sheets. Cease fire. Shift to the starboard guns."

Three more guns were fired. He had to repeat the order once more before all hands heard. *Resolute*'s guns fell mercifully silent. The sheets for jib and forestaysail cast loose, he turned the tiller downwind.

"Mainsail haul." Bringing pressure on her stern, her bow flew farther into the wind. Aloft, Hackett still worked to secure the foreyard.

As the bow swung into the wind, guns on the starboard side began to bear.

"Please, sir, fire?" asked Hopkins, the Gunner.

"By God, yes. What're you waiting for?" The words had barely left his mouth when the guns roared out, ripping once more into the brig's stern. Too late, the brig attempted to turn starboard, both to protect her stern and bring her guns to bear.

She must hope we aren't ready, or that she'll surprise us and get quickly around. Then she stopped swinging and sealed her fate.

"Back the jib and fore staysail to larboard. Back the mainsail to starboard."

The sail handlers responded, and *Resolute* began to fall ever so slowly back to starboard. Jonas glanced quickly over the side. Gathering sternway, he reversed the tiller to help bring the stern around.

He expected the brig would fall off immediately to rake his bow as he came back. He wanted to fall off quickly himself so they wouldn't get the chance.

Mad cheering interrupted him. Angrily, he turned forward. He found himself shouting as well.

The brig's mainmast had gone by the board, trailing off her leeward side.

Forcing her to swing around slowly, it allowed her starboard broadside to bear. Jonas realized with alarm that if they fired, it would be the raking shot he feared.

He shouted orders. The cheering died. The mainsail was brailed up. *Resolute* fell off the wind and gathered speed. Men re-manned the remaining larboard side guns and readied another broadside.

The brig didn't fire. Instead, a tattered ensign ran partway up her foremast, then came back down.

"Hold your fire!" Jonas shouted.

The order fell on deaf ears. The men had seen the gesture as well and broke out in renewed cheering.

The brig had struck.

Chapter Nineteen

Jonas sagged. *No time to be tired.*

There were orders to give and decisions to be made. Many were decisions he'd never made before. Some were ones he'd at least considered; others had never occurred to him.

"Do we have any boats left?"

Masefield stared at him. "Yes sir, I think th' launch is undamaged. I'll get it over the side. Will ye go aboard to take their surrender?" Masefield's speech was slow, his head slung low and forward. He blinked his bleary eyes.

"That'll be your honor."

Masefield looked at him and smiled slightly. "Thank'ee, Jonas."

Masefield and a twenty-man prize crew rowed across and climbed the side of the brig. Then Jonas turned to the task of beginning repairs to *Resolute*.

Hackett approached. "Sir, King was knocked on the head by a piece of deck beam. He's still unconscious, and we have wounded to be treated."

Hailing the prize crew aboard the brig, he asked about the injured prisoners and the brig's surgeon.

"Sir, he's workin' on 'em now. They have got about thirty, sir," Masefield replied.

Jonas recalled the launch and ordered his own wounded transferred to the brig.

Next it was the carpenter. "We've got a hole or two forward, low, below the waterline. There's two feet in the well and slowly rising, sir. We need to move some barrels to get at 'em."

Jonas gave orders for a small working party. Then Hackett was back.

"Sir, there's not a spar long enough to use to replace the foreyard. I can try to fish it, but I don't know how well it'll hold."

"See if the brig has one. If not, we'll fish it and see."

Jonas assigned four men to man the pumps and the remaining men were set to salvaging what they could of the wreckage strewn about the deck. What couldn't be reused went over the side.

Three bosun's mates were assigned the unpleasant task of collecting bodies of the dead and preparing them for burial.

In the Royal Navy it was common for the dead to be unceremoniously thrown overboard during a battle if the body were in the way. He hoped that had not happened on his ship today. A man deserved a decent Christian burial.

As he stood on the quarterdeck, more and more questions demanded his attention. He stayed busy through the long morning. Eight bells caught him by surprise. He hailed the brig again and requested Masefield return with the brig's commander. He had not yet received its formal surrender.

* * *

Long minutes later, Masefield followed a British officer into the boat. Jonas straightened his jacket as best as he could while they rowed across.

Aboard *Resolute*, Masefield led the officer aft.

The man was tall and angular. His uniform, though threadbare at the elbows, was in good repair, though smoke-stained.

Jonas guessed him to be about thirty. He momentarily pitied this man about to surrender his ship.

"Sir, may I present Robert Whipple of the—"

Whipple stepped forward. "Of the Royal Navy brig *Mythos*. To whom am I speaking?"

Jonas turned very deliberately to Masefield.

Masefield's eyes rolled. Then he said, "Sir, Mr. Whipple—"

Whipple leaned forward and growled, "*Captain* Whipple."

Masefield sighed. "Very well, *Captain* Whipple is the survivin' officer. Her captain was killed when we raked their stern. Their first officer was mortally wounded and died under the surgeon's knife."

Jonas's stomach lurched. But he hid his disquiet and turned to Whipple.

"I'm Captain Jonas Hawke, of the privateer *Resolute*, Norfolk, Virginia."

"Privateer? The governor of Virginia issued your privateering commission, yet you attack a Royal Navy warship? I believe, sir, that makes you a pirate." Whipple glowered, daring him to argue.

The man was full of bluster, fire in his eyes, but Jonas was no longer surprised by inane things cocky British officers might say.

Pirate? No, but equally predatory. Jonas sighed.

"My commissions come from the Colony of Virginia and the Continental Congress of the United Colonies. I am not a pirate."

"I do not recognize those 'august' bodies. It is my sincere hope that I see you hang." He turned his back on Jonas.

Jonas closed his eyes and took a deep breath. "Very well. If you refuse to surrender as an honorable man would, instead behaving like an insolent child, I shall treat you as such. Bosun. Clap this man in irons."

Jonas turned and walked to the rail to stare out to sea. Tilton and his mate took the now expostulating Whipple by his arms.

Whipple shook them off and stepped angrily toward Jonas. "You cannot do that. I am a King's officer. You wouldn't."

Jonas turned back to him and said tightly, voice low and

throaty, "I suggest, *Captain* Whipple, that you not try me." Stepping back and returning to a normal tone, he continued. "This attitude is what will cost England her colonies. Now, do you offer your surrender?"

Whipple stared at Jonas, jaw working furiously. Finally, his shoulders sagged. "Very well. I surrender *Mythos* to you. May you rot in hell, Yank."

He turned and stalked forward.

***

"MR. MASEFIELD, YOU MAY RETURN TO *MYTHOS*." Motioning Masefield closer, he spoke in a hushed tone. "Whipple will be confined below in *Resolute* until we send the prize home. The rest of his crew shall be held in *Mythos*. I am not certain I can trust our 'friend' to keep his word. However, he will be treated as a captured officer with all the respect due him. We will show him that we are men of honor, despite his disrespectful attitude." Straightening, he asked, "How do you find the brig?"

"She's got some damage to her hull but nothin' below the waterline. Well found with spare spars, too, sir. In a day, we can rig a new mainmast and repair the rigging." He paused, frowning. "How do we stow the prisoners, sir? They're mostly pressed men, so I'd not like to treat 'em as we were treated aboard *Otter*."

"How many are there?"

"Well, they have what Whipple called a 'large butcher's bill', sir. Nineteen dead, thirty-seven wounded out of a crew of eighty-one. Some of those were under the mast when it fell so they're pretty bad broke up. Not sure many will live. As I said, Whipple is the only officer. By the by, the helmsman was killed same time as the captain. That's why she stuck in irons." He rolled his neck on his shoulders. "Of the carpenter, gunner, and bosun, all are wounded, though the carpenter's only got a splinter in his arm."

"How many of the wounded will survive?"

"The doctor said he might save half of them, though he

wouldn't be certain. The sailing master, he lost a leg. Died below, too."

Masefield's report continued but Jonas only half heard it. He caught the important points but couldn't help mourning. His own toll amounted to eight dead and thirteen wounded. There were more than twice that many aboard the brig. He hadn't thought they'd hit them that hard, even discounting those killed or injured in the fall of the main mast. Of the thirteen *Resolute* wounded, only eight were likely to return to duty. That assumed no gangrene or other infection, Jonas reminded himself. The other five would have to be sent off in the prize.

Another question came to mind. "Did you find any dispatches aboard?"

"No, sir. I searched the captain's cabin. I believe if there were any, Mr. Whipple threw them over the side. However, she's got plenty of gunpowder, more than she ought for her size, far as I can tell. There's some stowed on the berth deck, even. She's carrying about two hundred muskets, along with flints, powder horns, and the like. They're down in the hold now, but I'll have 'em brought over here, if that's all right, sir. Better if they're not onboard with the prisoners, I was thinkin'."

Jonas held up his hand. "No, not yet. We can transfer some of the powder, but keep the muskets and all onboard. Post a watch if you think it necessary."

Masefield nodded. "There's also boxes and other baggage. One of the crew tells that they belong to an Admiral Graves. He says they're personal property, some foods and wines that the admiral particularly likes." Masefield grinned. "The brig was takin' 'em to New York."

Jonas was surprised but pleased. He hadn't expected they'd be so lucky as to capture even this small amount of military stores so soon. Getting them home became of manifest import.

It will also be the biggest challenge.

Jonas dragged. Finding it hard to think straight, he needed desperately to sit. While he and Masefield talked, two bells struck.

He held up his hand, interrupting Masefield's report. "Let's get all hands on both ships fed."

"Aye, sir. You should look to yourself, sir."

"Aye, I will. Will you stay and sup with me?"

Masefield politely declined, as Jonas knew he would. Jonas waited until all hands began to eat, then went below. Before laying aft to his cabin, he ordered the cook to take some food up to Hackett and those who remained on deck.

Masefield rowed back to the *Mythos* and took care of her crew.

In his cabin, safe from the eyes of his men, Jonas collapsed, dropping into the lone chair. He stared for a long moment out the stern window. Beyond, a beautiful day moved toward sunset. Hove to, *Resolute* rose and fell with the long swell. The clouds of earlier had fleeted past and hung low on the eastern horizon. A petrel flew lazily by.

Jonas was astonished at how quickly the battle had come and gone. Shortly after *Mythos* struck, he'd looked at his watch. The entire battle had taken two hours from sighting to surrender. The firing itself had lasted a little less than thirty minutes. He'd thought it much longer.

Slowly recovering, he rose and asked the cook to bring some dinner. A tin bowl of stew and ship's biscuit came, brought aft by the cook himself.

Jonas sat and stared at the food for a moment or two before eating. After the first spoonful, he found he was famished and quickly devoured it.

THE FOOD VASTLY IMPROVED HIS MOOD. STEELING himself, he moved out the cabin door and stopped at the scuttle-butt to drink the first water he'd had all day.

On deck, problems assailed him once more. Masefield requested *Resolute*'s carpenter and bosun to assist with repairs aboard *Mythos*. Significant progress had been made aboard *Resolute*, with the shot holes below the waterline plugged, so Jonas let them go. The bosun's and carpenter's mates could handle the remaining tasks.

At two bells, he suddenly found himself with a free moment and decided to visit the brig. He had the launch brought back, then returned with it to *Mythos*.

Climbing to the deck, the destruction shocked him, despite his crew's best efforts. While wreckage was no longer strewn all about the deck, plenty of damage remained visible. The carpenter had some of the prize crew hard at work restoring bulwarks, at least sufficiently to secure the remaining guns. Aloft, the bosun directed splicing and knotting both standing and running rigging and prepared to raise a new mainmast. The carpenter himself busily shaped that mainmast out of a spare spar.

At least five of the brig's guns had been dismounted as well, and the trunnion on one was shattered. It lay to the side, awaiting disposal over the side.

All around the deck, too, were bloodstains.

There had been aboard *Resolute*, as well, but they'd had time to scrub them off.

"Good afternoon, sir. Welcome aboard. Progress is slow, but we'll make it." Masefield took Jonas by the elbow and guided him aft.

"I need to talk to you about some of the prisoners." In response to Jonas's concerned look, he continued, "No, sir, none of 'em got into the spirits. But there's five of 'em claim to be Americans. They want to join us. I didn't want to commit one way or t'other, so's I could talk to you about it first."

Jonas blinked. "I suppose I will have to interview them directly. Where are they?"

"Down below. This way."

Masefield led Jonas forward to a hatch that led below to the tiny berth deck. The headroom was less than aboard *Resolute* and both bent low to avoid the deck beams.

Jonas paused for a moment to let his eyes adjust. The hatches were open but didn't admit much light. Once they could see, they moved forward to another hatch that led to the hold. Two men with muskets stood there. A swivel gun on a temporary mount aimed down the hatch into the darkness. Masefield motioned to one of the guards, who turned and descended into the murk. Very soon he returned, followed by a sailor in bloodstained shirt and trousers.

"This here's Delancey, sir."

Without waiting, Delancey knuckled his forehead and spoke. "We needs to speak w' you, sir, we do."

"That's why I'm here. What's on your mind?"

"Sir, we're Americans. I'm Patrick Delancey. Down below there's four more o' us. Esek Dibdin, Hoseah Jackson, William Roberts, Henry Dobbins. Well, sir, that's the five of us. Most of us 're from Massachusetts, though, Jackson, he's from South Carolina. Charleston, sir. We're Americans, sir. We was sailing out o' *Black Pearl*, from Kingston. The captain, he heard a press was bein' raised up an' tried to get the ship out o' harbor. Well, the fort fired on us and we was boarded." He paused and wiped the sweat from his forehead. "We want to join you, sir. Please. We can't go back to their damned navy, sir. They ride us somethin' awful, sir. Life's hell for us."

Jonas had seen a press gang in action. A midshipman had taken eight men into the pubs and taverns of Basseterre, on St. Kitts. There they'd essentially kidnapped men who were in their cups and taken them aboard a ship-of-the-line in need of crew. It didn't matter if they were sailors or not. The only requirement was that they appear healthy. Every sailor had heard stories of flogging captains aboard some of His Majesty's ships. In nearly all, the starter and cane were in daily use, ostensibly to "encourage the hands" in the performance of their duties. Jonas was certain all it did was instill a sullenness in the men, which led to inefficiency and sloth.

"Let's have the rest up here."

They waited while the named men were brought up. When they gathered on the berth deck, Jonas addressed them. "Is this right, men? Where were each of you pressed?"

All five nodded vigorously.

"That's right, sir. We was taken outta the *Black Pearl*, out of Newport."

"Well, men, I'll take your word and sign you aboard. But if you're caught, you'll likely be hung as deserters. If you want time to think, take it. I will tell you honestly I need you, but I'm not going to ask you to put your necks in a bight unless you know it."

To a man, they quickly agreed to sail with him.

Jonas would take them back to *Resolute* and enter them in the ship's books. He'd lost more than their number in the battle, but it was a start.

Finishing his tour of *Mythos* topside, Jonas next visited sickbay. Meeting the surgeon, he asked after the wounded.

"Sir, we need more air. The fetid air is no good for them and will putrefy their wounds." He waved his hand around the tiny space. "Of your men, one has died. The rest I've managed to keep alive, for now. I have thirty-five wounded of my own, too."

"I had been told there were thirty-seven wounded from *Mythos*, Doctor."

"Yes, well, two died. Of mine, there are nine who should return to duty. Nineteen will live. Of yours, six will return to duty. The remainder from both ships are all amputees. One of yours I fear for, as I had not only to take what was left of his left arm, but he's got a splinter wound in the abdomen. I've removed the splinter, but fear there's internal bleeding. Larson's his name, I believe."

Jonas winced. Larson had been the helmsman during most of the battle. "I'll see them, if you please."

Jonas walked among them, trying to be upbeat. To Larson,

who lay staring up at the low deck beams from his hammock, he said, "Larson, the doctor says you'll be fine. You'll surely see Virginia long before we do."

Larson didn't move for a moment, then rolled his head slowly to look at Jonas. "Aye, sir, t'at I will. But what's I to do when I get tere? I've lost me arm, sir. Ahnt sailin', sir, t'at's all I know."

"Aye, Larson, I understand. I'll see what I can do for you. At the very least, you'll get your share of this prize. That should set you up some. That's a good thing, right?"

Sighing deeply, Larson suddenly grimaced in pain. The wound in his stomach bled through the dressing. When his face relaxed, he continued, "Aye, sir, I s'pose it t'is. I'll be all right, sir. Tank you, sir."

Jonas moved on, more saddened with each hammock he visited. Despite their injuries, his men were generally upbeat, relishing the victory. Even those who'd lost limbs were somewhat cheerful, though obviously still in pain, despite the laudanum given them.

Back on deck he moved quickly to the rail to purge his lungs of the squalid sickbay air. Jonas was used to the mix of odors: unwashed bodies, stale air, rotten food, and a touch of human waste. But this odor was something new. He could only term it the smell of death.

In the late afternoon they held a burial service aboard the brig. Jonas let Whipple conduct the service for the British sailors, and had the prisoners brought on deck to pay their respects to their fallen shipmates. His own crew were armed and stationed on both forecastle and aft of the quarterdeck. He didn't expect any trouble, but it paid to be cautious.

Whipple read the service straight out of the Book of Common Prayer, the words containing little emotion. When he finished, he replaced his hat on his head and retired. But he'd been discreetly looking around all the while. Jonas motioned to Masefield.

"Our guest is very studious."

"Aye, sir, I know. I been watchin' him. I wouldn't trust him to buckle his own shoes."

———

Still later, Jonas held a similar ceremony on his own quarterdeck. The nine silent shrouded forms lay on planks, one end on a stand fashioned on the deck, the other on the rail. Two men, one on each side, stood beside each of the planks. The bosun had done well, he and his mates sewing each man into his hammock, with two round shot at his feet, to ensure that the remains sank quickly out of sight.

Jonas read the service from the same Book of Common Prayer of the Church of England. He felt the pain in the words as he spoke them, especially at the words "Forasmuch as it hath pleased Almighty God, in his wise Providence, to take out of this world the Souls of our deceased brothers...."

He wondered for the first time, but not for the last, at his own role in taking the souls of his dead from the world. He'd had occasion to conduct funerals before. In ships in which he'd served, there'd been occasional deaths. Sometimes a man fell from aloft or died of illness. But he'd never before felt he'd killed them. Today, he felt like the instrument of their death. It was an unwelcome feeling, one which he couldn't shake. He continued to read the names, pausing as the inboard end of each plank was lifted up, the body allowed to slide into the sea.

Larson's was the last. He'd died less than an hour after Jonas talked to him. When his canvas-shrouded remains slid off the plank and disappeared, dragged to the bottom by a cannon ball at its feet, Jonas concluded the ceremony. Most of *Resolute*'s repairs were well along or completed. The brig would take longer, but it would be ready to sail tomorrow evening.

Jonas needed to leave this place of death. He also had to decide where he would go.

In his cabin, he removed his best coat and hung it on the back of the chair. Removing the chart from the rack above his desk, he looked at where his morning fix had put them. They wouldn't have drifted far from there. By his calculations, they were only thirty miles north of Sombrero Island. To the west lay Puerto Rico and San Juan. To the southeast was Anguilla.

Jonas had been to Anguilla before. While there were two small towns on the island, there was nothing to trade. Thus, the only reason for ships to stop was to take on water. But the island was British. He could land his prisoners there, expecting them to be safely repatriated.

The only other option was St. Martin, either the French or Dutch half of the island. But beyond his distrust of the French, doing so would put him very much closer to the British ports of St. Kitts and Nevis where the Royal Navy often called. No, he didn't dare take that risk.

Moving to the chair, Jonas sat. His heart was uncharacteristically heavy, and he couldn't shake it. He wondered idly if this had affected his ability to make the decision.

He sat for some time, reflecting again on the battle. He saw nothing he could have done differently to try to save the lives of his men or of those in *Mythos*. Yet he felt there must be something.

The sun now sank toward the horizon. Rising, he re-fastened his collar, put on his coat, and went up on deck.

They would remain hove to through the night but would set sail for Anguilla as soon as *Mythos* was ready. There he would rid himself of his prisoners. Then *Mythos* would sail for the Chesapeake.

CHAPTER TWENTY

An overcast morning saw both ships still hove to, riding gently to the swells. The barometer had fallen through the night, and the wind backed until now it came from the west-southwest half west. Given the rate at which the glass dropped, Jonas didn't expect too big a blow. But he'd feel safer once they were underway. At least he wasn't on a lee shore. The nearest land was still Sombrero Island, now nearly forty miles to the south.

Jonas stood at the rail and stared across the water at *Mythos*. Nearly ready, her newly stepped mainmast was shorter than the original, only a foot taller than the foremast. The prize crew was just now sending up the main topmast. They'd salvaged the old one and so were able to re-use much of the topmast rigging.

There was one more thing to consider before the two ships got underway. He and Masefield had discussed the prize crew and agreed on its members. All were trustworthy, experienced men.

But they had not discussed who would command. Masefield had discreetly not brought it up, rightly judging it to be Jonas's decision. The natural choice was for Hackett to command their first prize.

However, in the weeks since they'd left Norfolk, Jonas had seen things in Hackett that gave him pause. While a right seaman and good officer of the deck, Hackett lacked imagination. He responded well to emergencies he'd seen before. But he needed guidance if something were out of the ordinary.

Jonas did not believe he was suited for command, at least not yet. The prize captain must be someone he could trust to handle crises and act independently. Jonas also didn't feel comfortable sending Masefield. He needed him on board *Resolute*.

Stepping back from the rail, he moved forward to the break of the poop deck. "Pass the word for Mr. Tilton."

Turning to Masefield, who stood to leeward on the quarterdeck, he said, " I'm sending Tilton as prize captain. Who do you want to fill the bosun's billet?"

"Well, sir, there's his mate, Hodges. He's younger than Johnson, but he's got more in his head, beggin' your pardon. And the others'll take orders from him. He's well liked, sir."

Tilton arrived on the quarterdeck and Jonas asked him, "Have you ever sailed as master or mate?"

Tilton cocked his head, pausing before he answered. "Yes, sir. I was mate once a few years back. I made a couple of trips to Jamaica. I didn't like it, though, sir, honest truth. The captain tried to talk me into stayin' with him, but, God's honest truth, sir, I like bein' a bosun."

"Be that as it may, I'm giving you command of *Mythos*. You'll accompany *Resolute* to Anguilla, where we shall put the prisoners ashore. After that, you are to take her home to Norfolk. I can give you one of your mates for a second, if you'd like."

Tilton thought about it for a moment.

"Aye, sir, I can do 't. I'd like to take Johnson, if you've no objection, sir. He's a right good seaman and that'll leave Hodges behind, sir. He'll take care of things for you, sir."

"Very good, *Captain* Tilton. Get your chest and assume command. We sail as soon as you're ready."

Tilton acknowledged and moved off to get his things.

Now Jonas needed to address Hackett. He'd never told him command of a prize would be his, but he knew the man expected it. Were Jonas in Hackett's shoes, he would have. Such an affront, left to fester, might destroy Hackett's trust in Jonas. It also had the potential to ruin Hackett's credibility with the crew. The men would also expect the second mate to command and would wonder. Rumors would start and the damage would be done.

"Mann, my compliments to Mr. Hackett, and his presence is requested on the quarterdeck."

"Aye, sir, your compliments to Mr. Hackett, and his presence is requested on the quarterdeck." Having faithfully repeated the order, Mann disappeared below, where Hackett led a working party in the hold.

Attaining the quarterdeck moments later, Hackett limped over to where Jonas stood.

"Are you alright?"

"Oh, aye, sir, I'm fine. A barrel shifted and struck my knee, nothing more."

"I'm giving command of the prize to Tilton, Enos. I need you aboard *Resolute*."

Hackett's eyes went wide at first, then cast downward as he tried unsuccessfully to hide his disappointment. His mouth opened, closed, opened again, then closed firmly.

"Aye, aye, sir. If that's what you think is best, of course. Tilton is a good man." He paused, apparently debating whether to add something else.

"Is there something else, Mr. Hackett?"

Hackett continued to struggle, then his face calmed.

"No, sir. I'm sure it's the right decision, sir. Will there be anything else?"

"No. How is it in the hold?"

"We've nearly got all the stores moved back where they belong. We lost three butts of water to a ball that came in through the starboard bow...." Hackett continued speaking, his end of the conversation more stilted than usual.

Finally, as he turned to go below again, Jonas added, "I know it's a disappointment, Enos. It's like enough there'll be other opportunities."

He didn't turn around, but paused, one foot slightly in the air for just a moment. Continuing to the hatch, he said, "Aye, sir. Thank'ee."

<hr>

By four bells, both ships were close hauled, headed south. The freshening breeze had backed farther, now coming from broad on their starboard bows. For now the swell remained on the starboard quarter as they made their way through the azure sea.

Heeling deeply to larboard, the long rolling swells overtook the ships, each rising up the front to the crest, then falling down the backs to the trough. The wind in the sails gave them stability, imparting a gentle roll with each wave's passage, but never past an even keel.

Jonas's noon sight showed them nearly halfway to Anguilla. If the wind didn't back further, they would make it by dusk. If he had to tack west, they would not arrive until morning.

The glass continued to drop through the afternoon. The wind freshened and veered a point, indicating the storm passing to the north. Jonas ordered sail shortened. As *Resolute* reduced sail, Jonas looked over at *Mythos*. She too took in sail, having taken *Resolute's* lead, snugging down to topsails and staysails alone. Tilton had immediately proven capable of handling her when he'd gotten her underway, the sail handling professionally done, especially considering the small size of the crew.

Jonas invited Masefield to supper and went below.

Masefield followed him into the cabin. "We're making nigh on ten knots now," he told Jonas.

As Jonas poured two glasses of wine, the cook knocked and came in bearing bowls of stew. They hadn't been to sea long enough to run completely out of fresh vegetables — moderately fresh, that is — and the meat was recently in the cask. In time, they'd eat the sweet potatoes they'd taken aboard in San Juan.

As they started to eat, Jonas got right to the point. "I mean to stand off and on just out of sight of the island until after dark. Then we'll close the shore and heave both ships to just off the town. An hour before dawn, I want you to use the two longboats to take the prisoners ashore. As soon as you set them loose, come back. When you're back aboard, we'll shape our course to the eastward until we are shot of the land, then come back around to the nor'west and resume watching the Anegada Passage. Tilton will then sail for Norfolk."

"Aye, sir. It's makin' the best of it. What about the lobster backs? Are there any in the town, d'ya think?"

"The one time I watered there, about eight years ago, there was a detachment of perhaps ten men, to keep the slaves in line. I imagine the fighting in the colonies has drawn away as many soldiers as they can spare."

Masefield grunted but said nothing.

"Besides, you'll be gone before they have a chance to muster." Seeing the corners of Masefield's mouth still drawn down, he added, "Still, if you see them, simply return. Then we shall find another way to release our prisoners."

"What about Whipple, sir?"

Jonas grimaced. "I will solicit his parole and demand his good behavior until released. Though I doubt I will get either."

The two fell silent. Jonas roused himself first. "Well, there's nought else to be done. Would you be so good as to join me for my interview with Whipple, after supper?"

Masefield nodded. They finished their supper in silence.

THE INTERVIEW DID NOT GO WELL. WHIPPLE ENTERED the cabin with his usual belligerent attitude and nothing he heard improved upon it.

"I have brought you here to ask for your parole until you can be properly exchanged." Jonas tensed as he asked, though he remained seated.

Whipple stared at him, eyes wide. "You wha-? What did you-?" His mouth hung open. Finally, he found his tongue. "You want WHAT?" His face grew redder by the second.

Jonas stretched his neck muscles and massaged the throb in his temples. "You heard me. I am asking for your parole."

"Never. Only a gentleman may ask for parole, and you, you bloody bastard, are no gentleman. And that does not even account for the fact that you are a dirty, foul rebel, not a real fighting man. I'll do no such thing." He clamped his mouth shut and turned to leave. Masefield placed himself between Whipple and the door.

"Get out of my way."

"No, sir, I will not. You will not leave this cabin until—"

"It's all right, John. I didn't expect him to behave with honor." Jonas stood and moved around the table. His face red, he said, "Mr. Whipple, I'll not demand satisfaction from you, because that would imply *you* were a gentleman." He stepped close, placing his nose nearly against Whipple's. Whipple's face had gone ashen.

"But if I find you've taken up arms again without a proper exchange, I will take great pleasure in hunting you down and treating you like the dishonorable dog you have shown yourself to be." Jonas continued to stare into Whipple's eyes, unblinking.

Whipple blinked first. Saying nothing, he backed away. Masefield stood aside, so when Whipple reached the door, he turned and stalked from the cabin. Masefield moved to follow him but Jonas bid him stay.

"Let the guard take him back to his cabin. We've more important things to do tonight. Have Mr. Hackett turn back to the nor'west."

Chapter Twenty-One

All through the night the two ships sailed over slowly rising seas, winds now out of the west. Shortly after midnight the ships tacked again, now steering southwest. The watch on deck adjusted the sheets once or twice each watch, bracing around until the wind blew off the quarter. This was where *Mythos* liked it best. However, *Resolute* had to brail up her mainsail to keep from steering large.

The gibbous moon sank below the horizon, leaving the ships bathed in starlight amid the darkness, their passage marked only by the phosphorescence in their wakes. At six bells in the middle watch, both hove to. Based on deduced reckoning, Jonas had estimated they would be ten miles off Anguilla at that time.

As dawn approached, the watch on deck manned the pumps. The bosun's mate rigged the hoses and the crew began to wash down the decks. Since leaving the colder water and weather behind, this daily chore assumed more pleasant aspects and the men skylarked under Masefield's tolerant eye.

"Pinkney. Keep alert. Captain expects landfall soon," Masefield called to the lookout, aloft in the fore crosstrees. Bringing his eyes back to deck level, Masefield signaled for one of the bosun's mates to come aft.

"My respects to the captain, and 'tis five bells. No sight of land yet."

Just before six bells the sun poked its orange head above the far horizon. The clouds of the previous day had for the most part cleared and the air began to warm.

"Land ho! Land right on the bow."

Jonas arrived on deck as the lookout's call surged down. "All is in readiness?"

"Aye, sir. I had the bosun's mates roust the prisoners a half glass ago. Mr. Whipple, too." He smiled for a moment.

"Deck there. Land's no mor' 'en a league away, sir."

Jonas waved at Hackett, who'd opened his mouth to shout up at the lookout.

"Never mind, Mr. Hackett. There's little on that island to make light. Like as not, it would have been hard to see until the sun came up."

Hackett closed his mouth and worked his jaw. "Aye, sir." He strode forward, back stiff and unbending.

Jonas shook his head, then climbed aloft to see the land for himself.

Anguilla lay dark and low against the horizon. Though still distant, Jonas could see a haze, the moisture of the jungle, that hugged the water. To the south, the short seaside cliffs showed brighter. Jonas knew South Hill village lay there. To the north of the cliffs was the largest of the towns on the island, known simply as The Valley. There was a fort on the other side of the island, but the steep beach on this side acted as a natural defense against invasion in force.

It was here he would land the prisoners. While steep, there were paths that would allow the men to ascend into the town and make themselves known. The island itself provided shelter from the stiff breeze. Thus the seas calmed closer to the beach.

Jonas hailed *Mythos* and had the prisoners rowed to *Resolute*. When the boats were alongside, he said, "All right, let us free ourselves of our burden."

"Aye, sir."

As Whipple emerged on deck, he asked, "What new depredation is this? I heard a boat go over side. Will you cast us adrift on the open sea to die, that we might not bear witness to your shame?"

Jonas snorted. "No, though I think it likely you would consider such a thing were our roles reversed."

Whipple bristled. "I'm a civilized man, you bastard. Not at all like you and your colonial brethren."

Jonas pointed over the side. "There lies Anguilla. Are you familiar with it?"

Whipple didn't speak. After a few moments he realized Jonas wouldn't continue without some response so he gave the briefest of nods.

"Good. Then once we have landed you on the beach, even you should be able to find your way to the village."

"You cannot be serious. This is an outrage. You would maroon us in this God-forsaken hellhole? You might as well slit our throats. You filthy coward!" Whipple shouted.

Jonas pulled himself up and moved forward. Whipple backed into Masefield, who'd positioned himself behind him. Jonas stared down at him. "Mr. Whipple, you will contain yourself. Anguilla is English, is it not? I am certain within just a few days you will be in St. Kitts. We are not marooning you. These are *your* people, though poor, and you will have the opportunity to return home."

"Bah. It's more bloody likely I'll be trapped there for weeks." Whipple stuck his jaw out and narrowed his eyes. "Perhaps you *do* mean for me to perish, lest I inform the Navy of your piratical acts, hmm?"

Jonas closed his eyes and took a deep breath. "I'll not dignify that with an answer. The fact remains, we will set you and your crew ashore. What you do or do not tell the Navy is your decision. Perhaps you think they will look unfavorably on the loss of your ship?"

"By God I'll see you hung, you bastard."

"Unlikely. Your men are already in the boat. Pray follow them and get out of my sight."

Jonas turned and walked aft to the companionway to his cabin, before Whipple could do more than gnash his teeth.

When the boat returned, Masefield came aboard and reported to Jonas on the quarterdeck.

"I left Whipple unleashing a flood of curses on us, sir. But we ignored 'em. When we was near out of hailing distance, he led his men up the beach. Good riddance, I say, sir."

"Aye, we agree. Courses and topsails, I think. Let us look for our next prize as we make for San Juan."

"San Juan, sir?"

"We were fortunate. We met an enemy who should have beaten us. We, I, was not prepared. I do not intend to allow that to happen again."

The day passed quietly, and Jonas allowed a make and mend. The men took advantage and brought their clothing up on deck. They sat in small groups, talking quietly while they made new or mended old clothes. Jonas watched them, weighing their morale. They appeared satisfied with their lot. There were no low growls or furtive glances to see who was listening. Those would have been indicators of dissatisfaction and potential problems. Satisfied, Jonas climbed aloft to watch the vast sea that surrounded them.

At noon, *Mythos* signaled she was parting company and shaped her course to the north. She would sail north for two days, then stand toward the American coast. Within a few hours, she was hull down over the northeastern horizon, and then disappeared altogether.

It took three days to beat upwind against the trades and round the northern coast of Puerto Rico. Shortly before noon of the third day, they raised the ramparts of El Morro. By midafternoon, Jonas perched aloft looking at the great fortress as his ship turned south to approach the channel. He estimated they would be in with the land in just two or three hours. A great weight lowered onto his shoulders as he gazed at the gray stone rising out of the sea. He hoped they would be welcome.

THREE AND A HALF HOURS LATER, *RESOLUTE* PASSED under watchful guns and opened the harbor of San Juan.

Jonas ordered the Grand Union flag flown, as the officially authorized flag of the Continental Congress. It received no recognition from the fort, but neither did it attract aimed fire. In fact, it attracted no response whatsoever.

To Jonas's mind, however, being ignored was far preferable to being fired upon. He'd worried about what might have transpired in the week since they'd last stood into the harbor. The customs official met them aboard another small guarda costa lugger. This time, Señor Padilla climbed heavily aboard.

"Buenos días, Capitán Hawke. Bienvenido de nuevo a San Juan. Welcome back to San Juan. It is very good to see you again."

Jonas bowed slightly and responded in Spanish, "It is good to be here, and to be welcome. I trust all remains well in the city?"

Padilla winked at him. "Oh, si, Capitán. You will find nothing has changed at all."

Jonas's heart sank. Some small part of him had hoped that the situation *had* changed. That San Juan would be more willing to help.

But it did not do to dwell on what might have been.

Padilla asked what flag it was that *Resolute* flew. When Jonas explained, he smiled.

"His Most Catholic Majesty's government cannot recognize your flag, of course. I am told that when you last visited us, you seemed to have many guns, and did not take on a cargo. Now, I find you appear to have suffered damages. What tragedy could have befallen you, eh?"

Jonas expected an unofficial expression of curiosity. "I would like simply to use your shipyard. As you have said, we must make repairs. I was assured you would not refuse me."

Padilla grinned. "Of course not, Capitán. You left last week in, shall we say, a great hurry. No matter, I chose not to be offended. Though, you must admit, it seemed unlikely that you could not hear me hailing you?" His grin faded for a moment but quickly returned. "We are friends, Señor. Let us speak no more about it. We will look at your certificates and proceed to clear your ship."

Documents examined, wine consumed, Padilla issued port clearance. He did not hesitate when informed they had made no port calls in the week they'd been gone, and he asked no further questions.

As he prepared to climb down to the lugger, Padilla looked at Jonas. "I am sure you would not do anything that might embarrass our royal governor, no? You expect to depart again on your voyage as soon as your ship is repaired?"

"Of course, Capitán."

Padilla grinned. "Señor Martinez-Leon is my second cousin. He has asked that I offer you his hospitality. This evening perhaps?" He departed.

There being little wind inside the harbor, *Resolute* lowered her longboat, ran a cable out of the hawsehole, and began the laborious task of warping the ship up the harbor to the yard.

Rowing to the first piling, or warp, Hodges made the cable fast. As the boat backed away, the men at the capstan hauled away. The pawls clinked, at first slowly, then more rapidly, and *Resolute* moved up to the warp. Meanwhile, another cable was looped around the next warp. The steps were repeated as they slowly moved to where Padilla had directed them.

Once anchored near the shipyard, Jonas ordered the men fed. Then he turned his crew to the work of repairing their vessel.

Chapter Twenty-Two

Jonas visited Señor Martinez later that afternoon. Masefield remained aboard *Resolute* to oversee repairs.

Martinez stood when Jonas was shown into the same room where they'd met before.

"Buenas tardes, Capitán. It is good to see you again, and so soon. I did not expect your return quite this quickly." Martinez smiled, though his eyes resembled flint.

"I did not anticipate such a thing, either, Señor. Fortune smiled on us, in a way."

"Fortune can be a fickle companion, Jonas, as I'm sure you realize. I understand you may have suffered in a, what shall we call it? A storm, which engulfed your ship? And that our shipyard assists your repairs?" Martinez waved at a chair. "Please, sit."

Jonas sat stiffly. As he did, a manservant offered him a glass. The beads of condensation beckoned his indulgence, and he took it gratefully.

"I am grateful for the shipyard's willingness to assist, Señor. I believe they can provide all we require."

"That is good news. I must ask, were there any injuries during the 'storm'?"

Jonas had carefully considered how he would address the

wounded and the prisoners. He brought out his story now, slowly and carefully.

"We had some, Señor. All were moved aboard another ship, *Mythos*, who had a surgeon. Those men who could be returned to duty have been. Those who are still healing but could soon return to duty will remain aboard until they are recovered. But, alas, there are those who were too badly injured to return to duty. They have gone home in the other ship."

Martinez leaned back in his chair, folded his hands, and steepled his forefingers. "Yes, well, this could pose an interesting problem. I had anticipated you might have injured men, and perhaps men who no longer could sail in one of the ships. The injured, of course, can be treated in the hospital. Transport home can be arranged for them in ships which leave here for many other nations, including America. However, I'm sure you'll recognize the danger of having many men, perhaps angry men do not wish to sail in your ships, here in San Juan? These men, they might challenge your right to our hospitality. They might find allies amongst those who live and work here. What would you do about these men? What would you ask us to do?" Martinez watched him carefully.

"Oh, Señor, we would not burden you with such problems. The injured, of course, we would welcome any treatment your hospital can provide. But I assure you there are no other men such as you mention here in San Juan. It would be too much for us to presume on your hospitality to encumber our friends with such trouble."

Martinez leaned forward, frowning. "But I do not understand. Jonas, I will speak openly. What of your prisoners?"

"Señor, I could not carry them here, for the reason I stated. And also because you have told me I cannot. I dare not send them on the long voyage home because there is too great a danger of them retaking their ship. Instead, I have put them ashore on an English island to the east, Anguilla."

Martinez sat back and laughed a short chuckle. "I see. That is a good solution for all of us." He sipped his drink. "Ordinarily, I would wait to discuss business until after we have dined. However, you have a certain air of stiffness that will, I think, be improved upon if I tell you my news now."

He leaned back and smiled. "It will interest you to hear that only a few days ago, the Dutch recognized the flag flown by one of your ships of war. *Andrew Doria*, I believe. In fact, it is the flag you fly now. She saluted the fort in St. Croix, which then fired a salute in return. Your colonies have found friends. A pity the British islands do not share your desire for independence. They are as badly treated by London as yourselves, perhaps worse."

Martinez shook his head. "This event was not lost on our governor. Further, we have heard that the French islands willingly provide assistance to your ships, including privateers." He grinned broadly. "I would not like to take too much credit, but there are those here in San Juan who have, shall we say, strongly suggested that such assistance would not only be expedient from a political perspective, but also profitable. As a result, the governor has let it be known that he will not interfere with any man's business affairs."

Jonas remained cautious. He thought he understood, but he was not steeped in the art of devious activity. So he asked, "Does this mean, Señor, that I can come and go freely and occasionally dispose of a ship and cargo here?"

Martinez waved his hand impatiently. "Yes, that is what I said. Discretion will still be required to avoid blatantly antagonizing the British agent here. But yes, you may consider San Juan your home." He paused, pursing his lips. "Your solution to the handling of prisoners has removed the one possible, what do you call it? Stumbling block. It would be impossible to argue for our neutrality were there British prisoners landed in San Juan. But you have taken that problem away. I salute you," he said, raising his glass.

Jonas relaxed the more Martinez talked. Now, he raised his

own glass. "I am deeply grateful, Señor. I will not do anything to damage the friendship that we share."

Martinez's eyes widened and gained a twinkle. He leaned forward, putting his hands on the arms of his chair. "Ah, Captain, it is well that we are friends. Let us dine together. I'm certain our business will be of benefit to us both."

THE NEXT DAY, WORK ADVANCED SUFFICIENTLY. JONAS thought it prudent to go ashore and make contact with the American agent to arrange for stores, and perhaps to send messages and post back home.

The agent, Andrew Fillmore, was a short, large man. His balding head sweated profusely in the heat, and he sat quickly after Jonas entered his office. Jonas carefully explained his needs, as well as what he'd done with the prisoners.

Fillmore mopped his head. Speaking with a Carolinian accent, he said, "Captain, I'd like to help you, but there's no British consul here at the moment. I therefore represent English merchants as well as the colonies'. How can I do that and help you? Do you not see the conflict between those interests?"

Jonas leaned back, eyes wide. "You represent English merchants? Why? We are at war with the British."

"No, Captain Hawke, *you* are at war with the British. I am a subject of King George. I do not share your enthusiasm for independence."

Jonas stared. "What will you do, now that you know I am here? That I operate from this port? Will you pass this information to the Royal Navy?"

Fillmore looked unhappily at Jonas, then stood and shuffled to the window behind the desk. He didn't speak for a time as he stared at the palm trees outside. Moments passed. Then he straightened his shoulders and turned to glare at Jonas. "I don't have an answer, Captain Hawke. In fact, I don't owe you one.

This infernal war is not of my doing. Reckless politicians at home have started it. Let them answer you."

Jonas stood and leaned across the desk. His eyes burned. "Will you betray your fellow Americans, Mr. Fillmore? That is the question I ask of you, and *you* must answer it."

Fillmore's glare softened, replaced by fear. "I cannot do what you ask. I will not be put in the position of lying. I will not help you." His eyes sank to the blotter on the desk, then closed. He turned once more to face the window.

"I'm not asking for you to compromise your beliefs. But I do ask you not to act as a spy for the Royal Navy." He paused, not wanting to speak the next words. But the silence wore on, and he said, "It could be profitable for you, you know." Money placed surreptitiously in the correct hands often encouraged both silence and on occasion outright cooperation.

Fillmore turned, face red as he glowered. "No, sir, do not say that. I will not be party to bribery. Nor will I involve myself in this conflict that you have taken up. I have a business to run." After a few moments, he added. "But no, I will not be a spy. If you do not make trouble for me, I shall let you alone, as well." He stood and leaned across his desk. "But I warn you, Captain, I will not lie for you. If I am asked, I will truthfully answer that you've asked me to help you, and that I've refused. Let the consequences be upon your head."

Jonas sighed. Fillmore wouldn't commit to independence for fear of losing money, not because he was loyal to the king. He would play both sides so long as it was to his profit. Yet he was terrified of anything that might place his own neck in a noose.

Jonas took his leave, disgusted by the man.

<hr>

On his way back to the ship, he found a small cantina. Taking a seat outside near the door, he ordered sangria, bread, and cheese. As he ate, he watched the business of the city.

The sun reflected off the whitewashed walls of the narrow street. Even under the awning Jonas felt the roasting heat, despite the time of year. Midday approached and street traffic dwindled as the inhabitants began the siesta. As he ate, he considered his options.

There would be no support from Fillmore. Moreover, he probably could not trust the man with post or messages home. He would also have to be careful when he brought prizes in to be sold. That would normally involve the American agent. He would have to find another agent, preferably Spanish. The British would make sure the Spanish officials were notified, officially, so he could not be too open in his dealings. His new country couldn't afford more enemies. They needed allies.

Finishing, he stood to leave. As he did so, Padilla walked around the corner.

"Buenos dias, Capitán," he said. "I thought I might find you along here. Señor Fillmore said you had left him, and I had not seen you return to your ship."

"You are well informed, Capitán," Jonas responded warily. He was not comforted by the thought of his every move being tracked.

"I am. I have interests, shall we say, in and around San Juan. As a result, I ensure that I know what is taking place. I have come not to discuss my business, however, but to discuss *your* business. It may be that I can help you." He sat and beckoned Jonas to do so as well. "But first, how does your refit proceed? I trust our humble services have been adequate to your needs?"

"Your shipwrights have been very helpful."

"Good, I am happy to hear that. It would not do to send such a fine ship out into the dangers of the sea unprepared. The dangers are great, are they not?"

Jonas carefully regarded him. He was grateful the man had turned a blind eye to the real reason for the damage to *Resolute*. However, gratitude did not necessarily lead to trust. Moreover, Jonas had the uneasy suspicion it placed him in Padilla's debt.

Jonas had always found the Spanish authorities an amiable group, friendly enough despite an air of indifference. They were also shrewd businessmen. "Si, the dangers are great, especially at a time such as this. Please, Señor, how can you be of assistance?" he replied.

"Very well, I will speak directly. You may recall that I told you when you arrived that the government here would take no official recognition of the new country you have created, and it will not publicly endorse your people's efforts to break away from the government in London, yes? You may also recall that I asked you about how your ship came to need repairs, no? Something about a storm, yes?"

Jonas said nothing.

Padilla leaned back in his seat. "Well, Capitán, we both know that what you said is not quite correct. Not a lie, certainly, but certain details were, shall we say, left out?"

Jonas didn't enjoy verbal sparring. He wanted the man to get to the point. As if reading his mind, Padilla did just that.

"Capitán, let us be honest with each other. As we have said, I know what happens in this place. I know Mr. Fillmore, while an honorable man, does not support independence for your colonies. I know your current occupation will likely result in a need to sell cargoes and perhaps even the occasional ship. And because of Mr. Fillmore's sentiments, you do not have an agent you can trust. You have a problem then, and I can help you."

As Jonas began to protest, Padilla continued, "No, Capitán, do not dispute the facts. We are both intelligent men."

He paused, taking in Jonas's sour look. "I see you are not quite certain about my offer. Remember Señor Martinez is my second cousin. He told you that you would be able to conduct certain business here. I am how you will do so. Now do you understand?"

Jonas sat back to listen.

Satisfied, Padilla continued. "Now, you must understand that we are not Bilbao. Our governor is not so willing to place his authority at risk to directly support your insurrection. However, he understands the advantages that would accrue to both our countries if you obtained your independence from the stifling regulations and taxes London imposes on your trade. There is a man I know who stands ready to help when the time comes. For now, we will not speak of his name."

Jonas was taken aback. The Guardoquis in Bilbao were helping American privateers dispose of captured prizes? Perhaps he had more friends in these waters than he'd realized. Perhaps he needn't risk his San Juan relationships by sending all his prizes here. If he spread his business more widely....

"I can see you are thinking, Capitán. That is good. A thoughtful man avoids trouble." Padilla sat back expansively. "Capitán, let me help you. No, let us help each other."

He'd little choice. Padilla was right, he needed an agent with the right contacts and discretion. The fact that he knew what had been discussed with Martinez gave him credibility. But Jonas did not know Padilla. He preferred to deal with Martinez. Nevertheless, he said, "Señor, I will be grateful for your help. I have a problem, one which vexes me. It requires resolution. But I must ask, Señor, what do you stand to gain from this solution?" Jonas asked.

"Ah, Capitán, you Americans are always concerned with the cost. Very well. I will require five percent of the value of what is being sold." Seeing Jonas's expression turn to horror, Padilla raised his hand. "Yes, yes, it is a large sum. However, I must ensure our *arrangement* remains unspoken in the halls of governance. There are many whose silent assistance must be obtained. This is expensive. And who knows what the value of future captures will be? You were away from us for barely a week and it appears you experienced good fortune. Surely, Capitán, this is a fair price?"

Jonas thought about it. He was accustomed to haggling for a better price, but haggling didn't seem appropriate just now. Arriving at a decision, he leaned forward again. "Very well, Señor,

I accept your offer. If I must send ships in by themselves, will the terms apply to the man I send in command?"

"Of course, Capitán, of course. My agreement with you will apply to any man you send to represent you. Upon occasion, I will send a trusted man of business aboard to handle certain details. However, the more rapidly such plans are enacted, the less likely that a situation might arise which would interfere. Also, the fewer who are involved in our arrangement, the less likely persons who should not will hear of it."

The two passed an agreeable hour, discussing the arrangements over sangria. When they'd finished, Jonas stood. "Very well, Señor. I will send a letter of greeting to you with my prize captains. I am grateful for your offer of assistance. Muchisimas gracias, Señor."

Padilla stood as well. Wishing Jonas a good afternoon, he left.

Jonas returned to *Resolute*, deep in thought.

He thought of *Mythos,* sailing toward Norfolk. He didn't know the status of ports along the coast, whether the British might have occupied or abandoned them. But he was certain they wouldn't occupy Norfolk anytime soon, not since the destruction of the town itself. It was safer to send her there, where the Virginia militia could take possession of the arms. There were also other ports in the Chesapeake, so if Norfolk were closed, the ship could go elsewhere.

Jonas walked up the brow of his ship and had the word passed for Masefield to meet him in his cabin.

<hr>

"Can we trust 'em, sir?" Masefield asked after Jonas explained the arrangements.

"I hope we can. Despite appearances, little happens on this island unless the governor approves it. It is likely the price for discretion includes some portion for the governor. Business here is based on relationships and reputation. Men rarely betray each other." He stood and looked out the tiny stern windows. "Padilla admits we may not get as much for a prize as if it were sold in an open market. But the alternative is to send it home to face the risk of recapture. Thus total loss." He turned back to Masefield. "Besides, I plan on further exploring the possibilities presented by Bilbao. It would be safest to have two, or even more, options."

Masefield grunted. "Aye. Well, sir, certainly t'will make it easier for the prize captains. To wit, sir, I've a list of those I think could take charge of a prize. Assuming, of course, that you don't want to use myself or Hackett." Masefield looked closely at Jonas, waiting.

Jonas looked away. "I will use you only if I absolutely need to. I'm not worried about your ability, but I need you aboard." Turning to look again at Masefield, he continued, "I trust you to tell me if I reach too far."

Masefield remained silent. Jonas turned away again and stood silently, weighing what he would say next. He suspected Masefield wanted to talk about Hackett.

Groaning slightly, Jonas said, "Very well. What's on your mind?"

"Well, sir, perhaps it might be Mr. Hackett."

Jonas fidgeted. Deciding that he needed to make what he'd said before the whole truth, he spoke. "Yes, Hackett." Jonas turned back to face Masefield. "He's a good seaman. But you know he needs guidance. He can handle the routine, even routine emergencies. But he doesn't think before he acts. He reacts randomly to circumstances he is not familiar with. That could be dangerous."

Masefield studied Jonas before he spoke. "Aye, what you've said is true. But we're all of us outside the familiar. Ye're the closest to a navy man this ship has. Yet even ye've no experience with war. Sure, some have fought the natives. A few were in the militia for a time. But this? 'Tis new for all of us. Who among us will do exactly the right things at the right time?" Masefield shook his head. "Hackett will do what he can. He will try to do what he thinks *ye* would do. He respects ye. But he isn't ye, and he knows that. You must trust him, just as you must trust this Padilla fellow. He will be better if ye trust him. And the men will trust him if ye do. Ye also know they will not if ye do not. That will be hurtful to the crew."

Leaning back, Jonas thought for a few minutes. The truth of what Masefield said warred with his native caution. In the end, he said, "All right. You're right. We will give him the next prize."

"Aye, sir. I'll go and see to the rigging, then." Masefield turned and left the cabin.

Jonas called after him, "This is why I need you aboard."

Three days later, the drum of hammers and saws was almost completely replaced by the ring of mallets on irons as the ship's hull and decks were recaulked. The yard had located new spars to replace those damaged in the "storm" that had officially ravaged *Resolute*. The new spars had been shaped and would be put in place and rigged over the next two days.

Jonas was exhausted. Hackett had been invaluable in supervising the men Jonas sent ashore to help the yard shape planks to replace those shattered in battle.

The Spaniards had been very cooperative, allowing him to use every facility, unofficially, to speed the work. They were more than happy to take his money, but they also wanted him to leave as quickly and as quietly as he'd come.

He was more than happy to oblige.

CHAPTER TWENTY-THREE

"Anchor's breakin' ground, sir," called Hodges, acting bosun. A bosun's mate played a weak, pulsing stream of water on the anchor cable as it came up in an attempt to keep muck off the deck. As the heavy rope ran in, men's feet sloshed on the treads on the deck around the capstan. The cable dribbled water as it tightened around the capstan drum. Grunting as they strained to push the bars, the capstan moved more easily as the anchor shook itself clear of the San Juan harbor mud.

When the cable tension relaxed completely, Hodges called out, "Anchors aweigh!"

"Mr. Masefield, please make sail."

"Aye, sir." Turning, he called out, "Back th' jib. Loose fore course and tops'l in the' gear. Set the mains'l."

All was ritual, and the orders flowed like a river. The topmen, already aloft and on station, had removed the gaskets, the lengths of rope that secured the furled sails to the yards. At the order to let fall, they pushed the mounds of canvas that were the square sails over, to hang in loose bundles below the yards.

As the jib raced, flapping up the stay, Jonas ordered the helm moved to starboard, turning the bow to larboard. Nearly simultaneously, Masefield had the jib sheet hauled to starboard to help pull the bow around. The sail filled with a sharp crack as the ship's head fell off toward the mouth of the harbor.

Resolute was alive again and under sail.

"Set the fore course and tops'l, starboard tack." Men hauled away on sheet ropes, blocks squealing in protest as the corners of the sails were hauled down to the yardarms below them, forcing the canvas to take the wind.

"Let go and haul."

As soon as the foreyards were braced around, the square sails filled. *Resolute* surged gently forward, away from her anchorage.

Despite the variable morning winds inside the harbor, she moved purposefully, responding to the helm. The air was bright already, though it was only five bells in the morning watch. A falling tide for the past three and a half hours meant a maximum velocity ebb current.

Soon she rounded El Morro and stood out to sea. Clear of the land, sail after sail blossomed and her bow rose and fell in rhythm with the swells.

Resolute continued northwestward, flying before the strength of the trade winds.

Jonas arose each morning with the sun and paced the deck. Periodically, he halted to scan both horizon and sails. Lookouts aloft took their signals from his restlessness and kept a sharp watch.

They sighted few ships, though, and all were Spanish or French coasting vessels, plying their trade between the islands of Puerto Rico, Santo Domingo, and Cuba. Jonas spoke to a couple of them but learned little. The one item of most value was that the British were not yet convoying merchant traffic. It would only be a matter of time, they told him though, as they'd heard of several American privateers preying on the Caribbean trade.

Jonas reasoned that the British wouldn't yet know about *Mythos*. She wasn't yet overdue in New York, her eventual destination. Even had she been, not enough time had elapsed for that news to get back to the Caribbean.

Jonas planned to cruise the Windward Passage between the coasts of northwestern Haiti and eastern Cuba during the day and retire to the southwest at night. It made it more likely that ships sailing through the passage during the night would still be visible at dawn. Jonas also chose to remain closer to Haiti, upwind of possible prey. It would be easier to run down on them quickly.

***

Four days later, *Resolute* hurried by Ile la Tortue on the larboard side, then rounded Cap du Mole on the northwest tip of Haiti and sailed into the Windward Passage. She rounded to and began her patrol.

The trade winds were perfectly suited for running up or down the passage. The fine days reminded Jonas why he loved being at sea.

With the exception of occasional isolated squalls, the sky remained clear and visibility good. In squalls, *Resolute* shortened sail and endured a soaking. But the sun shortly returned, the squall moved off, and decks began to steam as they dried.

But as the days turned into a week, frustration built.

On their eighth day, as *Resolute* worked her way back up from just west of Isle de la Gonave to their daylight station, they sighted a small brig on the larboard quarter, northbound. The brig flew no colors. Since it didn't seem inclined to hoist any, neither did Jonas.

"Mr. Hackett, let us slowly close the chase. Don't make it obvious."

Hackett ordered the yards braced around slightly to go with a small course change. Soon *Resolute* lay on a course to intercept far ahead in the pass itself.

Over an hour later, it became obvious *Resolute* was closing. When it did, the brig turned on her heel and ran to the west-northwest.

Jonas crowded on sail and wore ship. In a few minutes they

were overhauling the brig. An older vessel, she was slab-sided and bluff-bowed. Rather than cutting through swells as she churned across them, or even gracefully rising over them, she shouldered her way through them, slamming bodily into and thrusting her bow streaming through each. Jonas fancied he could see her masts and rigging shake each time she pounded. On her new course, she rolled and corkscrewed pitifully despite the press of sail aloft.

"Run up our colors. We do not want to be mistaken for a pirate," Jonas ordered. "Make sure she can see them."

She had little chance to escape, but her master tried.

As morning wore on, the wind freshened and veered until it settled almost directly from the east. The swells, made steep as they were herded into the passage by the islands of Cuba and Haiti, became longer as they made their way past Cap du Mole on the Haitian side, and Punta Morant on the eastern end of Cuba, back into open water. The sun shone down through a blue sky that saw only an occasional puffy cloud sail past.

The brig's master appeared to realize he wouldn't weather Punta Morant. He altered course again, steering southwest to pass south of Cabo Maisi, Cuba. Both ships ran now with the wind and the seas, their cutwaters pushing the water aside, the rollers coming up behind and passing beneath. *Resolute* benefited most, being somewhat less heavily burdened, surfing slightly down the fronts of the waves before they passed.

Two hours into the chase, the brig spouted pulsing streams of water from her scuppers.

"I believe he's started his water casks, is pumping it over side to lighten her," Masefield mused.

Jonas nodded. "We shall see if it benefits, and how much."

An hour later, she threw four guns over the side.

"That must have been a difficult thing to do," Jonas said. "She'll not be able to fight, even were she inclined to do so."

Shortly after the cannon went to Davy Jones's locker, she fired a small signal gun to leeward and hoisted a signal flag.

Masefield hailed the lookout. "Can ye read the signal?"

"No, sir. 'Tis blowin' straight away."

"See anything beyond the brig?" Jonas added.

The lookout stared for a long time, then said, "No, sir. Nothin'."

"Do you think there's someone over the horizon?"

Masefield rubbed his chin. "Won't know for a bit, sir. I'd hate to think it were a warship, though."

Jonas nodded. "If it is, they'll be beating upwind. We can steer toward Cuba, along the coast."

"Mebee. Depends on where they be. If there is someone there, they're in the same place we were, waitin' to catch somethin'."

"It could be a ruse."

Masefield said nothing.

A mere day's sail north of Jamaica, it was possible a frigate sailed below the horizon. If they kept going, it might snap them up, ending their privateering career, and perhaps their lives. The coast of Cuba was but four hours or so to the north, boxing him in.

Long minutes passed while Jonas considered whether to break off the chase. A circle of logic kept running through his mind as he weighed the likelihood of an enemy warship's intervention against the speed at which he was overtaking the brig. Maybe he could capture her and get away before the enemy could come up.

But if he fell afoul of an enemy warship, he'd have to beat upwind to escape.

Fifteen minutes later, the chase began to push the casks she carried as deck cargo over the side. Jonas watched with interest as they floated down *Resolute*'s side. He cautioned the helmsman to not hit them, while at the same time not yawing too much as to lose ground. In a collision between a cask and the ship, there was no doubt which would emerge victorious. However, such a blow could start a plank and allow a fountain of water to gush into the bilges.

Meanwhile, the jets of water from the chase's scuppers continued. Still, *Resolute* gained on her.

"Why throw their cargo over the side if there is help in sight?" he asked. "Wouldn't it be easier to allow us to take him, knowing he would be quickly rescued?"

Masefield nodded slowly. "Aye. That makes sense. Now ye say it, that's what I'd do." He turned to Jonas. "Yer thinkin' there's no one to help him."

"I am. We keep chasing."

He kept the whole crew on deck, ordering cold food served out at the guns. If an enemy were coming up, he would be prepared to flee. If he could not flee, he would do his best to fight a retreat.

Resolute wasn't speedy, but she was handy. The crew had come together nicely. She was newly refitted and most important, her hull was clean, having been scraped down in San Juan. Were an enemy sufficiently far to the south, he could perhaps run past him to the west and gain a port in Cuba, perhaps Santiago. Surely a British warship would respect Spanish neutrality?

"Sir, do you smell something?" Masefield crossed the deck from leeward to interrupt.

Jonas sniffed. There was something in the air. The back of his mind told him he'd been smelling it for a while. He'd been preoccupied with the dangers that might or might not lurk over the horizon. Suddenly it came to him.

"Rum?" Jonas and Masefield said the word simultaneously.

The chase was dumping rum. Jonas walked forward with his glass and focused on the stream of liquid flowing from her deck. Seemingly tinged with brown, bilge water was also brown. He shrugged. *We will know in time.*

Over the next few hours, Jonas's assumption proved correct. No enemy warship hove into sight.

By four bells in the afternoon watch, the brig lay within long cannon shot. Jonas ordered a gun moved to the unused port in the starboard bow bulwark. Struggling against the deadweight of iron in its wooden carriage, the sailors used ropes to bound the dangerous beast and contain it as the corkscrewing motion of the ship fought to release it. Thirty minutes later, it was secured in place. The first gun boomed out.

They fired seven rounds before they saw any effect. The eighth round seemed to disappear into the brig's hull. Another hour and at least ten hits later, the brig hauled her wind, raising and lowering her colors.

As the sun sank toward the horizon, Jonas ordered Masefield to go aboard and take possession.

Returning, Masefield reported her to be brig *Commerce*, carrying rum to England from Jamaica. Her master, a Sampson Merriwether, hung his head as he was led into Jonas's cabin.

"Good afternoon, Captain. I'm sorry we must meet under such circumstances," Jonas began. "War is an ugly business, harming mostly the innocent. I myself lost my ship to the Royal Navy just over a year ago. Won't you sit?"

Merriwether slumped into the chair Masefield placed behind him, then sat himself at the stern counter. "If you have such empathy, sir, pray why not then release me?"

"I would that I could. However, my country needs what we capture." At the man's skeptical look, Jonas added, "Perhaps not your specific cargo, but what we sell it for lets us buy other things we need." He leaned forward. "Did you know there were American ships of war about?"

Merriwether stared.

Jonas chose to wait.

Finally, the man spoke. "Aye, I know what you want. No, I didn't know you was here, but there's been word of privateers, pirates more likely, 'tween here and the Carolinas. There's not much them naval types doing 'bout it, though. Insurance is creepin' up, but 'til it gets high enough for owners to feel the pinch, nothin'll be done."

"Is that why you ran?"

"Thought you might be a pirate. Haiti's known for sheltering pirates. It's a fearful run through here. Whenever there's fighting, there's more that gets it into their head that they'll take some ship, blame it on war. The odds are still good for a ship makin' it through. Though I guess them odds is gettin' worse, now," he added.

"The Navy does not assist?"

"Well, that's a question, isn't it? They've not made any talk about convoyin'. The admiral talks a lot about fittin' out a squadron, to 'sweep the seas clean', he says." He seemed to think about that statement and how it applied to him, then sank lower in his seat. "Anyways, they say they can't. They say they don't have 'nough ships. Half the ones they's got sit there in harbor."

Jonas considered that for a moment. "Why? Aren't they ready for sea?"

Merriwether looked up and snorted. "Ready for sea? Not on your life. They're rotted, they are. Everyone knows the Navy's rotting. They used unseasoned wood to build them, then they's surprised when they rot out from under them."

This was news to Jonas. He needed to consider the implications of this revelation.

Returning his attention to Merriwether, he said, "I'm sorry. We will put you ashore as soon as we can. You will be well treated until then. If you give me your word to do no harm, I will allow you the freedom to come and go as you please aboard this ship."

Merriwether brightened slightly. "Aye, that's kind o' you. I give you my word."

Jonas asked him a few more questions about the actions of the British. In his despondency, the man willingly answered all inquiries. Merriwether gave him only good news, which was also fresh. While he still needed to exercise caution, there was less to fear. Although there was a small chance Merriwether had lied, his manner didn't indicate that to be the case.

Another piece of good news came when Hackett interviewed the brig's crew. Two more men joined *Resolute*. Jonas's battle losses were now nearly filled. He only lacked the men he'd sent in the prize crew.

Items of use to *Resolute* were transferred, then Hackett was rowed to take command of *Commerce.* She'd showed herself to be slow and unhandy, even without water and guns, so he told Hackett to sail her to San Juan.

Quite happy that Jonas had given him command, Hackett took his orders with appropriate seriousness. In the event of sighting a British warship, he was instructed to run for the nearest port. In the event he couldn't make port, he was to do whatever he could to make good his and his crew's escape, leaving the vessel to be recaptured.

In his cabin, Jonas took pen in hand to make log entries. As he did, concerns swirled in his mind.

If the British weren't yet convoying merchant trade, then he still had a free hand. He would have to exercise caution as one could never know when an enemy would sail up over the horizon. He'd been very lucky with *Mythos.* He could not, would not, take that kind of risk again. Each time he thought about it, he shivered. The likelihood another Royal Navy ship would be as unprepared was remote in the extreme.

He'd also been fortunate with the Spanish in Puerto Rico.

While the French appeared friendly to the American cause, he still felt wary of their intentions. Even if they did gain independence from Britain, Jonas did not think his country could fight France. If afterward the French moved to re-establish their own colonial empire by seizing former British colonies, he feared they might succeed. The new American nation would have to fight a fresh continental army with a war-weary army and populace. Whether England would allow such a thing he didn't know, but he was certain that in a conflict between the two great powers, the colonies had the most to lose.

There was some risk in Spain helping the colonies break away, too, though Jonas felt it less than with France. Spain had a large landmass under colonial rule themselves, and many of the inhabitants were less than pleased with that rule. If their own colonials learned their king had helped Americans achieve independence, it would almost encourage a revolt. Indeed, the Spanish Empire was fragile and didn't have the military strength to either defend its colonies or to put down a rebellion. Only the brutality often used, and the fact the colonies didn't know how truly weak the Spanish really were, kept them in line.

Jonas had no intention of looking a gift horse in the mouth. Yes, everything to do with *Mythos* had been very fortunate. He hoped that good luck continued. He wanted his crews back, and their cause could use the prize money.

More importantly, the militia needed powder and arms. But he knew he must exercise more caution and act with less abandon.

Chapter Twenty-Four

Jonathan Tilton, acting master of the prize *Mythos*, strode the deck of that lovely brig. He'd sunk the land hours before, and *Resolute* had finally faded over the southwestern horizon a mere thirty minutes ago.

Nineteen of Tilton's thirty-two years had been spent at sea. Despite his time as a mate, he'd never been in command. Yet here he was.

As an able seaman with mate's experience, he had a different perspective on how ships should run. He saw good officers and bad, and he learned from both. Thus, he came prepared. Not that he sought it, nor would he want to keep it long. *Perhaps that's what's attractive about it. It has an end.*

His job would end when he brought the ship into Norfolk.

"So what should we call you?" This came from his first mate. Johnson knew the answer, of course, but felt compelled to take a dig at his old friend.

"Now, Bill, you know better than that. You heard what I told them other fellows. I don't need no formal 'captain this' and 'captain that'. We's all shipmates, whether I'm in charge or not. Hell, Bill, I've always been in charge of you, anyway," he rejoined.

"Yes, well, some of us is content to work hard and don't need that fancy title stuff, nor the fancy food from the officer's mess. Others, o' course, are always lookin' for ways to get promoted out o' havin' to work."

Johnson winked. He was glad Tilton had been given the prize. Even more, he was happy he'd been chosen to sail with him.

"Damn you, Bill, you know I don't want to set up as master. As for you, the captain specifically asked me to get you off the ship, so's he could get some work done."

The give and take continued throughout the glorious afternoon as *Mythos* made her northing.

For two days she sailed with the wind on her quarter, now making three, now five, now four, now six, knots. The wind varied little. The crystalline blue sea mirrored the sky. Few clouds marred the scene once they cleared the more common tropical showers.

As the week wound toward its end, the mercury began to drop, though the barometer remained steady.

There was little to do as *Mythos* made her way slowly homeward. She wasn't as handy as *Resolute*, but that little mattered, as they rarely had to touch a sheet. The most significant change came when they turned westward toward the coast. They were now in the westerlies, having passed out of the tropics.

To pass the time, Tilton practiced navigation, taking several observations both morning and afternoon. He found the mathematics tedious and difficult, but he was determined to make himself expert. He'd come to the idea he'd be more valuable to Captain Hawke and *Resolute* if he made himself a highly competent prize master. There was extra money to be made as a prize master, too: the captain had told him he'd get an extra share for bringing *Mythos* in.

In any case, it filled the days.

TWELVE DAYS OUT OF SAN JUAN, HE JUDGED HIS NOON latitude to be right for Norfolk, and he ordered the course shaped due west. The captain had enjoined him to sail north for seven days, then angle northwest to the coast, following it northeast to Cape Henry. But as he'd gained confidence in his navigation, he'd decided to stay farther out to sea, the better to avoid Royal Navy cruisers. He planned to sail straight into the bay and up the Elizabeth River. There he'd meet with the commander of the militia, Colonel Snodgrass. He would take charge of her cargo, leaving Tilton to dispose of the ship.

As they approached the coast, the day grew more humid and the seas more calm. Despite the oncoming winter, the weather remained warmer than normal. The Gulf Stream ambled slowly northward, and Tilton ordered the course adjusted to compensate. They sighted their first land birds, and though they'd only been gone for a month, every man looked forward to landfall and a few days ashore before making their way back to San Juan to meet *Resolute*.

The night was spent sailing slowly westward. Tilton's evening star fix showed them somewhere around twenty-five miles east of Cape Henry, so he shortened sail to topgallants and fore topsail. At three knots, they inched their way toward home.

The gentle rhythm of *Mythos*'s movement lulled her crew. They were nearly home.

DENSE FOG GREETED THE DAWN. THE WARMTH OF THE Gulf Stream contrasted with the coolness of the air over land and combined to create pea soup.

No stranger to fog, Tilton ordered the deep-sea lead broken out and put into use.

The first sounding came in at twenty-seven fathoms, with mud and shell bottom. That was expected. He would approach the Bay cautiously, but he knew the entrance well enough to be confident.

Proceeding slowly under topgallants and jib alone, the leadsman's droning chant continued. The bottom shallowed to nine and ten fathoms with mud and shells, indicating they were in the approaches to the channel. The fog thickened by the moment, but Tilton knew as morning wore on it would burn or blow off.

"By the deep nine."

Again and again the rhythm continued. Drip, drip, swish, splash. Read the mark.

The back of Tilton's mind followed the leadsman's call while the front considered the next problem after they passed Cape Henry, that of getting upriver against the current. Unless the wind picked up, he might have to anchor until the tide turned. While it was flooding now, the ebb would start by the time they reached Willoughby Spit. They'd need a strong breeze to stem the current and stand upriver. But if they waited six hours, they'd have the current behind them.

He started badly when the lookout on the jibboom called, "Ship ahead! Ship half point on the larboard bow. Close aboard."

Tilton ran forward. As he did, the ship ahead emerged from the fog. He called behind him to put the helm over to larboard, to attempt to turn away. As he continued forward, he realized with a sinking feeling it was too late. *Mythos* had too little speed and so responded equally slowly to the rudder. He closed his eyes. He shouldn't have put it all the way over, either. The rudder was now like a sea anchor, slowing the ship and turning her even more slowly.

The slight flood current continued to push her toward the stranger, who it was now obvious lay at anchor. They were close enough to hear the startled cry of the other ship's anchor watch, and panicked orders from officers. "All hands for'ard to fend off, port side."

Tilton echoed those calls. The men around him, previously

frozen as they watched the approach of the unavoidable collision, sprang into action.

Grabbing rope mats, boat hooks, and anything else they could lay their hands on, they ran to the starboard bow to try to push off. Men aloft ran to ends of the yards to prevent the rigging from tangling. Men aft desperately braced the yards around to lessen the likelihood of their becoming entwined.

All to no avail. The collision was inevitable.

Just when Tilton thought it couldn't get worse, it did. He clearly heard a voice call "Away boarders." Only one kind of officer would issue that order — a naval officer.

Tilton was also certain only one navy would be so bold as to anchor in the mouth of the Chesapeake, and it wasn't any kind of colonial navy.

There were only two options: fight or surrender. Neither was palatable. To fight was suicidal and would only end the same way, but with far more bloodshed, mostly that of his men.

Surrender meant the loss of the ship, its cargo, and all the prize money. Worse, it meant imprisonment.

Tilton was ashamed, terrified, and enraged, all at the same time. He was trapped, a rat in a cage. Hoping against hope, he stood beside the larboard knightshead, staring at the stranger, willing *Mythos* to turn just a little bit more.

The captain of the other ship solved the problem for him. "Beat to quarters."

There was no longer a choice. If he didn't surrender, and by some miracle the two ships didn't collide, and the boarding party didn't get aboard, the enemy would still fire into *Mythos*. The result would be the same.

Then an idea burst forth.

Tilton cried out, hoping his men would catch on and follow his lead. "Ahoy the warship. Don't fire, your lordship, we're trying to fend off."

"Fend off, then heave to. I'm sending a boarding party. If you don't, I'll sink you where you stand."

"Aye, sir. We're bound to Baltimore with supplies for the Army. Please, sir, it'll be my life."

"Heave to, damn you. You run up on my ship and dare defy me?" The curse was punctuated by a crash as the two ships finally met. Aloft came the shouts of men trying to cut rigging that rapidly became a tangled mess.

Armed men now positioned themselves on the enemy's deck. As soon as the ships stopped grinding together, they leapt across the interval onto *Mythos's* deck. His shoulders sagged. He resigned himself to fate.

Johnson ran up from the waist. "We can fight, sir. We can fight."

Tilton turned slowly around, his face a mask of pain. "No. No. We haven't a chance. If they weren't aboard, we might have a chance to make like a merchant, but now they're here...." He shrugged. "It's every man to himself."

Johnson stared at him.

"Aye, sir."

Tilton moved to meet the boarders. He and Johnson ordered their men not to resist.

Most had the look of cornered rabbits staring down the muzzle of a gun. Ahead on the forecastle, a commotion broke out as several men leaped over the side. On seeing it, more in the waist and the poop deck followed suit.

But they had nowhere to go. While Tilton could sympathize, he couldn't do the same. He walked toward a just-arrived lieutenant to surrender.

As he moved, another British sailor knocked him down with the butt of a pistol. Shaking his head, he raised himself up with his hands. The point of a sword drew blood on his back, and he lowered back down. Face down on what had been his deck, he called up to his unseen captor, "We strike, sir. The ship is yours."

Tilton was taken to the captain's cabin aboard His Majesty's Frigate *Arimus*. Led by a midshipman and escorted by two Marines, he carried *Mythos*'s logbook.

The British had killed one man during the brief struggle on deck, shot by a Royal Marine. Four others had various injuries, none serious. Of the nine men that had gone over the side to avoid capture, one had drowned, his body floating just yards from the ship. Four had been recaptured. What might have become of the remaining four, Tilton didn't want to think about. The water was cold, and the shore, while not terribly distant, hidden in a shroud of fog.

Captain Canning emerged from his quarter gallery and looked Tilton up and down.

"So this is what pirates look like, what?" he asked rhetorically.

Tilton said nothing, but his heart sank. If this man determined to treat them as pirates, they were doomed.

After a moment, Canning sat down on a padded bench below the stern windows.

Short and portly, he was also bald and bewhiskered, bucking the trend of the day. When he grimly smiled, Tilton noticed his wooden teeth.

Taking the log, Canning opened it and began to read.

Time dragged interminably as Tilton stood there. His throat was constricted, feeling as if he already had a noose around it. Finally, Canning raised his head and said, "Come then, 'captain', tell me your name and what you're doing with that ship."

"Well, sir, if you know what the ship is, then you know what we're about. We took her, sir. We were bringing her in."

Canning looked thoughtfully at Tilton, then moved to a chair near his writing desk. Finally, after an uncomfortable pause, he spoke again. "You best tell me all about it. It's likely it'll be your only chance to speak. There's many among us want you rebels hanged as pirates."

Tilton didn't know what to do. If they were to be tried as pirates, anything he said would simply damn them at trial. If he chose not to speak, that too would be used against them. Between a rock and a hard place, he decided it would be better to speak and at least give them the truth rather than let them make false assumptions.

"I'm Jonathan Tilton, late the bosun aboard the privateer *Resolute*. I was chosen prize master for *Mythos*, which we captured in the Caribbean nigh on a fortnight ago. I was to bring her in for sale, sir."

Canning listened interestedly. "You claim to have captured her in a fair fight? Hard to believe a rebel could match a packet commanded by a naval officer, what?" Canning cocked his head wonderingly. "No matter, what did you do with her crew?" he continued.

"We released them, sir, on Anguilla. It was a fair fight, sir. The brig's captain, he was killed early on and she got hung in irons when she tried to tack, sir. They was unlucky."

Canning leaned far back in his chair, which threatened to topple.

"Who did you release them to? You didn't just turn them ashore?"

"Well, sir, in a manner of speaking, we did. We put them ashore in a fishing town on the north part of the island. I can't say as I know what they did after we let 'em go, but the captain, that is, Captain Hawke, said it was a British island. He wanted to make sure they was well treated and could get back whence they came." He leaned forward. "Sir, we're not pirates. Captain Hawke's got a privateering commission from the Continental Congress and one from Virginia. We're all legal, sir."

"Then why did your crew abandon ship so quickly? Makes it look damn suspicious, jumping overboard rather than be captured, don't it? They had to know we'd catch 'em."

Tilton hung his head. "We'd been told by the lieutenant from *Mythos* that you all would hang us as pirates if we was ever captured, sir. Most of the men'd heard that, and, well, no one wants to dangle."

Canning smiled. "No, I suppose not." He continued, "All right. I know you're not pirates. You kept a good log of your voyage. Pirates don't do that. And I read the final entry from Captain Bell prior to the battle. I know you were flying the colors of this damned Continental Congress, for all the good it'll do you." He closed the log and flung it on the desk. "However, I'm not the one to make that decision." The smile faded. "Regardless of your intentions, you are rebels, and thus in name you are traitors to the crown. It might be you will wish you were a pirate. It might go easier on you," he added ruefully.

Canning dismissed him, calling the sentry to take him back. He was taken forward and clapped down on the orlop deck along with his crew.

In all, fourteen men crammed into the tiny space. For those who'd been with Jonas in *Elizabeth* the year before, there was a sense of déjà vu.

In such confined conditions, fear fed on itself. They were even more despondent when he told them about his interview. Sailors are either very optimistic, or pessimistic. The former prize crew of *Mythos* saw nothing good about their future. As the evening wore on, fear magnified the possibility for ending their days at a rope's end.

Even so, as the night wore on, eventually one by one they dropped off to sleep, exhausted by the day's events, and by the workings of their own mental terror.

Chapter Twenty-Five

Tilton stirred when the hatch lifted. He'd spent the night berating himself for entering the channel when he couldn't see.

Despite the darkness, the vague shape of a man appeared in the opening.

"Up and out," ordered the shadow.

"Where are we going?" Johnson's disembodied voice answered.

Hearing the belligerence in his tone, Tilton spoke up. "I'm the captain. What d'ye want?"

The shadow stormed, "By God, you are a brazen bunch of bastards. You're going ashore, and now. You can walk, or we can carry you. I do not care which. Move."

Arimus had remained at anchor after the collision. Once they'd freed the ships from their mutual embrace, *Mythos* had been anchored a few hundred yards away. The hit on the head Tilton had taken during the boarding and subsequent surrender combined with the previous day's events to drain his every fiber. Now his natural suspicion was heightened. Tilton told his men to get up and follow orders. They did, grumbling dangerously.

Still dark on deck, the moon shed enough light to see the pale shadows Tilton assumed were marines. Over the side he heard cursing, the coxswain trying to keep the boat from smashing up against the ship's hull.

"All right, let's go." He led his men down the ladder into the boat. Timing his jump with the rise and fall of the craft, he dropped gently to the bottom. Armed sailors roughly pushed him to the bow. Despite agility gained over many years at sea, Tilton nearly stumbled as he was thrust forward. His discomfiture earned him laughs from the British seamen.

"Well, Jonathan, yer no sailor, are ye? Can't e'en stand in a longboat."

Holding his tongue, Tilton sat just aft of the sailor holding the bow hook.

Once he and six others were safely ensconced forward, the coxswain ordered the lines cast off. The men at the oars gave way and the boat pulled gently away from the frigate.

Tilton's head sank onto his chest. He didn't watch the second boat pull alongside and the remainder of his crew loaded.

The walls were to be closing in on them. There appeared to be no escape.

•

AFTER A SHORT ROW ACROSS THE SLOWLY ROLLING SEA, the boats made up alongside *Mythos,* and the men boarded the ship that had until the previous morning been theirs. Packed below once again, they felt the ship weigh anchor and get underway.

Hours later, they heard the anchor let go. The ship had tacked back and forth several times, apparently sailing up the Chesapeake. Even before the anchor took hold, the hatch rose and the men trooped out on deck again. It was sunny with a noticeable nip in the air. Around the anchored ship, trees no longer sported the golds and reds they'd worn when *Resolute* had sailed. Most stood bare-branched, only a few leaves remaining, and the grass had donned its brown winter coat.

Tilton tried to determine where they might be. It looked like the York River near Yorktown. Once more they were herded into boats.

Tilton watched the shore pass peacefully by, looking no different than it had for years. No sign of the struggle with England marred its beauty. He was struck by the thought it might be the last he saw of the world before he was hung. Without thinking he reached up and rubbed his neck.

The officer in the other boat hailed an empty pier. In response, men faded out from the woods to take the lines thrown from the boats. Well short of Yorktown, the pier looked to belong to a homestead, out of sight in the trees. It was well maintained, though rough-hewn; two planks had been recently replaced.

Marched along a dirt road, the group reached and passed the home the pier served. A small but stately affair, two columns supported an ostentatious porch above the front entry. Beyond the home fields lay strewn with the detritus of a tobacco harvest.

As the day wore on, they were marched through more Virginia farmland. No longer certain where they were, Tilton tried whispering to Johnson, his reward a crack on the back of his head with the flat of a cutlass. He spoke no more, but held his head until the bleeding stopped.

Finally around a turn in the road, a small town appeared. There they were marched to the gaol and placed in cells.

Grabbing what space they could, most promptly faded off to sleep.

They saw no food the rest of that first day. A bucket of stale water was quickly emptied by thirsty sailors. The waste bucket soon overflowed.

Midday on the second day, guards entered their cells and shackled them. Then they were taken to the public house next door, to what passed for a courtroom. Ordered to stand on one side of a long table, they faced three seated naval officers, all captains, and two civilians. They stood for some time while the civilians shuffled papers and the officer in the center seat signed them.

Finally, he addressed them.

"Who is the head of this lot?"

Tilton spoke up. "I am, sir, Jonathan Tilton, late bosun aboard privateer *Resolute*, prize master for brig *Mythos*."

The captain, obviously the president of the court, looked up angrily. "Don't you speak to me of privateers. You're pirates."

Tilton saw one of the captains roll his eyes discreetly skyward at the outburst. The other officer just nodded slightly.

"Now, then, since you are in charge, I assume you speak for the others?"

Tilton hesitated, but answered, "Yes, sir, I do."

"Very well. This court charges you with piracy in that on the 15th November last, you did engage, board, and illegally seize the Royal Navy Packet *Mythos*. Also, that you did illegally and with surprise and clandestine action capture and murder..."

Tilton jumped at the word murder, raised his hands and leaned forward. "No, sir, we did no—"

He was cut off mid-sentence when he was hit from behind. He nearly fell but caught the edge of the table and steadied himself. He shook his head and again faced the president, who looked down and continued.

"As I was saying, that you did illegally and with surprise and clandestine action capture and *murder* the crew of said vessel. Finally, that you did illegally seek to transfer her cargo to rebellious traitors within these colonies."

Tilton couldn't believe they were being accused of murder. Sounds of blows silenced the grumbling from those behind him.

The president looked back up and sneered, "Do you have anything to say? That is, something we can believe? It is now your turn to speak. Keep it short."

Tilton repeated what he'd told Canning. Then he said, "Sir, we didn't murder anyone. We're no pirates, sir. I swear it. And the crew of the brig, sir, they're not dead. We set them loose in Anguilla, sir."

"Enough. Neither of those traitorous groups you name can issue a privateer's commission. Only the crown in England, or a Royal governor, can do so. Therefore, you admit you are pirates. And do not pretend to tell me that you captured *Mythos* in a fair fight. She was a well-found ship, ably commanded by a naval officer. The only way scum like you could take her would be by trickery and treachery. I believe their bodies are most likely decaying at the bottom of the sea." He snorted. "Released them in Anguilla, indeed."

"No, sir. They were put ashore—"

"Silence. I will hear no more of your damned lies. Captain Bodkins, Captain Temple, are you ready to issue a verdict?"

The officer called Bodkins quickly answered, "Yes, sir."

Temple, the one who'd rolled his eyes earlier, held his answer for a few seconds. Then he said, eyebrows raised, "Captain Ross, are we to deliberate in front of these men, or behind closed doors, as is customary?" The words were spoken quietly and firmly, but with no animosity.

Ross sneered at him. "I anticipated your holding back. Very well, dismiss these animals and we shall deliberate. I, for one, know how I shall vote."

Tilton and his men were ushered out of the room to stand in the street. Almost immediately, they heard Ross roaring loudly. While they couldn't make out the words, they were vehement. A low voice argued in response. Tilton assumed it to be Temple. Bodkins looked like he would eagerly do whatever Ross told him to.

The guards moved the men farther down the street out of earshot. The guards gave them no chance to escape.

Within ten minutes they were pushed back into the room. Ross stood and spoke stiffly and formally. "You are found guilty of piracy, and of the further charges and specifications noted by this court. However—" Ross glared at Temple before continuing.

"However, in view of unusual circumstances, this court waives the death penalty, and orders you transported to New York to be incarcerated in a prison ship. May you rot in hell."

He was nearly jerked from his feet before Tilton could move. From the moment they'd run upon *Arimus*, everything had seemed unreal. Prison ships, especially in time of war, were known as "hell ships" by sailors the world over. He knew their life expectancy to be far lower in one. He'd seen those who had survived, and they were never the same again.

He slumped as he and his shipmates were led from the courtroom.

THREE DAYS LATER THEY WERE MOVED TO THE HOLD OF a packet. Shortly after being brought aboard, it weighed anchor.

Three days passed with agonizing slowness. The routine never varied: at eight bells they were given a poor gruel of watery oatmeal. In the evening they got boiled dried peas. Only once did they get a small piece of salt pork.

On the fourth day, the swells and wind increased and the packet ran from a gale. The men wedged themselves in wherever they could to keep from getting banged up. For those two days, they went hungry and thirsty.

As the days lengthened into a week, the men grew weak. Three men sickened and were removed to the sick berth. Tilton hoped they would survive. But no one in the ship's crew would tell him their fate.

On the eighth day, the hatch opened.

"Hoy. Your mate, the one with the scar on his face?" came the question from above.

"His name's Reed. What of him?" asked Tilton.

The disembodied voice laughed. "He's gone to Hell, Jonathan." Still laughing, the hatch slammed shut again and the dark returned.

"Bloody hell," Johnson muttered.

Tilton sat, head in his hands. Eventually, he said. "What they'll do with him, d'ya think?"

Johnson snorted. "Likely as not he's been over the side for hours. Not even a Christian burial."

Later that day, the men heard the cry "land ho." Just after six bells the next morning, the anchor was let go. There was no food.

In the afternoon the hatch rose again. "Up and out. Ye're going home." Laughter followed.

Sunshine blinded them on deck. Squinting, they stretched cramped muscles as they awaited the boat. Most could barely stand and were helpless to keep their footing as the packet rolled gently. The British sailors poked fun at them, though more muted than during the voyage. *Perhaps they know what's in store for us and have at least some sympathy.* A gentle breeze tugged at their clothing. Tilton shivered after the warmth below.

"Where are we?" Johnson sidled up to him.

He'd caught sight of what had to be the prison hulks across the bay to the south. "It looks like New York to me. Wallabout Bay, perhaps."

Three ships stood out, stunted with only some of their lower masts in. Two anchor ropes extended out from each bow, one to each side. A third anchor rope reached out from their sterns. Other ships, fully rigged, rode to single anchors from the bow.

He pointed at the largest of the three. "She must have once been a proud ship. She's a frigate, twenty-eight guns. Look at her now." A sad shell of her former self, she appeared rotted and rotting, gunports boarded up, nearly mastless. Only the bowsprit itself and the stump of a mizzenmast remained, the latter rigged with a boom for hoisting stores aboard.

"I'll be damned. You can smell them from here," Tilton said, mouth agape. "Those are the prison ships."

"Wish we was anchored upwind of them."

Tilton looked at him, head cocked to one side. "We won't be upwind once we're aboard."

Johnson closed his eyes. "No, we won't."

An hour later, they stood on her deck. The stench was horrific. The deck gave beneath their feet in places, the sponginess of rotten planks. From below came the sound of wet coughs of misery. Forward, a man cried out, begging his wife to bring him wine for his supper. Delirium flowed in his words. Aft, a chorus of sobbing wafted up, mixed with prayers and supplication for release. A black pall descended on the former crew of *Mythos* as the reality of their new life surrounded, pounded them from every side.

The lieutenant in charge read them the rules of behavior. Tilton only needed to hear half. Nearly every punishment for almost every possible offense was "death by hanging" or "death by flogging."

When the lieutenant finished, they were led below to their fate.

It wasn't long before they all wished they'd been sent to hell, instead.

Chapter Twenty-Six

Jonas looked to the south. Nearing noon, there was still no sun to shoot.

Cap a Foux, the northwestern tip of Haiti, lay on the horizon off the larboard quarter. Great Inagua Island loomed over the horizon on the starboard quarter, some fifteen leagues distant. An observation of the sun coupled with his known position would validate the time on his watch. However, the thick gray overcast prevented it.

The wind had veered back to the northwest through the night. Now it blew directly from Cuba. Thus whitecaps lacked time to build. Still, *Resolute* rolled heavily despite the press of sail. She carried as much as Jonas dared in order to remain well clear of the Haitian lee shore while the storm blew through. The glass had dropped continuously over the past two days. It would not be good to be caught close in to land.

They'd patrolled the Windward Passage now for ten days. They'd seen seven ships in that time, but none had been legitimate targets. Though the second they'd sighted had at first looked to be.

Ship-rigged, perhaps twice the size of *Resolute,* she'd not raised a set of colors as they'd approached. When he'd fired a gun to leeward, she quickly raised Dutch colors. Not trusting, he'd still closed to where he could speak to her. But the accent of the mate and the orders shouted in Dutch convinced Jonas. The master spoke little English, but the mate had enough to tell him that she was *Angelica*, forty-two days out of Antwerp, bound for Aruba.

A disappointed Jonas allowed her to proceed. The mate was indignant at being threatened, but upon learning the American character of her pursuer, he softened his tone. He'd told Jonas the Dutch sympathized with the American cause.

Jonas hoped their luck would change. This morning, he and Masefield discussed supplies.

"Beggin' your pardon, sir. Mr. Hodges looked over the hold, like you wanted. We got plenty of salt meat, dried peas, flour, and the like. The rice we took in San Juan will last a few months. It's the water, sir. Like it always is."

"How many weeks?"

"Oh, probably four. Less we reduce the daily ration."

Jonas shook his head. "No. We're too close to a friendly port for that."

"What about them islands?" Masefield pointed first at Haiti, then toward Cuba.

"Not many springs or streams on my charts in Haiti. None along this part of the Cuban coast." He stretched his arms over his head and yawned. "At least, none that would be easy to get to. We would have to drag the casks a half mile or more inland, then bring full ones back."

Masefield grunted. "That coast don't look all that easy, not for moving hundred-pound casks of water. There's always collectin' rainwater."

"I would rather return to San Juan."

As the storm passed to the north, the winds continued to veer and strengthen. As it did, larger seas accompanied it.

Resolute left the northern end of the pass behind, sailing south-southwest. The seas grew larger and steeper, funneled through the Pass itself.

With the seas now on the larboard quarter, *Resolute* corkscrewed. Her stern rose reluctantly to the crest, then dropped sickeningly into the trough behind. Throughout, the helmsman fought the tiller, trying to keep her on course as she yawed back and forth.

By midafternoon, Jonas was compelled to shorten sail to double-reefed mainsail and fore topsail, with the main staysail set for balance. Wearing to the west to gain sea room, *Resolute* now lay over heavily to larboard, her lee deck edge often awash as she labored, beam to the seas. She could not yet clear the Cuban coast, and as the storm blew through, Jonas would need to alter course once more southerly to keep well clear of reefs and shoals.

Concern about the crew lay foremost in Jonas's mind. Morale climbed with each ship sighted, and sank with each released. Grumbling grew louder and more urgent. Even some of his more loyal followers joined in.

Still, he'd always lived by the tenet that it was only of concern when sailors stopped grumbling and became silent. That was when sedition came aboard.

Jonas possessed no personal experience with a serious breach of discipline, not in any of the ships in which he'd sailed. There were very few mutinies in merchants. Since he found himself in that nether land between the two types of ship, he worried even more. Perhaps a good blow would help. There was nothing like heavy weather to bring out the best in a crew.

"Sail ho! Sail one point off the larboard bow," the lookout on the mainmast called, pointing.

Everyone on deck immediately looked aloft, then followed the lookout's finger. With nothing yet visible from the main deck, Jonas took his glass and began the laborious climb up the windward shrouds. As he climbed, he prayed the other ship's lookouts were asleep.

Once outside the protection provided by the bulwarks and rigging, the wind's power became manifest. Climbing the shrouds to windward ensured that power pushed him against the shrouds and in toward the ship, instead of pulling him away toward open sea.

Gaining the top platform, he rested briefly before raising the glass to scan the horizon. *Damn me, I'm tired.*

He'd been tired before, during and after storms, long days and nights spent laboring to save his ship, his crew, and himself. This was different. He felt the tiredness more in mind than body, though there was plenty to go around. Over the past few days, he'd noticed he thought more sluggishly.

Now here was the physical manifestation. Labored breathing told the tale.

Refocusing, he scanned the horizon, beginning at the bow and moving ever so slowly to larboard.

There, a fleck of white more consistent than the surrounding whitecaps. Turning the glass to focus, he saw only the highest of the other ship's sails. The lookout, posted higher in the rigging, could see farther. Jonas would have to wait until the other vessel closed. Unless he climbed higher. He chose to wait.

Lowering his glass, he looked aloft. *Resolute* would also be visible. The head of his fore topsail stood ten feet higher above his head. Worse, its face was toward the other ship.

Jonas called up to the lookout. "What d'ya make of her?"

"Little hard to see, sir. Keeps dippin' below the waves. Looks to be gettin' closer, though."

Several minutes later, he again looked. The other vessel was indeed closing on them, fast. He could also see she was square-rigged. He still couldn't tell if there was a third mast or not, but that would resolve itself soon enough.

The lookout confirmed it to be a three-masted ship-rigged vessel, and that *Resolute* was on the other ship's larboard bow. That put the other ship close-hauled on the larboard tack, while he was close-hauled on the starboard.

Jonas returned to the deck and ordered a sail change. Assuming the other ship hadn't yet seen *Resolute*, he wanted to keep it that way for as long as possible. He set the foresail, double-reefed, and took in the fore topsail. *Resolute* would be a little slower, but if it delayed being sighted, it was worth it.

Fifteen minutes later, the ship's topsails were visible from the deck. The other ship couldn't help but see him now. At the last heave of the log, *Resolute* made six and a quarter knots. Jonas estimated the other ship to be somewhat faster, though she carried less sail, relatively speaking, only reefed topsails, forestaysail, and jib. The wind veered another point and a half, and Jonas had steered *Resolute* a half point higher to get to windward of the stranger. When she decided to run, he would alter course at her, putting the wind on *Resolute*'s beam. The other ship would have to carry a cloud of sail to run away from him. Despite his heavier spars, doing so risked carrying something away as the wind continued to strengthen.

But the same applied to *Resolute*. Jonas would need every bit of luck he could get.

The other ship didn't change course, steadfastly maintaining her head. As they closed, Jonas wondered again at the lack of caution among the merchants. He closely examined her as they drew closer. He wanted no more surprises like *Mythos*. She had no more gunports than expected, three on each side.

"Mr. Masefield, run up our colors."

As the yellow bunting climbed the mast and blew clear, the stranger suddenly reacted. Men scurried around on deck and climbed aloft. She tacked more quickly than Jonas would have expected, and set more sail. Now she shaped her course to the southwest.

Jonas had the advantage for the moment, and it became quickly apparent the other captain knew it. The commotion on deck continued. Soon, gunports opened and she showed her teeth.

Jonas altered course slightly, more paralleling the chase than before. He was slightly faster. He would slowly overtake her unless the enemy (for he now thought of her as such) did something to change the situation.

As afternoon wore on, *Resolute* continued to gain on the chase. Jonas began to feel more confident.

At five bells, *Resolute* fired a gun to leeward, but she ignored it. Three more times Jonas ordered the gun fired, with the same result.

The wind veered a further, settling in the north-northwest. At seven bells, it began to diminish perceptibly. The storm center had moved off.

Turning again, the chase finally had the wind at her best point of sail. She kept even with *Resolute*. Jonas shook out reefs, first in the foresail, then in the main. With each sail he added, so did the chase. Still, Jonas had the initiative. He could gain for a short period until the chase added sail. By eight bells, *Resolute* was two points abaft the stranger's beam.

"Mr. Masefield, standby the guns. Helmsman, bring her into the wind."

All his careful planning fell apart. The chase suddenly and with great skill wore ship, coming around to nearly the reciprocal course. Her move caught Jonas flat-footed. Not quite close-hauled, the ship rapidly passed down *Resolute*'s unmanned guns.

Cursing, Jonas ordered *Resolute* to tack. It would be faster, and he wouldn't lose his upwind position. Between orders, he berated himself for being taken in and made a fool. The other captain had lulled him into a false sense of security. Allowed him to grow overconfident. At the right moment — Jonas admitted the other man had chosen exactly the right moment — he'd made his own move. It would take *Resolute* hours to make up what they'd lost, and by that time it would be dark.

There was now a very real possibility they would lose her during the night. Jonas cursed himself anew. The only thing in his favor was they both would need to turn back to the west-northwest to clear Cap a Foux.

Resolute barely avoided being caught in irons, so much way had she lost. Backing the jibs helped swing her bow through the wind. Angry men hauled braces around smartly. Spars were briefly endangered as they came up sharp against the shrouds.

Settling on the new tack, Jonas ordered more sail set. A reefed topgallant and the main gaff topsail made their appearance. The ship heeled right over, the leeward rail disappearing for long seconds beneath the foam. He drove her hard, perhaps too hard, but he was angry.

Masefield hovered to leeward, hesitant to recommend against the press of sail. Finally, he resolutely stepped forward. "Sir, perhaps if we rigged preventers on the backstays, we might ring an extra knot or so out of her."

"Make it so. God in heaven, I want that man."

Jonas's breath came in gasps, his fists clenched. *I should have thought of the preventers myself.* He would continue this chase. It already grew dim beneath the overcast. The sun set as he watched.

An hour later, the darkness was complete. No starlight, no moon, just the inky black of sea as it faded without seam into the night sky.

Jonas doubled the lookouts in hopes of keeping the other ship in sight through the dark of night.

Through the long evening and night, he paced the forecastle, pausing every few minutes to look forward to find the enemy's loom. It grew more difficult with each passing moment.

At four bells in the evening watch, Masefield joined him. "Sir, might I interest you in a bite?"

"No, not now. I'm not hungry right at the moment. What do you think he'll do tonight?"

"I don't know, sir. I've been tryin' to put myself in his place, but that turn of his caught me aback. I think if I was him, I might try it again, but we're astern of him, so he'd not gain anything by it. We would likely see him as he passed down the side."

"That's what I've been thinking, too. But he's already shown he's too cunning to simply let us follow him all night. He'll do something, but what? By my reckoning, we have both got to tack to weather Cap a Foux."

"Aye, sir. I wouldna want to get too close at night, if 'twas me."

"Nor would I, were I not being chased by a hungry wolf. But if I were, and I were as stubborn as that fellow has shown himself to be, and as cunning, I would hold my course as long as possible, hoping my pursuer would be more cautious."

"Aye, sir, it's possible." Masefield shook his head. "But there's no knowing. Still, sir, you should eat somethin', if you're plannin' to stay up here all night. I can have cook bring you up somethin'."

"All right, that's fine."

A few minutes later the cook brought Jonas a bowl of cold stew. Moving back to the quarterdeck, Jonas laid into the stew, hungrier than he'd realized.

"Deck there, we canna see the chase, sir."

Jonas dropped the bowl and ran forward. "Damn. All hands, prepare to come about."

Jonas whipped through the orders, the watch on deck hard-pressed to carry them out so quickly they flowed.

While *Resolute* steadied on her new course, disbelief showed in the men's faces. They were convinced he'd lost them the chase.

Jonas couldn't help but think that himself.

THE LONG HOURS PASSED AS THE SHIP MOVED THROUGH darkness. The winds abated further. By two bells, Jonas had the reef shaken out of the topsail. He sensed the anger that surrounded him as the men tried to figure out why he was concerned about maintaining a high speed. As far as they all knew, they simply sailed toward empty ocean.

The sky began to lighten to the east, and Jonas shook himself awake. He'd leaned up against the foremast and immediately fallen asleep. He didn't know how long he'd slept, but the sky was perceptibly lighter. He swore he wouldn't allow that to happen again and moved forward. He'd stand away from anything and force himself to remain awake.

His tired eyes strained as he reached forward. Insufficient light meant he stared into uniform gray. Moving around made him both more alert and warmed him, so he paced the forecastle.

"Sail ho! Sail broad on the starboard beam."

Silence reigned aboard *Resolute*. Finally, the lookout called, "Sir, it's the chase."

Jonas couldn't stop the smile that sprang up. Quickly suppressing it, he forced himself to casually raise his telescope. His hands shook. Finally, he could focus.

His gamble had paid off.

Cheering broke out. It was too early for that, though. "Silence. She's not ours yet, lads."

The chase also saw him. She'd carried as much sail as she dared and more all through the night in her attempt to pull away. Now she shook out all the remaining reefs, heeling steeply as they filled. She surged ahead, and Jonas despaired of catching her, though it would take her all day to pull away from *Resolute*.

But the wind was still too strong and the chase hadn't rigged preventers. Glee rose in his chest as her main topmast snapped at the cap. It took with it the fore topmast.

The wreckage crashed to the forecastle. Relieved of the pressure of sail forward, the chase spun as her bow rounded up into the wind. Her helmsman fought bravely, but she continued to steer large, veering to one side then the other as the seas threatened to throw her on her beam ends. The enemy captain tried to compensate by setting the foresail. It lessened her gyrations, but did not give her back the speed she'd lost, the speed she so badly needed to escape.

Her crew went aloft to cut away the wreckage. Jonas's throat tightened. One man, inching his way onto the main yard, was tossed off as the ship pitched. *Resolute*'s crew watched in agony as he fell, twisting in midair. He hit the rail and bounced horribly into the sea. The broken body passed down *Resolute*'s side, white-caps washing over it.

Jonas broke the silence. "I hope they strike soon. 'Tis a pity to risk men's lives needlessly."

A few minutes later, the enemy crew, more careful now, finished cutting away the remnants of the mast and its rigging.

By eight bells, it was obvious the cause was lost to all onboard *Resolute*. Jonas imagined it must be obvious to those aboard the chase, but not apparently to the captain. Still, he sailed on.

At one bell, Jonas ordered the bow chaser to try a ranging shot. Fired at maximum elevation, with the bow rising on a swell, the shot pitched over the enemy ship, raising a spout fifty yards ahead. That finally convinced her master the pursuit was over. The enemy struck her colors, rounded up, and heaved to.

When he was brought before Jonas, he was torn between congratulating the man on the chase or upbraiding him for risking his crew.

Choosing the former, he said, "You nearly escaped, sir. I thought you'd get closer to Cap a Foux before you tacked."

"Weal, ah thought that meself. Then, ah thought, weal, he'd do the same. So, ah had all but the fore tops'l clewed up, ta make it harder ta see. We tacked quick and waited 'til ye was past us ta set sail again."

Jonas's eyebrows rose, and he smiled. Then in his mind he saw again the body float past and his frown returned.

Stetford was filled with flour and sundries from Jamaica, bound for New York and the British army there. Jonas felt a renewed sense of accomplishment. He'd prevented supplies from getting to the British. By doing so, he helped the Continental Cause.

RESOLUTE'S LUCK HELD FOR THE NEXT THREE WEEKS. She captured five more prizes.

With each, Jonas became more concerned about a British reaction to his presence.

Meanwhile, morale soared with the captures. If anything, the griping worsened when potential prizes were let go. They'd disliked it even more when Jonas burned prizes after removing everything they could. Jonas took to keeping one prize, schooner *Katie*, with him to offload ships he felt weren't worth sending into San Juan. Twice he'd dispatched her with prisoners to Anguilla, then to San Juan to sell cargoes and retrieve prize crews.

Padilla had been true to his word, arranging quick sales for cargoes and ships. Jonas was also pleased by the prices he'd gotten for both. He'd been afraid the discount for disposing of what amounted to seized property would be substantial. Instead, he was getting close to half again what he'd expected.

Each time he captured a ship outbound from Jamaica, he questioned the master and officers closely. Most refused to answer questions, but a few spoke willingly.

What they told him increased his concern. The British were prepared to institute a convoy system, though they still didn't have the ships to do it. Their few sound ships had gone north to join the fleet in New York. The Royal Navy was doing what it could to make the remainder ready for sea.

At the end of December, *Resolute* captured a ship laden with powder and a load of twenty 24-pounder cannon, along with gun carriages, destined for a new fort at Kingston, Jamaica. The enemy put up a good fight, and it took Jonas three days to complete repairs on both vessels. However, thanks to the prizes, he was well found with cordage, canvas, and spars.

He sent this ship directly to the colonies. On the second day of January, he detached it to proceed to Philadelphia. His final direction to Wynn, the master's mate he'd chosen as prize master, was to determine what might have happened to *Mythos*. Sufficient time had passed for the crew to return to San Juan, and he was worried.

The day Jonas dreaded finally came in the middle of the

month. They'd just taken a small schooner filled with molasses and were in the process of sending over the prize crew when a strange sail hove into sight from the southwest.

His fear of a Royal Navy warship showing up had come to fruition. The ship was not so large as a frigate, but a sloop of war.

Jonas detached his latest prize. He took *Resolute* to the northwest, hoping the enemy warship would follow him and not the prize.

It did.

CHAPTER TWENTY-SEVEN

Resolute sailed with a fresh breeze broad on her starboard beam. Jonas stood at the weather hances, scrutinizing the stranger. She was likely to be British, of course. He eliminated Spanish or Dutch as soon as he saw the shape of her topsails. There were no French colonies in the direction whence she came.

That left only the question of her character: merchant or warship. Unwilling to take the risk, *Resolute* kept her distance.

When it turned in pursuit, the stranger confirmed her identity. Jonas ordered *Resolute*'s course shaped just east of due north, close-hauled.

This was the situation he'd dreaded when fitting out his ship as a privateer. A warship carried vastly more sail for its size than did *Resolute*, and despite larger size and greater displacement, was like to be faster, up to a certain size. He could outrun the largest ship of the line. However, a ship that size would likely be accompanied by frigates, which Jonas could not easily outpace.

It would require his best to avoid being brought to an ill-considered action. What they'd done against *Mythos* had been purely lucky. They could not, and he would not, count on such fortune again.

The ships drove through gathering seas. The trades freshened and a long swell ran as a consequence. They met *Resolute* broad on her starboard bow. She pounded into the occasional whitecap, throwing up a fine spray, instantly grasped by the wind's claw. Flung inboard, it coated both men and ships with dew-like drops.

Jonas had his sextant brought topside and took the angle between the enemy's topgallant and fore yards. An hour later, he took it again. They were closing, albeit slowly.

"Mr. Masefield, see if she'll take the fore t'gallant and the main tops'l."

"Aye, sir," replied Masefield. He turned and shortly the sails appeared. *Resolute* heeled further to larboard, the water rushing now past her gun ports, its swift passage audible. Instead of fine spray, large beads of water came over the weather bow. The ship trembled with each impact. Looking aloft, the masts moved perceptibly as she rose and fell, despite the extra preventers he'd had rigged. He took another sextant reading and waited.

Afternoon passed into evening. Jonas kept a running measure of their progress. They'd begun to pull away after setting more sail, but the enemy soon spread more sail herself and halted *Resolute*'s flight. They no longer gained, but neither did *Resolute*.

As soon as he judged themselves well past Punta de Maisi, the northeast tip of Cuba, Jonas turned northwest. He knew it would disadvantage him in the long run, putting him out of position to quickly return to Puerto Rico. He'd have to beat to windward, a long, hard road in the narrow waters between Cuba and Florida, with Great Inagua Island and its smaller islands and reefs, between him and his destination. But he needed to give the schooner and her prize crew time to escape. During the night, he reasoned, he would turn, as had the master of *Stetford*. He could lie closer to the wind than his pursuer. He would use that to his advantage. *Resolute* also drew less water than the enemy. While he did not relish the thought of threading his way through the reefs to the north, perhaps the British would be even more wary.

The sun set and night threw its velvet cloak over the small region of ocean the two ships occupied. Jonas got a good look at

Punta Maisa to the southwest just prior to the sun's departure. He reasoned if he remained on this course for an hour more, then turned north, he would have at least nine or ten hours of deep, clear water ahead.

On the deck of His Majesty's Sloop *Glamorgan*, Commander Wilson waited for the vessel he chased to do something. Thus far the enemy had done nothing but run. Eventually, he'd run out of sea room.

Wilson was still a commander after more than thirty years at sea. A barely competent seaman, he nevertheless considered himself poorly used, convinced of his own brilliance. Spare of height, overweight, he drank and ate too much, and knew too little of seamanship and navigation, though he believed he hid it well. He owed his current post to a lenient old captain in poor health who cared little for his own legacy.

Commanding an old, rotten sloop of war in the cursed West Indies squadron made Wilson bitter. Real action and opportunity for promotion had always lain in European waters, particularly the Mediterranean. Thus, Wilson viewed the rebellion as his opportunity to finally advance, the victor in some heroic single ship action. Ordered to pursue the rebel ship raising Cain in the Windward Passage made his heart leap. He would not allow the abysmally poor excuse for a warship he commanded to interfere.

Glamorgan was not sound of hull nor was she well-rigged. Her hull timbers and backbone rotted, having been cut and assembled from unseasoned wood nearly fifteen years before. She was overpowered for her size, with masts and sails sized for a vessel a fifth again larger than she, so was crank under full sail. Wilson didn't understand sail balance well enough to realize that simply by trimming her more by the stern, she would behave better and sail faster. Instead, he concentrated on keeping her painted waterline exactly parallel with the actual waterline, frequently having his men roust out stores and restow them in his efforts to maintain her beautiful but detrimental trim.

Today Wilson stood quietly on his quarterdeck, arms folded across his chest, feet wide apart in a feigned stance of power. He never went forward to the forecastle. If asked, he would have said it was because a commander should remain coolly near the helm. He would never admit that he feared being among the men.

Unsure if he was gaining on the enemy, he also didn't know how to figure it out, though he fancied he wasn't. Turning to his long-suffering first lieutenant, he said, "Mr. Barry, I want the mizzen tops'l and t'gallant set."

Barry opened his mouth, thought better of it, and answered, "Aye aye, sir."

Barry was the antithesis of his captain. A first-rate seaman and leader, the fact that he served under an officer who was neither irked him. He looked on it philosophically, though, knowing that someday this too would pass.

He moved forward to give the orders, despite knowing the additional sail area aft would simply make *Glamorgan* steer more wildly, without a compensating increase of speed.

As *Resolute* rounded Punta Maisi, the enemy delayed his own turn. Thus when Jonas turned north, they would cross the enemy's bow.

Now well past Punta Maisi, they neared Punta Guarico to the west. As the sun touched the horizon, Jonas fretted about sea room. The farther west, the more it necked down.

Meanwhile, Jonas would do what he could to discourage his adversary. He had a gun moved aft to pepper her with shot. It was fully dark by the time the last breeching and gun tackles were made fast and the gun ready to fire. The white water at their enemy's cutwater was just visible several hundred yards aft and to starboard.

"Give her a salute, Mr. Hackett."

Hackett, ten days back from San Juan, and with newfound confidence, grinned broadly. "Aye, sir, a salute indeed."

The gun spoke, its crew momentarily blinded by the orange flash. Jonas had closed his eyes so when he opened them, he caught the splash of the ball. "Short, Mr. Hackett, perhaps by a cable's length and a half. Try again."

In only a short time, the gun crew was in a rhythm. Load, run out, train, wait for the right moment, stand clear, fire, swab, reload.

"They don't seem to like bein' shot at, sir." Masefield stood, as always, at Jonas's elbow.

"No. Would that I could see aboard her. She steers slovenly, and I can't help but wonder why he carries so much sail aft."

The enemy almost seemed to be dodging their shots, making aim more difficult.

The gun belched fire again, but Jonas saw no splash this time.

"I believe you may have hit her, Mr. Hackett."

The men cheered without breaking stride as they began the cycle again.

Aboard *Glamorgan*, chaos ensued when *Resolute* began firing.

"Damn them to hell," shouted Wilson.

Barry winced but turned to his captain.

Wilson stared wildly forward. He turned to Barry, eyes wide and filled with fury. "D'ya see that, Mr. Barry? The damned whelps are *shooting* at us. How dare they? I want a gun set up for'ard, now. We must shoot back."

Barry closed his eyes, grateful that in the dark Wilson probably couldn't see it.

"Aye aye, sir," he replied and went forward to see to it, grateful to be off the quarterdeck. Behind him Wilson continued to cast invectives at the colonials.

A half-hour later the bosun came up to him as he supervised the work on the forecastle. Knuckling his forehead, the bosun said, "Sir, the captain's compliments, and he wants you on the quarterdeck 'forthwith', sir."

Barry's head hung down. "Very well, thankee, Drake." Turning to the gunner, he said, "As soon as the ringbolts are put in, get the tackles rigged and the gun moved. I believe the captain is impatient to be returning their fire."

On the quarterdeck, Wilson fumed. Seeing Barry, he exploded.

"Just what did you not understand of my order to fire back, Mr. Barry?"

"Sir, the gun forward is not yet ready. The carpenter finished cutting a port a few minutes ago. The gunner is installing ringbolts for the tackles." He did not mention that the ports had been there six months ago but had been removed by the very same Captain Wilson because he'd felt they spoilt the clean lines of the bow.

"I will not tolerate such slovenly work, Mr. Barry. It should not take this long to accomplish such a simple matter. See to it they work faster. Use a starter; there is nothing so much motivates a man to overcome sloth than a knotted rope across his stern sheets." Wilson turned to face forward again in dismissal.

"Aye aye, sir." Barry returned forward just as a ball came across the bow. Decapitating the gunner, it spattered blood and brain matter over his gunner's mate, who'd bent low to slip the breeching rope over the cascabel. The ball traveled aft, spending its final energy against the fife rail at the foremast, shattering the pins that held the sheets for fore topsail and topgallant. Chaos attended as the feet of those sails, freed of restraint, flew up and spilled their wind.

Barry turned from the spectacle and closed his eyes. Quickly surveying the destruction, he called, "Clew up the fore tops'l and t'gallant." Having strove to minimize the damage, he ran aft to Wilson.

"Sir, we must—"

"Who in God's name is reducing sail? Hmm? Tell me, damn your eyes."

"I did, sir. That bastard's last shot shattered the fife rail and the sheets are loosed. We need to get the sails off the mizzen, too, else—"

"No. We will fall behind if we shorten sail."

Barry moved closer to Wilson, his voice low and urgent. "Sir, if we do not, the helmsman will be unable to steer. Look, sir. See how he struggles."

Wilson turned around. The helmsman quickly spun the wheel, spokes flying through his hands. "Steer small, damn you. I will not lose the enemy because you cannot hold the ship's head."

Barry drew in a breath and put his face into Wilson's. "Sir. You must shorten sail aft until we get the forem'st rigging sorted out. Just a few minutes, sir." He squinted and hissed into Wilson's face. "*Now.*"

Wilson looked Barry in the eye, saw his intensity and blanched. "Oh, very well," he stammered. Backing away, he regained his composure. "But get it done quickly. And tell the gunner I want him to return the enemy's fire immediately."

Barry snorted. "Sir, the gunner is dead." He turned and ran forward again, leaving Wilson staring after him.

Jonas paced the deck. They'd stopped firing after the enemy dropped back. It appeared they'd gotten one hit, and it must have been a lucky one. He had to take advantage of the fact they could no longer see the enemy.

"Mr. Hackett, come around, if you please. Due north."

"Due north, aye, sir."

Leaving Hackett to see to the course change, Jonas moved aft and stood at the taffrail. He hoped the enemy was far enough behind them not to notice the course change. If all went well, *Resolute* would have nearly seven hours on this course before the enemy realized it. That would leave him almost directly downwind of *Resolute*, unable to catch them.

At six bells in the evening watch, the clouds that concealed the waxing quarter moon moved on and it shone some light on the scene. Though they'd only changed course two hours earlier, the enemy was not in sight. Jonas would not be satisfied until he could see to the horizon. He resolved to remain on deck.

Sunrise found Jonas asleep on the fiferail, leaning against the mainmast. Stretching, he stood and moved aft. To the south lay a line of clouds, rain slanting down. A rainbow colored the sky toward Cuba. Even if the squall hid their enemy, it would take him all day and well into the night to make up the lost distance.

Resolute was safe.

Jonas sent his crew to breakfast. He would maintain this course for a few more hours, then begin the long beat to windward.

He and Masefield shot the sun for their first line of position of the new day. In ninety minutes, they would observe it again and use it for a fix of their location. While he worked out the math, he pondered his next move.

He and Masefield studied the chart to north and west of their estimated position. No matter how long he stared, it showed the same thing: islands and reefs to the north, though sufficiently distant to give him plenty of sea room. To the northwest lay the Bahama Channel, narrow and dangerous. He hoped the British captain continued that way.

But for *Resolute*, it would still take days to beat back to the Windward Passage. By the time they did, they would require water and stores.

When they got back, then what? Jonas wondered. The Royal Navy had taken notice of him. Even if their pursuer had only stumbled upon him through misfortune, he discounted that possibility. He'd taken enough prizes and there were enough released prisoners in the Caribbean now that word must easily have reached Jamaica.

Time to change his hunting ground.

It had been a longer night in *Glamorgan*, less so for the captain than for Barry. When Wilson had yawned and informed him he would retire for the night, Barry knew someone must remain awake and continue the chase. Better it be himself. So he'd remained on deck all night, trying to keep the ship's speed up to make up for the lost distance. He'd taken in the mizzen topsail and set the windward studding sails on both fore topsail and topgallant yards. With the improved balance, the ship had picked up nearly a knot. Barry hoped that by the time the sun rose, they'd be close enough to open fire with the bow chasers.

But when the moon broke through the clouds, there was no enemy ship ahead of them. In fact, no enemy was in sight.

Even assuming they'd lost a full half hour when they'd been hit, they'd still managed about three knots. Prior to being hit, they'd been making eight and a half knots. That meant the other ship might have been able to pull ahead by five or six nautical miles, but they'd still be visible, even in the dim light of the moon.

If they'd changed course, the only direction was north. Cuba was too close to the south, and there were squall lines that way.

He wrestled with altering course to the north on his own. The punishment would be severe even if he was right. In the end, there was only one thing to do. "Mowey, my respects to the captain, and I request he come up on deck."

Nearly fifteen minutes later, Wilson's head emerged from the hatch. He didn't look around, instead angrily stumped over to Barry. "What is the emergency that you call me up here?"

"Sir, it appears the enemy has altered course to the north.

They are no longer ahead of us. In fact, they are not to be seen at all."

Wilson's half-open eyes wavered for a moment then flew wide. "How could you have lost them? I demand to know where they are."

Barry gritted his teeth. "Sir, as I said, I believe they altered course once they were out of sight of us last evening. When the moon came out a few minutes ago, they were no longer in sight."

Wilson's jaw worked, then he looked forward. Finding nothing, he looked to starboard.

Barry continued, "The moon was obscured behind clouds, as you recall. If it pleases you, I recommend we also turn north. If we are fortunate in hopes of their being within sight at sunrise."

Wilson continued to stare at him. Finally, he answered, "No, I think not. They could not have altered course. There is nothing to the north for them. They must sail for the Bahama Channel to escape. Therefore, we will remain on this heading. Is that clear?"

"Yes, sir, perfectly."

Wilson retreated to the hatch and disappeared below. Barry put his hands behind his back and stared out over the bow.

Chapter Twenty-Eight

Resolute fought seas that flung themselves violently at her, attacking her port bow and spending their energy on her planks and frames. On impact, they flew apart, drenching her sides, her crew, and her lower rigging with spray that dripped to the deck and ran in rivulets to the scuppers. All of these things made her crew miserable as they huddled in the lee of the windward bulwark.

They'd been four days making their way north to the southern tip of Aklin Island, then tacking southeast to Great Inagua, then north again, and finally southeast once more until they finally cleared the northern tip of Little Inagua Island. Now they were beating along the western side of the Caicos Bank.

Jonas expected they'd make San Juan in three or four more days. For now, they beat into a growing storm. He'd rigged preventers and shortened sail at noon. There was nothing for it now but to wait it out and make what easting they could.

After supper, Jonas sat back in his chair, which was now made fast to a deck ring so it didn't slide more than a foot or so in any direction. The ship's motion was wilder than it had been all day. But the glass was rising, meaning the storm was passing. Jonas looked forward to the respite San Juan would offer.

Following a refit, he would reposition once more to the Anegada Pass.

He pulled out pen and ink and trimmed the quill. Wedging his feet around the table legs, which were nailed to the deck, he wrote a short note to Mary. It was the ninth he'd written since they'd left Norfolk. Finishing, he rose and staggered to his cot. Sleep came quickly.

With the new day arrived the first sun in three days. Accompanying it came moderation of the wind as the storm blew itself out. *Resolute* rounded the southern tip of the Caicos into more open waters. Jonas's noon position showed them at the midpoint between Faun Shoal to the north and Monte Cristi shoal off Santo Domingo Island to the south.

"Sail ho! Sail on the larboard bow."

Jaded, Jonas simply waited as the two ships closed the distance.

Forty minutes later, the lookout identified the sail as their own *Kate*, a captured schooner Jonas had made *Resolute*'s tender.

Soon the two ships lay hove two, and a boat rowed across to *Resolute*.

"Welcome back, Wallace," Jonas said as the tall gangly sailor, most recently prize master of a small captured brigantine, stepped aboard.

"Thankee, sir." He indicated a canvas bag tossed up behind him. "I've got letters, sir, from home. Mr. Padilla, sir, he sent word back home that letters here would be got to us."

Jonas had to restrain himself from grabbing the bag. They'd not had post since they'd left. He'd told no one where he intended to go, lest word get to the British.

"That is good news. Let's have the bag. Tell me, did all go well with you and the prize?"

"Aye, sir. We moved the prisoners to *Kate* just afore were got to San Juan, just as you told us. She went on to let 'em go at Anguilla whilst we took the brigantine into San Juan. Mr. Padilla met us at anchor in that boat o' his. He walked around 'er an' looked at the cargo papers. Then he told us to leave 'er to him and go ashore. He had some men with him — a rum lot they were, sir — and they turned to roustin' out the cargo. We went ashore an' got some lodgin' to wait for *Kate* to come back. Mr. Padilla came an' gave me a letter for you with how much the brigantine and cargo was worth. This here's the letter, sir." He handed Jonas a thin oilcloth-wrapped envelope.

"Well done. You may stow your chest."

Jonas took the bag and went below. Once in the cabin, he summoned Masefield. Together, they sorted the mail. When finished, Masefield took the letters for the crew and departed. Jonas sat to look through his own.

He quickly reviewed the letters from Padilla and Martinez. They detailed sales of cargo and ships to date, and the funds Martinez held for Jonas. They amounted to some forty thousand Spanish dollars, which pleased Jonas immensely.

Then he turned to his personal mail. There were three letters from Mary and one from Jonathan Trimble. He opened them in order from earliest to latest.

The first was what he expected. It detailed life in Newport and how the children were getting along. The second was more of the same, though Jonas sensed a growing darkness in Mary as he read it.

The third caused him to leap from his chair.

The British had occupied Newport and taken his brother-in-law's business. Nearly all the shippers in town had lost their businesses, their ships left rotting at the wharfs. While Mary struggled to assure Jonas all was well with her and the children, it was impossible to miss the despondency and fear.

He hurriedly opened the letter from Trimble. It contained much the same news but added a warning. He told of the recapture of *Mythos*. The British now knew he was at sea as a privateer. Trimble feared it was only a matter of time before they discovered his family was under their control. He urged Jonas to return and get his family to safety. He himself could not, as the British watched his activity.

He threw open the skylight above his head and called, "Ask Mr. Masefield if he has the time to join me in my cabin."

In a few moments, Masefield stood before him.

"As soon as we complete our stores here, we sail for Philadelphia."

Masefield's head jerked backward and his eyes widened. "Philadelphia? Will we refit first?"

Jonas shook his head. "No. There's no time." He showed Masefield the letter from his brother-in-law.

Looking up, Masefield said, "But sir, what can we do? We're more useful here, takin' British trade. Our ten cannon can't stand up to a single fort around Newport. And why in God's good name Philadelphia?"

Jonas stared at him. "Mr. Trimble tells me that Philadelphia is the nearest port to Newport not yet controlled by the British. As to going home to fight, no, you're right about that. But my family is in danger. I can't stand idly by and let come what may."

Masefield took a deep breath. "Jonas, I'm proud o' what we've done here. And we ought to keep doin' it. Ye are lettin' your personal worries blind ye to what good we're doin'. What good *ye're* doing. Every enemy ship we take makes it harder for them to win. We ought to stay here an' fight."

Jonas found he couldn't meet Masefield's eyes. "I hear you. But I wasn't home when the twins died. I can't let something terrible happen again while I'm away."

The two men stood silently for a few moments. Jonas finally broke the tension. "John, we will sail home."

Masefield sighed. "Aye, sir, home it is."

Four days later found *Resolute*, with *Kate* in company, standing into San Juan.

No secrets exist aboard ship. Word got out they were going home. That, coupled with thoughts of a coming run ashore in Puerto Rico, assuming Jonas granted them one, raised spirits among the men. Jonas did not share them.

A drenching rain began to fall as they left the harbor mouth. The rain streamed from his face and clothes, deepening Jonas's black mood. The stiff breeze necessitated *Resolute* sail in under fore staysail, reefed mainsail, and fore topsail alone. The rain and accompanying reduced visibility made the transit that much more harrowing, and more than one pair of eyes on deck glanced occasionally back at their captain with concern as he drove her hard.

Fetching up to the anchorage, the lookout reported the familiar port captain's lugger departing the quay. Hackett called attention to it as it approached. Jonas moved to the side to meet officialdom.

As Padilla climbed the ladder to the deck, he looked up and grinned in greeting. His grin died as he beheld Jonas's face, however.

"Capitán Hawke, it is good to see you. But your face... it holds much unhappiness. Has some misfortune befallen you?"

"Nothing of great concern, Señor. We have enjoyed much good fortune in our cruise, in fact."

"You have, indeed. I see the fine ship *Kate* is with you. I trust you have received my messages?"

"Si, Señor, I have. Perhaps we could adjourn to my cabin?"

Jonas led Padilla below to his cabin. He removed his dripping outer garments, took Padilla's as well, and hung them over the bench below the stern window.

Jonas spoke first. "Señor, I must make this visit to San Juan brief, only to take on stores. Mr. Masefield will—"

Padilla waved his hand casually. "Must we speak so quickly of business, mi amigo? You have enjoyed success. Let us hear tales of your conquests. My responsibilities do not allow me to pursue such adventure, nor even to leave the city often for the countryside. Certainly not to sea. Yet I find that I am strangely enamored of sea tales."

Jonas regarded him silently, then rose and drew two glasses from the locker.

"Very well, Señor...." Jonas told of the captures, though he kept the tales short. Padilla listened politely and asked astute questions. His keen interest in the details of a sea chase prompted Jonas to warm to his topic.

Half an hour later, Jonas finished the story of his escape from the British sloop. As he did, his memory of the letters thrust themselves to the front of his mind.

Padilla noted the change. He cleared his throat. "On to business then." He drained his glass. "It is well that you have returned. Only a half day after *Kate* put to sea, three days past, the British agent returned. He told terrible stories of marauding pirates who captured ships in the Windward and Anegada Passages. Pirates who marooned crews on Anguilla Island. And he warned us that these pirates might disguise themselves as privateers to avoid punishment for their evil deeds." Padilla's eyes sparkled as he spoke, his grin unabashed.

But Jonas was himself too anguished to appreciate the humor. "I understand, Señor. May I presume his return may affect your ability to assist me?"

Padilla frowned, his eyebrows coming together into a single bushy line. "No, Capitán. The presence of the British agent will have no effect. Well, perhaps a little. It might be wise to send some of your future prizes to Ponce, a city in the south of the island. This would make less the chances that he would see an unusual number of ships, some perhaps having suffered damage, coming to this port and being sold. But this can be arranged easily." He leaned forward. "There is one other thing you must know, Capitán. In the past three weeks, two British Navy ships have been seen, and one made a short visit to San Juan. It is he who delivered the agent. The other, however, has three times been reported to, how do you English say, remain 'in the offing,' that is, pass north of the city, on the horizon, but in sight of the fortress."

Jonas bristled at being labeled "English" and Padilla noticed. Very quickly, he said, "I mean no offense, Capitán. I apologize. I know you are American, not English." Slapping his hands on his thighs, he said, "While the English seem concerned that so many of their ships are disappearing, there is nothing to tell them we assist. The governor has assured their agent that no colonial *warships* are permitted to operate from this port." He paused, then continued. "The governor has no information to the contrary and speaks the truth." Padilla held Jonas's eyes tightly.

Jonas nodded slowly. It would be in both their interests that the governor not be given any direct evidence to the contrary. Both men understood that what the governor might suspect was a far different matter than what he knew.

Padilla smiled for a brief moment. Then his eyes narrowed and he leaned forward. "Capitán, you are not of a mind to pay attention to such details, yes?" In a moment of inspiration, he continued, "You have perhaps received unpleasant news from home?"

Jonas glanced sharply at him, but quickly relaxed. "Yes, Señor, I have, though there is little to be done. However, it necessitates that I return to the colonies. I would like to take on stores quickly, that I may depart as soon as possible."

Padilla leaned back, sadness crossing his face. "I am sorry to hear of it, amigo. Of course, we will get what you need quickly. The first may perhaps be delivered tonight. I am certain your very able Señor Masefield has already provided my man with your needs." He stood and held out his hand. "It is likely I will not see you again before you sail, as I have business in Caguas, in the center of the island. I shall be gone for several days. When you return, as I hope you will, we will renew our acquaintance, and our business. Vaya con Dios, Capitán."

Jonas escorted him topside and saw him down into his boat. Padilla gave a last wave as the boat sailed back to the quay.

Turning to Masefield, he said, "Padilla told me the first of our stores might be ready by this evening. Will we be ready to stow them?"

"Aye, sir, we will." He clasped his hands behind his back. "Beg pardon, sir, but I recommend we give the hands a run ashore. They'll nought have the chance until we are home. Who knows what awaits us there? We can let half a watch go for a few hours at a time and still get stores aboard, sir."

He looked closely at Jonas, adding, "And that goes for you, too, Jonas. Ye're wore thin, Captain. Too thin. The crew needs you at your best. *I* need you at your best." He turned and walked forward, ostensibly to prepare to take on stores.

Jonas watched him go, then stood by the side looking up at the city.

CHAPTER TWENTY-NINE

The morning dawned cloudy and gray. The fine weather of the past days was gone, replaced by a gloom, and the falling glass told of the coming storm. Arriving on deck, Jonas read in the sky that before nightfall, it would rain.

Half the crew had gone ashore the night before. All were back aboard, a bit worse for wear, but nothing fresh air and hard work wouldn't cure.

"Good morning, sir." Hackett made his appearance and briefed Jonas on the ship's standing. They'd finished stowing barrels of ship's biscuit and water that had arrived last evening.

When finished, he added, "Sir, while we was rousting out the cables up for'ard, Page noticed there's a couple of sprung butts near the bow. Up high, just below the berth deck. I went below and looked. They don't leak much, but they ought to be fixed, sir."

While Jonas considered the report, Masefield joined them.

"I was just tellin' the captain about the sprung butts for'ard," said Hackett.

"Aye. Sir, I don't know how they're fixed for plank stock after our last visit. They barely had enough for what we needed done then."

"I remember. Well, I'll be seeing the yard this morning." He sighed. "It appears fate conspires to force at least some of the refit. We'll have to careen her to get at those planks. Too bad last night was the full moon. We'll only have a couple more days of good spring tides to do it in," Jonas answered.

Later the shipyard office gave him good news. "Si, Capitán. We have the wood you need. It is a local wood, called guaraguao. It will no swell like oak or pine, but we make thinner the seams. We can careen your ship at the end of the bay in the flats. The mud is no too deep and there is a good channel to float the wood to you."

Jonas made the arrangements. His carpenter would inspect the plank stock beforehand to select the right lengths. Then, he made his way back to the wharf.

As he neared the wharf, a full-rigged ship made its way to anchorage. She looked familiar, but he couldn't place her. As it closed the anchorage where *Resolute, Kate,* and three merchant ships lay, a flag broke out from the halyards. They were the colors of Jonas's fledgling nation. His heart leapt. Another American ship was a welcome sight.

Jonas continued to watch the newcomer as he was rowed out to *Resolute.* No one in his boat crew recognized the new vessel, so Jonas decided to call upon the master later in the afternoon, after they'd had a chance to snug down and get their ship settled.

ARRIVING ABOARD *RESOLUTE,* JONAS FOUND THE master of the other vessel had already made a call upon Jonas, coming across as soon as his anchor bit.

"Jonas, my son, I'm damned glad to see you," Scoggins declared as soon as Jonas stepped on deck. He rushed forward, gripping Jonas's hand with both of his.

Jonas was equally glad to see him. He returned the hard grip, smiling fondly at his father-in-law.

Down in his cabin, he asked, "What news of home?"

"I've letters from Mary. She'll be telling you herself, but the last we got before I left Gosport was they were doing well. Your William itches to go to sea with you. And your Rebecca grows again. Mary wishes you were home, of course, but sends her love. Elizabeth sends hers, as well." He leaned back in his chair. "Damn me, I'm glad to see you, boy."

Jonas pursed his lips.

George noticed. "What's wrong?"

"George, I had a letter from Mary, and one from Trimble. The British have taken Newport."

George shook his head. "But why would the lobsterbacks go there? They have it blockaded. There's very little shipping left. No reason to hold the town."

"Trimble thinks it is to cut the flow of money from there. And, despite the blockade, there are a few ships getting in and out. From there it is little matter to get powder, shot, and food to the army."

Scoggins sat and stared out the stern windows, lost in thought. Jonas hated to interrupt, but he had other news. "Trimble also tells me the Royal Navy has a list of those who have taken to the sea as privateers. I captured a Royal Navy brig, *Mythos*, back in November. She was retaken. From her log, they obtained my name. He believes I must return home and remove Mary and the children to safety, away from Newport."

Scoggins closed his eyes in pain. Mary was his only child, William and Rebecca his only grandchildren.

"When will you sail, then?"

Jonas turned to look out the stern windows. "As soon as I make certain repairs, and finish loading stores."

Scoggins rose and moved to stand next to him. He put his hand on Jonas's shoulder. "I know what you feel, truly I do. Your family is as dear to me as life itself. You must do what you think best. But know that what you, what we, do is also important. It is difficult for a man to believe that what he accomplishes is significant. But for each of us who take the war to sea, who take from the king some small sum, contributes to his downfall." He squeezed Jonas's shoulder. "I will stay here and do what I can to fill your shoes. But you must return, as soon as you possibly can."

Jonas cleared his throat before he spoke. "Thankee, George. I am grateful for your understanding. I will return. That, I promise." Changing the subject, he asked, "What other news of the war, then?"

"Ah, Jonas, that's also not good. General Benedict Arnold fought an action in the great lakes, at a place called Valcour Island. Sadly, he was beaten. We got word of it a week after you left. The British continue to move down the lakes to come at us from the north. With Howe in New York and General Washington running from him at every turn, it may be the death of us. New England will, in all likelihood, be under their control soon. Washington was going to encamp for the winter in Pennsylvania, just across from Camden."

Jonas considered this. So much of what the embryonic nation had to offer other world powers came from New England. So did much of the support for the war. Washington had done little but retreat since the heady days of the Boston siege. At first his actions had been excused as a necessary but very temporary strategy. As the long months dragged on, each one saw a new home for the struggling Continental Army, each move ceded more territory to the enemy. It became obvious the colonists really couldn't stand and face the might of the British Army, after all.

"There was a bit of odd news, Jonas, which you'll find amusing. When the lobsterbacks put their soldiers ashore in New York, a young man by the name of Nathaniel Hawthorne attacked their fleet, all on his own. He took a barrel and made it into a strange craft that floated below the water. He attached a powder charge to the hull of a ship of the line, and returned to tell the tale. What an adventure. The man's a genius, though he didn't quite sink anything."

Scoggins had a gleam in his eye as he talked. He relished invention among men, equating it with the noblest of endeavors. He roused himself. "Seems you've seen a bit of fighting yourself."

"Not so much, really." Jonas relayed the story of the capture of the *Mythos* and the others.

"Aye. Very bold, taking on a ship of the Royal Navy," said Scoggins. "You were fortunate, and you handled it well."

"Ah, less well handled, and far more fortunate than I deserved, I'd say, sir. Had I known, I would not have attacked. When finally I recognized what she was, I felt like I stood on an icy hill, sliding toward a rock, unable to stop. Had her captain not been killed early on or her crew been newly formed and raw, it likely would have turned out very differently," Jonas responded. His face darkened.

"But what of your success?" Jonas asked, drawing in a deep breath and smiling, though it didn't touch his eyes.

"Ah, Jonas, would that I'd had the success you've found. We've had naught but troubles since we left Norfolk." Taking a long sip of wine, he continued. "I sailed the twenty-third last, taking advantage of heavy rain. Little good it did. I ran straight away into the blasted *Otter* just off Cape Henry. Your Captain Squire dogged me for nigh on two days before I could run him hull down. 'Tweren't for the rising winds and seas, he'd have still been on me all the way here. He finally had to shorten sail. Thanks to God for my new rigging."

"There was little enough good rope available when I refitted *Resolute*," Jonas commented.

"Aye, true enough. I thought myself fortunate for many things during the building. Now 't seems I'm paying for that fortune. We've sighted only three sails the entire time we've been out. One was a Spaniard, the second a Portugee, and the third another Royal Navy patrol." Scoggins turned to face Jonas. "You pay heed to this one. I ran into her just five days ago, near the Eastern Passage. She's a 28-gun frigate. Fast and well handled. She found me during another of the bloody storms that's bedeviled me since we left home. Came out of a squall less than a league to windward. We saw what she was and made sail, but not fast enough. She carried more than ourselves, and set even more. I wore around to run, but damn-me, she's fast. She got her guns out and got two broadsides in on me. Thanks be to God for the seas running, as she missed with nearly all the shot. They did take my mizzen tops'l, and *Reprisal* got downright crank. I thought us finished, but we managed to get the mizzen t'gallant set. I headed into a squall, hoped that it might to carry something away 'board the chase. Well, it's what saved me. When I came out the other side, she wasn't behind. When she did come in sight, she was well away to port. She'd thought I'd wear away again, and so she wore to larboard herself."

Scoggins refilled his glass. His hands shook as he did. "He gave me far more credit for craft than I deserved. I turned away then, you can be sure. He came around, too, but he'd lost too much. When opportunity presented another squall, I took it. Again, though, I didn't turn. Maybe he would think I'd learned from the first and turned, so I thought. It worked. He came around, again. But now he was well to looward. *Reprisal* goes to windward well, and we were able to lose her. She no more fell for tricks in squalls, but she couldn't make up the distance to windward. I lost her the second night. At dawn she was not to be seen. We were in need of water by then and San Juan was the easiest port to make. That's how I found you."

"A harrowing tale, George. I came across a Navy ship recently, a sloop. Not nearly so well handled. Alas, my success here may have nipped the pie for you. The Port Captain tells me the Royal Navy knows there are privateers about."

They talked for another hour. Jonas told him about Padilla and Martinez. Scoggins was happy to learn America had friends in San Juan.

Finally, the two men agreed to meet for dinner before Scoggins took his leave.

The next day Jonas, Scoggins, and Masefield dined with Señor Martinez. Padilla was already there when they arrived at the Martinez home.

Scoggins and their host hit it off well. Jonas's recommendation was enough for Martinez, and he greeted Scoggins as an old friend. Throughout supper they shared deep conversation about trade and the advantages to both nations if America won its independence. Jonas was content to sit back and listen. It amused and intrigued him, so he enjoyed his evening without being an active participant.

Masefield entertained Padilla with his trove of sea stories.

"Jonas, the wine stands by you. Will you join us and drink a glass to the confusion of the enemy?" Scoggins asked.

Jonas roused himself and smiled. "Of course." He grasped the bottle and topped off all five glasses.

"Confusion to our enemy." Each echoed him, and all drained their glasses. The bottle went round to refill them.

Martinez addressed him. "George informs me you will depart our glorious island for home. Your family is held by the English?"

Jonas looked hard at Scoggins, who shrugged. "I know of no reason it should be kept secret, Jonas."

Jonas turned back to Martinez. "Yes, Señor. They are not being held, but are in a city that is occupied by British soldiers. Because the Royal Navy knows my name, it is of concern."

Martinez smiled and nodded. "Of course, you must protect your family. The war will go on without you for a time. When you return, you will continue to bring fear to English shipping."

He nodded toward Scoggins. "In the meantime, your father-in-law will terrorize the English. And we will support him." He raised his glass to Jonas. "Vaya con Dios, Capitán Hawke. May you find safety for your family."

After the toast, Martinez continued. "But you must return as quickly as possible. My friends who make it a habit to gather information tell me that the Royal Navy is discomfited by what you have done. The English shippers are not happy with *them*.

English merchants have great power in their government. This is an important way to win this war, by making them angry." He smiled and turned back to Scoggins.

As they dined, the full moon climbed higher. Despite its coolness, the still night air combined with the wine and relaxed Jonas. When they eventually left, Padilla escorted the sailors to the sea wall where *Resolute* and *Reprisal*'s boats lay. Shaking hands, the men said their goodnights.

Once more aboard his ship, Jonas undressed and lay down. Within seconds he fell asleep, his first truly relaxed and sound sleep in months.

EARLY NEXT DAY, *RESOLUTE* WARPED ONTO THE MUD flats at the far eastern end of the harbor. While they waited for the tide to go out, her boats busied themselves placing the trunks of great palm trees between her hull and the harbor bottom to limit how far over she would heel. Onboard, the rest of her crew secured everything that might move with stout ropes, and lowered her topmasts to the deck.

By midday the planks in her bow were above water and the carpenter's mates, assisted by the yard's men, were hard at work. Both planks were worm-eaten and had to be replaced in their entirety. Jonas worried they wouldn't finish before the tide came back in, so he watched in silence from the jolly boat.

By midafternoon, the last treenails were driven into the new planks and the caulkers were beating out their unique rhythms.

Jonas came back aboard. "I will be below until we are afloat once more."

It was only an hour before he felt *Resolute* begin to sit upright again. By sunset, she was warped once more to her anchorage. Tomorrow they would get her topmasts aloft and re-rigged.

While *Resolute*'s rigging was set up, Scoggins and Jonas met for a final time.

"I feel the need to get to sea, George. We sail on the afternoon tide," Jonas said.

"Aye. I'd have been happy to see you tarry a while longer. When you return, perhaps we should sail together a bit, to cover more area, eh? But for now, I'll be away myself in a week or so. I will leave word with Padilla where I will be."

"Fine. We can sail together, and perhaps enjoy good fortune. Meantime, I leave *Kate* with you. It has paid handsomely having another ship to bring prize crews back."

"Thank you. You take with you my prayers for a swift passage."

"Aye, sir. And I will give Mary and the children your love when I see them. God willing, when next we meet, they will be safe."

Just before two bells in the afternoon watch, *Resolute* weighed anchor and stood out to sea.

Chapter Thirty

Clear skies followed *Resolute* as she made her way northwesterly. A fresh breeze whipped up small whitecaps, stark against the infinite indigo of the sea. The sky was bereft of clouds and intensely blue. While not what might be called warm, the humidity stayed low for a change, a welcome break. Heeling far over, she made good speed, an easy nine knots, rising and falling with the swells, her lee rail buried occasionally beneath the warm blue Atlantic waters.

Departure from San Juan had proved uneventful. They'd not seen a single sail, but Jonas really hadn't expected to. He'd chosen a route directly toward a point at thirty degrees latitude, fifty leagues east of the Florida coast. From there, he would take advantage of the westerlies blowing off the continent, and the great coastal current, remaining twenty leagues off the coast until he reached Cape Hatteras, where he would shape his course north to Delaware Bay. The winds would remain just aft of the starboard beam until they left the tropics.

Along the way, they would pass just east of the Bahama islands. There they might pick up a prize or two.

THE MORNING OF THE THIRD DAY DAWNED AS HAD THE others, clear and warm with the wind steady out of the east-north-east. Jonas stood to the windward side of the poop deck, leaning against the rail. Despite the fair weather and good sailing, his mind was in turmoil. There he remained until time for the noon sight.

The lookout hailed from aloft as Jonas raised his sextant. "Deck there, sail ho! Sail broad on the starboard bow. Looks a warship, sir," hailed the lookout.

Jonas immediately ran to the taffrail with his glass. Just on the horizon, a spot of steady white that didn't come and go like whitecaps.

There were only two directions to go. Southwest toward the Bahamas. Southeast toward the broad Atlantic. The Bahamas consisted of shoals, reefs, and tiny islands, risk to be avoided. The Atlantic led to winter storms, and assuming they escaped their tormentor, having to beat back for days, perhaps weeks, to North America. Jonas's mind harkened back to what Scoggins had told him of a well-handled enemy frigate. If it were, they were unlikely to outrun it.

He turned to Masefield. "Wear ship. We will sail toward the Bahamas." Then, to the helmsman, "Make our course southwest half west."

Resolute crowded on sail. So did the assumed enemy. Despite Jonas's best efforts, the pursuer slowly gained on them. Jonas finished taking his sunline and went below to the chart.

Afternoon turned to evening, then to night. Hull up now, sure enough, the vessel hounding them was a small frigate or sloop. Both flew before the wind, the enemy closing in. The moon, just past full, rose an hour after sunset, eliminating any chance of escape under cover of the dark.

"Land ho! Land broad on the larboard bow," came the call, a little past one bell in the middle watch.

Jonas hoped that would prove to be San Salvador Island.

As they sailed past, he caught sight of what he decided must be Cockburn Town, confirming the identity of the island in his own mind. He was running out of sea room.

"Hands to wear ship." He'd decided to take the deck himself, though neither Hackett nor Masefield had gone below. "Steer west-southwest." As the yards braced around and the mainsail swung to larboard, *Resolute* put her stern toward San Salvador and sailed on into the night.

When eight bells sounded, no one moved. All hands were on deck already and intended to stay there.

The cry of land minutes later started those few who'd fallen asleep between the guns. Jonas went aloft to look. There were no lights on the low-lying land. Breakers extended well out from the tip closest them. This then had to be Conception Island.

He kept silent, and *Resolute* passed between Cat and Long Islands, into Exuma Sound.

CAPTAIN WILSON CAME ON DECK SHORTLY AFTER sunrise. He'd gone below to sleep shortly after they'd passed Conception Island. No matter that he'd had to rely on Barry to confirm what island it was. As captain, he had greater concerns.

Such as the certainty that the enemy brigantine couldn't escape this time. He smiled grimly.

The American ship was trapped. It was a matter of time before it was forced to surrender. He'd looked at the chart himself once he'd been certain where they were. The enemy had sailed into Exuma Sound, surrounded on three sides by islands and reefs. *Glamorgan* was the fourth side of the box into which the vile pirate had sailed. He would take great pleasure standing into Kingston with the American trailing astern, the British ensign flying above the rebel rag. Justice for the depredations the Americans had wrought on trade in the Caribbean, and on Wilson and his ship.

It still rankled him the rebel bastard had escaped the last time.

The fact that Barry had actually recommended the right course of action, and that he'd ignored it, only made it worse. Wilson had laid the blame for the enemy's escape on Barry in his report to the admiral commanding the West Indies squadron. But the laurels for their capture would be his own.

"Mr. Barry, shorten sail, if you please. We needn't try to overtake her any longer. She'll either run aground or realize her predicament within the next several hours. Either way, we'll have her by midday."

"Aye aye, sir." Barry moved forward. The bosun's pipes twittered and men broke into motion. Canvas flapped and was reined in. *Glamorgan* slowed.

Wilson took pride in how well his crew performed. Perhaps he would have an extra tot of rum issued this day when they took the prize.

He stood on the quarterdeck, thoughts filled with images of the commendation he would receive from the admiral.

Twilight before sunrise found *Resolute* in what appeared to be open waters, though Jonas knew better. Looking aft, the enemy continued to follow them, perhaps two leagues astern, not yet in cannon range.

Masefield came up to him. "Sir, I don't know these waters as well as ye, but methinks we're trapped here. Ahead lies only reefs and islands."

Jonas gave him a weary smile. "So it would appear. However, there are a couple of passes with sufficient water for us to pass. But I don't believe our friend can. It waits only for us to find them, and to ensure we pass on high tide."

Masefield stared at him, jaw working. Finally, he said, "By the Lord, I hope you are right."

The two men stood watching their adversary. "Sir, d'ya see that? Why would he be reducing sail?"

Jonas smiled. "Because he, too, believes we are trapped. Perhaps he does not know these waters, either."

"But why not keep up with us, that he might more quickly take us when we run out of sea room?"

"Perhaps he waits for daylight. I don't know. But I've been considering this might be the same ship that chased us before. Her captain proved easily misled then."

"You had this in mind yesterday when we turned toward the Bahaman Islands?" Masefield asked, eyebrows raised.

Jonas shook his head. "No. I wish I could lay claim to such diabolical plans. But no."

"What did you hope for then?"

Jonas shrugged. "I had not devised a plan. It seemed better to at least turn in a direction that would allow us to continue our voyage, were we to escape. Returning toward San Juan was too difficult to stomach. We had no choice but to run. When after moonrise found him still on our stern, I looked at the chart and hoped for the best."

Masefield shook his head. "A very great gamble, sir. I hope that it pays."

Jonas rubbed his hands together. "So do I. So do I."

RESOLUTE CONTINUED WEST UNTIL FIVE BELLS, THEN turned north, close-hauled and skirting a lee shore more closely than any aboard felt comfortable doing. Daylight made prominent breakers between the several low islands less than two leagues to larboard. The lookouts, of their own accord, spent more time looking at the water directly ahead of the ship than for sails on the horizon, hoping not to see the lightening that indicated shallow water.

Jonas shortened sail as soon as they turned north.

The enemy continued to fall behind. When *Resolute*'s turn

became obvious, she followed suit, though she remained significantly further off the reefs than did her quarry.

At noon, Jonas shot the sun for his latitude.

"I'm going below to my cabin for a few minutes. You have the deck."

In his cabin, he pulled out the chart. There was good water close in, perhaps thirty minutes ahead, but it shoaled quickly, with reefs on either side. The depth in the channel should be near two fathoms at high tide. That would be in a little more than an hour. But there was less than a fathom on either side. If he ran up on a reef, his escape would end very quickly. Worse, the channel was less than a hundred yards wide at its narrowest point.

He only hoped his nearly seven-year-old chart was accurate.

Masefield was right. What they were doing was a tremendous gamble. He would have to thread his way through the reefs. If he succeeded, there were more reefs beyond, more danger, though the channel would be much wider, nearer a half mile and opening. He would have to hold his course for at least an hour before he could make his turn northwest.

If the enemy were as feckless as he hoped, they would try to follow him and find their bottom ripped open. But he couldn't count on that. In the event they did not follow, it would take them a full day to beat back to the bay entrance, and another to go round. All that time, *Resolute* would put distance between them.

He put the chart aside and went up on deck.

At three bells, *Resolute* turned west to run nearly downwind. The frigate held her course for another fifteen minutes, then hove to, waiting for *Resolute* to ground.

As they ran toward the reef, Jonas tried to gauge by how far they would weather it. "Mr. Masefield."

"Aye, sir." Masefield joined him by the larboard knighthead.

"Place a good hand in the chains with the lead. We will not have much warning before we're upon the reefs. I also want the best lookouts in the fore crosstrees watching for shoal water.

Ensure they understand that we all count on them for our lives. I shall join him in time, and pilot the ship from there. Meantime, I want no unpleasant surprises under our keel."

Masefield moved aft to see to it.

The rhythmic cry of the leadsman began.

"Twenty-eight fathoms, sir. Sand bottom." The lead was flung forward again.

Jonas began the long climb to the fore topsail yard. Achieving its great height, he settled himself with his back against the topmast, legs hanging on the forward side of the yard, the billowed sail against his heels. Settling his head against the mast, he looked for the telltale breakers and spume that marked reefs.

He closed his eyes and prayed silently as they hurtled toward them.

AHEAD, ALL HANDS SAW THE BREAKERS, THE deceptively beautiful white menace that drew ever closer. Periodically, a crashing wave ahead or on either bow told of an otherwise unseen obstruction waiting for the mistake that would rip into their bottom, impaling the ship. Unaware of Jonas's intent, some wondered if he planned to drive her onto the rocks to avoid capture, their worst fears breeding irrational conclusions.

"By the mark nine, shoaling fast, sir," called the leadsman.

Jonas digested the information and called up to the lookout a few feet above him astride the topgallant yard.

"No, sir. No rocks ahead, that is, not right on the bow, sir — wait, sir, yes, sir, about two cables lengths, sir. Mebee one point to looward, mebee less, sir."

"Very well." Now, shouting down to the quarterdeck, "Helmsman, steer nothing to starboard of the current heading, d'ya hear?"

Receiving a nervous shout of comprehension, Jonas returned to considering the way ahead. In his mind he saw the chart, and he overlaid it with what his vision gave him. He could see the passage. It was narrow, but it was clear.

Looking back at the enemy, muzzle flashes and smoke erupted as the frigate fired. It had to be born of frustration as the range was too great to hope even for a hit from a skipping ball.

They continued threading their way through the shoals. Even the wind seemed aware of the tension and fear aboard, for it came in throaty gusts and its burden belied the bright sunlight.

As they neared the narrowest point, their pursuer hove to and began lowering boats filled with the red coats of Royal Marines.

Jonas smiled without mirth. *He must think they'll have a wreck to board and take as prize.*

Nearing the bottleneck, Jonas had the helmsman steer slightly starboard to give them greater distance from the final reefs.

Finally, after nearly an hour of high tension, the water ahead colored the darker blue of deep water. Jonas breathed deeply and descended to the deck. As he reached it, the lookout drew his attention to the enemy ship.

"Deck there! They're settin' sail."

Jonas raised his telescope and pointed it astern. They were indeed setting more sail. No longer hove to, she was also attempting to retrieve her boats as she began pointing toward the gap in the reefs.

The question was, would she try to follow *Resolute*? Or was she breaking off the chase?

"God damn them to hell."

Wilson's eyes were wide and his mouth hung open after he delivered his epithet.

He couldn't believe what he'd seen. The damned rebel had actually found a passage through the reefs and was sailing away from him on the other side.

"Sir, we should recall the boats. There's nought we can do now." Barry spoke warily, cringing against the expected eruption.

Wilson's eyes shifted from the enemy to Barry. At first he only stared, then he shouted, "Yes, damn you, get them back. And get us under sail again. Follow them."

It was Barry's turn to stare. He could take it no longer.

Lowering his voice, but with an urgency that could have singed Wilson's eyebrows, he said, "Sir, no. I will not. We cannot go through there. He draws much less water than *Glamorgan* does. We will find ourselves aground. We cannot."

Wilson's eyes grew impossibly wider, though he whispered his response. "You would declare mutiny? Damn *you*, sir. Do your duty. Follow that ship."

"No, sir. I *am* doing my duty, to the ship and to the Crown. If we follow, you will lose your ship. You will never get another."

The two men stood, eyes locked, for long minutes. Then Wilson looked away. He turned and stalked to the taffrail, looking astern.

Barry looked after him for a moment, then turned.

"Make sail. And get those boats aboard."

Glamorgan put her stern through the wind and turned south, making a lee for the boats on her starboard side. Once they were recovered, she shaped her course close-hauled to the southeast.

It would take her more than a day to get back into open waters. Once there, Wilson could decide whether to search for the enemy or not, and Barry would support that decision. But he knew everything had changed for him. Wilson could destroy him for what he'd done. No court-martial could overlook the fact that Barry had not only disobeyed his captain's orders but told him to his face that he would. They would see why Barry had done it, but they would not sanction it.

He would find himself on half-pay on the beach. His service was ended.

Chapter Thirty-One

The next several days were uneventful as *Resolute* made her way north through the Bahama Islands then along the Florida coast and north. Then, one day out of Delaware Bay, the rising sun brought with it a call of a sail in sight to leeward.

"Sail ho. Sail, broad on the larboard bow."

Hesitant to commit to a chase, Jonas nevertheless altered course toward the stranger, edging carefully in, ready to run at a moment's notice.

Jonas looked around on deck. So many missing faces, most absent serving in prize crews. Too many were dead or so badly wounded he'd had to leave them behind, some in a prize to make their way home, or in Puerto Rico in the care of his Spanish friends. He sighed. "I'll go aloft. Set a course to intercept her, if you please."

"Aye, sir."

Jonas hoisted himself into the rigging and slowly made his way to the crosstrees and the lookout.

Minutes later, he called down, "She's a topsail schooner, steering southerly. She's going somewhere in a hurry."

Jonas made his way back down as their maneuver completed.

"She's carrying a great deal of sail for this breeze," Jonas said, moving to stand next to Masefield.

They stood silently for many minutes, for one, then two bells. The schooner was still hull down but barely. Her sails resembled dirty white stones in the freshening breeze.

"Wind's picked up, sir. I'd like to think about putting that reef back in," said Masefield.

Jonas was silent for a moment. He trusted Masefield's seamanship implicitly, but the other ship wasn't shortening sail. If *Resolute* did, it would mean a much longer chase at the least, and they'd most likely lose her after dark.

"No, not yet. There's only three hours until sunset and I don't want to lose her."

"Aye, sir, I understand. But she's only a coasting ship, methinks. She may not be worth the effort."

Jonas had thought of that, too, but he meant to try. "We'll keep at her for now."

NOW HULL UP, THE SCHOONER POUNDED IN THE seaway. Nearly every rise and fall released an explosion of spray from under her stern. The waves overtook and threatened to poop her, grabbing her stern, throwing it leeward. It was a high risk the schooner's captain ran. For Jonas, that risk proved that whatever she carried was valuable.

Given she sailed along the coast she was likely British, most American shipping having been swept from the sea. Assuming she was British, she would probably not feel threatened by *Resolute*'s approach. They'd reached the point where the chase couldn't escape. It was time to reveal their identity.

"Run up our colors, Mr. Masefield."

"Aye aye, sir. Hopkins. Run up our colors."

The flag climbed to the top of the gaff and streamed briskly off to larboard.

The chase reacted quickly.

"Deck there! She's alterin' course, sir, away. Towards the land, sir."

Jonas and Masefield exchanged glances. She had done the one thing Jonas hadn't expected. Turn toward the dangerous shore. Granted, it wasn't a lee shore, as the wind blew off the land. Nevertheless, they were south of Cape Hinlopen, and this part of the Delaware coast was known for its treacherous shoals and shallows.

"Better send the crew to quarters. I wouldn't think she'd run herself ashore. Maybe she's simply trying to give herself time to prepare for battle. Either way, she's made it difficult," Jonas said.

"Even if she is trying to win time for herself, that's a foolhardy way to do it," responded Masefield.

The two men stared out at the chase as around them *Resolute*'s reduced crew cast off extra lashings from the guns. They'd been put on only a few hours before, to keep the metal behemoths restrained despite the motion of the ship.

Resolute's motion was now similar to the schooner's, though with the extra headsail Masefield had set and the reef he'd kept in the mainsail, she carried more sail forward than aft. The greater pressure forward kept her bow off the wind, and she was less inclined to yaw strongly as the seas beat on her starboard quarter. She still rolled mightily. It was this that threatened to break guns and men loose.

Afternoon wore on. The chase continued to close the coast. Jonas continued to close the chase. Both ships had been forced to shorten sail by the steadily rising storm. In the interim, the chase had run up the anticipated Royal Navy ensign.

By six bells in the afternoon watch, he concluded he'd be able to open fire and gave the order.

The wind, nearing a full gale, shredded the smoke, casting it away as if it had never existed. Jonas tried to see the fall of shot but could not.

"Aloft, there. Did you see anything?" he called.

The lookouts had been staring at the chase, but quickly answered, "No, sir, not a thing. But they're runnin' their guns out, sir. Three this side, sir."

They were, indeed, and soon the schooner returned fire. Both crews struggled to reload against the wild gyrations of the decks beneath them, and to aim across a raging sea. Following the third broadside, Jonas was sure he saw splinters fly from the enemy's bulwarks, but her fire didn't slacken.

He gave the order to have every other gun fire high to target the schooner's rigging in the hopes of hitting a sail. With the tremendous pressure on the sails on both ships, a single hole would be a catastrophe as the sail blew itself apart like shattered glass.

A cheer forward broke his rumination. He quickly scanned the enemy vessel. There was one less headsail on her, the shreds blowing out from the stay toward *Resolute*.

The chase turned directly toward *Resolute*. He willed his crew to be faster on the reload, enabling them to fire as the enemy's bow pointed directly at them, sweeping the deck from fore to aft and wreaking a terrible slaughter.

The enemy captain was quick. He immediately put the rudder over to counter the greater pressure aft that threatened to jerk her bow into the wind. He also had the mainsail sheets started, and the sail quickly brailed up to reduce her resistance to the rudder. The schooner whipped around once the pressure came off.

Jonas reacted, too, but not as quickly. The schooner's captain had caught him by surprise. It cost Jonas precious seconds.

"Put your helm up. Mr. Masefield, wear ship, quickly."

"Hands to the braces. Start the mainsheets and brail up. Now, move!" shouted Masefield.

Slowly at first, then more rapidly, *Resolute* wore round. The gun crews made their guns fast and shifted sides, to try to get off a broadside as soon as the guns would bear.

But they didn't, and the schooner pulled ahead. A new headsail broke out forward, and would soon be bent on, raised, and set.

Jonas cursed himself and his slow reactions. Worse, the schooner had fallen off the wind further once she'd passed astern of *Resolute*, and was now to seaward, with an avenue of escape open.

With *Resolute* now astern of the schooner, neither ship could fire. Jonas considered yawing to open his broadside, but knew he'd lose too much distance. Serving the chaser was impossible with the spray coming over the bow.

As night closed in, the schooner achieved what had eluded Jonas throughout the afternoon. A chance shot flew high, struck *Resolute*'s fore topsail, which split, and with a thunderclap, shredded and disappeared. The men on the poop deck reacted immediately, not waiting for the order to release the mainsail sheets. But they couldn't move fast enough, and *Resolute*'s bow swung violently into the wind, taking the square foresail aback, throwing her into irons.

"Brail up, brail up!" bellowed both Jonas and Masefield. Even as they shouted out orders, men grabbed coils of rope off belaying pins and hauled like madmen to spill the wind from the sail, gathering it in bunches where gaff met mast. Masefield ran forward. The foresail was quickly clewed up.

"Back the heads'ls. Leave the tops'l yard alone," he cried.

Three men had grabbed the topsail halyard and were preparing to lower it. But with only ribbons and shreds of the sail flying from the yard, there was no need.

It took long minutes to get it sorted out. With the mainsail no longer acting as a weathervane, the wind on the forward faces of the fore staysail and jib thrust the bow back off the wind, though on a larboard tack. Once the mainsail was set and drawing, this time deeply reefed, *Resolute* gathered way. Soon she had enough way on to tack and resume the chase. Jonas had the foresail reset, though with such a reduction in sail, he no longer had any hope of closing to gun range before dark, let alone taking her. And it would take nearly a half an hour to get the new topsail bent on and set.

"Damn, sir, that was a lucky shot," Masefield said.

Jonas didn't answer but stood closing and opening his fists. Anger would not get him anywhere, so he pushed it aside and applied himself to deciding his next steps. As he deliberated, Masefield set about getting the wreckage of the old topsail removed and the spare one bent on and set.

The schooner had been sailing south along the coast when they'd sighted her. Therefore, it was likely she would try to continue her voyage, especially given how hard the captain had driven his ship. *He must be carrying important cargo.* Jonas assumed it must be military.

Regardless, Jonas wanted it.

AS THE STORM GREW AND THE SUN SET, THE GRAY SKY turned first darker, then to black. There were no stars, and the schooner did not deign to be helpful by lighting a stern lantern. Thus the chase disappeared, one moment a vague mass a few miles ahead, then gone.

Jonas ordered *Resolute* put about on a southerly course. The wind veered farther north as the storm center passed to the northeast, so she sailed with the wind abaft the beam, only a point to starboard from dead astern. He ordered lifelines rigged as *Resolute* gyrated like an unbroken horse.

If the schooner did what he thought she'd do, he'd given himself the best chance to find her again in the morning. He would parallel the coast. Only the morning would tell if he'd guessed correctly.

Daylight revealed an empty sea.

Jonas came on deck just before sunrise and climbed the foremast slowly and deliberately in the pre-dawn gloom. The wind had not abated, blowing still from the north. The seas were less confused and swept along with the swell from the north.

As black became gray, lightened by the hidden sun, he scanned horizon to horizon, hoping to see the white spot that marked a sail. But he saw nothing. After two hours he came stiffly down.

"I think she's slipped away. Let us close the coast a bit. Steer west-southwest for an hour. If the lookout spies the coast, come back to the southwest. There's no point getting too close," he said.

"Aye, sir. Steer west-southwest for an hour, or if we sight land. It's a might perilous if she's spent the night that close in."

"Aye. But if by chance she's farther offshore than ourselves, we'll catch her as she closes the coast at her destination."

"There's that, sir. But if her destination is as far south as Charleston? Or Savannah?" asked Masefield. "Do we want to settle in for that long a chase?"

Jonas had considered that. "I'll decide in two days' time."

Masefield gave Jonas a sidelong glance, and asked, "There's somethin' bothers you about that ship?"

Jonas didn't answer at first, looking out toward the still invisible coast of Delaware. "I'm not sure what it is. Perhaps it's that I'm not quite ready to risk going into port and finding we have run into a blockading squadron, or once we are safely alongside the quay, finding we can't get out again. Maybe it's something about how she behaved yesterday. But there is something."

Masefield said nothing. After a time, Jonas went below to look at the chart.

They saw nothing all day save storm clouds and high seas. *Resolute* labored along the coast, now and again catching a glimpse of breaking waves as they passed close to one of the barrier islands. By Jonas's reckoning, they would be at the same latitude as Cape Henry by dawn.

Night fell once more, and Jonas's hopes sank with the sun.

WATERY GRAY MARKED THE DAWN, DRIVING RAIN having been added to the wind. A second storm appeared to have followed the first, for Jonas's glass had begun to climb slightly but had sunk again.

Once more Jonas climbed to the crosstrees. Within minutes he was soaked through, but doggedly wiped his glass as he continued his slow and careful search.

Before he'd combed even a quarter of the sea around his ship, the lookout perched in the shrouds just feet above him called, "Sail ho! Sail broad on the starboard beam."

Jonas whipped his telescope around and looked. The lighter smudge on the horizon he'd been hoping for.

"On deck. Steer west-southwest. If this is the schooner, we have her!" he shouted.

Masefield gave the orders, settling *Resolute* on a course to intercept.

Jonas could immediately tell when the other vessel finally sighted *Resolute*. She put her own helm down and made for the coast again.

Unlikely she had any better idea than did Jonas where along the coast they were. It appeared to be a move of desperation rather than a deliberate attempt to make a specific port or inlet. That convinced Jonas that this was likely the same ship. As they closed her and made out her rig, he became certain.

Back on deck, he said to Masefield, "It's unlikely she'll escape us again."

Masefield looked out across the water at the chase. Hull down from the deck, he could see her sails clearly. "Perhaps, sir, but it may not be that he's desperate to get away. He might just be fool-hardy. Running toward the shore like this doesn't strike me as wise," he said.

"Nor I," said Jonas. "But I'd be surprised if he actually ran her ashore."

The chase continued through the morning and into the afternoon. Just after one bell sounded in the afternoon watch, the lookout above called, "Breakers! Breakers dead on the bow."

The cry galvanized the crew into action. Jonas ordered the helm put down toward the chase, while Masefield got the hands to the braces to avoid running aground. *Resolute* quickly turned west. Once settled on the new course, Jonas ordered sail shortened and climbed aloft to take stock. They'd made between six and eight knots for the past two days, so Jonas reckoned they now approached Cape Hatteras.

The schooner still ran along the coast. Perhaps she'd seen a gap in the barrier and was trying to make it into the shelter behind. She pulled ahead of *Resolute*, crossed the bow. Jonas worried she might escape after all.

An hour later, as all hands watched, she sailed into the breakers, apparently trying to thread her way between low lying islands. She veered suddenly to starboard. Her masts whipped forward, and first the fore topmast, then the fore topmast, fell. Her hull came to a sudden stop and slewed.

"Mr. Masefield. Heave to," Jonas called.

Masefield complied while Jonas returned to the deck. The seas were too high yet to launch boats in order to try to help the now stranded crew of the other ship. They would have to wait until the storm subsided.

They watched helplessly as the schooner's hull was beaten by ferocious seas.

Calmer seas arrived and the overcast began to break up. The wind was down to a fresh breeze and Jonas judged he could launch boats to aid the stricken ship. As dawn broke, he saw she'd been pushed farther up on the small island, and her back broken. Her rigging was a shambles, with even the lower masts broken off at deck level. Farther up the beach, a small cluster of survivors huddled miserably in a makeshift shelter comprised of wreckage from their ship.

"I'll go with the landing party. I want to meet this captain. Find out why he was so determined to escape."

"I don't believe that to be wise, sir," Masefield said.

"I understand. But I trust you will retrieve us if need be."

Masefield snorted. "Sir, ye'll be takin' most of the crew with you. How exactly will I retrieve ye?"

Jonas smiled. "Well, perhaps not quickly. You could anchor for a day or two, if you needed to."

Masefield shook his head, took his leave, and moved forward to ensure the boat was launched.

The survivors barely looked up as the boats grounded the leeward side of the island. At the height of the storm, the waves must nearly have washed across it.

"Who's in command?" Jonas asked as they neared the group. Several men were injured, and the clothing they wore showed the effects of shipwreck and nearly fourteen hours' exposure to the elements.

A man rose unsteadily and said, "I guess I am, sir. Who may you be?"

Jonas responded, "I'm Captain Jonas Hawke, privateer *Resolute*. I must ask, sir, why you chose to go aground rather than let me take you."

The man grunted and sat back down, now facing Jonas.

"I didn't 'choose' to go ashore. The captain did. 'Twas the last act of 'is life."

"Then who are you?"

"John Wade, late sailing master of 'is Majesty's schooner

Shark. Captain Townshend died, though I don't think 'e'd have lived much longer, even 'ad 'e not driven 'er ashore. The same ball that took our first lieutenant's 'ead also took the captain's arm. Seeing as 'e refused to go below, 'e bled rather much. I don't think 'e was right in the 'ead by the time we sighted you yesterday morning, sir," came the rough reply.

"Why drive her ashore? Why stay on deck? Surely he could have turned command over to you."

Wade looked at Jonas and shook his head. "I've no idea, sir. 'E were a quiet type. No man aboard knew him well, not even Lieutenant 'Igby. Since we sailed from New York, 'e's been driving 'er and 'isself right 'ard, 'e was."

"What was your cargo?"

Wade looked strangely at Jonas. "That's a mystery, init? We don't 'ave no cargo, sir, not really. We 'ad a 'undred extra barrels o' flour and salt pork, but no cargo to speak of."

Wade answered a few more questions as Jonas's men took possession of the few arms the survivors carried.

"Can we help bury your dead?" Jonas asked Wade.

"No. We did it ourselves, early this morning," Wade responded.

Jonas nodded. "We will take you aboard. Gather what you want to take."

"As prisoners?"

Jonas shook his head. "As shipwreck survivors."

The group moved back across the island to the boats.

As they moved away, Jonas and his coxswain walked to the wreck. The sea had left off trying to erase it from the face of the earth, at least for now, and the low tide had left it high and relatively dry. Jonas climbed aboard and made his way carefully and slowly aft to where the captain's cabin, or what remained of it, was. Entering it, he began methodically looking through drawers. Coming upon a locked drawer in the desk, he looked around for something with which to pry it open. Taking up the dead man's sword, he used it to pry the drawer open. Inside lay a package wrapped in oiled canvas with a wax seal. Jonas broke the seal and read:

From His Majesty's Commander in Chief,
North American Station

To His Majesty's Commander in Chief,
West Indies Station

I have the honour to be, etc...

Jonas's eyes widened as he read, and his hands began to shake.

He held in his hand the coordination documents for an invasion of Maryland from the West Indies.

Calling to the coxswain, he made his way back on deck. Barrett had checked the hold as best he could without becoming tangled in wreckage and reported that anything below was likely spoiled.

"Never mind, I've found what they were carrying. We need to get back aboard and make for home."

CHAPTER THIRTY-TWO

Resolute took three days to win back the distance she'd lost chasing *Shark*.

The storm had blown itself out, but the wind remained stubbornly out of the north. *Resolute* was forced to tack twice a day to obtain the vicinity of Cape Hinlopen again to enter Delaware Bay and the Delaware River.

She was fortunate in that she saw no other sails save small coasting schooners, until she was on her last leg, steering west-northwest toward the entrance of the bay. With the clearing weather, Jonas had been able to take a sight on the sun at sunrise to get a firm latitude, and a good estimate of longitude that placed him ten leagues from land.

"Sail ho! Sail three points abaft the starboard beam."

"Our fortune has run out, John. I feel it," said Jonas. The two men stood on the quarterdeck, each hoping that as they closed the coast they'd not be seen by, nor see, any other ships. Each knew the odds were that any sail sighted was more likely an enemy than not.

"Perhaps, sir. Maybe it's another trade ship, though. Why d'ye feel that way with this one?"

"Because we're so close to Philadelphia. You may be right, but I'll not make a wager on it."

Forward, nearly all hands on deck looked off to windward, even those working on make and mend. They couldn't yet see the stranger, but their eyes were irresistibly drawn toward what they all suspected was danger. They'd been that way for days, ever since entering colonial waters, well before they'd chased *Shark*.

"Let's get another headsail on her, and the t'gallant," Jonas directed.

As Masefield moved forward calling out orders, Jonas turned to the stranger and waited.

The next hour dragged by. Bells sounded and the watch changed. The stranger had altered course to intercept them shortly after they'd sighted her. Jonas went aloft to look for himself.

A full rigged ship, his heart sank further.

Now the sails were visible from the deck. Anxiety grew.

Jonas ordered the main staysails set aloft and alow, and *Resolute* heeled farther over. She sailed as close-hauled as she could be made to go without loss of speed. Spray careened over her starboard side as the seas pounded her hull, and her larboard rail occasionally went under as the seas passed beneath her.

The stranger no longer closed as quickly, as she couldn't point up quite as close to the wind.

Though the courses of both were shaped toward the shore, there was a limit to how far Jonas could run. He hoped his position allowed him to make the bay. If he needed to, he could run her ashore there and get the crew safely away. He hated such thoughts that protruded into his mind, but he had to consider every option.

"Land ho! Land one point off the starboard bow."

Jonas found himself halfway up the starboard shrouds. His heart beat wildly as he raised his telescope. He nearly laughed with relief. Cape May, lying low to the horizon, right where it would do the most good.

The larger ship, whatever it was, must have a greater draught than did *Resolute*. Thus, the stranger had to pass further south to remain in deeper water. It would be like the chase they had escaped in the Bahamas only a fortnight before.

It would also be a near run thing. Jonas could gain distance on her, perhaps even getting to the mouth of the Delaware River.

Of course, where do I go after that?

The two ships continued their approach to Delaware Bay, *Resolute* in the lead. Jonas estimated the flood had just started and would be near its maximum as he entered the mouth of the river.

If he were able to get that far. He hoped there hadn't been much rain upriver, so the flood would better counter the outflow from the river.

With Masefield periodically reminding the lookouts to keep a sharp eye out for shoal water, Jonas kept *Resolute* as close to the wind as possible. The hours dragged by with the speed of a glacier.

Just as four bells were sounded, two o'clock, Jonas and Masefield stood at the taffrail looking aft. A distant gun sounded forward. Both men whipped around with their telescopes, searching for telltale smoke. They saw none, but the lookout had.

"Deck there! There's a fort on the point to starboard, sir."

"Cape May?" asked Masefield, his face showing his puzzlement.

"Apparently. But whose?" replied Jonas. "Raise our standard. We'll know soon enough if they're friend or foe."

As the flag rose snapping up the halyard, they waited. No more gunfire erupted. With the passing minutes, their hope for an escape rose, though the bay entrance was wide enough for the stranger to avoid coming under fire.

As *Resolute* passed clear of the fort, Jonas made out the yellow flag flying above it, similar to his own and confirming the fort's allegiance. Moments later, they heard more gunfire, this time to the south. Jonas turned just in time to see the smoke from what appeared to have been at least four cannons whipped away from Cape Hinlopen.

Next to him, Masefield spoke. "They're firin' at the stranger, sir. Three splashes 'bout half mile off her larboard bow. We have friends on both sides of the water, t'appears," he said.

"The entrance is too wide to hit her, but they could drive her toward the shoal that's mid-channel, if they keep up their fire. Let's hope they can."

The fort did keep up their fire, forcing the stranger to give up. When she rounded to and stood back out to sea, Jonas's crew gave a ragged cheer.

Grinning, Jonas crossed to where Masefield stood, saying, "We've been blessed by the Almighty with good fortune, again, having done nothing to deserve it. I feared we would be taken, having gotten so close. Now, I believe we will make it."

***

RESOLUTE ANCHORED BEYOND PHILADELPHIA'S teeming wharves as there was no room for her pierside.

In fact, there was precious little room for her to swing at anchor. It was fortunate that the flow of the river left all ships dangling at their anchor rodes with bows pointed upstream, not needing the span they'd require in a roadstead.

They'd passed one more fort on the river bend below the city. As before, their flag had gotten them through. The anchor secure, Jonas had a boat lowered and went ashore.

The smoke hung low over the city, fed by myriad hearth fires blazing in homes and shops against the midwinter chill. The gray overcast threatened snow and contributed to the pall that lay just above the rooftops.

Jonas had been many times to Philadelphia and recognized the major landmarks that climbed above their neighbors. Both St. Peter's and Christ Church stood out, as did the Pennsylvania

State House. There was a tall, new brick building in between them, looking like it was along Chestnut Street, and Jonas wondered idly what it might be.

Gaining the quay wall, he ordered his coxswain to make fast and wait. He allowed the men to adjourn to a small shack just off the quay, placed for boat crews to keep warm and out of the weather. Moving off, he walked toward the State House. It was where he thought he'd find the Congress and its Marine Committee.

It came as a shock when he found no such thing.

Searching the empty State House, he finally found a gentleman in the courtroom at a small desk.

"Can you tell me where I might find someone from the Marine Committee?" he asked the man.

The man, middle-aged, and nearsighted with white powdered wig, peered over his spectacles, regarding Jonas as if he were daft.

"Well, you've missed them by, oh, I'd say nearly six weeks," he responded. Raising his head, he put his quill in its holder and leaned back in his seat, stretching his shoulders.

"Don't you know the whole kit and caboodle moved to Baltimore? The British were up in Trenton, you know, until Christmas Day when General Washington captured them Hessians. They're still just the other side. If they attack, they could be here in days." Leaning forward once more, he moved whatever document he'd been writing and folded his hands on the desk. "Of course, they 'could be here in days' for the past two months, now. What with moving them out of Trenton, I think it's a bit less likely," he added, his mouth quirking in a sardonic half smile. "There's been a lot of fighting this month, with the British trying to retake Trenton and chase General Washington back here. I think they are worn out by now, though. Meantime, what can I do for you?" he asked.

Jonas considered before answering. "I believe I have business with the Committee. I've come into, er, information, that they might desire."

The man tilted his head slightly, eyes lighting up with interest for the first time. "Very good. First, of course, who are you, son?"

"My name is Jonas Hawke. I've a privateer's commission and have been these past four months in the Caribbean." Not wanting to simply share his information with just anyone, he held back how he'd come by it. "I thought this information important enough to return here immediately," he prevaricated.

The man studied Jonas. After a moment, he appeared to reach a decision. "Well, as I said, you can find them in Baltimore. Congress has relocated. I'll give you the man to talk to there. Note, sir, that I'm also not asking you to reveal your information. While the British have shown only a little interest in actually moving on Philadelphia, at least not until after the winter is over, we are ever cautious, lest loyalists find their way into our confidence and betray us."

Jonas was grateful for the man's reticence to reveal confidences.

"You may want to go overland, Captain Hawke. The Royal Navy has a squadron in the Chesapeake, two ships-of-the line and several frigates. I would avoid them, if I were in your shoes."

They spoke for a few minutes more about how Jonas might get to Baltimore and avoid entanglements with the British army.

Then, retrieving the paper on which the man wrote a short letter of introduction for Jonas to a Mr. Johnson, he thanked him and departed.

As he returned to the quay, it began to snow.

Aboard *Resolute* he took Masefield aft to the stern rail.

"The British army is near Trenton, so Congress relocated to Baltimore. I need to meet with someone from the Marine Committee. I'll go overland while you begin the refit."

"Aye, sir," Masefield responded, then paused. Clearing his

throat, he continued. "Sir, I've never questioned ye, and I'm not questioning yer orders now. But what drives ye to seek out the Committee? Ye were hell bent on getting to Newport before. Now ye've got this errand with the Marine Committee. I know what they're about. They're building frigates and making a navy. Are you thinking of putting us in that navy?"

Surprised, Jonas answered, "No." He shook his head. "None of you signed up to join any navy, and I don't see myself doing that, either." He paused briefly. "I'm sure Barrett told you I found a document in the wreck of the *Shark*. It contained an order from Admiral Howe to bring a fleet up from the West Indies and use it to move an army to Maryland. They plan an attack on Baltimore and Philadelphia from the south. I need to get that information to the Committee. I've met Mr. Hopkins before, when I was in Newport. They must have time to prepare as best they can."

Masefield grunted. "Aye, there's no secrets aboard ship, sir, as you well know. Barrett mentioned it to his mates. I heard about it in due course. I don't blame you for holding it close to your chest."

He looked off at the brown haze covering the city and the falling snow. It had begun to coat both running and standing rigging, the guns and bulwarks, and the deck threatened to grow slippery. "You need to tell them about it, sir. But why go over-land? *Resolute* could land you near there in a few days."

"No. I also learned the British have a strong naval presence in the Chesapeake. It would be worse than foolish to try to get to Baltimore by sea. I'll get my seabag and hire a horse. Please have the boat and crew ready by eight bells. The crew may have liberty, though I'd like you to keep half of them on board and sober, in case the British do come. Until Christmas Day, they were *in* Trenton, just upriver. General Washington rousted them out, but they're still near there. I'm told that if they were to attack, it might not be difficult for them to take the city." He pondered what else could be done. "See what you can get done by way of refitting, too. Nothing that would keep you from standing out to sea again, if need be. But whatever you think we ought. Here's the key to the strongbox with our funds."

Masefield took the key and acknowledged Jonas's orders, then left Jonas to pack.

Chapter Thirty-Three

Three days later, Jonas stood on the street outside Mr. Henry Fite's tavern. The Continental Congress was supposed to be in session.

A large stone edifice, it took up nearly the whole block in length, and appeared half a block deep. Saving the steeple of St. Paul's, it was the tallest building in Baltimore. Jonas could see why Congress had chosen this site. He opened the door and went inside.

He entered a long hall that looked like it went all the way to the back of the building. Paneled in rich, dark wood, there were four doorways down the length of the hall, two to each side. The one to Jonas's immediate right had no door, only a frame. It entered into the public room, which was populated by tables and a long counter set against the back wall. Three small groups of men with drinks sat at the tables, talking earnestly. Jonas did not recognize any of them and moved on.

To his left, the frame held a closed door. Behind the door, he heard seemingly several voices, and at least two were raised in what might be called passionate speech. He judged this might be the main meeting room, but as it was closed, he forbore entrance.

Continuing to the back, the second door was the entrance to a kitchen area, while the door across the hall opened into a stairway to the second story. Jonas returned to the public room.

Moving to the first group nearest the door, he said, "Excuse me, gentlemen, I was looking for Mr. Stephen Hopkins."

The men stopped talking and all four looked at him, clearly sizing him up. A rather large man with a rosy, sweaty face that glowed above a ruffled shirt and brown waistcoat answered him. "Who might you be, sir?"

Jonas introduced himself, to which the man replied, "Well met, Captain Hawke. If you're one of those giving the British hell, we'll all be glad to meet you, especially members of the Naval Committee. Mr. Hopkins is across the hall. I'll take you to him."

He rose and introduced himself and the men he was with. "I'm Benjamin Harrison. This is Mr. Johnson, across the table is Mr. Jay, and to my right is Mr. Morris."

Mumbled greetings from the men rose to meet Jonas: "Your servant, Captain.", "A pleasure, sir.", and "Privileged, Captain."

"Your servant, gentlemen," said Jonas. Turning back to Mr. Harrison, he said, "I thank you, sir. I do not mean to be rude, but time is short and the information I bring is of uncertain value. I wish to convey it to those who might determine its value and if it must be acted upon."

Harrison looked shrewdly at Jonas, and said, "Well, gentlemen, I for one could stand to step away from our little debate for a moment or two. Pray do not take any hasty decisions in my absence."

Morris and Jay both snorted, and Johnson nearly laughed out loud. The three men nodded to Jonas and returned to their drinks and conversation. Harrison took Jonas's elbow and walked him across the hall. Not stopping to knock, he opened the door.

Entering, Jonas saw that the room was actually divided into three. The main meeting hall had two doors opposite the main door through which they'd entered. Both doors were open and showed smaller meeting rooms where groups of men talked. From the one on the right issued loud, discordant voices, clearly arguing.

In the main meeting hall, three of the corners were occupied by small groups of men speaking in more hushed tones to avoid creating a cacophony.

Harrison led Jonas to the group in the far corner, where Jonas recognized Stephen Hopkins's face.

"Hopkins, I bring you a sea captain who actually fights the enemy while we only talk of it."

Hopkins turned from where he appeared to have been making a point to the others and straightened.

"Mr. Harrison, if I took you at your word that it was important every time you interrupted a meeting, I would get nothing done. Yet, here I am, again, assuming the worst, that it is indeed important." He turned to Jonas and said, "Your servant, sir. What brings you to me?"

"You won't remember, sir, but we've met before in Newport, early last year. I worked with Jonathan Trimble, my brother-in-law, who introduced us at a shipper's ball. I also talked to your brother about service in the navy. My name is Jonas Hawke, of the privateer *Resolute*."

Hopkins's face took on a speculative look. Slowly recognition dawned. "I certainly remember Jonathan. I believe I remember you, as well, though it seems so very long ago. What can I do for you, sir?"

Jonas told his story and pulled out the package he'd found in the captain's cabin aboard *Shark*. Hopkins took it eagerly and opened it, reading silently. The men at the table stood to read over his shoulder. Only the low conversations from the other two groups remained to break the silence.

After a few minutes, Hopkins looked up. "Good heavens. You were right to bring this to us. General Washington has successfully defended Philadelphia to date, though that situation remains delicately balanced. Such a move would cause a collapse of our army in Pennsylvania and New Jersey. Congress would be forced to move further south, perhaps to Richmond. Worse, it would destroy the morale we've only just begun to rebuild in the army and with our people." Hopkins sat. "You say you've just come from the Caribbean. Do the British have the forces there to carry out this plan?" he asked.

"Sir, I can't say for certain. As you might expect, I have tried to avoid British forces. But I have friends in San Juan, who have passed information to me, though primarily of naval forces."

"Well, come, Captain, what do your 'friends' tell you? Did they say anything at all of the land forces?" asked another man.

Hopkins introduced him. "This is Mr. Richard Lee, another member of the Committee. He is from Virginia. He would not, I believe, like to see the British in Maryland."

"Indeed, I would not, not only for Virginia's sake, but for our independence. If we cannot hold in New England, we cannot win. If the British chase our army into and then through the south, where will we end up? In Florida? Louisiana, perhaps? The French and Spanish will not abide that."

Lee smiled, though his smile didn't reach his eyes. He sat back in his chair. "In all truth, Captain, if the British are able to bring another army to bear, it is questionable whether we could prevail. This information is possibly key to our survival."

"Mr. Lee, I can only say that it appears there are no large land forces in the Caribbean. Of course, each island has soldiers, but I'm told they are under strength, having little in the way of enemies about. As to ships, I have been chased twice by a sloop and was able to make good my escape. They suffer from rot, having been built of green wood. However, even a rotting ship with cannon is a threat, sir, and cannot be discounted. Are there enough ships to move an army to Maryland? I believe there are." Jonas paused to think.

"Having said that, I also believe that they must begin to occupy at least some ships in convoy duty, the result of our privateering efforts. I make no boast of my own small efforts. But the Spaniards say there are large numbers of American private ships of war, who have taken or destroyed a great many ships. My friends in San Juan tell me insurance rates have doubled, and British merchants are demanding protection by their Navy. Necessarily, any invasion of Maryland would take from those convoys. In addition, to carry soldiers and their supplies means they must acquire merchant hulls, which would likely take some time. Yet, it could be done."

Hopkins and Lee regarded Jonas, then turned to confer.

The third man, a Mr. Heyward, spoke first. "We must bring this to the attention of the general assembly, of course, but also send a dispatch to General Washington. He must know the risk. General Howe will have sent more than one copy of the order to Admiral Gayton in the West Indies. It is likely to be enroute even now, or possibly might have arrived. We must be prepared."

"I do not think informing General Washington is a good idea. He is ill prepared for the fight he has and cannot prepare for a fight behind his position. It would divide his force and leave both even more vulnerable than they already are," said Hopkins.

Lee sat back and listened to the other two as the discussion waged back and forth. At one point, he smiled at Jonas, who remained standing, unsure whether to leave or to stay. Lee's demeanor didn't indicate he should leave, so he didn't.

At last, Lee said, "Gentlemen, we are not the proper decision-making committee. You both make good arguments, but the decision is not ours. Let us make the arguments to the general assembly and seek a decision there. I, myself, will argue that we call on the Carolinas and Georgia to raise another army, quickly, and send it north. I will send to Richmond and Williamsburg to see if Virginia can raise another regiment or two, though to say it would be difficult is to underestimate the situation."

Hopkins and Heyward both nodded. Hopkins turned to Jonas. "It is greatly to your credit to bring us the information you have, and you have our..." When he glanced around the table, his companions nodded. "... thanks."

Turning back to the others, he said, "And now, I think it is time to sup. I for one am peckish, and I'll wager that Captain Hawke has not eaten, either?" He looked the question at Jonas, who shook his head. "Very well, then, we will adjourn and return in an hour. Gentlemen."

Hopkins took Jonas by the elbow and led him to the public room, where he sat at one of the few unoccupied tables in the far corner of the room. Despite the shutters being open, the room was dimly lighted, the fire in the hearth providing more illumination than the windows.

"You've done well, Captain, and if we can guide the assembly to actually making a decision, it will help not just find a way to face this new threat, but also help with our unity. We still find ourselves not entirely comfortable with our independence, let alone fully prosecuting the war."

"Even with the Declaration, sir? There are those who would rescind it? How? The king would not forgive it so easily, I suspect," Jonas replied.

"Oh, no, he would not. Nor is there anyone in Congress who, if put to the test, would repudiate the document we signed, for we signed it in our own blood. That does not prevent some, shall we call it hesitation, when it comes to taking more bold measures to win this war." He took a long pull from his beer. "We are the naval committee, yet we have no real navy to manage. Some of the ships we've procured have sailed, some have met with a modicum of success, and others have been captured. Of frigates, three have launched and three more burned to prevent capture. Only one is fully armed and ready. You might have seen her anchored north of the city. She's the *Delaware,* and she supports General Washington. Two more have been commissioned but are blockaded in Narragansett Bay. *Randolph* is also anchored off Philadelphia, fitting out. We hope she'll be able to get to sea in the next month."

Hopkins shook his head and looked around the room. "There are three more we hope will commission in the next few months. Four more we had hoped to complete, but with the British pressing near where they're being built, we despair, and they may have to be burned. We even have one which we cannot get to sea at all. It seems when she was laid down, no one took account of the depth of water across the bar, even at spring tide. She draws too much. In the end, it is the privateers that have truly taken the war to sea. Men like you and your crew. They — you — are truly our best hope, for you take the war to the English merchant in the form of increased insurance, and to the English public in increased expense. Oh, we have a few other vessels in commission, and they've had some successes, some even markedly so. It will ever be to their credit that they've done so well against one of the premier navies in history. But they are few and far between, and they cannot do the economic damage the privateers can."

"I thank you for the kind words, sir. I assure you we are doing our best. But for every ship we capture, many others get through. Even those we capture are sometimes recaptured and arrive at their destination with their cargoes intact or nearly so. It often feels like we are a flea attacking a very large dog."

Hopkins laughed and sat back. "Well, even fleas can bring down a large dog, if there are enough of them. Here's to the fleas," he toasted as he raised his glass.

Jonas raised his as well, and the two men spent an amiable hour.

As he and Hopkins rose to depart, Hopkins said, "You know, Captain, you should consider joining our nascent navy. You strike me as a straightforward man, and you think clearly. You also seem to have a view of how difficult this war will be. We need captains such as you, who are able to fight. We pay the navy prize money, too, though, of course, you keep more as a privateer."

Jonas did not hesitate. He said, "No, sir, though I thank you."

As Hopkins moved to speak, Jonas raised his hand. "No, sir, it is not the money, though I need to provide for my family. It is that I have been my own master for fifteen years and more. I do not suggest that you or anyone else meddles in how the ships are run, but I want to be able to decide whence I go, and what to do when I get there. Once more, I thank you, but I cannot, not now."

Hopkins sighed. "I understand, though I cannot but wish you would choose differently. However, may God bless you and your crew, and bring you success."

With that, the two men parted. Jonas began the return journey to Philadelphia.

BACK IN PHILADELPHIA AND KNOWING NOW WHAT TO look for, he saw *Randolph* anchored off the builder's ways on the southern side of the city. Her masts were in with standing rigging set up, and most of her running rigging, as well. But she had no sails yet adorning her yards. Her bare masts resembled the winter trees that lined the riverbanks. She also rode high enough in the water that she couldn't have stores aboard, though through the open gunports he could see she had at least some of her guns in. He heard the thump of a carpenter's mallet from her direction. He estimated it would be another month before she was ready for sea.

He found *Resolute* easily enough, though she was now alongside the quay. From her, too, issued the thumps of carpenter's hammers, and he saw that Masefield had the fore topsail yard and topmast down to be replaced. He went aboard.

"Pass the word for Mr. Masefield, Simpson," he said to the first man he saw.

Simpson sat on a bucket near the capstan, mending a seam on the fore topsail, which was spread on the deck forward of where he sat. Simpson looked up. Upon recognizing Jonas, he immediately stood.

"Aye, sir, I'll get him," he said and disappeared down the nearest hatch.

"Welcome back, sir," said Masefield but a few moments later, rising from the same hatch with Simpson right behind. The sailor settled back on his bucket and took up needle and palm once again.

"It's good to be back. I see you've wasted no time. I take it that the topm'st was as rotten as we feared?"

"Aye, it was, and there was a weak spot in the t'gallant yard, too. But if we cut down the topmast, it can be a new t'gallant yard, so we really only need a topm'st," he replied.

"Very good, very good indeed. Have we any word on our prizes?" Jonas asked.

Masefield sighed and gave him the bad news. "We already knew *Mythos* was captured when she came into the Chesapeake, sir. But we got word her crew were sent to New York, to a prison ship. We've had four of her crew rejoin us. They went overboard when she was captured. They say Tilton had no choice but to strike. He entered the bay in a fog and ran straight into an anchored warship."

Jonas looked down at the deck. He pictured the situation, men doing their best to save themselves while realizing their ship was doomed.

It was a blow, indeed. Like all sailors, he knew of prison ships. Their reputation was widespread as a place where many men who disappeared aboard never came ashore again. There were daily burials aboard those hellholes.

"Are they aboard now? I'd like to meet with them later."

"Aye, sir, they are. If ye don't mind me asking, what's next?"

"We refit here. I'm going up to Newport to bring my family back. It appears that Philadelphia is as safe as anywhere. That is, not very. Now that Congress knows about the British plans, they will have to deal with them, though I do not know how. General Washington has done well, apparently, to keep the British out of Pennsylvania. If the British are able to land an army in Maryland, it could be the end. If that comes, I'd prefer Mary and the children were here. I can make arrangements for them to escape back to Virginia." He looked at Masefield. "What about Sally and your children?" he asked.

Masefield grunted. "They'll be safe in the Shenandoah Valley. I know you thought I was crazy to send them there with the problems with the Indians. But, as I said then, I feel better with them out there than near where the British are. With Norfolk gone, there isn't anything to keep them there."

Most of his crew, those who were married, at least, had moved their families farther inland, going against the sailor's grain. He wished he'd done the same.

"I'll depart within the hour, John. If there's need for a man to go home, have him paid off and signed out. We should be able to replace small numbers here, at least. Word will get around that we've had some success and it should make recruiting easier. I'll be back in a few weeks. That should be plenty of time to get at the hull seams and replace what planks need it, and overhaul the rigging. If there's need for me to return immediately, send word. I'll only be there for a fortnight to conclude any business there and get them moved."

"Aye, sir. Godspeed, sir. We'll get her ready for sea again."

Jonas went below to pack.

Chapter Thirty-Four

Jonas crept through the trees, careful not to make noise and to remain on the animal path he'd been following the past several miles.

It was approaching dawn, and the sky was lightening to the east. He worried about having the light behind him, but he couldn't stop, not now. He was so close.

He'd been on the road for ten days now. The first nine had been fairly easy, walking the high road between Philadelphia and Newport. He'd skirted Trenton, New York, and Hartford to keep away from the British. A few times, he'd taken coastal vessels or boats for short distances.

At first, he'd stopped and slept at inns, as did normal travelers. But that had ended yesterday midday. He'd stopped at an inn in Tiverton and taken a room. The innkeeper hadn't shown any surprise at Jonas taking a room so early in the day.

"Thinking to start traveling after dark, are ye, sir?" the innkeeper had asked.

Taken aback, Jonas had responded, "What makes you ask such a question? I'm simply tired is all."

The innkeeper had winked at him and smiled. He said no more, simply brought the ale and meat pie that Jonas had requested to the room and left silently. When he'd finished his meal, Jonas had slept.

He had left just an hour before midnight, hoisted his small sea bag onto his shoulders and disappeared into the night.

Since then he'd kept to the shadows and the woods as he made his way south along the western side of Narragansett Bay. He was fortunate. There was no snow on the ground and the soil was sufficiently frozen to keep from showing too much of his footprints. He knew approximately where the British would have skirmishers and patrols out, having asked the Continental soldiers whose lines he'd crossed yesterday morning.

Technically, he found himself between the two armies, though there was little fighting at this point. The Continental Army was willing to besiege the British occupying Newport, and the British were too small in number to break the siege. Most importantly, the British General Clinton had found Newport to his liking and had no desire to leave.

Jonas heard a twig snap ahead and froze.

After a minute, a hare came down the trail toward him. Standing up on its hind legs in the dimness, Jonas could imagine it wrinkling its nose. It turned suddenly, bounding off to the right and into the underbrush.

Jonas began to move again. Rounding a large boulder, he found himself at the water's edge. Beyond were the lights of Middleton, just beginning to waken.

An hour later found Jonas pulling a boat he had appropriated up into the grass along the water's edge. He pulled bushes from the sand and hid the boat. Done, he began to walk south.

His information thus far about British patrols and sentries had been accurate. The British, believing the Continentals could not mount an invasion of Aquidneck Island across the lower half of East Narragansett Bay, had placed minimal fortifications or watches.

Jonas imagined that the smugglers and spies who moved along

the path he also trod had great incentive to ensure it remained that way.

He continued quietly south, toward Newport.

It was midmorning when he arrived at his sister's home near South Street. It sat quietly in the cold morning, though smoke curled gently from the south chimney. He'd passed several British soldiers as they made their morning rounds or carried out errands on behalf of their officers.

The door to the house suddenly opened. Out of abundant caution, Jonas ducked behind an oak tree at the corner of the yard. He saw with dismay and growing fear that a British officer came through the door, walked down the steps, and strode off in the direction of the waterfront. Stupefied, he realized he couldn't risk going to the door.

Jonas turned and moved off down the street toward Taylor's Wharf, the location of his brother-in-law's shipping office. Arriving, he stood across Thames Street to observe before he tried to go in.

Traffic was much reduced by the waterfront from what Jonas remembered when he'd previously worked here. There were ships moored at the wharves but not very many, and nearly all had their sails stowed, their topmasts down and looked laid up.

He waited.

Nearly twenty minutes later he saw a man emerge from the office near the foot of the pier.

He was clad in a long coat against the cold and walked with a limp. Tall and thin despite the bulk of the coat, he was the right height for Jonathan Trimble. But Trimble had been an ample man.

Jonas moved down the street and crossed so the man would have to walk by him going the opposite way.

The man kept his eyes to the ground as if deep in thought, but Jonas recognized him.

"Jonathan. Jonathan," he said, carefully keeping his voice low, while urgently trying to get his brother-in-law's attention.

Trimble looked up and recognition slowly dawned. "Jonas. Thanks be to God, you're alive and safe. We hadn't heard for months now and feared you lost. What are you doing here?"

"Looking for Mary and the children. I went by your home, but saw a British soldier come out, so I stayed away," Jonas replied.

Trimble gave Jonas an anguished look and Jonas's heart sank.

"What's happened, Jonathan?" Jonas's question came out in an agonized whisper. He felt the buildings and the street swirl around him as he awaited the answer. The few people who hurried along on their business disappeared. For Jonas, it was as if the two men stood alone.

Trimble stared at him for a long moment, then sighed and closed his eyes. Through clenched teeth, he said, "Mary is dead, Jonas. Dead these past three months and more. I'm sorry."

Trimble opened his eyes. Jonas saw the pain seared into his soul.

Reaching out to put his hand on Jonas's shoulder, Trimble continued. "Come, come to the house. We'll talk and get you food and something to drink. The children are there." Getting no response from Jonas, he repeated, "Do you hear? The children are there."

Somewhere deep inside, Jonas heard, but his mind was still dealing with the blow.

Mary was dead.

She'd feared for so long that he would not come home, having been killed at sea. Yet here it was. He was alive and had returned. It was she who was gone.

"Jonas? Come, man, come home with me."

Trimble took Jonas by the arm and steered him along Thames Street, toward and then up Queen Street. Very few people were about this morning, and the silence of the street screamed of death and fear.

After a couple of blocks, Jonas found his voice.

"How, Jonathan? How did it happen? And the children, are they alright?"

"The children are healthy, though destroyed, of course. We'll talk when we're inside. It's not always safe to talk in the street."

Jonas held his questions for the rest of the ten minutes it took to reach Trimble's new home. Entering a building through a side door, the two men climbed the stairs to the second floor. Trimble entered the door to the left, toward the street. The door to the right must be another set of rooms, Jonas thought idly.

Entering the Trimble home, Jonas saw his two children on a settee in front of a fire. William read quietly to Rebecca, who was covered in a blanket with her eyes half closed. The room was chilly, despite the fire.

At that moment Martha walked in from the back and nearly dropped the mugs she carried. "Jonas."

At her exclamation, the two children looked up. William stood quickly, dropping the book to the floor. Rebecca's eyes grew wide and a large smile lit her face. She ran to his embrace.

William did not smile, his eyes nearly vacant as he looked at his father. Jonas moved to him and gathered him up, as well.

They stood that way for long minutes, sorrow and joy mingling and washing around them like the confused waves of a storm. Finally, they separated, and Rebecca lay back down under the blanket. But her eyes never left her father.

"Martha, I've told him the worst already," Trimble said gently.

Martha looked first fearfully at Trimble, then at Jonas. As Jonas released his children, she hurriedly handed the mugs to William, who made Rebecca take one. Rebecca's smile faded as she gazed at her father and saw his tortured expression.

She began to cry softly.

"Rebecca has a cold, Jonas, so we're keeping her warm. You're welcome to some tea. I may have some biscuits from breakfast, if you're hungry," said Martha.

Turning to her, Jonas said, "That's fine." Even to himself, his voice sounded hollow.

"I'm so sorry, Jonas," she whispered. She reached out, hugged him tightly, and then turned and left.

Trimble moved to a chair and sat. Jonas turned back to his children.

Rebecca stared at him. William's eyes were now downcast, and a tear dripped off his nose. "I'm so grateful you both are alright. I know it's been hard since I left, ever so hard. But we're together again," Jonas told them.

William's shoulders sagged even further. Finally lifting his eyes to his father, he said, "But it's my fault she's dead, sir. All my fault."

Jonas was taken aback by the ferocity in his son's tone.

"No, William, it's not. I've told you, it's not." This came from Trimble, his gentle voice firm.

"Of course, it's not, William. How could it be?" added Jonas.

Jonas hadn't thought it possible for his son's face to look more agonized.

William took long moments to gain sufficient control of his voice. "Yes, it is, father. I was there. *I was there.*" He could no longer speak, but simply stood there, eyes begging, pleading for forgiveness, his stance begging for punishment.

Trimble sighed and took up the tale. "It were December, Jonas, the 10th day. The British and Hessians sailed boldly right up the bay and landed south of town. The militia wasn't prepared and fired hardly a shot. Mostly, they tried to get their cannon out of the town. They still left many behind." He looked out the window.

"Seeing the militia retreat, many of us tried to leave as well. We expected the loyalists to turn on us, and that the British would do what they've done elsewhere. Confiscate our property and turn us out. God's truth, Jonas, it was shameful. No one defended our city at all."

Trimble stood and moved to look out of the one window in the room. He appeared to be reliving the day the British had come. Martha returned to the room. "Rebecca, come with me, dear. We'll get you to bed."

"But I want to stay with father." Martha ignored her pleadings and picked her up, carrying her from the room.

Jonas was grateful.

Trimble continued. "The British had been here a week. I was at the house when one of Clinton's men told me the general wanted my home. We began to pack just the barest of things we would need. I had to go back to the office to get money from the strongbox. By the time I returned home, it was too late."

He turned to face Jonas. But before he could continue, William took up the story. "I was taking our things down the stairs to the carriage in back when I heard mother shouting at someone on the front porch. She was telling them to get away from the house, that they could have it when we had left. I heard a man laugh and say that they'd have it now." A sob escaped. "I came out on the porch from the back just as a soldier pushed mother away from the door. I got angry..." William's voice faltered and he cast his eyes downward again. Another tear rolled down his cheek and off his chin.

Jonas put his arm around him, but William pulled away.

Taking a deep breath, the boy continued. "I ran to push the man away from mother. There were two other men on the porch, and—" He paused again, but quickly pushed on. "One of the men called me a rapscallion and picked up his musket. I expect he planned to hit me. I heard mother cry out—" He couldn't continue, but stood there, his body wracked with silent sobs.

"Mary stepped in front of the musket, Jonas. William was right, the soldier was going to strike him down, a boy, for God's sake. Instead, Mary was hit in the head. She must have died quickly, may God rest her soul."

Silence reigned. Jonas could see in his mind Mary throwing herself between her son and the enemy. He could see the musket swinging, striking. He could see her falling, and the blood.

The blood.

He reached out for William.

William could stand it no longer, and he shouted, "It was my fault! I should have hit him. I should have killed him."

Jonas jerked him into his arms. William fought against it for a time. But in the end, he gave in and collapsed against his father.

Jonas thought of this boy, *his* boy, trying to be a man. A boy who'd lost his home and his mother, and thought he'd lost his father.

And he wept for him.

———

Jonas went alone to the cemetery to find Mary.

He didn't tell anyone where he was going, though he was certain Martha knew. William hadn't known, but had wanted to go just to be with him. As gently as possible, Jonas had put him off, telling him he could come with him the next time.

Turning left off Thames Street onto Farewell Street, he came quickly upon the burying ground.

Martha had described her grave as being beneath a young elm near the low wall that ran along the back of the grounds.

The grass was all yellow and brown, dormant for the winter. It was clumped here and there, having been long when fall and the cold weather came. Now frozen, the clumps made walking treacherous, and Jonas nearly fell twice.

He found two young elms, but the first was not the one beneath which his love lay.

The second was.

Jonas saw the newly carved granite headstone. It already leaned as the ground settled over her coffin.

He did his best to straighten it, then knelt on the cold ground.

The words were simple:

Mary Rose Hawke

B. 1746

D. 1776

Their simplicity struck Jonas's heart like a knife, burying deep in his soul. For the second time this day, he wept.

***

As he walked back through the lonely streets of wintery Newport, chaotic emotion first tugged, then yanked firmly at his heart. Part was dreadful sadness born of loss and more loss.

And there was anger. A towering rage built inside him. A fearful, burning, raging flame.

He'd never been so angry in his life. A small part of his brain feared this powerful anger, afraid of what it might lead to. Jonas had never felt a desire to kill before, but he felt it now. First and foremost, he wished he could identify the soldier who'd killed his wife. If he were able to find that man, he'd kill him with his bare hands.

As he walked, he seethed.

He must go to sea again and destroy his enemy. This war was personal now. No longer was he looking to hurt Britain's trade or to hinder the resupply of their army in the colonies.

Now he wanted to kill the enemy and burn his property. Purely for the sake of revenge. And he knew exactly how to do the most damage.

He would take the war to the enemy, to his shores, to the very gates of his cities, and the doors of his homes.

Jonas walked on, completely absorbed in plotting his vengeance. Men and women who saw his face moved aside, shuddering as he passed.

Chapter Thirty-Five

Later, as the adults ate, Trimble continued the tale of woe that Newport and his family had endured. "The British couldn't very well admit one of their soldiers had murdered a woman, so they arrested me for treason when I arrived home. In fact, I've only been released a fortnight ago. I've lost my business, my ships, my home. Thank the good Lord I have my family."

He suddenly realized what he'd said and looked down at his plate. "It's alright, Jonathan. You mean no harm. It's true. I, too, thank God that your family and my children are safe." Jonas sighed. "But why did they hold you so long? Surely they didn't suspect you of fighting with the militia?"

"No, not given my age, and my gout. Nonetheless, they gaoled me in an old distillery in Middleton. My gout flared up something fierce in there."

Martha spoke up. She'd been quiet thus far, concentrating on her plate while the men talked. But she needed to speak. "Jonas, Rebecca is a strong child, and she's growing used to her mother's absence. But William, as you saw, blames himself for Mary's... loss. We've tried, but we can't seem to make him understand. And he hates the British, with a burning hatred that I fear knows no bounds. He's talked often of joining the militia himself as soon as he's able." She cleared her throat and took a sip of water. "He doesn't hide his hatred from the soldiers, either. They know him and they watch him, as if a twelve-year-old boy could do them harm."

Jonas thought as he chewed. Trimble had told him game was becoming scarce with the added burden of the British soldiers feeding off the local woods, and there was no meat coming in from the surrounding countryside.

William was old enough to go to sea, and with what he'd seen and experienced, it would be good for him. He'd certainly matured this past year and a half since Jonas had returned home in *Elizabeth*.

Was it only that long? Not quite even that.

"I'd thought to come here to visit, and to remain here while my ship is refitted. To move my family—" His voice caught. "—my family to Philadelphia. Now, it is doubly important that I get back. I will stay for a few days. I know it's an imposition, but can you help me find a room for while I am here? I cannot put you to trouble."

Trimble and his wife shared a look. Clearing his throat, Trimble said, "Jonas, we would do anything for you. As Martha's brother, you are also mine. But if you move into lodgings, even for a night, it will draw attention to the fact that there's a new man here in town, and the British assume all new arrivals to be spies sent by the Continentals. You can, of course, stay here, out of sight. We will make room for you."

Jonas began to speak, but Martha held up her hand. "Jonas, Rebecca and her cousins get on famously, and I think it best she remain with them. They — help her to deal with her emotions," she added.

"I can't impose on you like that," Jonas replied. "I can see you have little enough as it is without adding another mouth to feed. I have some money. It's Spanish dollars, thus I fear it will be of little use here. Nevertheless, I will leave it with you."

"No, I'm sorry, that's out of the question. You are right, the money would be useless. If you remain too long, the British will discover you. If they do not, someone will turn you in. There's precious few of us left in town, and the loyalists insinuate themselves with the British, and even with the Hessians, to gain favor and access to food and clothing. They even entertain them in their homes. No, you must stay with us while you are here, then you must go." He folded his napkin beside his empty plate. "That sounds harsh. But there is little else to do. We make do and we can feed another mouth. And it will do the children wonders for them to spend time with you. Perhaps you can even get through to William and help him realize there was nothing he could have done, save die himself."

"Stay with us, Jonas. I believe Mary would have wanted you to do so," added Martha.

This last shot hit home, and Jonas looked down at his plate. Not for the first time since the war had come did he feel he had no choices, no good options. Events drove his life, and he lacked any control over them.

Looking up, he said, "Very well, I will stay. But only for a few days. Then, I must leave."

"Rebecca must stay here, Jonas. If you go back to sea, she'll need family around her. But I believe William best go with you. I know, a ship of war is no place for a lad of his age. But he needs his father. And if he remains, I'm afraid he will come to grief. It's dangerous for him to stay," Martha said somberly.

Looking first at Trimble, then at Martha, he agreed. "I will take him with me. You are right, he needs me. And I need him. Not just for another hand aboard ship, but because I need him to grow up, to understand what it is we fight for and why we are willing to die." Jonas's voice caught again. After a moment, he continued, "And why his mother died. If we succeed, these are days of which men will speak for centuries. And if we fail, it will fall to William and those his age to renew the fight when they are able. For we must succeed. We cannot go back to the way things were. Neither side will accept that. One side must vanquish the other. There is no middle ground. And I would see us succeed."

Martha and Trimble exchanged looks, Martha's one of fear and resignation, Trimble's of relief and pride.

"You're doing the right thing. It will be hard for both of you. But you go with our blessings and with whatever else we can gather to send with you. I would that I could come with you, Jonas. God's truth, I do. Know that my heart goes with you."

"I have no way to repay your kindness, save to say 'thank you'."

"Pshaw, Jonas. Thank us by setting us free."

***

JONAS STAYED LONGER THAN HE'D PLANNED. He needed time with his children, and his children needed him. Rebecca was quiet, withdrawn. She'd seen too much for one of such tender years. It took nearly a week for Jonas to coax another smile out of her. He read to her or told her stories of his time at sea every night.

"—and the monkey threw water on the boy below."

Rebecca smiled, and Jonas's heart melted.

"Papa, did he really?"

"I promise, it happened just as I said."

"How do you know? It's just a story."

Jonas smiled. "I was the boy, you see."

Rebecca smiled again and hugged her father. Jonas quickly wiped his eyes and gently pushed her back in the bed.

"It's time you slept, my sweet. I will see you in the morning." He covered her and tucked her covers under her.

As he blew out the lamp, he heard her ask, "Papa, will you leave us again?"

He closed his eyes and laid his hand on her head. Her hair was soft. Kissing her forehead, he gently brushed her hair back.

"Not yet, my dear, not yet."

A week later, Jonas and William packed small sea bags and walked out of the Trimble home bound for Philadelphia.

Rebecca stood trembling next to her aunt, but she refused to cry.

GLOSSARY OF NAUTICAL TERMS

Anchor Rode - The length of rope between the bow of a ship and its anchor lying on the sea bottom.

Batavia - Modern-day Indonesia, the island of Java.

Belaying pin - Solid wooden peg used on traditionally-rigged sailing vessels to secure lines of running rigging.

Bells - Used to tell time aboard ship. The ship's bell would be rung every half hour during a four-hour watch. Odd numbers of bells indicated the half hour, even numbers indicated the hour. Eight bells (four double strokes) indicated the end of the watch. Eight bells sounded at midnight, at four and eight in the morning, at noon, at four in the afternoon, and at eight in the evening.

1 single stroke - half an hour into the watch
1 double stroke - one hour into the watch
1 double stroke and one single stroke - ninety minutes
2 double strokes - two hours
And so on

Boom - The horizontal wooden spar that holds the bottom of a triangular or gaff-rigged sail.

Buntlines - Small diameter ropes attached to the bottom of a square sail then run up through blocks. The buntlines are used to pull the bottom of the sail up when furling a square sail.

Cable - A thick natural fiber rope of three inches or greater in diameter. So called to distinguish from a hawser, which was greater than one inch in diameter, but less than three inches.

Careening - Placing the ship on the beach at high tide. When the tide runs out, the ship careens to one side, allowing the hull to be scraped clean. The process is reversed the next high tide to clean the opposite side.

Cascabel - The hindmost knob of a cannon.

Chains - A platform outside the ship's railing where a Leadsman would stand to heave the lead.

Chandler, or Ship Chandler - A retail and wholesale source of supplies, including food, for both individual seamen and vessels.

Clewlines - Used to lift the bottom corners (clews) of a square sail up to the yard. To "clew up" means to haul on the clewlines, spilling the wind from the sail.

Deduced, or Ded Reckoning - Using knowledge of local currents and how much leeway (drift due to the wind on the side of the ship), a means of estimating position based on course steered, speed, and time sailed.

Forecastle - The forward part of the main deck on a ship.

Gaff - A wooden spar used to hold the top portion of a gaff-rigged sail, for example, the main sail on a brigantine. When set, the gaff is usually at a roughly forty-five degree angle from the mast.

Gaskets - Short lengths of braided rope used to secure folded/stowed sails to yards and booms.

Hove to - The sails and rudder are set to keep a ship in place without having to drop anchor.

Knightshead - One of two timbers, one on each side of the bowsprit, rising from the deck just aft of the bow on a wooden ship.

Larboard - To the left side of the ship. Modern day sailors use "port."

Lead, or Lead Line - A lead weight, usually hollow on the bottom, attached to a rope. The lead is thrown well forward of the ship and allowed to settle to the bottom. The rope is marked so a sailor, or leadsman, can read the depth.

Leech or Leechline - An arrangement of rope used to keep the side of a square sailed stretched to better capture the wind.

Lines vs. Ropes - A rope is a stored object. A line is a rope in use, for example, a mooring line or a part of the rigging.

Messenger, or Messenger Rope - A small-diameter rope used by sailors to assist in moving larger ropes, hawsers, or cables.

Offing - Over the horizon.

Packet - A small, fast ship used to transport messages, mail, and other lightweight important cargo.

Points - An angle of eleven and a quarter degrees. A full circle consists of thirty-two points on the compass. Thus, two points off the starboard bow indicates the object is approximately twenty-two and a half degrees to the right of directly ahead, or off the bow.

Poop Deck - The raised portion of the after deck of a ship. Not every ship had a poop deck. The poop deck was also the quarterdeck.

Quarterdeck - The after portion of the main deck of a ship. Often reserved for officers, though seamen with work to do were also permitted there for the duration of their task. The quarterdeck is also where the officer of the watch would stand his watch, and where the helmsman would steer.

Robands - Short lengths of small rope used to secure a sail to the yard. They differ from gaskets in that robands keep the sail set when in use, and gaskets stow the folded sails.

Scope, or Anchor Rode - The length of cable between the anchor on the bottom and the ship's bow.

Sheets - Lines used to position a sail to best capture the wind.

Slow Match - A hemp or flax rope soaked in resin to slow its burn rate. Used to fire cannon, one end would be lit when clearing for battle, then stowed in a bucket near each cannon. Typical burn rates would be one to two inches per hour.

Speak (also to speak, spoke) - To maneuver close to another ship and heave to in order to hold a conversation and exchange news. In context: "*Resolute* closed *Mythos* to speak them," and "*Resolute* spoke the Spanish ship."

Starboard - To the right side of the ship.

Starter - A short length of thick rope, often braided. Used by the Bosun and sometimes his mates to hit sailors, usually on the backs of their legs, to "encourage" them to be more attentive or faster with their duties.

Tender - A small vessel used to ferry supplies and men to a ship operating at sea. Often a schooner would be used to "tend" a larger ship, such as a sloop, frigate, or ship-of-the-line.

Tiller - Wood bar attached to the top of the rudder, used to steer the ship. To turn right, the tiller is moved to the left, and vice versa.

Triangle Trade - Trade route that took rum and other goods from New England to Africa, where they were used to buy humans for enslavement. The slaves were then taken to the Caribbean, where they were sold, and the profits used to buy molasses, sugar, and other raw materials, which were then taken back to New England.

Waist - The middle portion of the main deck of a ship.

Warp - A piling, part of a set of pilings, placed in a harbor that allow a ship to tow itself between locations, usually an anchorage and a quay, pier, or wharf.

Well - The very bottom of the ship, where water collects in the hull.

Well found - In good shape or well-equipped.

Wind direction - Always named for the direction the wind is coming *from*. Veering indicates the wind is changing direction clockwise around the compass. Backing indicates the wind is changing direction counterclockwise.

Yard - A horizontal spar made of wood from which hang square sails. The yardarms are the ends of the yards.

Acknowledgments

This story took longer to write than it should have, or than I would have believed possible: almost thirty years. There were obviously lengthy interruptions along the way, for deployments, other writing, work, life. But it's finally complete, and I'm a better writer now than when I started it.

No writer writes in a vacuum. At a minimum, they have an editor who believes in them and their story. Even more important is support from family. As I've matured, I've realized that I also need support from a host of friends and acquaintances. As John Donne so famously said, "No man is an island...". And so it is with me.

I must thank my wife, Elisa, and daughter, Emily. They have suffered and supported me, giving up hours and days I could have spent with them to allow me to put words on paper. They make my storytelling possible.

To my late parents, Bill and Donna, goes my gratitude for telling me that I could do anything, be anything. I wish I'd listened sooner!

Next, to my late writing mentor, Richard Keith Taylor, to whom this book is dedicated. He read an earlier incarnation of this story and told me it was worthwhile. Without his encouragement (really, kicks in the ass), it might still be collecting figurative electronic dust in my hard drive.

To my extended family and friends who have put up with my requests for readers, and for reading not just one draft, but in some cases, several drafts. In no particular order... David Wallace,

Don Ditko, Tammy Taylor, Kathy Taylor; and finally, my oldest friend, Fred Page. Also, to my writing community. Again, in no particular order, Seamus Bierne, George Galdorisi, Ara Grigorian, Janis Thomas, Isaac Lee, Patrick Holcomb, Dennis K. Crosby, Kim Moreno, Rick and Linda Ochoki, Jennifer Silva Redmond, Laura Rader, Gene Desrochers, Megan Haskell, Simone Berkowitz, Cherie Kephart, and so many more from the Southern California Writers Conference. Each has assisted to make what you, gentle reader, hold in your hand into something worth reading, if indeed that is your judgment.

I also could not have finished this effort without the tireless efforts of two extraordinary editors: the late Jean Jenkins; and the fabulous Laura Taylor, herself an award-winning author, and my friend. Laura doesn't just edit to identify plot holes, grammar errors, and lack of consistency. She teaches and works with me to improve my writing. She also talks me down when frustration hits a high note and I'm ready to throw in the towel. I owe her an enormous debt of gratitude. Thank you!

To my illustrator, Lorelai Thrasher, and map maker, Devaun Longley, much gratitude for their excellent work.

It goes without saying that I am indebted to Acorn Publishing for taking a risk on me. Holly Kammier and Jessica Therrien have built an incomparable team who take a manuscript and turn it into art! My Project Manager, Jessica Hammett, worked tirelessly, and patiently put up with my questions and worries. Kat Ross and Laura Rader put their attention-to-detail to work to expunge every error in the draft. And Damonza created a cover beyond beautiful. Thank you all!

I must also note that while each of those whose names appear here have striven to make this novel of a certain quality, my own efforts, and very likely my pride, have pulled in the opposite direction. Any merit you find in these pages is the result of the inputs that these kind people have provided; the corollary is that all errors or failures are mine and mine alone.

Finally, I must thank you, the person who holds this book in your hand, or on your screen. You've taken the risk of opening it to perhaps read it, and thus I am indebted to you, as well.

Naval Academy and Naval War College graduate Thomas M. Wing retired after thirty-two years as a Navy Surface Warfare officer. He served more than ten years at sea and twenty-two years ashore in increasingly important tactical and operational billets. A dedicated sailor for half a century, he created the Continental Navy Foundation, served as its executive director, and commanded its brigantine, *Megan D.*

He wrote *In Harm's Way* from a desire to explore the topic of America's early sea warriors and how they struck fear into the hearts of British shippers around the globe.

Thomas's award-winning first novel, *Against All Enemies*, was released in 2023 by Acorn Publishing. He resides in San Diego with his wife and daughter and a cat and a dog. Whatever free time he has is spent on the water.

For more updates, follow the author at: ThomasMWing.com